African Harvest

by

Terence Reeves

Grosvenor House
Publishing Limited

All rights reserved
Copyright © Terence Reeves, 2011

Terence Reeves is hereby identified as author of this
work in accordance with Section 77 of the Copyright, Designs
and Patents Act 1988

The book cover picture is copyright to Terence Reeves

This book is published by
Grosvenor House Publishing Ltd
28-30 High Street, Guildford, Surrey, GU1 3HY.
www.grosvenorhousepublishing.co.uk

This book is sold subject to the conditions that it shall not, by way of
trade or otherwise, be lent, resold, hired out or otherwise circulated
without the author's or publisher's prior consent in any form of binding or
cover other than that in which it is published and
without a similar condition including this condition being imposed
on the subsequent purchaser.

A CIP record for this book
is available from the British Library

ISBN 978-1-908447-57-9

I dedicate this book to Ann, her courage, love and selflessness

*"When I feel the wind on my face,
I know you are there at my side."*

About the Author

Terence, known generally as Terry by his family and friends was born and lived his early years in Weymouth, Dorset. Loving the freedom of the countryside he took up a career in agriculture, starting out in West Dorset before going on to run a leprosy centre farm in Tanzania through Voluntary Service Overseas where he developed a lifetime passion for Africa. He later lived and worked in the Seychelles, and at the University of Malawi in central Africa, returning to spend twenty four years in North Yorkshire, before taking early retirement in France and now east Devon.

Acknowledgements

Over the years pressure has mounted from friends and family. "You should write a book," they said. So I did!

My wife Andrea was the driving force with her encouragement and inspiration, convincing me that I could and should reveal my life and times through a book to the world and the next generation. This set me on the path.

There is a time in life for everything and the space allotted me to write this autobiographical story revealed itself to me. There was no need to create the story that had been done by life with all its twists and turns. The meticulous diaries that had been kept by my wife for most of her life which I had never read, letters and scrapbooks retained over the years all provided a rich source of information and insight to dip into. It only remained for me to dig deep into those places and memories, places I had previously feared to tread.

My deep gratitude also goes to Margaret and Philip Cox, who not only shared part of the life journey, but also volunteered to use their expertise in editing and proof-reading my recording of events. My thanks go to the Honourable Jenefer Farncombe for her kindness, generosity and help with valuable comments and suggestions relating to that part of my life and allowing me to tell it exactly as it was.

To my children Paul and Lynda who travelled life with me, through many places and events they would have preferred not to have had to pass. They did it uncomplaining and with great courage. I wish it had been different at times and my thanks and love go out to them. Unfortunately the choice is never ours to make, but we need the courage to walk the path.

I would also like to thank you the reader for spending your time looking into this window of my life and I only hope by doing so you find something to help you in your own.

Website for your comments www.terrysworld.co.uk

Chapter One

He found it strangely eerie being back in North Yorkshire again, enjoying a June afternoon walk along the River Ure calmly winding its way through Boroughbridge. He was never able to pass the town without stopping to take a walk along the footpath that held such deep and painful memories. It was as if one more visit would somehow provide the answers, explain the reasons why, and finally make clear to him the justification for the events that destroyed his world and changed his life that October in 1981.

Some people are said to be born with a silver spoon in their mouths, Terry's was more of a wooden one! His Mother, one of a twin, was born the result of an "Upstairs Downstairs" relationship in 1912. At birth she was immediately separated from her twin brother Arthur, when they were taken off to different Children's Homes as they did in those days. The fees for their care had been paid for a period of eighteen years; a person with much to lose must have been responsible for such a generous gesture.

Terry's mother, Daisy, never really recovered from this all her life, and of course never knew her parents. Her mother, Lucy Player, had come from a family of fourteen children and spent most of her life living in Wiltshire. Lucy married Albert Bowles in 1921, but she did not have any more children; dying at Bodmin in 1973, sadly never having been united with her children. Terry's father Frank, was the third and youngest child of an ex Royal Marine and public lamplighter for Portland Urban District Council in Dorset, so no silver spoon there for sure! Frank & Daisy brought up their two children Esmee and Terry in the light of this background with all its hang-ups, hardships and difficulties.

Terry's education was poor: it began at St Augustine's Catholic Primary School, in the back streets of Weymouth in the 1950's. The school, unusually set in a row of terraced houses was near the railway sidings on Walpole Street.

Emotionally his qualifications were little better. His family background had hardly been very stable or indeed very affluent. His mother had suffered severe depression after his birth, so much so, that for the first five years he was brought up by his father's only sister, Bess, who lived in Wyke Regis, Dorset. Educated by the Sisters of Mercy, they taught him about this God he had to fear, that if he did certain things, then terrible happenings would befall him.

At school Terry was given endless lists of things that had to be learnt and undertaken, as well as things that he was never to do, half of which he had never even heard of or knew the meaning. After all, what was sloth? Would he enjoy it? Where is it? How could he find it and would he even know he had done it? This was all very confusing when you are so young and brought up in that culture of fear as he was.

School life seemed to also revolve around the dreaded 11-plus: it hung over Terry and his fellow pupils like a sword; the fear of it took away the ability to learn and perhaps to pass. However, he did not disappoint and as predicted he failed it spectacularly.

Terry had to come to terms with the fact that, as he had failed his 11 plus there really was no further point in him living; he was made to feel a failure, with no hope, written off by society. The 11 plus, he was led to believe, really was a point in your life that determined your success or failure forever. This was very much the sentiment of the day, leaving him feeling empty, frustrated and totally useless.

"I think it would be good for you to become an altar server," his Mother suggested, having seen him so bored sitting with them in church each Sunday.

So at the very young age of five years, Terry became an altar server, at St Joseph's Catholic Church, high above the Westway Road in Weymouth. The Parish Priest Monsignor Ryan, on being confronted with him at the Crib that Christmas night in 1950, carrying the baby Jesus, said he hardly knew which one to place in the Crib, Terry or the baby he carried.

He grew to enjoy the feeling of being involved and of being "on stage and different," even at that early age. The feeling of Ceremony, that something special was taking place on that altar, during those services, stayed with him always.

He went on to realise how right he had been to feel that way: it was the seed of his faith, a faith that would be tried and tested to the full during his life.

Being an altar server gave Terry good reason to go to other services during the week and to ride off on his bike to the church, giving him a sense of freedom in those early teenage years. No longer did he have to sit in the pew, pinging the name tab holders on the benches, as he always had done and feeling terribly bored.

It allowed him to go out at night during the week and at weekends to serve at different services. It provided an opportunity to go off with Peter Costello, a fellow altar server afterwards to the Swannary where they would have a cigarette before going home, a vice Peter introduced him to. It gave him a wonderful new freedom and independence, following his instincts to be out and about, with a good reason for doing so.

He played endless football, at home, for the school and the local boys' team attached to Weymouth FC. Like all young boys, he enjoyed it far more than studying and as he had already been written off by society, why not enjoy life he thought.

From Walpole Street School in September 1957 Terry moved to the Holy Child Catholic Secondary School after his failure of the 11-plus. It was situated on the Wyke Road, in the posh area of Weymouth. Terry felt uplifted going there, and proud to wear a uniform of grey jacket, bright red tie, grey trousers and a grey cap with the red school badge, all proudly worn, unaware that it took every spare penny his parents had to provide it. Life at Holy Child School, once he had come to terms with having failed and being a failure, was not so bad as he settled into it, as long as he could avoid "Aggie's " cane, then he felt he would survive.

Aggie was the Head Mistress of the school, Sister Mary Edmond Campion, to give her full name, "Aggie" to all the pupils. She was of course a Sister of Mercy, the Catholic Order that ran the school, but she never showed Terry very much mercy. She was in her late 50s, therefore old in his eyes and she seem to spend long hours sitting in a store cupboard where it was rumoured she drank bottles of Guinness – purely medicinal of course!

Her lunch hour in the summer months was spent sitting outside on the playing field at a table, watching over the pupils, while reading the Daily Telegraph. It was well known that she was an ardent supporter of "Cambridge" at the annual University Boat Race. This rubbed off onto the pupils, humanized her and was the reason why, to this day, Terry supported Cambridge in the race each year.

In every institution, there is good and bad among the individuals and to be fair there were some lovely sisters who formed part of his education and his life. One in particular came to Terry's rescue and to some of his school friends, pointing them to the future with some hope.

Just six months before he was due to leave the Holy Child Secondary School, Sister Magdalene, a beautiful young Irish sister with a wonderful glint in her eye, bravely went to a gang of six lads that hung around together.

"Now, boys, it's just a few months before you all leave school. What are you going to do?"

"Play football, of course, Sister."

"Now you know you can't do that. How will you feed and care for yourselves? You have exams coming up soon and you must work and pass them if you are going to do anything with your lives."

They all laughed but felt some fear at going out into the unknown away from the shelter and protection of school life.

"If you boys are prepared to work hard, from now until you leave school, then I'll help you," Sister Magdalene volunteered to the gang one day. "I'll give up my holidays and weekends to get you to a standard that will enable you to pass the entrance exams to the

Technical College, but you have to work! Then you will be able to take further training at college in a subject like plumbing or electrical engineering."

So the six boys, Steven, Patrick, Mac, Christopher, Dennis and Terry took up Sister Magdalene's challenge and worked hard for the last six months of their school life, harder then they had ever worked and studied before. They in turn all rewarded her with their success, passing the entrance exam to the Technical College with flying colours. To see sister Magdalene's face on hearing of their results was for the boys reward enough.
"Right boys, will you get out there now and show the world that Holy Child Boys are the very best."
"We will Sister," they all replied in one voice.

That was the first exam any of them had ever passed in their lives, not the stuff of those that were supposed to be rated as failures! They had amazed themselves!
They were elated one and all and so grateful to Sister Magdalene and the faith she had shown in them. As to what they might all do with their new found wealth of qualifications they were not sure?

Terry was not very inspired with going to be a builder or an electrician and was eaten up with the urge to do something else, something different, something exciting, but what?

His mother, who always wanted the best for him and his sister Esmee, in part due to her own background, wanted them to have a better life than she had been able to have.

"What are you going to do with your life and with your future?" she would often ask him. "It's no good just aiming to be a footballer, that's just not on so get used to it."

"Why not? It's what I enjoy doing." Terry always replied to her questioning on this subject.

"I know you're not so keen on the Technical College thing, but it would give you a good foundation."

"Yeh! Maybe it would. But it doesn't really appeal to me somehow, not exciting enough."

"Well it's no good you talking like that. I want you to do something with your life, so I've made an appointment for you to visit the Employment Exchange with me tomorrow and we can talk to them and see what jobs they have."

"Aaaaaaaah Mum! Why are you coming?" he protested.

"To make sure you attend of course. I know what you are."
So on a very warm July morning in 1961 they both set off along the Chickerall Road to attend the interview, Terry dragging along behind not really wanting to be there.

"Come on," his Mother called back at him. "It's no use. We have to get you interested in something and into a decent job."

They walked on up the steps past the old Town Hall building that went to Chapaley Heights, where the Employment Offices were situated on the edge of the bombed out remains of High Street.

"One day Mum, I'll be able to take you to work in my Rolls Royce," Terry said as they were walking along!

"Well I hope if you have a Rolls Royce, I'll not be going to work!" she responded sharply.

They went on up a few more steps onto a cleared area where bombs had destroyed most of the buildings during the war years, except it seemed, for this long stone building that was now the Employment Offices along side Holy Trinity Church on Weymouth's harbour side. They took the few steps up to the entrance and went in.

A tired, dull, uninspiring, slightly grubby looking man watched as the unlikely couple entered his seedy little office.

"Sit down," he commanded. They dare not do otherwise!

"Well, son, what do you want to do? What do you want to be?" he fired the straight questions at Terry.

Huh strange, Terry thought, I'm not his son. I had hoped that he might tell me what was available, or at least give me a few ideas.

"Well, I have passed my entrance exams to the Technical College," Terry stammered.

"Good, well you can go there, can't you, so why are you here?"

"I don't want to do that," Terry explained.

The man looked puzzled with an exasperated expression on his face.

"Well, what do you want to do?" he snapped, with a 'tired of all this' sort of tone in his voice.

"I don't know," Terry replied. "What else is there?"

"Do you have other interests?" the now sweating man asked with some impatience.

"Well, some weekends I go to help on a farm at Osmington just outside Weymouth," not being very sure if that was at all relevant or indeed helpful.

By this time the man was getting very red faced and sweaty, replying with an element of frustration in his voice.

"Well there is a new Agricultural Apprenticeship Scheme coming out. Would you like to do that?"

Terry looked at his Mother for some inspiration and approval.

"You're always up at that farm, you must enjoy it," she said, "but it's a poor job and you'll not be paid very well. It's a well known fact that agricultural workers are very poorly paid and always have been."

The somewhat confused man was now getting a little irritated, so Terry agreed that he would give this Agricultural Apprenticeship thing a try.

"Yes, I know, but I do enjoy the outside life; think I'll have a go at that Mum."

"I'll get you an appointment with Mr Schrock who is to run the new scheme from Dorchester. He'll tell you all about it, and what you must do if you want to join the scheme."

Eager to get this problem boy out of his office, the man wished them 'Good Morning.'
He seemed relieved to show them the door, shook them by the hand and showed them out on to the flattened dusty bombsite once again.

From there, Terry followed his interest in the countryside and wide open spaces to become one of the first of four agricultural apprentices that passed out in the County of Dorset at a ceremony on 1st September 1964 in front of the blaze of the press! He also gained a selection of City & Guilds examination passes, obtained in Day Release classes, while he had been working for three years at Denhay Farm, Broadoak, near Bridport. He went into lodgings at 'Oakhayes', an old rectory in Symondsbury, owned by the Barnes family, who are related to the poet William Barnes. Terry lived there happily for the three years of his apprenticeship, enjoying the idealist life of a west country farming family.
He followed that with a year at the Dorset Farm Institute, in Dorchester, where he was awarded a National Certificate in Agriculture. It was not much, but it provided all the tools he had, with the exception of enthusiasm and an inbuilt desire to do something different.

With two or three fleeting relationships with the opposite sex that touched him deeply, but were now behind him, he ventured out into the world, ill equipped, but with determination to improve his lot.

Terry had always remembered a talk they had received by a very enthusiastic young lady during his college year. She had returned from Voluntary Service Overseas and had really inspired him with her tales, her wonderful enthusiasm and the excitement of travel. It had made him aware that there was a lot of poverty in the developing world, which to him, a budding farmer, surely did not need to be.

So he decided to take himself off to resolve the problem of world poverty once and for all, to remove this evil that caused so much suffering and then, after that, go on about his career.

It sounded like a good and useful thing to do, exciting and worthwhile.

He applied to Voluntary Service Overseas at 3 Hanover Street, London, W1 (VSO.)

Within weeks the VSO Director and the interview board summonsed him to London for an interview.

"Which country would you like to serve in?"

"I'd like to go to Jamaica please!" Terry replied.

He did not really know why he had said that. He must have been reading something about it at the time, or more likely it was the first place that came into his head.

"You do realise young man that this is not to be a holiday?"
"Yes I do," he shyly replied, wondering why he had said Jamaica.

He wondered if he had blown it with such a thoughtless comment, but a few days later he was thrilled to receive a letter dated 21st August 1965 telling him that he had been accepted as a volunteer with "Voluntary Service Overseas" and would be sent to Tanzania, East Africa.

They were unable to tell him exactly where in that country he would be sent, or to which project it would be, but that information would follow.

Terry, feeling swept along by events, wondered if he had the capability or knowledge to do the task before him. After all, he had not come from a very inspired background or had a grand education, even if he had a loving family, but he did not lack determination, a quality inherited from his mother. At this point he was just so excited, as was his mother, if a little dazed and concerned at her only son going off to foreign parts.

Terry's Sister Esmee was in the WRAF, based in Norfolk, so he saw very little of her. They never really had that much in common, Terry being the one to enjoy the outside life and Esmee to sit and read, always fearful it seemed to him, of going out or taking risks.

She had attended a private school, at the Sacred Heart Convent, and had gone on to study and pass her "A" level exams, so she was the one with the brains and the education!

He didn't see very much of her, their age difference of nearly four years contributed to their separate interests. Esmee met Roger while serving in the RAF and went on to marry him at St Joseph's Catholic Church in Weymouth on 29th December 1962. It was deep snow that day, the first year for a long while that snow covered Weymouth, even the sea froze on the railings along the esplanade, a winter to remember.

Anna-Marie their first born, Terry's niece, was really the first baby that he had ever had anything to do with or had paid much attention to. He fell in love with her as soon as he saw her, the most unlikely thing for an eighteen-year-old youth to do, but somehow, unexplainable, he really bonded with her, and could spend hours just looking down at her, gazing into her cot; she was the most beautiful thing he had ever seen.

He loved the occasions when Esmee & Roger would come to visit Weymouth and stay with his mum & dad at their home on Tennyson Road, giving him the opportunity to see Anna-Marie again. Everywhere he went he carried her picture with him, even to Africa. The love grew and still today he has a very special bond and relationship with her.

His nephew, Craig, entered the world on the 10th November 1965; he made his entry in Norwich, Norfolk. Terry's mum and dad decided to go and greet the newly born Craig on the 17th November. This turned out to be the very day that Terry was due to leave for Tanzania and the Leprosy Centre. So instead of them waving him off, it was he that went to see his parents off on the bus to Norwich, not quite what he had expected.

Daisy and Frank were convinced that they would never see their son again, that if he didn't catch Leprosy, then a lion or hyena would surely eat him.

Terry shared some of their fears too, going out into the unknown with both excitement and fear in his heart. He could never have imagined that the momentous decision he had made to go to Africa, would have such far reaching effects on him, that everyday after it would be in his thoughts, the people, the places, the sounds and smells of Africa would haunt the rest of his life.

He waved them a tearful goodbye, that crisp sunny November morning in 1965, at the Southern National Bus Station on Upwey Street, Weymouth, for them to make their journey to Norfolk, while Terry set off on his big adventure to Tanzania, East Africa.

Standing in the isolation of the bleak bus station that morning, wondering if this was to be the last time they would ever see each other, he felt alone and a bit sad, but with the feeling that this had to be done. His life was about to undertake a sharp and profound change.

Carrying his case, packed with his few worldly goods (44lbs) he staggered across the road from Upwey Street to the green wooden shed that was Weymouth's railway station and boarded the train to start this new exciting period of his young life.

When he had first imagined leaving home to travel across the world to live, he had pictured at least a tearful family on the railway station waving him goodbye, maybe aunties, uncles, friends, lined up on the platform, but not this.

Here he was, sitting on the train with the sun pouring through the window and not a soul to wave him off on this journey of a life time, a journey that was to become the most profound experience of his life, taking him from boyhood to manhood and beyond.

He was feeling very alive, excited and on the edge of an adventure, although he had no idea where it would lead, having only just planted the seeds with his application to join Voluntary Service Overseas.

The thrill of going into the unknown, to a place and a people he knew so little about, the travel, the new life, was quite overwhelming, but he felt elated too; it was a very big step for this inexperienced boy from a council estate, but a fantastic opportunity.

He felt good, if a little sad to be leaving Weymouth, the place of his birth, where he had lived with his parents and was brought up in those difficult days after the war: he was going now from the familiar into the unknown.

The throbbing GWR steam engine prepared itself for the long journey ahead to Waterloo, steam pouring out of its sides, the smoke belching from its chimney, as if it too knew that it was off on a special mission.

It slowly and purposefully steamed on out of Weymouth Station, under Alexandra Bridge, up past Radipole and Upwey Wishing Well stations, where Terry and his school friends had so often stood watching the trains in their teenage years. Then on through the long Ridgeway Tunnel to Dorchester, Bournemouth, Southampton and Winchester to the edge of London, slowly pulling into Waterloo Station with the great gusto of power and might. There the engine seemed to just collapse at the end of the platform like an exhausted beast, panting, expelling smoke and steam with a great feeling of accomplishment.

He made his way through the underground system for the first time alone, remembering the instructions his father had given him on how to negotiate the tube to get to the London Airways Terminal Office on Buckingham Palace Road, London SW1 without getting himself lost.

He checked in soon after 17.00 hours and sat waiting for the coach that took all the passengers to the airport on that dark wet November evening.
Out of the windows he could see the rain soaked streets in the lights, making him look forward to the warmth and the sun of Africa. A coach soon arrived to take him on the short journey out of London into the excitement and business of Heathrow Airport, where he boarded the BOAC VC10 that was to take him to Africa, stopping at Rome, Cairo, Nairobi and finally Dar es Salaam. The adventure had begun!

Chapter Two

Terry settled into the unfamiliar surroundings of an aeroplane and for the first time in his life, he prepared himself for the flight ahead. Then, over the plane's speaker system there was an announcement, "Would Terry Reeves make himself known to a hostess?"

"What now?" he thought, with fear rising within him.
"Were my parents ill already?" He had always feared that they would die whilst he was away. Had VSO decided not to send him? There had been so much confusion surrounding his posting.
He made himself known to the hostess, " I'm Terry Reeves. You called me?"
She passed him a telegram. Telegrams always were the carriers of bad news he thought! His shaking fingers took the telegram, which read on the envelope,

"Mr Terry Reeves Flight to Dar Es Salaam 7.45pm. TRY BA 165 Heathrow Airport, Central Hounslow".

He managed to rip open the envelope and read the following message:-

"SORRY UNABLE TO COME THE BEST OF LUCK. Arthur"

It was a message from his uncle in Horsham – what a kind thoughtful gesture - at least someone realised that he was about to step off the world!

The excitement mounted as the BOAC VC 10 sat at the end of the runway, engines throbbing in their position at the rear of the plane, sounding like a huge Volkswagen car with wings!

It shot off down the runway and catapulted into the air like nothing he had ever experienced. Terry hung on tight, trying not to show his fear. The lights of London were now below and fast disappearing from sight as the plane rose higher and higher and on up to 35,000 ft.

It was time to read the large blue glossy Menu and see the delights that were before him: it all looked majestic as he viewed the contents with amazement,

London - Rome
DINNER

Canape Choisis

Lamb Cutlets Reforme
Buttered Green Beans
Saute Potatoes

Gateau Majestic

Cheese – Cream Crackers

Coffee

Rome – Cairo
Evening Refreshments for joining passengers

Cairo - Nairobi
BREAKFAST

Compote of Fruit
Tomato Omelet with Buttered Mushrooms
Rolls. Croissants. Butter. Preserves
Coffee - Tea

Nairobi – Dar-es-Salaam
LUNCH

Coupe Florida

Cold Roast Breast of Turkey
Kenya Ham – Ox Tongue

Mixed Salad

Cheese - Cream Crackers

Coffee - Tea

He was overcome at the style and amazed that he was taking part in it all, a real dream.

In a matter of two hours he was landing in Rome, then on to Cairo, followed by Nairobi.
There he really felt that he had arrived in Africa and far away from home. It was wonderful to feel the heat of the sun, the change in the light, which lifted the spirits, after the darkness and gloom of London.

Terry sat drinking a large glass of orange juice, sitting in the airport lounge and chatting with other passengers. He discovered that there were two other VSOs on board so they sat and exchanged views on their respective projects. He really began to feel part of something big, something good, as they all shared their various talents, discussing the work they were to undertake and all with the same exuberance.

They were called to board the flight again and strolled out from the lounge to the plane some two hundred yards away from the main buildings. The plane roared off on its way to Dar es Salaam, the last leg of their journey.

The VC 10 circled Dar es Salaam, giving the most amazing and beautiful views from its small windows, of both the city and looking down on the harbour. It was absolutely breath taking as it twinkled like a jewel in the sunlight below.
Slowly it came in to land and taxied to the small range of buildings that formed the airport. He had made it, the flight of a lifetime was over; he was in Tanzania, in East Africa, and it felt unbelievable!

As Terry stepped out of the giant VC 10 and down the steps he felt the moist heat that he supposed was coming from the plane's engine, after its long journey, but no, it was the climate of the country on this November day, humid, sticky and very very hot. Wow!

Richard Denyer, a tall quiet man, with large biblical beard, met them – he was the VSO Representative for Tanzania and based in Dar es Salaam.

"Welcome to Dar. How was the trip? How is London?"
"The flight was fantastic – London cold and wet, it's so good to be here in the sun.
Is it always as hot as this here?"
"This is nothing, wait until January comes. That really is hot and humid," Richard replied with a smile.
He then greeted the others that had also been on the flight, one a young doctor and the other a teacher. Then from nowhere appeared two people who introduced themselves to Terry, "I'm Guy Timmis, the doctor in charge of the Leprosy Centre at Hombolo where you will be stationed," he said. "We were in Dar today and thought we would welcome you."
He was a very colonial looking figure in shorts, long white socks and safari boots. His wife Dawn then introduced herself, a pleasant, friendly deeply tanned lady in a full cotton dress.
"We will meet you in Dodoma when you come up on the bus, then take you to the Leprosy Centre from there. Look forward to seeing you then and welcome!"
They were gone from sight as quickly as they had arrived.

The three VSO's then climbed aboard a grey Land Rover and Richard drove them off to the city suburbs where he and his wife Sue lived.

Terry and his fellow VSO's were amazed as they were driven down the straight road from the airport. There at the sides of the road were people carrying things on their heads, very poor looking people, some just squatting in the heat of the day. There were mud huts with grass roofs all around. He felt ill prepared for all this and could hardly take it in.

They arrived at Richard and Sue's house situated on a street that could have been any suburb in England, not here in the centre of Dar es Salaam, except for a magnificent red flame tree in the garden that overshadowed the house while at the same time keeping it cool.

Sue welcomed them, she was a very slim pretty lady with dark hair, in her mid to late twenties. She looked a bit strained and tired. They noticed during their stay that she often went to lay down of an afternoon. The heat of Dar and the humidity was clearly getting to her.

After a long cold drink Richard explained to them that they would all stay in his house for three or four nights, but would have to sleep on mats on the floor until they were dispatched to their respective projects. However, first of all it was necessary to go to the British High Commission to meet the High Commissioner and make their presence known in the country, as he was responsible for all British people in Tanzania.
Richard drove them into the city through a suburb covered with tropical palms among some very smart houses and offices. They drove up the driveway of a palatial white property and parked the landrover under the trees in the shade.

It all seemed very grand and important and in a strange way made them feel proud to be British. Richard seemed to know the way around the offices, as he went to the reception desk.
"Will you find out if Mr Jones is able to see us now?" he asked the man in a white suit at the desk. The floors were all highly polished and everything bright and clean; large potted palms around the reception area gave a very tropical feel to the place. Wow Terry thought, what am I doing in a place like this?

Mr Jones sat behind one of the biggest desks he had ever seen, a jolly, short portly man who welcomed them as if they were royalty.

"Do sit down. Would you like a drink? 'Fanta' or 'Coke'?"

A young smiling African man distributed the drinks. Terry found since he had arrived in Tanzania that he had a totally unquenchable thirst, so he accepted a drink whenever it was offered.

Mr Jones went on to fill in all the details of the three VSO's, which had to be registered to show they were in the country and explained that they should always remember that they were guests in the country and to behave accordingly. They were to respect the customs of the country at all times and avoid discussing or commenting on politics.

"On no account must you get involved with the local women," he told them.

Dave, the teacher and Don, the doctor, Terry's fellow VSO's smiled and looked somewhat surprised.

"I've heard all the stories and all the excuses," Mr Jones explained.

"Don't come to me in a few months time telling me that you acquired any sort of V.D. or sexually transmitted diseases from the toilet seats. There are only two people living that I would believe that from, one is the Archbishop of Canterbury and the other is the Pope. NOBODY else."

With the formalities out of the way Mr Jones relaxed and discussed the projects they were taking up, explaining how they were ambassadors of their country and to always remember that. They discussed how long each of them planned to stay in the country and he expanded on the joys and beauty of Tanzania.

He described some of the history of the area, how the Slave Trade had been largely run from Bagamoyo, just north of Dar es Salaam, with all the horrors attached to it. David Livingstone had passed through the region, so had Henry Morton Stanley, as well as Burton and Speke who had discovered the sources of the Nile and so many African explorers in the 1840's and 50's, when carrying out their epic travels deep into the continent. Terry already had a great admiration for the work of those men, having read something about a few of them. It was difficult enough in our present day, but in theirs? However did they manage it? True adventurers, brave and courageous men, with such great powers of endurance and commitment, the like we see so little of these days and who perhaps will never be matched again?

Mr Jones explained he had a boat that he kept in Oyster Bay and invited them all to join him Sunday morning on the beach, when he would take them out on a fishing trip. This sounded fantastic, but there was just one problem for Terry, he had to catch the 10.00am bus to Morogoro and on to Dodoma that Sunday morning, so he could not join them. Rotten luck. The others were to go to their projects in the following week, but he had to leave on the Sunday and so would miss the fun.

On the Sunday morning they all went down to the beach to meet Mr Jones, who was waiting for them attired in his shorts and tee shirt, looking very different from the man who had been behind his desk in his official capacity. He was more relaxed and at ease. They stepped into the serving dingy in turn and paddled it out to the yacht, as Terry waved them all goodbye from the shore! He felt sorry not to be able to go with them and was somewhat aggrieved to miss such an opportunity, a bit of fun and relaxation, but the time had come to face his new project and new life and he was looking forward to that.

After saying goodbye to them all he made his way along the beach to St Joseph's Catholic Cathedral near the Old Boma on Sokoine Drive over-looking the sea. It was his habit on a Sunday morning to attend Mass and being in Africa was no exception. He just had time to attend Mass, before going on to the bus station where he found the bus, together with a bicycle that had been supplied by VSO. This was now sitting on the top of the bus along with every sort and type of luggage from the other passengers. With a "Jambo" (Hello) he offered the driver his case containing all his worldly goods; it was easily thrown onto the top of the bus, to find a space for its safe passage to Dodoma. The driver directed Terry to the entrance of the bus, as he knew hardly any Swahili at that stage so was totally dependent on the universal language of hand signals!

He gathered the bus was nearly ready to leave so climbed aboard, the only white man on the bus; everyone was curious as to why he should be travelling in that way, their expectation being that every white man had a car and did not ride on buses.

This clearly was not the Southern National bus service in Weymouth, which became very apparent as he stepped over goats, chickens, large baskets of vegetables, sugar cane etc to his seat about half way down the packed bus. He took a seat by the window where he could open it to get some air as the smell was somewhat over powering due to a combination of sweat, animals, vegetable matter and the heat of the day!

The bus pulled slowly out of the station in a heavy well-loaded manner, rocking from side to side under the weight of the assortment of people, animals and baggage. Terry looked longingly towards the sea and all the boats in Oyster Bay, just wishing he too had been able to spend the day on Mr Jones's yacht, along with his fellow VSOs. It had looked so inviting.

The bus drove along the rough tarmac road in the direction of Morogoro, which was to be the first stop. The heat was oppressive, but there was a flow of air now that they were on the move. He looked around at the mixed bunch of passengers. There were two Masai warriors, very tall with their hair coated in red mud, and beads around their necks. They were carrying long tubes made of bamboo, which he later found out was probably full of a mixture of urine and blood. The Masai carried long sharp knives and looked quite savage and somewhat out of place on this otherwise relatively civilised bus journey. There were an assortment of ladies all with babies and some with several young children too. Men with large looped ears, some with the most unusual items in them like torch batteries hanging as ear rings. There were also two goats that seem to have the freedom of the bus, pacing up and down and sniffing everything in sight.

In the seat next to Terry, was a very old man with very tatty blue shorts, rather more holes then material. He had a skin like a rhino and viewed Terry with some curiosity as he chewed on his sugar cane. Every so often he would tire of the cane he was chewing as it lost its flavour, lean across Terry and spit it out towards the open window. Unfortunately for Terry he was not a very good shot and it often landed on his leg and didn't make it out of the window!

Becoming a bit fed up with this he indicated to the man that he'd like to change places with him so that the man was next to the window. There he could spit as much as he liked. He seemed happy with the new arrangement as he smiled at Terry with the few teeth he had left in his head.

The bus continued on its journey, the tarmac soon ended and was replaced by a red murram substance, becoming rough and dusty; the passengers seemed to be floating along in a cloud of dust. Every time a vehicle passed in the opposite direction they were showered in more red dust as it swirled into the bus covering everything and everybody in more fine red dust. He was getting desperate for a drink but foolishly had not thought to bring anything with him.

He was amazed at the flat dry lifeless countryside with mud huts and baobab trees all around, trees that looked as if they had been planted and grown upside down! Poverty was all around with half dressed people, children in rags playing with hoops and old tyres and a few cattle that had the appearance of walking hat racks with their bones pushing up through their skin. They all had humps between their shoulders, like camels, something Terry had never seen before in cattle.

This was Africa in the raw and it was only just beginning.

Chapter Three

The arduous one hundred and twenty one miles to Morogoro were completed, with everyone and everything having survived the journey, but covered in a layer of fine dust. They pulled into the centre of the town to a parking area under trees that created a welcome shaded area, giving some relief from the unyielding heat of the sun.

As Terry gladly stepped out of the bus, he was amazed at the beauty of the place; there was a haze of purple mountains high above the town, with flame trees everywhere displaying their rich red flowers in avenues along the road side, with the purple flowers of the bougainvillea, trailing around fences and gardens.

Such astonishing beauty, amongst the poverty that is Africa's, it was rightly a country of contrasts.

Red dry dusty roads seem to be the order of the day, with small wood shuttered shops along each side of the street. People started to approach the bus selling their variety of wares, from small black round cakes, cabbages, tomatoes, pawpaw, melons and wood carvings of every shape and form, expertly carved from black mahogany.

This band of sellers followed Terry as he made his way to a fallen tree a few yards from the bus where he sat in the shade. He was careful not to go too far away from the bus, as he had no idea how long it was to stay before taking off on the next leg to Dodoma and not being able to speak Swahili he could not ask the driver. He managed to buy a Fanta drink from a small and typically African shop and sat on the tree taking in his new surroundings and all that was going on around him, as he tried to brush off the red dust and come to terms with life in Africa.

The sun continued to beat down unmercifully with the dust flying whenever a vehicle passed its way down the quiet street. After thirty minutes he returned to his seat on the bus, to continue the journey to Dodoma. The old man next to Terry had given up the sugar cane and was now chewing tobacco, but it did nothing to improve his aim!

They set off again along the dusty roads in the heat, mile after dusty mile, the diesel engine throbbed on, a general fatigue seemed to have come over all the passengers, even the goats were now laying down in the aisle of the bus. Terry sort of wished he could join them, feeling tired, with a headache fast developing, the lack of drinking water and the heat being the most likely cause, these and all the events of the past few days since leaving London.

After four hours the bus stopped again, where there was a small run down shed, set back from the road. It seemed to sell a few things, so everyone got out to stretch their legs and to buy a drink. All they had were bottles of Coke, and not cold ones either; they had been stored on the shelves in the sun. In desperation Terry bought one, for there was nothing else and for the first and only time in his life he knew the unpalatable taste of warm coca cola that did nothing to quench his thirst. By this time his head was pounding and he began to feel very low, just what had he got himself into he wondered.

The bus droned onwards, another three hours passed. Terry had fallen by this time into a semi-conscious state, trying not to feel the pounding in his head. His ears, nose and hair were full of the dust that had now changed to a dirty grey colour, as the soil changes of the journey, indicated the miles that they had travelled.

Eventually after nine hours the bus pulled into a large lifeless compound on the outskirts of Dodoma, the light was fading and the sun sinking below the horizon, giving welcome relief from its fierce heat.

Terry was relieved to get off the bus, but exhausted.

"Jambo, Terry," a voice called out.

He spotted the face of Dr Guy Timmis, who he remembered from the brief meeting at Dar es Salaam airport on the day of his arrival. He was the doctor in charge of the Leprosy Centre at Hombolo.

"Am I glad to see you?" Terry said. "What a long journey it's been."

"Yes, it's over 300 miles," Guy replied with some pity in his voice.

Guy looked so clean and tidy in his light grey hat, long white socks, shorts and corduroy jacket, very colonial looking.

"Come on, let's get your case and I'll take you to the Bishop's House where my wife is. You can have a meal and freshen up there before we go off to Hombolo."

They loaded the case into his Peugeot Estate car and made arrangements for the Leprosy Centre's Farm Manager, George Hart, to collect the bicycle the following day.

The Bishop's house was in a suburb of Dodoma not far from the Post Office, off Kikuyu Avenue; they parked in the drive and joined everyone in the dining room.

Doctor Timmis introduced Terry again to his wife Dawn and then to Bishop Stanway. They both welcomed him and said how delighted they were that he was to work with them. "Welcome to Tanzania and to Dodoma. You must be feeling very tired. Would you like to use the bathroom?" Dawn asked.

The answer to that was obvious as he stood there rather resembling a wild bushman, red hair, dust covered and exhausted. He asked Dawn for something for his headache and she gave him two aspirin and lots of sympathy as he made his way to go and clean up. Dawn was something of a motherly figure, very caring and kind. Terry felt they would get on well together and immediately warmed to her, as he did to Guy.

After dinner he began to feel human again, as the aspirin, the food and drink started to kick in. He was not looking forward to yet another journey, but at least it was with friends and in a car.

"How far is it to Hombolo Leprosy Centre?" Terry asked the doctor, as they drove out of Dodoma along the now familiar dusty, bumpy roads.

"About thirty five miles but the road will get quite bumpy as we progress towards Hombolo. Once the rains come next month the roads will be graded and it should make driving conditions much better."

Terry was seated in the front, typically Dawn had given up her seat and sat in the back where the bumps in the road were more exaggerated. They discussed his journey from home, the flight and how he found being in Africa.
They were keen to hear about his family's reaction to him giving a year to work in Africa, especially their concerns and his own at living and working with leprosy patients at a Leprosy Centre. He too was keen to hear about the Hombolo Leprosy Centre, its people and all about the life he would find there.

They told him how he was the answer to a prayer by the missionaries! The Centre was part of the Diocese of Central Tanzania and run by Christian Missionary Society (CMS) under the direction of the Australian Bishop, Alf Stanway. Terry had never been the answer to anyone's prayer before, as far as he knew? What would Aggie have thought of that?
They explained how they had, for so long, needed someone to come and take over the farm to enable George Hart, a New Zealand missionary and the Farm Manager to take seven months home leave with his wife and two girls, but until Terry came they had not been able to find anyone to do it.

The road seemed to go on and on. All Terry could see in the headlights were the deep ruts of sand that seemed never ending, mile after trying mile as they ploughed their way along in the darkness of the African night. He was very very travel worn by this time, but they chatted and he tried to keep his eyes open as they explained all about the centre, its people and its original creation.

When they finally arrived at Hombolo Leprosy Centre at about 22.30 it felt very deep in the heart of Africa. The Leprosy Centre was in darkness; Guy explained this was because at 22.00 each evening the diesel engine that provided the electricity was turned off in order to keep the costs down.

The Centre seemed to consist of just a few dwellings. They pulled up in front of a bungalow where they got out of the car. A short, tired looking, almost wild, but gentle lady appeared, holding an oil lamp. She approached nervously as Dawn and Guy introduced Terry.

"Sorry we're so late Joan. This is Terry. He's had a very long day."

As they shook hands a short very weathered looking man came out of the darkness with another oil lamp. Guy introduced Terry.

"George this is Terry, just arrived from U.K."

"Good day, mate," George replied. "Come on in."

Guy and Dawn then left for their own house a few yards away, leaving Terry in the hands of George and Joan Hart who were CMS Missionaries from New Zealand and from who Terry had come to take over, allowing them to take home leave.

George had developed the farm from nothing but overgrown bush land and lived there with his wife Joan and their two young girls, Anne and Margaret since 1963. He was a builder by trade and was responsible for all the building work at the new Leprosy Centre, as well as carving out a farm in this semi-bush country. Terry's admiration for him was already growing.

The Bishop of Central Tanganyika, by chance, had met Guy & Dawn Timmis in 1958, when they had taken leave from their Government work in Uganda and had gone to visit the hospital at Mvumi, near Dodoma in Tanganyika, the place where Jungle Doctor Paul White had worked and based his popular books.
"You must let me know when you are leaving Uganda," the Bishop had said to Guy and Dawn. They had been greeted by Bishop Alfred Stanway while at Mvumi, with that command. Consequently, four years later in 1962, when Guy and Dawn Timmis heard about the need for help from C.M.S. for assistance in developing a new Leprosy Centre in Tanganyika at Hombolo, they decided to

postpone their early retirement and offer themselves for two years to help get it started. They in fact finished up staying there fourteen years, the happiest and most fulfilling of their lives they later said!

They went on to develop a one hundred and fifty bed centre and to carry out the supervision of some one hundred Government Dispensaries in that area, requiring many long and dusty safaris. They were supported by the C.M.S and the Leprosy Mission and showed great spirit in their response to that enormous challenge.

They were assisted in their task by a fellow Australian, Staff Nurse Win Preston, who was also a C.M.S. missionary, who had years of experience working with leprosy in that part of the world and here at Hombolo, with the assistance of numerous other African staff that she trained and worked with to develop the hospital.

George and his wife Joan played no mean part in this development work, spending tireless hours, building houses, hospital buildings, farm buildings, and clearing the bush to grow crops and feed the patients of the Leprosy Centre, working alongside those leprosy patients that were able to assist in the work, giving them new hope and the chance to learn how best to help themselves.

It was into this life Terry had been thrust by joining VSO and by this time he was beginning to understand something of what had gone on here to get the project to that stage, the problems and the courage shown by the individuals involved, as well as the obvious needs of the people in fighting Leprosy. He was beginning to feel very humble indeed.

That night he did not so much sleep, as fall into unconsciousness on this his first night at Hombolo. He was absolutely exhausted, and did not awake until eight o'clock to bright sunshine and a noise that seem to be saying, "Go away" "Go away?" He wondered just where he was for a while. This noise continued and came from the tree outside his bedroom window. A greyish bird about eighteen inches long with white neck and a loud penetrating sheep-like bleating call, "gaarr, wayyyy" - "gaarr, wayyyy." It seemed determined to get him out of bed to face the day!

Joan welcomed Terry again. She explained that he was to stay with them for a few weeks as the bungalow where he would live was having a veranda built on the side, but was not quite finished. It was to be used as a guest house in the future, but for the length of his stay he would live there. After breakfast of pawpaw, egg and toast he went off to find George at the farm.

Everything seemed so strange, the light so bright; the heat of the day was building up as it does in those open bush landscapes. It was already eighty degrees and it was only ten oclock.

George spent the morning showing Terry around the Centre, and the boma where the beef cows lived and were herded at night, an enclosure made of thorny branches. He showed him the fields where maize, groundnuts, millet and beans grew, the vegetable garden and the water supply system. The water supply was essential for them all of course and came via a diesel pump from the dam, about a mile from the centre. It was why the leprosarium had been built in that position in the first place, being near to the newly formed dam of some six square miles, built in 1957 by the government.

What an energetic and enterprising man George was, a real New Zealander, burnt a rich red brown by the sun under which he was constantly working. He stood in the field in his long laced up leather boots, dusty khaki shirt and shorts and a large Anzac slouch hat shading his eyes. George had the most amazing piercing blue eyes, like sapphires that seemed to look right through you. He seemed to be curious about the fact Terry was a Catholic.

"Don't you Roman Catholics pray to Mary?" he asked. "Why do you do that?"

Not a question Terry had expected, standing in the middle of the African bush!

"Well it's not quite like that," Terry replied and passed over it for the time being.

But he noticed over the next few days that George was very curious and somewhat apprehensive about Catholics, perhaps he had not really met any before, hardly surprising where he was living.

He took Terry to see his new home situated about three hundred yards from where George and family lived and the same distance to the doctor's bungalow, with Sister Win Preston's house in between the two. The building team were busy doing the extension to what had been a house used by two African nurses. Terry was looking forward to moving into his very first home and establishing his independence, it was so exciting.

"Now mate," said George, "there is to be no girls staying with you in the house when you move in. I hope you understand?"
This was George's humour, which surprised Terry, with him being a missionary; he really didn't know why he should have thought that. Perhaps being a missionary he did not expect him to make such comments.

George had a good sense of humour and over the five months that he and Terry worked together before he took his leave they became quite close, something that it was not easy to do with George. They enjoyed a banter and had a mutual respect for each other, even if they did have different approaches to the work and religious views.
George had come from a narrow low-church background and had a strong faith in God. He had never been afraid of hard work and his time in Tanzania had seen him turn his hand to most things, his strong point being the building work at the Leprosy Centre as well as many town houses including the Bishop's house in Dodoma, where the CMS mission headquarters were based at Mackay House. It was he that discovered that to build a bungalow on the usual foundations was not acceptable, as the walls would soon crack and the houses fall down within six months, as many did.
Instead, he discovered, it was necessary to first place at least a foot of sand under the foundation to act as a cushion with the concrete foundation poured onto the top. This allowed the house to float in the movement of the soil, causing little or no cracks to

appear in the walls. With the severe changes in weather conditions, dry from April to November, then extremely wet from November to March, it was a very difficult place to build, or to grow crops, but something George had worked out how to do, despite the elements.

That was the nature of this remarkable man and in this way he was able to demonstrate to the local people just how much it was possible to achieve in such a poor environment.

It became very apparent to Terry, but he was never sure that George fully appreciated the fact, that without the support of many, firstly his hard working wife Joan, who kept the house going and produced good meals in the most difficult of conditions with limited supplies, and his sister in-law Meg from England, who so often took care of their children Anne and Margaret when they were on school holidays in England. Many others in the long support chain helped him to continue serving at the Leprosy Centre, which he could never have done without their assistance and support. One of the last people to come into George's life to complete the support mechanism that was so important, in fact vital to him in his retirement years, was to be Terry, but that's another story!

"Whatever you do, mate, while you're here and I'm away on leave, take good care of the vehicles. This landrover is quite old and parts are expensive and difficult to come by. The CMS mission has very limited funds, so you must take great care of it. You'll be asked to pay twelve cents a mile for your private use."

Out of Terry's pay of £1 a week he could see that he would not be travelling very far!

As George was explaining this he reversed into a tree stump and put a large buckle in the bodywork at the side!

"Yes," Terry smiled, "I'll take great care!"

No more was ever said on the subject!

Electricity for the Centre was supplied by a large generator that was driven by a huge diesel engine standing in the centre of the area between the farm buildings and the hospital administration buildings, contained in its own purpose built building.

"Every night at around 6.45pm you must come and start the engine, without fail," George explained.

He unlocked the door of the generator house, where there was a large board of controls, dials and meters. George went through a list of things Terry must do and NOT do, if he was to be successful in starting the monster and keeping the supply going!

The weight of responsibility began to feel heavy on his shoulders as he tried to take in all that George was telling him.

"I'll give you a demonstration, mate."

George took a large starting handle, placed it in the middle of the huge flywheel and started to turn it. First it revolved slowly, then faster and faster as George went redder and redder in the face. When it was going as fast as his little body would take it, with a free hand, he quickly pushed a lever while still turning the flywheel causing the engine to roar into life.

"There you go. That's all there is to it!"

He then showed Terry how to adjust the voltage, so that he did not blow all the light bulbs and motors in the centre by running it at too high a voltage. They then closed the door on the throbbing monster that Terry had to keep fed and running during his stay. Never again would Terry just accept mains electricity and take it for granted.

"So, mate, at night Guy will turn off the engine: there's a small bell push by his back door and in order to conserve the expensive diesel he turns it off at ten o'clock every night without fail," he explained. "If you want to stay up longer then you have to use an oil lamp, so make sure they are lit by then or you'll be plunged into darkness!"

Slowly all Terry's new responsibilities were loaded upon him as George went over all the necessary details of keeping the farm and the Leprosy Centre going on a day to day basis.

At the same time local men were being employed to clear the bush to increase the land available for cultivation and cropping; these had to be monitored and paid at the rate of seventy shillings an acre (£2.50) having cut and removed all the trees and dug up, by hand, the roots so ploughing could take place.

Of course one of the most difficult tasks was to learn Swahili, a language Terry had no knowledge of, little of that was spoken in Dorset! Slowly he picked up some of the language, but it was a major problem for anyone working out there. Terry loved the sound of the language and admired George who seemed to speak it well and could certainly get his point over to the men in his employ and the people in general.

About fifteen men were employed from outside the Leprosy Centre, with the Leprosy patients doing some of the cultivation and clearing work. The groundnuts that were grown on the farm were harvested and shelled by the patients, as they sat in the shade of the farm buildings. This provided them with valuable finger exercises and made them feel that they were doing something in return for the treatment they were receiving.

A man approached Terry with a note in his hand; he beamed a wide and toothless smile at him and said, "Jambo Bwana," as he passed him the note.
It was from Dawn.

"Would you like to join us for dinner this evening at 7.30?"

He was able to communicate his acceptance of the offer to the man. How completely bizarre he thought, to be holding a sort of conversation with this man who had only a few fingers and toes, and was covered in scars from his leprosy. It felt unreal, but there it was right in front of him, fresh from England, a reminder of why he had come to Africa, if he needed it.
How far removed it all seemed from his life in Dorset and the U.K. quite unbelievable really, and it had all taken place in such a short time.

The remarkable thing about the few leprosy patients he had seen so far was that they were all smiling and seemingly happy. Terry was not sure he would have felt the same in their position.

Chapter Four

There had been much to take in and to understand: Terry was fast learning there was a great deal involved in the day to day running of the Leprosy Centre. He was unused to the heat and was glad to return to his room and lay on the bed to try and absorb it all.

"You want a bath mate?" George called to him from the hallway.
"You bet."
"Well it's all yours; the water should be hot enough as the fire was lit early today in your honour!"

Terry went to the bathroom and ran the water; it was the colour of tea, a reddish brown. He wondered if he would come out dirtier then when he went in. It also had a very strange smell like rotting vegetables. Ah well, he thought, at least it's wet!

As he lay in the bath, getting some relief from the aches and pains of the day and washing away the dust, he spotted up on the windowsill a glass jar with a screw top. It looked as if it contained a sample from a science lab. Wonder what that is he thought. I must ask George.

Having cleaned up, Terry and George sat chatting in the sitting room area while Joan busied herself in the kitchen preparing the evening meal.
"Never go out at night without a torch, mate. Apart from the off chance of a leopard, hyena or lion being around, snakes are everywhere, dangerous and fatal.
The old lion loves a tasty piece of meat from the 'Old Country' you know!" George said laughing.
"The leprosy centre has been so recently carved out of the bush, there are still many of its natural inhabitants around. They don't like us being here and you need to take the utmost care." George explained with concern, a rough smile on his sunburnt rich red brown face and twinkling deep blue eyes.

He showed Terry the twelve bore shotgun, where it was kept and how he should use it.

"Have you ever used a twelve bore before mate?" George enquired.

"Very little, just for the odd pigeon or pheasant when working in Dorset," Terry replied.

"Well take the greatest care mate, always keep the safety catch on when it's not in use, it's no toy. It can kill you know!"

More of George's humour, but it was serious humour on this life saving subject. Terry smiled and hoped that he would never need to use it, but it was comforting to know it was there should he need to.

"Tell me, George, while in the bath I noticed a jar with a strange looking item in it on the windowsill. Is that Ginger Beer?"

"Ha Ha! You English are real nosey. One day I'll explain to you, but not now mate."

It was time to get over to the Timmis's house, where Terry had been invited for dinner, so he set off the few yards to their beautiful bungalow, set in a garden of trees, shrubs and flowers that Dawn had built up in the short time they had lived at Hombolo; it was her pride and joy and rightly so.

The lights of the house drew him to the welcome that only Guy and Dawn could give, always warm and kindly. Guy responded to the usual African greeting that everyone made when approaching a house.

"Hodi." (Hello, anyone there)

"Karibu," was always the reply. (Come in)

"Wonderful news about the cricket isn't it," Guy said excitedly, as he opened the door that was made of wire and mosquito netting. This allowed the air to flow into the house but not the insects.

"Sorry I don't follow cricket. My father watched it every minute that he could and it's rather put me off," replied Terry.

"We are winning against the West Indies; it's been so exciting."

Dawn appeared from the kitchen with a beaming smile, "Come in. You must be hungry? I do hope George didn't work you too hard today, your first day. He works so hard himself and drives everyone the same way."

"Would you like a Fanta or a Sprite?" asked Guy.

"A Fanta for me please."

The room was homely with a piano in the corner; the table was laid with candles and flowers, with a napkin in each place. Dawn liked to present everything well and was known amongst her two sisters as the 'Duchess,' due to the fact that everything had to be just right, with a place for everything, in the Victorian manner.

Dawn and Guy had no children. They had worked in Government service, spending sixteen years in Uganda from 1946, and told wonderful stories of those times with nights spent sleeping in the bush under canvas, as they went from one place to another across seven different districts, dealing with every medical condition, from smallpox and sleeping sickness to an epidemic of pneumonic plague.

Guy first met his wife to be, Dawn Brewer, while working at C.M.S. Mengo Hospital that had been started by Sir Albert Cook. Dawn's Mother had worked with Sir Albert at the time of the breakthrough for African nurses, when they were first given the freedom to touch a sick person! Guy and Dawn were married at Namirembe Cathedral in Uganda in 1948.

"I'd never really had much involvement with Leprosy in the past, it was more general medicine," Guy explained.
"Of course I came across it everywhere we went in Africa. It still has the same effect on people as it did in biblical days you know, with families turning people out if they thought they had the disease."

"Can it be cured?" Terry asked Guy.

"Yes, it can mostly. It's contracted by prolonged contact, like mother and child and husband and wife, that's why you are unlikely to pick it up. I wrote to your mother and father to reassure them on that point by the way."

"The two main types of this bacterial disease are Lepromatous and Tuberculoid Leprosy. In the Tuberculoid form sensation is usually lost within a small patch of skin where the pigment is lost, the tiny nerve endings being damaged. If not controlled, it spreads, causing loss of touch, and loss of pain, hot and cold in that order. This causes the possibility of burning and cutting without the feeling being present as normal; causing a great deal of the disfigurements, the type you will often see around here at the Leprosy Centre amongst the patients."

"Lepromatous leprosy causes more nodules and ulcers to appear on the skin as well as the same loss of sensation. The main problem is that the sufferer loses the sensation in their fingers and toes, with the result that they cut or burn themselves without knowing and so often have fingers or toes missing."

"If it can be cured with such ease, why was it so widespread?" Terry asked.

"For many reason really. First they have to admit and know that they have it. Then they have to be able to find treatment. Some are living far from any form of dispensary or hospital. Even when they have been given pills to take, you cannot be sure they have always taken them; they are so poor that sometimes they will sell the pills the doctor has given them in order to buy food. In a way, who can blame them? The whole point of the Leprosy Centre is to go out and bring to our hospital all the worst cases from the surrounding countryside, treat them and let them return to their communities and villages. While here they help us grow food and learn more about providing food for themselves when they return home," Guy explained.

Terry was somewhat taken back by this insight into leprosy, he knew very little about it, never having given it much thought until coming face to face with it.

"Well it's fascinating as well as sad and I look forward to seeing around the hospital with you tomorrow. Perhaps you would take me out to some of the villages next time you go to the dispensaries; that would be interesting."

"Sure I will. It'll be chance for you to see the countryside and to meet some of the Wagogo people of this area. In a way they are the lucky ones, there are fifteen million leprosy sufferers in the world and only one in five gets any sort of treatment. Anyway don't let George work you into the ground and take time to learn more about your surroundings when you can. We're just so grateful to have you here." Guy told Terry.

One of the major projects for Terry was to lead a group of men in the construction of a wire fence around the farm to secure both the land and the cattle within. The Diocese had been given more land and the materials to fence it off. Wooden posts with barbed and plain wire had been donated to the Centre; it was a long and back-breaking task of clearing a bush track around the boundary, then endless hours digging in posts and straining wire, all in the heat of the day, week after week and not with the best team of workmen in the world!

Having become a bit fed up of seeing his men dig the wrong depth hole for the posts, Terry devised a method he felt was fool proof. Each of the men was given a stick; the length of the stick was to determine the depth of the hole required. When the top of the stick was level with the surrounding ground the hole was the right depth and the man could stop digging.

One day when he returned to see how things were progressing, one of the men was out of sight, deep down in the hole with soil flying out with the man having dug over six feet deep?

"Where is your stick?" Terry asked him in his best Swahili.

The man pointed to it stuck in the ground about 2 meters away. He had used the stick as a sort of clock and then when the shadow was in a certain place he knew it was time to knock off, just like a sundial!

He was more concerned with leaving on time then he was in doing the job!

Terry worked long hours with the men, learnt their ways and some Swahili too. He worked alongside George, ploughing with the huge disc plough on the back of the Fordson Major Tractor, discing large areas for planting new crops, cutting the grass to make hay, planting and harvesting vegetables, spraying and caring for the livestock, not forgetting dear "Buster" George's Alsatian dog, who was a wonderful companion and character.

At the same time Terry had to make sure the day to day activities like keeping the water supply going and the electric generator working were never forgotten, for the consequences of a failure would be drastic for everyone, to say the least.

In late November Terry experienced the first rains of Africa; slowly the heat had built up until everyone felt their heads would burst with the humidity. Then with a crack of thunder the heavens opened and gave the great relief they had all waited so long for. The evocative smell of the rain on the soil of Africa, after seven months dry would stay with him always.

George and Terry were busy sowing grass seed on some newly cultivated and cleared soil, walking up and down with sweat pouring off them as they spread the seed in handfuls, like two old yokels from another age.
"You get to see nature in the raw here, mate," George exclaimed.
"Nature will always fight back, seeking to reclaim the land; if a cleared area is left neglected for very long, wild grasses and small shrubs would soon creep back and spread. The dormant seed of the thorn tree can lie in the soil for years, then germinate and spring up reclaiming the land again in just three to four years. If we didn't keep it under control it would soon take over. A seed that gets in a crack will grow and force apart buildings, with all their built in strength. If we do nothing the whole place would quickly return to bush again!
There is wonderful power in nature and that's a fact mate, it's a beautiful country, but hard and cruel. There's little sign of nature helping man, but rather a long tough struggle for space, light and life," George pointed out, as he stood there in the field in dusty khaki shirt and shorts, an Anzac slouch hat shading his dazzling

blue eyes from the blazing sun. Terry became aware that this was a very special man!

With the grass sowing complete the two of them walked through dense bush land adjoining the cleared area where they had been working; the ground was rock hard, shimmering with heat and the silvery gold sheen of drying grasses and shrubs all around them. Acacia trees writhed under the sun with their long wicked thorns covering the branches; there was a tangle of thorny undergrowth, ready to tear at the hands of anyone trying to remove it. "The soil is poor, the humus burnt out by the power of the sun, the top soil blown away by the winds of these plains over the generations." George took pains to explain.

"There are no farming rules here, you just have to try and then try again, work it out for yourself, its tough mate, it's really tough."

"I've had to experiment; groundnuts grow quite well here, although the big Pied Crows think they are grown for their benefit. The birds move along the rows as you watch them and calmly dig out the seeds before your very eyes. The shotgun scares them for an hour or so, but they soon come back again, for they too are fighting for survival. Soya beans also make a good crop if the conditions are good. It can be very frustrating mate, at times, but when I think of the patients in the bush who have nothing and see them coming here to the hospital, weak and sick, then going out better - well it has to be worth it, doesn't it?"

George was a deeply thoughtful man and would often be found just standing and staring at something as if it were the first time he had ever seen it. That was part of his nature: he would be trying to fathom how it worked, or how it was made, deep in thought and looking on in wonder and amazement.

"You know mate, he said to Terry. "There has to be a God, how could there not be when you look around and see what you and I see in this raw tough countryside around us here today."

"There has to be," Terry agreed, as they stared out across the grass that formed the savannah landscape, endlessly stretched out before them in the sun.

Terry was aware he had shared a very deep and meaningful moment of wisdom and understanding with George, a moment that passed between them, and was then forever lost.

It was sometimes easy to forget that these were missionaries working here, people who had given up everything to follow their deeply held beliefs to share them with others, trying to make their lives better, brave and courageous people who were totally fulfilled by their mission in life, an example to the world. Content people who in today's language were real celebrities.

Each morning there was a short service at the hospital conducted by George or Guy for the staff, if they wished to attend. On Tuesday evenings they had Bible Study for a couple of hours and on Thursday a prayer meeting. On Sundays at 5pm they held a service at Guy and Dawn's house with George and Joan and Win, when they gathered to pray and sing hymns. Terry did not join in with them at these services; his Catholic upbringing did not encourage him to be involved in or to mix with non-Catholics. He later regretted the fact that his church had taken that view, instilling it into him as they had done. It felt and was wrong, very misguided of the Catholic Church.

Instead, Terry attended the only Catholic worship there was in the area, when he walked the five miles to the village of Hombolo on the first Sunday of each month to attend a Mass, the only one around. He would set out on foot along the dirt road in the hot sun of the day, with no thought of the wild animals around that may fancy him as a snack. Walking along through thick bush over bridges and sometimes through flooded river beds to the village of Hombolo.

An Italian Priest would arrive by landrover at the village community centre/school at two o'clock where a small group of local people and Terry would hear Mass, under the heat of the galvanised roof, and kneeling on the hard concrete floor, before turning back to walk the five miles home to the Leprosy Centre again.

By the second week in December Terry's house was complete. Dawn had made it very homely. Curtains at the windows, two easy chairs and a large coffee table furnished the small sitting room, almost filling it.

The kitchen had a Belling bottled gas cooker, just large enough for one person, as well as a stand-alone Kerosene fridge with a water filter standing on the top. Every drop of drinking water had to be boiled and filtered before it was drunk. Each evening after his meal he would set to and boil the water for the following day and pour it into the filter and then into bottles which stood in the fridge, for the next day, a much-needed source of refreshment.

He grew to love the little one bedroom house, which gave him a sense of belonging and safety, as well as sometimes a feeling of loneliness, but after a busy day in the heat he was exhausted and glad to return to his haven of peace.

At the weekends in the afternoons he would often be found sitting on the gauzed veranda writing to his family on a small blue aerogramme or reading a book. This was always a relaxing pleasure and on a Sunday around 5pm as he sat there he would often hear the music and singing that came from Dawn and Guy's house when they held their Sunday Service.

Mail was one of the greatest of luxuries. On average a letter would take ten – fourteen days, so to receive a reply to a question would take a month. The excitement would mount when it was known someone was going to make the thirty-mile trip to Dodoma.

"Don't forget to post my letters."

"Don't forget the mail bag," the cry would go out.

In the bag was always the key to Box 301 at the Post Office, where the mail was collected, then carried back to the Leprosy Centre, like a bag of gold, awaited hungrily by all, like water in the desert.

Terry's mother often sent him bundles of the Dorset Evening Echo that she had tirelessly rolled up and sent off. He would unwrap them after their long journey and iron them, just like a Victorian butler he thought, having seen this done in films. Many evenings were spent scouring the newspapers for information of past friends and places. His mother would never know the great pleasure she provided by her task and expense, one she could ill afford. It brought him closer to home and provided entertainment and comfort while sitting out in the middle of the Tanzanian bush.

Dawn and Guy loved to entertain; Terry always found it very pleasant to spend an evening with them, as well as an opportunity to get to know each other and to listen to their wonderful stories about their life when working in Uganda. It was on such an occasion and after a wonderful meal of liver and onions that Dawn gave Terry a plate with some of the leftovers from the meal.
"It's not enough for us for tomorrow, perhaps you could use it?" Dawn suggested.
Mmmmm "Yes, please, that will be just right for me."

"Do please be sure to bring back the plate when you are passing the house again," she asked Terry.
He left with his plate of liver feeling that they were such a kind devoted Christian couple and how fortunate he was to have two lovely families and the nursing sister Win to share his year in Tanzania, although of course, in March George and his family would be off on leave, so the numbers would be much reduced.

The next day, Terry could hardly wait to get home and prepare his evening meal with the wonderful left over liver and onions that Dawn had given to him. He prepared some of the vegetables that came from the Leprosy Centre garden, took the plate of liver and onions and placed it in the oven.

He prepared his table, had a shower and went to remove the liver and onions from the oven thinking how proud his mum would have been to see him preparing such a meal. To his horror, he then realised the plate was plastic and had melted into a strange fluted shape; most of the contents had run off into the bottom of the oven and dried-up! The loss of his dinner was bad enough, not to mention the mess he had to clear up in the oven, but what about the plate.

Dawn had particularly asked him to return it. The edge of it was just a wavy line and the heat had buckled the whole thing into a boat shape. How on earth was he going to give that back to Dawn who had been so insistent on his returning it to her? She, 'the Duchess', who had to have everything just right, would be so aggrieved.

For many days he walked swiftly past their house, hoping that they would not call to him as he passed by; he even tried going on a different route. However, he knew he could not go on hiding. Sooner or later he would have to face the music and the day very soon came.

"Bwana" a voice called, as Terry was collecting eggs at the farm hen house. He froze, there was Dawn's houseboy Petro, this was it, he must be after the plate.
Petro handed him a note, I bet she wants that damn plate Terry thought, quickly reading the note.

Terry

"Could I have the electricity on please.
I need some power for the washing!"

Dawn.

PS "Would you like to come for lunch at 1pm."

"Help!" He thought, "I 'm trapped."
He managed to convey to Petro, in his poor Swahili, that he would like to attend for lunch.
He returned to his house later, to collect the remains of the plate to take with him. The time had come: he had to own up and face Dawn.
Terry approached the house in fear, clutching the bent and buckled plate.

"Come in quick the BBC news is coming on," Guy said as he greeted Terry with the now familiar tune played before the news sounding out of the short wave radio.

Dee dee dah dee dah dee dah dee dee dah dee dah dee dah dee dee

Suddenly there she was, Dawn, standing by the table beaming at him.

"Welcome, we hadn't seen you for a few days and imagined you must be busy and might like to have lunch with us. How are you?"

Terry swallowed, handing the plate to Dawn. "I'm afraid I have a confession to make. You know the plate you gave me and asked me to return, well I'm afraid I didn't realise it was plastic and I put it in the oven!"

"Oh dear," she replied, looking at it in dismay, and then quietly took it off to the kitchen.

Guy was going on about the Irish situation while he was listening in to the BBC news, while Terry sat there feeling greatly relieved that he'd at last disposed of the dreaded plate.

"These Catholics" Guy said without thinking, "What are they going to do with them in Ireland?"

As was the custom in Dawn and Guy's house a small hand bell was rung by Dawn for lunch to commence. "Please turn off the radio Guy and come and say grace will you?"

They all stood around the table as Guy said his favourite version of the Grace.

"For Food & Friends and Fellowship, we give you thanks oh Lord."

As he was saying those words, Terry cast his eyes down on to the table and there in the middle of the table was 'THE' plate.

Dawn had filled it with frangipani flowers and was using it as a centrepiece for display! Nothing in Africa is ever wasted, especially in Dawn's house!

Christmas approached and the rains had turned the surrounding landscape to a lush green. The rate of growth of the crops and livestock was amazing. Unfortunately the rain caused many problems too: bridges washed away, roads rutted by the flow of the water, crops washed out of the ground, but on the whole the benefits were paramount. Insects were in abundance, especially at night as they all swirled around the lights and tried to get into the house. The bird life was astonishing and, being near to a man-made lake, the birds enjoyed the insects and the fish that it provided. The lake had been created by putting a dam into the river, which then flooded the low area surrounding it, eerily leaving trees growing out of the water where the riverbank had been.

George asked Terry to fit the grader blade on to the rear of the tractor, and pass it over the road into the Leprosy Centre, as the rain had caused the road to break up making it very bumpy for everyone trying to get in or out.

"We are off to do some shopping in Dodoma, so if you could do that and start the electric engine this evening for me, as we'll be late back."

"Just drop the blade down and scrape a few inches off the top mate, you know the sort of thing," were George's instructions.

So Terry spent the afternoon driving the Fordson Major tractor up and down the road, trying to make the surface level. It was a task that had to be done several times a year, as the road in was their lifeline for supplies.

When the task was completed, in the failing light he drove the tractor back to the shed where it was stored. He was tired from the heat of the day and ready to go and start the electric generator, if he could summons the necessary energy. He was more then ready for his supper. He leapt off the tractor in the half-light and as he did so was aware that he had nearly jumped onto what at first looked like a long black inner tube.

Yuram, one of the farm workforce was waiting there to collect keys from Terry to go and lock the chicken houses for the night. He saw Terry return with the tractor and leap from it. He screamed at him, "Nyoka, Nyoka," and pointed at the tube on the ground two feet from Terry's foot.

He was very excited, dancing around and shouting in Swahili and pointing, as if doing a tribal dance?

It was then Terry realised that he'd landed inches from a very large Black Mamba the width of a man's arm and two meters long. It slid off into a pile of wood near to the tractor. Yurum watched the snake hide in the woodpile, shouting, "Hatari! Hatari!" (Danger) while Terry rushed off to fetch the twelve bore shotgun.

Still shaking with fear and shock he returned with the gun, Yuram bravely removed some of the timber hiding the snake and "Bang, Bang," the snake rose up in the air and rolled over onto its back twisting and turning. Terry reloaded the shotgun trembling, but the Mamba was dead.

Yurum, was still dancing around and shouting, "Ukubwa sana, ukubwa sana, Bwana," (very big, very big).

Terry shook Yuram's hand. "Asante, Asante," he said to Yurum in thanks, for he had saved his life by pointing out the snake that he'd thought in the half-light was just an old inner tube.

They chatted and examined the snake as it lay there: it was the first Terry had seen so close, he hoped the last, too; it looked evil. Yurum poked the dead snake with a stick and suggested it was taken over to the hospital for Dr Timmis to see, as it was so unusually large. Together they lifted the heavy lifeless snake into the back of the Landover and set off to the hospital buildings a few hundred yards away.

They drew up out side the administration building where Dr Timmis was winding things up for the day in his office before going home. They called him over to show him the snake, then, as they looked into the back of the land rover, the snake, like Lazarus, rose up and slid out onto the ground before them, twisting this way and that. It was still very much alive! Yurum, quickly and bravely took the long Panga knife that was in the Land Rover and hit the snake with it on the head with repeated blows!

They all gazed at each other in utter shock and amazement at the now dead and headless snake.

Chapter Five

A month had passed since Terry had arrived at Hombolo and Christmas was creeping up fast, not that it felt anything like Christmas or showed any of the usual signs of its pending arrival. The heat at that time was in the 90's most days and since the rain had arrived it was very humid, that plus being 4000 ft above sea level sapped all his energy.

Guy and Dawn were always so concerned for Terry, inviting him to meals and taking him out.

"How'd you fancy going to a Christmas Party at the Bishop's house in Dodoma?" Guy asked as they were sitting on his lawn one afternoon having tea and listening to the BBC World Service News.

It didn't sound too exciting to a then 20 year old, but, well, it was different Terry thought and it gave him a trip into Dodoma.

"Yes love to. When is it?"

"Sunday evening at 5pm. You can use the Leprosy Centre Landrover, collect the mail and call it a business trip."

"Ok great I'll look forward to it."

Sunday arrived and off Terry went in the Landrover feeling a sense of freedom to be driving out of the centre and making the long bumpy, dusty journey into Dodoma on his own. Arriving at the Bishop's House there were lots of cars and people milling around and Terry just mingled.

There was the Bishop's Secretary, Mary Punt, whom he had met a few times, both in Dodoma and when she had visited the Leprosy Centre. There was the Headmaster of the local mission school, teachers and government workers, people of all colours and creeds, altogether quite an interesting gathering. There was a wonderful array of food on the table much to Terry's surprise and delight. Feeling hungry after his long trip, he took a plate and helped himself.

"Can you tell me what's in these sandwiches?" asked a friendly dark haired man.

"I really have no idea," Terry replied, "but these sausage rolls are pretty good."

"I'm Philip by the way. Are you a CMS missionary here?"

"Pleased to meet you Philip, I'm Terry. No, I'm a VSO, you know, Voluntary Service Overseas, a volunteer from England, from Weymouth in Dorset, but working at a Leprosy Centre thirty miles north of here. So what do you do here Philip?"

"I teach at a Catholic Mission at Bihawana, twelve miles south with my wife Margaret. We're from Grimsby."

With that a lovely slim lady in a pale biscuit dress joined them, "Hello there."

"This is Terry," Philip explained. "He is a Volunteer from England and working with the CMS Mission at a Leprosy Centre."

So it was that a new and lifelong friendship began between them, as happened to so many when they were living far from home.

The tempo of Hombolo was a mix of hard work, fighting to keep everyday needs going like electricity and water supplies, times for rest and sleep as well as keeping their own food supplies topped up by trips to Dodoma. Relaxation consisted of chatting with visitors to the center, of which there was always a regular number and the odd trip out. Otherwise they made their own entertainment. Often slide shows when one of them had a box of slides returned from Hemel Hempstead, where they were processed. This caused great excitement. They would all get together for a meal at Guy and Dawn's house and the latest slides would come out receiving both critical and complimentary remarks.

Guy had found an old Belling 16mm projector, which Terry repaired, much to Guy's admiration, which enabled them to watch reels of films from the British Council and the American Embassy. These were relished at the get togethers and, if suitable, shown later to the leprosy patients at the home made outside cinema, which consisted of a large white area painted on the side of one of the patients' houses. Everyone brought along a seat and the latest film was projected on the wall with sound, for all to watch and enjoy, including the mosquitoes, the uninvited guest that was Africa's greatest killer which insisted on joining them!

One of the other most enjoyable highlights was to go out in a small homemade, wooden flat-bottomed punt, which George had made, to fish on the lake. The lake, about two miles long and half a mile wide, had lots of ugly catfish in it, but also the most succulent and sweet tasting Tilapia. Whenever they all could find time, a Saturday afternoon would be spent quietly sitting in the punt a few yards off the shore, tied to one of the old trees that was still standing half-submerged in the water, letting the peace of the day wash over them, while pulling out twenty to thirty lovely Tilapia on a rod and float line. The occasional appearance of a Catfish with its long ugly facial whiskers on someone's line would throw the boat into chaos and laughter.

Otherwise it was all very relaxed. They enjoyed seeing the bird life attracted by the water, Black Cormorants, Black and Brown Divers, Spoonbills, Cranes, Fish Eagles and many others. It was a time to take in the wonderful scenery that surrounded them, for it was such a beautiful spot with the flat plains of the Wagogo Country stretching out to the purple mountains far out on the horizon. As they returned to shore the sun would be setting, turning the water deep red and old gold, the half submerged trees black against the skyline.

Terry could feel the history of the place, where the slave traders had marched with their captives in yokes and chains along endless bush trails, through this very area to the coast at Bagamoyo to an unknown future. You could almost hear the cries and the clanging chains of the slaves.

What a tough background there was to this country, what beauty, what depth, what hardship and bloodshed there had been an unforgettable land of contrasts. He could feel Africa moulding a warm and lasting place in his heart. This was an experience that would never be forgotten, one he could never ever forget; he could already feel the hold of it eating into his very being, like a madness!

It was Richard Burton, the great linguist and African explorer of the 1850's who said, "All madness comes from Africa." Terry could feel himself being taken over by that madness; it would make him want to return again and again, as indeed it had for so many before him. For countless numbers it had taken a hold, so much so, that they threw all caution to the wind, just to 'be' in the country, to feel it, see it, experience it and renew their individual love for it and its people.

"What was it? Why was it? What caused it?" He felt engulfed by the experience that was "Africa."

These deep melancholy thoughts were a feature of life at Hombolo, the inescapable solitude and often loneliness, it was something else that had to be lived with and understood by all that experienced it. Sometimes it hit you hard and with such a force, like a deep depression, an inner torment. David Livingstone spoke of it, as did Henry Morton Stanley.

On Saturday 18th April 1874 after David Livingstone's funeral, when Stanley walked solemnly out of Westminster Abbey into the bright London sunshine he was already planning to throw away wealth and fortune and return to Africa. Henry Morton Stanley was going back to Africa, as David Livingstone had done with that same madness working away inside them, something they carried to the end of their lives.

Christmas served to highlight these thoughts with its sentiment and memories of home. Sitting outside the Leprosy Hospital on a starlit Christmas Eve, with the coloured lights strung across the trees, singing Christmas carols with the leprosy patients, brought tears to Terry's eyes, he could hardly bring himself to sing. He really hadn't expected all this, to feel as he did, to love as he did all that was Africa.

Years later when in England, George said to Terry, "You know mate, the first thing I think about when I awake in the morning is Africa. I remember every tree and almost every bump in the road; it totally possesses me."

The New Year opened with heavy rain, the routine of life continuing. George, Joan and their two girls Anne & Margaret prepared for home leave in New Zealand. Guy and Dawn and Sister Win worked long hours at the hospital and Terry continued learning about all the responsibilities he had to take over. He tried to learn more Swahili, while working on the seemingly unending fence around the centre and working alongside George in the daily tasks of running the farm.

There was some interesting news coming from CMS office in Dodoma. Apparently there were now sufficient funds to commence the long awaited Occupational Therapy building at Hombolo and Kevin Engle, from the Bishop's office, and his team were going out to Hombolo to set out the site and get the contract underway. It was too big a task for George who not only had the farm to manage but of course was also off on leave for seven months.

Having an Occupational Therapy building at the centre was an important step forward in the treatment of leprosy, providing a place where the patients could practice skills that would give their limbs exercise while at the same time teaching them new skills that could help them to earn a living once they left to return to their villages. In the new therapy building they would carry out hand exercises, make items from clay, weave cloth and make rush mats. Old car tyres were to be cut up and from them they would learn to make flip-flop type shoes, which are so popular and durable in Africa.

The excitement from Terry's point of view was the news that there was to be another member of the team join the small number living at Hombolo. Even better from his point of view was the fact that she was a single lady from the U.K. She had been working in Canada for four years and was now on her way to visit her Aunt, a well known and respected Church Army Missionary, who worked in Western Tanzania at a place called Kalinzi, just north of Kigoma and Ujiji, the place where H M Stanley had found David Livingstone on the morning of Friday 10th November 1871.

"Would you like a cup of tea?" Guy called out, as Terry passed his house on the way home. It was often the cry when Terry passed in the late afternoon, by which time Guy would often be found sitting on his lawn with a tray of tea, relaxing after a busy day. Terry always hoped he might be there and they could have tea and a chat, he so enjoyed those occasions.

"Would love to Guy. Thanks."

The two of them sat there looking out towards the beautiful mauve coloured hills in the far distance, with Guy in a high old state about the cricket, which seemed to be his number one interest. He could never really understand that Terry knew nothing about 'Maiden Overs,' well at least not in that sense!

Dawn rounded the corner of the house in a somewhat exhausted state and called to Petro, their houseboy to bring another cup and a fresh pot of tea.

"Have you heard yet when the new therapist is to arrive? I understand that work on the new building is soon to start," Terry asked Dawn, who was responsible for all the employment matters.

"She is staying with her auntie for six weeks at the moment, over near Kigoma in the west, then coming here in April if all goes to plan."

Her auntie, Lesley Bangham, was a formidable lady who first came to Tanzania in 1946, set up her own hospital on the border of Rwanda with the help of the CMS. But the Bishop withdrew support for her because it was getting too dangerous to safeguard and be responsible for her. When told by the Bishop that she must leave, she refused and would not hear of pulling out and stayed on for a year supporting herself from funds raised by friends in U.K.

"My people need me so I am not going to leave them." Lesley had told the Bishop.

"In the end the Bishop agreed to renew her support, such was her determination. So she is a very strong-minded and formidable lady! You may get the chance to meet her," Dawn said, "as she is going to bring her niece Ann over to Hombolo in April. Ann, when she arrives, will share Win's house as she has a spare room and they'll be company for each other."

Terry was already beginning to look forward to Ann's arrival, what ever she was like, and at least she would be another person with whom to share day to day life and to exchange views with and, he thought, someone who is not a missionary!

Meanwhile Terry was due some time off work and decided to take up the offer of Margaret and Philip Cox, his new English friends whom he had met at the Bishop's Christmas Party. They suggested he may like to have a few days with them at the Bihawana Mission and school, before he went to Nairobi to see something of Kenya. He had been told that 'The Kenya Young Men's Christian Association' in Nairobi was a good place to stay, at only twenty three shillings a night. So he booked himself in there for five nights, planning to stop off at Arusha on route, as he was keen to see Mount Kilimanjaro, the highest mountain in Africa at 19,340 feet, which was not far from Arusha at Moshi.

On Friday 18th March, Sister Win took Terry into Dodoma where he had tea with Mary Punt the Bishop's Secretary and met Margaret and Philip at the Dodoma Hotel. They had a drink in the colonial surroundings of the Hotel, sitting on the veranda among the tropical vegetation. It was heaven and a light relief from life at Hombolo.

They then went to the local cinema to see the film 'Huk.' Attending an African cinema, run by an Indian man, is in itself quite an experience compared to the cinema at home. Philip was up and down to the projectionist throughout the film asking him to focus the lens and turn the sound up or down.

At the interval Margaret wanted to use the toilet and asked Philip if such a place existed and where it was. He asked the projectionist who sent him to the Manager for the key to the private lavatory, but the manager said that he did not have the key and told him to ask the man in the shop next door! So out he went to ask him, but no good, so in the end Philip took Margaret five minutes down the road to the hotel!

After the film they all went to Margaret and Philip's place at Bihawana travelling in their yellow Ford Anglia car, very smart and up to date for Africa.

"But how does it survive these roads?" Terry asked Philip.

"It has telescopic suspension on the front and that helps glide over the corrugated road surfaces," Philip told him as they ploughed their way south along the twelve-mile road through sand, dust and corrugations from Dodoma to Bihawana.

Terry spent a wonderful weekend with these new friends, there was a common bond between them, with both being from England, living in a foreign country and being Catholics. They sat until the small hours enjoying wonderful food, Carlsberg beer and a few Sportsman cigarettes as they chatted and got to know each other, having only met once at the Christmas party at the Bishop's house.

On Saturday morning they went to the market in Dodoma to buy local produce and in the afternoon played tennis on the court at Bihawana, followed by films at the school in the evening.

On the Monday morning Terry was due to leave Bihawana at 7.30am and go into Dodoma to get the East African Railways Bus to Arusha. They found there had been an almighty storm and the main road out of Bihawana Mission was flooded, with the bridge washed away. Margaret and Philip were so upset that he should be losing a day of his holiday, but Terry had enjoyed his time with them so much and felt so at home that he was quite happy to have it extended by a day.

By the following morning the water level had fallen and Philip was able to negotiate his car over the riverbed, quite a normal practice in Africa when bridges were washed away, and drive to Dodoma where Terry was able to catch his bus and embark on his journey north.

Terry arrived in Arusha after the long and dusty journey from Dodoma, where he once again shared the bus with dogs and goats on an over populated bus. He tried to find a place to stay for two nights, as he wanted to visit Moshi nearby to see Mount Kilimanjaro. However, apart from the very expensive Safari Hotel in the middle of town, there was nowhere.

A well-meaning man directed him to "Liberty Hotel" halfway between Arusha and Moshi, which, he said, provided overnight accommodation. Terry went off in search of the "Liberty Hotel" with high expectations. He found it at the side of the main road to Moshi, a run down building with rooms going off a long corridor on one side. A single room for the night was five shillings, but you had to share the bathroom. Feeling desperate, what else could he do? He was tired and worn from the journey and was desperate to both clean up and to get some sleep. So he paid his five shillings to a rough grubby man who shuffled along the corridor, like a character from Dickens, to show Terry the room.

"There you are, you can wash next door," he said. A man of few words, who then shuffled off back to the entrance of the 'Liberty Hotel.'

Terry stepped into a small narrow room with no light or window. There was a very weak light bulb, probably 25 watt hanging from the ceiling and a single bed along the wall. That was it. The heat was unbearable and there was no air. The sheets were reasonable and seemed at least to have been washed recently, but the one and only other bedcover was brown and well used.

He noticed that there was no way of locking the door which did not really close properly or latch.

"How grim," he thought to himself, but tiredness was taking over.

He went to explore the bathroom that was next to his room. He carried his case with him, not daring to leave it in the room. He may not have had much of value in it, but to a passing African it would be wealth beyond their dreams.

"Bathroom?" It was another small dark room, no electricity, with a small window high up in the eaves. A pipe came out of the wall with a tap underneath. In the floor was a hole for the water to run out; that he worked out must be the place to wash or shower.

Over in the opposite corner of the bathroom was a large hole in the ground: the WC. Bizarrely on one wall there was a huge decorative mirror, six feet high with a wooden decoratively carved frame. It seemed strange, as there was no light to see in the mirror, even if you wanted to. The concrete floor had a slippery film on it and Terry found it difficult not to slip over.

As there was no lock on the door he stood his case behind it to prevent unwelcome visitors. He just had to wash off the dust of the day. He turned on the tap only to find that the top came off in his hand and dropped to the floor, narrowly missing the hole. Water spurted out from the pipe above, a dirty brown cold fluid that trickled down. If Hombolo water was like tea, then this was like Mum's best and thickest gravy. Terry decided only to wash his face and hair that were covered in red dust from the day's travel. Having reluctantly done so, he realised that he had no towel and of course no towel was provided. Perhaps that was a blessing.

He returned to his room and tried to prop the door closed with his case together with a length of timber he found lying in the corridor. Taking his wallet and passport he placed them under the mattress for safety, as surely he would get some sleep in this hellhole. As he lifted the mattress two large brown cockroaches ran out, across the room and under the door. How much worse could it get, he wondered.

Terry was horrified with the accommodation, but felt trapped, what else could he possibly do? He was desperate to lie down and was so weary. After examining the bed he lay there listening to the sounds around him. It was surprisingly quiet. There was the odd drunk that seemed to go into one of the other rooms off the corridor, but it was not so bad, with just the constant jabber of conversation in the distance, all of course in Swahili. He very soon slipped into a deep sleep waking every hour and checking that the door was still propped close, which it always was.

At 4am he awoke with a stabbing pain in his side. He turned over cursing the bed; it felt like a sting from a hundred nettles as he rubbed his side while lying in the bed. By 4.30 the feeling of nettle rash was more like a bee sting and the pain grew slowly worse. With the aid of his torch he could see that his side was red and blotchy and had several holes in it with white rings around them. Then he spotted the culprits: in the bed flattened by his weight were the bodies of four small brown dead scorpions. Somehow they had got into the room and onto his bed where they had stung him with their vicious tails as he slept and then had been killed as he turned over onto them in his sleep. Terry shot out of bed clutching his painful side; he had no idea what to do next.

He looked into his wash bag and all he could see that was remotely able to help him was a small tin of Zambuck he had brought from the U.K. He rubbed it into his side watching the red area swell and the pain in his side increase. There was no question of him laying on that bed again he thought, so he packed his case and rubbing his side, left the 'Liberty Hotel' and walked down the road, stopping to rub his side from time to time like a man possessed.

It was cold and misty at this early hour and a thin fog hung over everything. He sat by the side of the road on a tree stump feeling very very low not really knowing what to do next, wondering if it had been very wise to embark on this journey without any resources. After a local goat had come along and showed far too much interest in him, he decided it was better to walk on towards Moshi, so with his case and his low spirits he staggered along the road some two miles towards the town.

On arrival there he spotted a bus stop and wondered if any buses ever passed that way through this sleepy small town so early in the day. He sat there looking up towards where Mount Kilimanjaro would normally be seen, but that morning it was hidden by the morning mist.

He perched on his case for half an hour, then slowly like the curtain on a stage the mist rolled back and revealed the most incredible sight he had ever seen. There high above Moshi was Mount Kilimanjaro in full view, with bright blue sky behind it; the top was covered in snow like icing on a cake, the view every bit as beautiful as the pictures he had seen of it. He sat there amazed as the sun burnt the mist and coldness away. Then another miracle, up the road a bus approached and yes it was going to Arusha. He was so relieved to see it. The ride to Arusha felt like being in a Rolls Royce after the events of the night.

"So here I am back again," he thought, as he arrived in Arusha. "What now? I've seen Kilimanjaro and I've seen the Liberty Hotel!" He was not due to arrive at the YMCA until the following day; he had to find somewhere else to stay the night. There was only one thing to do; he would have to blow some of his holiday money on a night at the 'New Arusha Hotel' which was 47/- shillings a night!

After a luxurious night there he felt so much better and able to face the next one hundred and seventy two miles of the journey to Nairobi. The long red murram dirt road stretched out before him through Namango and across the Tanzanian – Kenyan Border post in the Amboseli Game Reserve. All went well, once they joined the A109 Mombasa to Nairobi road, which was tarmac. What a blessed relief that was although, because of the state of the surface, it was still very rough and bumpy. The bus passed along Haile Selassie Avenue pulling into Temple Street and on into the bus station at 4pm, Nairobi at long last.

Terry gathered his case and set off in the direction of the YMCA. He laboured on walking in the heat of the afternoon sun and out of the bus station and down the road. As he did, a car pulled along side him and he heard someone shout, "Can I help you? Where you heading?"

Terry was surprised and a little wary at this greeting. He stopped and looked into the car where he saw a pleasant looking European man.

"I'm booked into the YMCA. I understand it is in this direction and up the top of the hill."

"Yes it is," the man replied, "but it's a long way from here up on Hospital Road. If you would like to jump in I'll take you there."

Terry was a bit uncertain about taking a lift from a stranger, but he did seem pleasant enough and by this time the man had already got out of his car and was opening the boot. "O.K." Terry said, "thank you. It's very kind of you."

He stepped into the car, wondering if he was doing the right thing. They chatted as the car roared off through the crowded streets. Terry was relieved to see the car pull up outside the YMCA and quickly got out.

"By the way," the man said, "my name is Tony Cunningham. I work here in the government offices and have done so for five years now."

"Pleased to meet you and thanks a lot for the lift."

"What are you doing tomorrow?" Tony asked.

"Nothing planned. Have a look around the city I guess."

"Well how about if I take you to see the animals in the National Park as I'm not working in the afternoon?"
Terry was again unsure, but he did seem like a genuine kind man.
"That would be very kind of you, I'd love to see the park as I've heard so much about it."
"Right," Tony said. "I'll pick you up here tomorrow afternoon at 2pm. Look forward to seeing you then."
The following morning Terry explored the city. He was amazed at the contrast with sleepy Dodoma; there was a busyness and order about the place, all the buildings were in excellent decorative repair, clean and tidy. There was a policeman standing in a raised box with a sun shield over him in the centre of the road directing traffic with the cars obeying his hand signals: it seemed amazing to see it here in Africa somehow. The population was over 300,000 and the altitude 5,500 ft above sea level, so it was often cool in the mornings and evenings. The long rains were from March to May with an average rainfall of thirty five inches, so on the whole the climate was very pleasant with temperatures rarely above eighty degrees.

Along the pavements, outside the shops were lines of carved wooden figures, animals, men and women, bowls, wooden knives, salad tongs, small chairs and three legged stools. Hundreds of them, making a magnificent display of ability and talent in producing such items, aimed of course at the tourist. There was the general hustle and bustle of city life giving the feeling of lots of trade going on, not a city of great wealth as there were vast slums all around the edge of Nairobi, but a lively busy agreeable and safe feeling place.

Tony arrived at the appointed time and they had a most enjoyable and successful visit to the National Park just seven miles from the city, an area of some forty four square miles where an astonishing variety of wild life lived, including lion, hippo, giraffe and all kinds of antelope, carnivore and birds; it was a truly wonderful opportunity to see the park. If Terry had not met Tony then he, having no car, would never have seen the inside of the park.

Tony seemed to enjoy the visit too. He suggested they might like to go to the 'Drive-In Cinema,' of course Terry had never even heard of a 'Drive-In' let alone been to one. Together they sat in the back of Tony's car, eating a burger and watching the film.
After the film he took Terry back to the YMCA having spent a full and enjoyable day together.
"Would you like to have a trip out tomorrow to see Lake Naivasha? It's a really beautiful area and you can see the grand Kikuyu farm lands, then you can come and see my flat and have a meal with me in the evening?"

Terry agreed, but was still not totally certain that it was the right thing to do, wondering where all this might be leading, feeling still a little apprehensive about this sudden friendship that had grown from nothing. He was concerned, too, that Tony was paying for everything and he was not able to contribute, especially after the unexpected cost of the night at the Arusha hotel.
On Saturday morning Tony arrived at the YMCA and they set off on their tour, calling in at the beautifully kept War Cemetery and on through the Kikuyu country to the beginning of the Great Rift Valley, the giant crack, a mysterious geological fault in the earth's surface that runs through three territories; at the viewpoint it is forty miles wide, with the extinct volcanoes of Suswa and Longonot seen on the rift floor. The road to the viewpoint passed through fertile coffee, tea and dairy farming areas as well as the Kikuyu reserve with their splendid sweeping views, lush trees growing so tall they seemed to touch the sky. The people looked far better fed then those in Tanzania, but then the climate was so different and the rainfall more evenly spread throughout the year. Tony seemed to know a great deal about the area and its people;

he explained about the Mau Mau uprising that was still fresh in everyone's minds and along with the Second World War, never far away.

They slowly took the steep hill pulling into a small chapel on the edge of the ever-twisting main road. "This chapel was built by Italian prisoners of war who'd worked a lot in this area," he explained. "They built roads, houses and cleared forests. This chapel was built in memory of their countrymen and all they had done here in Kenya."

It was very tiny and seemed far from any sort of population that may wish to use it, constructed of sandstone, probably locally excavated.

"Would you like a picture taken?" Tony asked.

"Please," Terry replied and stood on the step by the door while Tony took the picture.

"I'd like one of you too, as I don't have your picture."

"Sorry, I don't like having my picture taken," he said surprisingly.

A fact that Terry would always regret as he never did have a picture to remember him by.

They drove on along the long straight road towards Naivasha, turning left onto the lake road to the 'Lake Hotel' at the side of Lake Naivasha where they enjoyed a wonderful lunch sitting on the veranda looking out over the beautiful lake and surrounding countryside: it was like a dream, the charm and natural beauty of the place. Terry thought how it was a million miles from his night at the 'Liberty Hotel' at Moshi!

It was all too soon time to return and make the steady climb back up to Nairobi taking a loop road to see the Ngong Hills then on through the district of Karen and back into the city.

Tony had a government flat in a block that had security guards and a gate where you had to enter a number to obtain access, all very impressive Terry thought. The flat was furnished with style having been Tony's home for four years. He told Terry how his wife had died two years before from cancer; hence he was now living on his own. He loved Kenya and had decided to stay for as long as his contract continued to be renewed by the Kenyan Government. He worked in the President's office on the security side and worked closely with the Mayor of Nairobi, Charles Rubia.

The following day, Sunday, Terry attended Mass at the Holy Family Cathedral in the centre of Nairobi. During the Mass on the other side of the church he saw a familiar face; it was his friend Tony Cunningham. What a surprise to see him. The two of them had never discussed their religious beliefs, but it turned out he was a true Christian man, well he certainly had been to Terry.

It was time for Terry to return to Hombolo, so on Monday a glorious, warm and stimulating day, he had arranged to travel off down to Arusha and to stop off at Tengaru a government station for research. Terry had met a couple on a visit to Hombolo who offered him a bed there on his return, so he had no concerns about accommodation this time!

Tony took him out of Nairobi to the junction of the A109 with the A104; there in the interest of economy Terry had planned to try and hitch a lift from a passing motorist.
"Well, what can I say?" Terry exclaimed as he stepped out of the car. "It's been a most fantastic experience. Thank you for everything you have done to make my visit to Nairobi such a memorable one. Without you, Tony I would have seen little and I thank you for everything and your kindness to me. I hope we will keep in touch, that one day we'll meet again." The two of them said a sad farewell taking their different roads; fate never allowed them to meet again, although they did keep in touch for many years.

After two days of travelling through the dry open country from Nairobi, with thorn trees all around, passing groups of Masai, the men tall and willowy and carrying long staffs, the women with shaven heads, their wrap-around clothes dull and plain with the dirt and dust, but with colourful bead necklaces, copper bangles and enormous copper wire ear-rings. Terry arrived again in the Wagogo region of Dodoma at 4.30pm where he was met by George and Joan Hart with the now familiar call of, "Good day, mate, how was your holiday?"

All the way back on the road to Hombolo Terry caught up on the events since he had left for his holiday. So that by the time they arrived he felt it was business as usual. Joan made a delightful meal for them all as soon as they arrived back at Hombolo, despite the fact they were leaving the next day to start their seven months leave and most things were packed up. She had always made wonderful ice cream and that night somehow Terry felt it was exceptional as they enjoyed it with fresh mango at this memorable last meal together.

George and Terry had, over the months together at Hombolo, built up a strong bond and respect for each other, a father/son like relationship based on their common interest in agriculture, their Christian faith, and Terry's admiration for all the work that George had done in the development of the Leprosy Centre, with his dogged determination and ingenuity. Neither of them admitted their exceptional relationship, but both were very aware of it. They enjoyed that last evening together as they sat there talking everything over, knowing that the next day, Terry would have to take the responsibility of George's job on his young shoulders and pick up the load that had been until then George's.

"Before you go George," Terry asked, "I have one more question, that's been bugging me since the day I arrived."

"OK, fire away, mate."

"On the night I arrived at Hombolo, what was it in that jar on your bathroom windowsill? You always said you would tell me and I'm just fascinated."

"Right, I'll tell you, but it's a bit personal, mate!

Ten years ago I had to have a colostomy and ever since I've had to use a bag that was my spare!"

Terry was quite taken back as he had never come across anything like that before and regretted forcing George to reveal his secret.

"I'm so sorry to hear that George, it must be extremely difficult to work here in Africa with that condition and dealing with it."

"Well mate you get used to it, you know, and most of the time everything is all right. It's never easy, but you see I love Africa and I came here to serve the people and make a better life for them. The cost of doing that is high, both for my family and for me, but Joan and I decided that it's what we wanted to do."

Terry did not know what to say and was amazed how George had worked so physically hard over the years with such a serious health problem. It only served to show the depth of his commitment and love for Africa and its people. Terry found that very humbling indeed.

George and Joan, with their daughters Anne and Margaret left Hombolo for their home leave in New Zealand on Thursday 14th April 1966 with everyone feeling a bit sad.

"Well, mate," George said, shaking Terry's hand, "I've done my best and taught you all I know, just keep it all going for me, take care of dear old Buster and I hope you don't have too many problems. See you in November."

He loaded up his black Volkswagen and drove off down the road in a cloud of dust. They had to drive into Dodoma where they would pick up the MAF flight to Nairobi for their flight to N.Z.

Guy, Dawn, Win and Terry waved the Harts a tearful farewell: they all felt the depleted numbers that the Harts' departure caused, but with loyal determination and George's courage and inspiration they carried on with the daily tasks.

Chapter Six

Within twenty four hours of the Harts' departure Terry was in trouble. He began to feel very feverish, hot then cold and quite ill. It turned out that he had a mild attack of malaria. If that wasn't enough the bearing on the main water pump that supplied the Leprosy Centre's water, situated at the dam developed a knock and needed attention. So he dragged himself out of bed and down to the pump to establish the problem. He found the housing of a bearing was loose so attempted to tighten the bolts, but in doing so snapped a steel bolt, bringing the water supply for the whole Leprosy centre to a halt for twenty four hours, while he tried to find a new steel bolt in Dodoma.

This was not a good start to his term in office as Farm Manager. Fortunately a garage run by a man from Germany, Bert Swzster, who did a lot of work for the Diocese, agreed to make a suitable bolt and the next day sent out someone to fit it and get the water flowing again, much to everyone's relief. Africa is like that; just when you think it is hopeless, something or someone comes along to resolve the problem or provide just what you need.

Temperatures were in the 90's in mid April, with the hot sun beating down mercilessly everyday. The leprosy patients were harvesting the millet that George had planted. It is not a grain that the Africans favour for their flour; they prefer maize flour for their porridge meal of Ugali, their staple food. However, it was a good stand-by when there was little else; otherwise it was mainly used for animal feed. The heads of the millet were cut off, and then carried back to the farm where they were laid on a raised wire rack to dry in the sun. When dry, they were laid-out on an area of concrete and beaten with sticks by the women, to thrash out the grain for storage. Apart from the millet, harvesting of the hay continued, collecting it and taking it to be stored near the cattle enclosure for use in the long dry season by the forty head of Zebu cattle. The grass dried so quickly here in Tanzania's heat, the quality of the hay was good with little of the feed value lost from cutting to harvest.

Fencing of the farm boundary continued, with the new fence having to be patrolled each day to be sure no damage had been caused, either by people or animals, for the fence was never an obstacle to either or a deterrent for large animals like rhino; for them it was like strands of cotton, so it was necessary to check the fence every few days and make the necessary repairs.

At the hospital the day to day routine continued for Guy and his team. He showed Terry how he took a photograph of each patient when they were admitted to the centre and another when they left: the difference was often remarkable. Guy loved his photography as a hobby too, and had a good eye for a picture; he made all their Christmas cards often using a scene from the open bush land. He developed and printed all his own black and white pictures, but had to send coloured films away. He and Dawn had a vast range of colour slides recording their travels and their work over the years in Uganda and Tanzania, a wonderful collection that was a joy to view and to hear the stories surrounding them.

During one of their afternoon tea sessions on the lawn outside Guy's house, he asked Terry, "Would you be able to come out with me tomorrow to visit Humakwa? It's a dispensary that I'm due to visit, which I try to do twice a year. It would be interesting for you to see what goes on. That's if you are over your attack of malaria and feel like making the journey. It's quite a long and rough road. Win is coming with me too, as we like to take a close look at those that might have signs of leprosy and see if we need to have them attend the Leprosy Centre, if we have the space to accommodate them."

Not wanting to turn the offer down and keen to see more of his surroundings Terry arranged things so he could leave the farm to take the trip the next day. Yuram, the foreman, was an able man and Terry was happy to leave the day-to-day activities of the farm with him. So at eight thirty the next morning, Guy, Win and Terry set off on the hundred mile round trip to visit an area north of Hombolo to a dispensary where a trained Tanzanian health worker checked those people that came to him for help and were in some way sick. He would then refer them to a hospital or arrange for Guy to see them on his visits as necessary.

"Told you it was a rough road," Guy explained as the car bumped along the corrugated surface of the dirt road, throwing a large cloud of dust up behind. "You should see it in the wet season!"

The countryside was quite flat and from time to time you would see a giraffe or a gazelle right along the roadside and of course monkeys were everywhere. All this was so different, exciting, and something Terry had only read about before this day.

It was hot and the roads dusty, but it was interesting to see the countryside around, to see the square mud huts, their grass thatched roofs, all with a small patch of maize growing around their house, providing the basic food for the year, the difference between life and death.

"This is the Kongwa area," Guy explained. "It has a fascinating history and was part of the area where the British Government's Groundnut Scheme of the 1940's and 50's had taken place. An amount of forty-nine million pounds had been expended on the failed scheme, typical of politicians, don't you think? They should have had you out here then to oversee it. So much hope had been placed in that scheme, so much time and money invested, to be abandoned in 1951 at considerable cost to the British taxpayer.

The area chosen was subject to drought; groundnuts require at least twenty inches of water a year, which they rarely have in this area. Some idiot forgot to put out a rain gauge!"

"What do you make of Africa so far?" Win enquired. "Is it how you imagined it to be?"

Terry considered the point. "Well it's such a beautiful country full of need and challenges. I do love the huge Baobab trees, the birds we have at Hombolo and the sounds of the bush. It's a country full of contrasts. The heat is far more intense then I thought it would be, the people are poorer, but at the same time so much more cheerful then I imagined, with their being so poor and with all they have to put up with."

Win explained how the people expect so little. "The Wagogo tribe of the area are a Bantu ethnic group, cattle people; cattle are a sign of their wealth, but food and water, a dry house and enough land to grow their annual maize is all they really ask. I have worked with the Tanzanian people now for thirteen years in this area both at Kilimatinde and Makutopora and now Hombolo; they love to keep grazing cattle if they can afford them. They're an amazingly happy and a peaceful people asking so little from life."

Win continued, "Our Bishop, with the support of Mission to Lepers, set up the Leprosy Centre. Until then most of the leprosy in the area just spread and spread, with little control. Now at least they have somewhere where they can receive patients providing some help and care."

The little dispensary at Humakwa was a small single storey building in the middle of nowhere. They pulled off the road and greeted the medic who was in charge and waiting for them. There was a long line of people of all shapes and sizes waiting in the heat of the day for the doctor to arrive. They went into a small room and sat there while the doctor discussed the condition of each patient in turn, in Swahili of course. Therefore Terry had little idea of what was happening, having only a very limited vocabulary of the language.

As this was going on, they all suddenly leapt up and rushed out of the room exclaiming something in Swahili. Terry didn't understand so he just sat there. He was aware of a noise that sounded rather like a train passing, then after a few minutes he thought he would investigate to see why everyone had gone outside, thinking it may have been to see a train. As he stepped out a big cry went up.

"Oh my goodness!" Guy exclaimed, "We forgot you didn't understand Swahili. That was an earthquake! We had shouted, 'Get out quick.' Didn't you hear the quake?"

"No," Terry responded anxiously, "I thought it was a train passing, I wondered where you had all gone?"

The doctor conducted the rest of the examinations outside, just in case another wave of the earthquake should shake the building and cause it to fall in on them.

Life continued at Hombolo with its steady routine and Terry settled into his new life and responsibilities, but always missing George's support. The days were hot and long with the odd light shower as the rainy season drew to a close. Terry continued to organise the clearance of the bush ready to cultivate more land for cropping, the men being paid seventy shillings an acre to cut the bush trees and dig out the roots. It seemed hard work to him, but that was the going rate. On the whole there was a real feel of the farm developing and progress being made which gave Terry a real buzz and the feeling that he was doing something positive.

News came through that a new occupational therapist Ann Bangham was due to arrive on Monday 23rd May 1966. That was a day he really looked forward to. It would mean another young person and a European to share the loneliness and isolation that was Hombolo, as well as someone who was not a missionary. Terry could not help but wonder what Ann would be like; clearly she enjoyed travel having worked in Canada for four years. He sort of felt that they would get on, that they were destined to do so, or was that wishful thinking he wondered.

On Monday 23rd he kept an eye open for Ann's arrival but by midday there had been no sign of the car arriving when Terry went home for his lunch. On his way back to the farm, he took the same path he always did, past the Harts' house. As he did, he saw two people at the front door.

"Hey. Young man," a booming voice rang out across the plains, "come and help us open this door at once."

There stood a short portly lady in a cream dress and brown hat with another tall slim lady with long fair hair tied back in a pony tail, both looking a little concerned and anxious.

Terry went to the front door of the Harts' house to meet them, "Hello, you must be Ann and Lesley Bangham?"

"That's right young man and who are you? Do you know how to open this door?" Lesley bellowed at him. Terry shook them by the hand, introduced himself and unlocked the door for them, as they were to stay in the house for a few days, while Ann was settling in and for the length of Lesley's visit.

Ann appeared to be a little apprehensive about the whole situation and a bit embarrassed by her auntie's forthright manner.

Fortunately Terry had been warned about Lesley Bangham, the big woman with the big heart and even bigger demands, now he was meeting her in the flesh!

Dawn invited Terry to afternoon tea to officially meet Lesley and Ann, so at four o'clock he presented himself at their house looking forward to enjoying one of Dawn's wonderful high teas and of course getting to know Ann. Dawn's teas always seemed so unreal with the bone china and napkins, not what you expect when sitting out in the middle of Africa, but Dawn always made everything feel special!

They all sat out in the garden in the shade of the acacia tree having their tea, the table covered with a beautiful African print in the usual style of Dawn with the finest china, silver teapot and jug.

Terry learnt that Lesley had been in Africa for some sixteen years, in the west near Kigoma, where she lived and worked at a hospital that she had herself set up on a hill near the small village of Kilinzi. She was the only European, but enjoyed the love of the local people there for her devotion and work; she was really one of them. Indeed she was a very formidable lady with terrific determination and character and she as they say, 'took no prisoners' nor suffered fools. She had a gentle side too, and would do anything for anyone, but was never backward in asking for something if she needed it and by the sound of it, usually got it!

Ann was somewhat in her shadow during this afternoon tea party, but told them that she was from Bristol where her parents worked as teachers. She had trained at St Loyes College near Exeter and then went to Canada where she spent four years working at the "Workingmen's Compensation Board" near Toronto, helping lumberjacks recover from their injuries through occupational therapy. She had then decided to come to Africa for a few years, spend some time with her aunt and then wanted to do some voluntary work, which brought her to Hombolo.

"Perhaps you would like to take Ann to where her occupational therapy building will be," Guy suggested to Terry.

"Yes, sure, I'd, love to."

Ann, of course, was very keen to see the new building and went with Terry to the hospital complex.

"What did he mean by saying where it would be?" Ann asked.

"Ah," said Terry. "Just what have you been told then?"

"Bishop Stanway gave me the impression that it was almost ready for me to occupy, that they needed someone straight away. Is that not the case then?"

"Well," Terry hesitantly replied, "you could say that, let me show you."

They walked along to the administration building, next to it they stood by the side of trenches dug out in the ground that were part filled with sand.

"This is it," Terry explained! "It's progressing slowly. The builders have gone off to get more sand today to put in the foundations, but they should be here again tomorrow. They have to put sand in before putting the concrete foundation in, that way the building sort of floats on the sand and does not crack as much; simple, but very effective."

Ann stood there with a surprised and despondent look on her face when she saw just the foundations of the building.

"How disappointing," she exclaimed to Terry, "I thought everything was ready to move in. Where am I to work until this is finished and when will that be?"

"Well, there is a small room in the admin building, but that's all. It'll be two months at least before your new building is completed."

Ann's start as occupational therapist at Hombolo was not what she had expected, but in Africa that's how things often are: progress is slow, as she was beginning to learn.

Over the next few weeks she settled into her new life at Hombolo, sharing Win's beautiful bungalow and garden situated between the doctor's house and Terry's. Living with Win was not easy for her: Win had very strict routines as a result of living for so long on her own, and the age difference created different needs but on the whole it seemed to work out.

Win loved her garden and spent all her free time there, as well as employing the services of a 'garden boy' so it was full of colour and every sort of shrub, from Bougainvillea to a plant that devoured flies, a type of Venus Flytrap, a truly amazing little plant that by evening was full of dead insects floating in its lethal liquid. They would float there in its open jaws until dusk when slowly and almost undetectably the lips would close over the cavity entombing its contents that were then somehow digested over night.

Amongst the fruit trees of the garden there were mango and pawpaw, each fruit slowly swelling and ripening in the heat of the African sun. However did they grow in the semi desert conditions Terry wondered – the marvel of Africa!

"Would you like to have a pawpaw?" Win shouted across to Terry as he passed her garden on his way home.
"Mmmmmm! Yes please, I've no fruit and it'll be days yet before I'm due to go into Dodoma."
"Don't forget that the Bishop is coming tomorrow to see around the centre. Isn't it exciting?" He could feel the admiration she had for him in her voice, 'worship' almost of this 'Great Man.'
"Do you know he has a special car, with special gears?"
"No can't say I did," he replied, not really being a contributor to the hero worship given to Bishop Stanway, a man he had only met a couple of times, but this visit to Hombolo seemed to have him treated almost like the second coming!

Win slipped into her kitchen and brought him out the most beautiful deep orange coloured fruit, the shape and size of a rugby ball, which Terry carried home like a trophy, sliced it into quarters, covered it with lime juice and sugar and devoured it for his tea.

Mornings in the heat of Tanzania were very special: the coolness, the blue sky and the expectation of the heat to follow by 10 o'clock when it would be well up to twenty-five degrees centigrade. It was a competition with the elements to get the main activities going before the heat of the day sapped all of your energy.

The Bishop duly arrived mid morning from Dodoma, thirty miles away, where his main office and those of the Christian Mission Society were situated. Terry was busy cultivating a ploughed field that had recently been cleared of thorn trees, when he saw the dust clouds that followed the entourage as they approached the Leprosy Centre.

The Bishop was greeted by Dr Guy Timmis and his wife Dawn and Sister Win. They showed him around the hospital and administration centre before whisking him off to lunch at Dawn and Guy's house.

After lunch Terry and some of the staff had all been told that they could meet the Bishop before he returned to Dodoma, that if they were to gather in Guy and Dawn's garden he would see them there. The main African staff from the farm, Ann Bangham, the new occupational therapist, and Terry with the farm guard dog 'Buster' waited in the shade of the trees in the doctor's garden for the Bishop to reappear after his lunch.

"This is a right carry on," Terry said to Ann.

"Yes," she replied, "bit like waiting for the Queen, isn't it?"

Terry was curious about the man that everyone held in such high esteem, even if he was a 'Protestant' Bishop!

Well at least, Terry thought, as he had given up a year of his life to come and help the Bishop and his people at the Diocese Leprosy Centre, he surely would want to say a thank you to him, even if Terry was a Catholic. That would at least make Terry feel kindly towards him and his endeavours at Hombolo even more worthwhile.

The Bishop appeared out of the house from his lunch, his car and driver awaiting him in the drive under the shade of a large tree. Terry couldn't see any sign of the special car or special gears that Win had spoken of. Had she made that all up?

The Bishop was dressed in his smart black suit with maroon inner shirt. He was a tall Australian man of average build. He stopped along the little disheveled row of gathered people and said hello and a few words to each of them. Stopping in front of Ann he said, "Hello, Ann, nice to meet you. How are things? Are you settling down to your new life with us? I understand your new occupational building will be completed soon."

Without waiting for a response from her he moved on to Terry, who was standing with the dog Buster at his side. "Hello Buster. How are you?" the Bishop said to the dog, as he passed by! He then stepped into his car and drove off into the dusty afternoon sun, leaving Terry in total disbelief, wondering if he had suddenly become invisible!

In the absence of a building, Ann was often seen working with some of the patients under the shade of a thorn tree near the hospital. She would be doing hand exercises, making rope from the Baobab tree bark with the blind men, or cutting up old tyres ready to make into shoes. Or collecting canes from the lake side making them into baskets of all sizes for use by the farm and the hospital. She was always busy.

She was so full of new ideas and was an inspiration to all the leprosy patients having a particular rapport with the young ones. She developed a small band of musicians that played local instruments, as they marched around in their uniforms that she had made with them. It was difficult with no premises to work from, but she made the best of it. The building was finally ready for part use by the middle of July to her great joy and excitement. It would be towards the end of August before the whole building was complete.

Terry and Ann quickly became good friends and most evenings were spent in each other's company, either in her house or at his, chatting into the small hours. It brought a new dimension into Terry's life at Hombolo, which was something of a lonely and challenging one. They got to know each other well, which was almost inevitable, both working and living in such close proximity. They consoled each other when they were fed up, something that they both felt frequently, probably as a result of living in such a remote spot, together with the effect of the Paludrine tablets, which they had to take for protection against malaria.

They enjoyed each other's company and to being with someone other than missionaries all the time, as well as supporting each other with their different work interests and talk of home.

Ann loved the bird life around Hombolo and going out in the punt on the lake on a Saturday afternoon with Dawn and Guy, where they could fish and observe the many varieties of birds: the Red Billed Hornbill, the Von Der Decken's Hornbill, the Barbets, the White-Bellied Go-Away-Bird, the Crowned Plover, the many Storks and the Spoon-bills to name but a few. They loved to witness the amazing sunsets and enjoy the fun and laughter of those days in the remote wildness and in the sun. It was always such a joy and a pleasure, not to mention the wonderful fish suppers they often devoured around Dawn's Victorian style table, while listening to the many stories and adventures of their days in Uganda.

Terry and Ann were often invited to enjoy a weekend with Philip and Margaret Cox, (Terry's new English friends) at Bihawana Mission, south of Dodoma. The chance to get away was so welcome, with time to enjoy life, play tennis, have a beer or a whisky and to hear of new and different experiences while building lifelong friendships of a deep and meaningful type.

Working at Hombolo was lonely and both felt the inescapable solitude and isolation of the place, sometimes causing a sort of depression: they started to call it 'Homboloitis.' They took their pleasure in listening to music, chatting together, going for walks in the bush in the clear cool air of the evening, visiting others working in the area at schools and the agricultural training centre a few miles away, making other new friends in the process. In doing this the time passed, as week followed week, every day a new experience, Ann always being keen to share Terry's problems and he hers, knowing the difficulties that each had to face on a daily basis; they became a great support to each other in the everyday events of life in the bush.

Early one morning, around 2am, long after the electricity had been turned off at 10pm, as it was every night, Ann awoke to the sound of the chickens screeching at the farm about five hundred yards from her house.

She rushed over to Terry's house, "Wake up!" she shouted at his window, "You must come quickly, something is attacking the chickens. Wake-up! Wake-up!"

He awoke with a start, jumped into his long leather boots and grabbed the twelve bore shot gun as he rushed out of the house.

As he did so Sister Win drew up in her car. He and Ann jumped quickly into her Volkswagen and they shot off to the chicken houses. They found dead chickens scattered everywhere, in the trees and on the ground. They approached the area slowly and carefully not knowing what to expect. Terry loaded the gun while Ann held a torch. Slowly Win drove the car towards the chicken houses, inching her way along in the darkness having turned her headlights off so they could see around them, just using the moon light and the sidelights of the car.

You could smell the fear in the car as they all peered out, minds racing, searching for a sign of movement in the surrounding bush. Win turned off the engine and they sat there in the moon light, waiting and alert as a cat after its prey. The noise had died down, but they could see the carnage of the dead chickens, but no sign of the cause of the slaughter.

Win, Terry and Ann were all somewhat terrified, not knowing if it was safe to get out of the car. George had told a story of coming face to face with a leopard when he was out one night and they knew that lion and hyena were often heard in the distance. They sat there hardly daring to move! Then as they looked around they had to smile as they viewed their situation. Win was in the driving seat in her nightdress, just as she was when she had leapt out of bed and with a very gummy smile as she had no teeth in. Ann was sitting in the back seat in her nightdress and Wellingtons, gripping a torch. Terry sat next to Win holding the twelve bore shotgun, wearing just the bottom half of his pyjamas and black leather boots! What a comic trio they looked. Dad's Army in the bush!

"Right Win," Terry instructed, "keep your hand on the light switch and if you see anything move out there switch the lights on full beam; I'm going out to look around. Ann, you be ready with the torch and if you see anything shout and shine the light on it so I can see where to shoot."

He opened the door and slid quietly out, fortunately the moon shed some light around, but also made shadows. The wire side of the chicken house had been ripped open and there was a large hole in its side where the beast had got in. Terry approached in the half light, but saw nothing just dead birds everywhere. He walked around the chicken house with his hair almost standing on end with fear, but saw no sign of any animal that might have been responsible.

"Can't see anything, just dead chickens everywhere, poor things," Terry said as he returned to the safety of the car with some relief. "I wonder what it could be that kills so many, yet eats so few; it seems totally pointless. There's not much we can do now, perhaps we should go home and clear this up tomorrow in the day light."

They drove around the area to see if they could see an animal but no, so the three "Big White Game Hunters" returned home all feeling a bit shell shocked by the night's events.

The next morning over forty six chickens were found dead as a result of the break in. The skilled African trackers on the staff looked around but they were unable to find any sign of the animal that was responsible, so the mystery remained.

"I suggest we are better prepared tonight," Terry said to Ann as they had coffee later that morning. "I'll keep the Landrover at my house as Dawn and Guy are away. I'll put the large torch in the cab, then, if we hear anything in the night we're ready to move quickly."

The next night they all slept with one eye open, but it was a quiet night with no developments. Maybe it was just a one off they began to think.

But a few nights later Ann was again at Terry's window in the middle of the night shouting for him to wake up! She had woken to the screeching of chickens again and leapt from her bed with no fear or concern, bravely running in her shoes through the bush to Terry's house, madness in itself with the number of snakes there were around!

The two of them drove down to the farm, Ann driving and Terry sitting in the back with the twelve bore shotgun in hand. Ann pulled in at the chicken house where the noise was still coming from. "Reverse back towards the chicken house," he shouted his instructions. "I'll open the rear door. You reverse but very slowly, while I sit with the gun ready to shoot whatever is in there."

Ann reversed slowly, while shining the torch. Terry was sitting aiming the gun towards the chicken house out of the open back door of the landrover. Something was still in there running around causing the few live birds to squawk. They could make out the dust and feathers flying around inside.

Suddenly with a crash the beast flew out of the large hole it had made for itself in the side of the hen house, landing on its feet on the ground, frozen in the light of the torch as it just stood there, dazed, looking at them.

"Shoot! Shoot!" Ann screamed at Terry. "For God's sake shoot it. What the hell are you doing? Shoot it before it kills us."

Terry was squeezing the trigger, but nothing was happening. "I'm trying to," he yelled back, "but nothing is happening?"

He suddenly remembered that he had the safety catch on; George had always instilled in him the necessity of keeping it on when not in use!

He released it and shot directly at the animal that was only yards from them both. It seemed to have no impact on it at all as it moved forward even closer to the rear of the landrover and the open door where Terry was sitting with the gun.

"Shoot again, shoot again," Ann screamed. Terry fired the second barrel at the beast and quickly reloaded. It did not fall but ran off into the darkness of the night.

Terry quickly closed the rear door of the landrover. A wounded animal, as it surely was, would be an extremely dangerous one. They turned the landrover around and put the head lights on to see if they could find what they had shot, but there was no sign of it anywhere and, not daring to scout around on foot, they returned home.

"Surely it must be dead," Terry said. "I'm convinced I hit it at least once; it couldn't live long after that. Sorry about the safety catch, Ann, I couldn't make out what was happening for a minute. I hope it didn't scare you too much."

"You idiot," she said. "I was terrified and thought it was going to kill us both."

By then it was 3.30 in the morning so they drove back to Terry's house both feeling very high after all the excitement of the night, so they did what the British always do in times of crises, they made a cup of tea!

A few hours later at first light, Terry was up and out to see if there was any sign of the animal. There were dead chickens everywhere and he collected up twenty dead bodies and saw just a few terrified birds sitting up in the trees near by.

A few metres from the chicken house towards the bush lying there in the dust was a long haired grey/white body about the size of a large dog. It turned out to be a Honey Badger, a fearless animal with long powerful claws. Despite their name they do not rely on just honey, although the highly nutritious bee brood is certainly a sought after delicacy. They are great opportunistic carnivores and it must have been out at night looking for a nice meal, but why did it have to kill so many and eat so few?

Chapter Seven

In the middle of July Terry and Ann heard from the Diocesan office in Dodoma that eighteen year old David Warren was to come to stay at Hombolo Leprosy Centre for five weeks at the beginning of August. He was from North Wales. His parents were keen to give him an experience in Africa after having met one of the missionaries while they were in U.K. Nobody knew much about David, but Ann and Terry were delighted to be having another young person at the center, if only for a short time and a non-missionary too. Dawn and Guy had invited him to stay with them at their house, quite a challenge!

Terry was becoming very aware that his relationship with Ann was changing; all the trials and experiences they had were bringing them closer. This concerned him somewhat with the perils of getting too close in such a restricted environment. He did not want to get deeply involved only to find on return to U.K. that it had all been the result of the closeness of their life style in Africa. After all he had just extracted himself from one close relationship before leaving England, where his ex-girlfriend's father had him ear marked to take over the family farm in West Dorset. So he was not too keen to get in so deep again, where he and others might all finish up getting hurt.

The more he thought about it the more concerned he became: Ann was a very lovely and special person. He liked her very much and they got on so well together. They were sharing such a close life together at Hombolo Leprosy Centre, very quickly growing in their knowledge of each other, warts and all; it was a special relationship.

Ann could sense that Terry was experiencing some sort of inner conflict as he looked so absorbed whenever she saw him, not his usual exuberant and light hearted self. She was concerned for him, while at the same time not daring to hope that he was beginning to feel something for her. She was confused, flustered and bewildered, while at the same time she felt it probably was their relationship that was causing him to be as he was and wished he would speak to her about it.

On the last Saturday in July, as they walked back from a fishing trip on the lake she felt it was perhaps a good time to approach the subject with him, with their being away from work and in a more relaxed frame of mind.

"What is the matter with you?" she asked him gently. "For days now you have looked so far away. Have I upset you? Are you all right? Are you unwell? Is it the malaria? Why have you been looking so glum? Please talk to me, please."

Terry dismissed it. "It's Homboloitis, and you know how it is living here in this place far from anywhere, the work, the tiredness, the challenges, and the heat. I've had to go into Dodoma three times this week and had punctures twice, repairing them at the side of the road in the midday sun; I'm just very tired. On top of that I've had to find some more chicks to restock after the visit of the Honey Badger, and I'm concerned for the cattle at this dry time: there doesn't seem to be enough hay to last the dry season."

Ann heard what he was saying and true it had been a difficult week for him, but felt there was more to it and wished he would tell her what was really on his mind as it frightened her a bit. She had become very fond of Terry and wanted to feel, with a deep longing, that what they had together would become long lasting. She, too, was aware of the pitfalls of living and working together. Before leaving Canada, she had left behind a broken relationship and it hurt too much to let it all happen again.

The two of them were feeling so stifled: the pressures of their work and now the weight of all this, the late nights and the heat and the isolation were dragging them down.

Ann had started teaching English to some of the young leprosy patients and was enjoying that very much, despite the extra hours. The work in setting up the occupational therapy unit was also very demanding, assembling the items of machinery that had been donated from charities, then finding that parts were often missing. Trying to get Doctor Timmis to refer patients to her and working alongside him, had its problems too. She had worked hard getting an old man on to his feet after his long illness with leprosy, but had made some progress there, so she too had put lots of extra hours in and was feeling the strain.

Living with Sister Win was all right, but they were very different in age and at times things were strained. How good it was to be able to go to Terry's house of an evening, to chat, laugh and unwind together. Ann did not want those times to ever end; without them she felt she would go mad.

Life was quite demanding for these two young people in the heart of Africa and did not look like getting easier anytime soon.

"Shall I come around tomorrow afternoon?" Ann asked. "Being Sunday I'm fairly free. I've just a couple of letters to write home, or are you going to Hombolo Village for Mass?"

"No, that's next Sunday," Terry replied. "It would be nice to see you, perhaps you would like to walk around the boundary with Buster in the late afternoon. How does that sound?"

"Yes fine, should be a bit cooler by then too. Try and get an early night. You'll feel much better. See you tomorrow." Ann left him to make his way home. She hoped that on Sunday afternoon she could get him to open up and talk to her more.

She was up early the next morning and washed her hair. It always seemed to be full of dust these days and needed continual washing. She decided not to go to the usual little service held at the hospital each Sunday morning and started to prepare a roast dinner of pork for her, Win, Dawn and Guy, which was superb and enjoyed by all. Terry had, unusually, declined to join them and that worried Ann somewhat, as she busied herself in the kitchen.

In the afternoon she went over to his house around 3.30 as had been arranged and found him sitting on his veranda writing letters home, as normal for him on a Sunday afternoon, it was really the only free time he had to do it.

"Hodi," she called, as she approached the house. "Can I come in?"

"Yes do, nearly finished, just writing to my sister; let me just finish off."

Ann sat on a chair looking out from the veranda, towards the bush on one side of his house, while Terry finished his letter. It was very cosy there, peaceful and in the shade, with just the humming bush noises; she was happy just sitting there by his side looking out onto the African landscape. By the look of the pile of letters at his side Terry had been busy. She understood how important it was to keep up with the correspondence, as, if you did not write letters, then you did not receive any and they were their lifeblood!

He soon completed his writing and quickly stuck stamps on the little blue aerogramme letters, leaving them ready to go off to the post with the next person that went to Dodoma.

"Would you like to see the baby ducks that are in the incubator? There are about thirty eggs and some are already beginning to hatch," Terry asked Ann.

"Oh yes, I'd love to."

He opened the drawer of the incubator that was kept on the veranda and there were two tiny ducks just breaking out of their shells.

"Ah they are sweet, so tiny. I love them. Do you hatch out the chicks for the laying hens like this too?"

"No we usually fly them in on the Mission Aviation Fellowship plane from Nairobi to Dodoma at a day old. It's why I had to go in to town so much last week; they were not on the first flight so I had to go again the next day."

"How long is it before the chicks are big enough to lay eggs then?" Ann enquired.

"Usually about eighteen weeks. I hope this new lot have a better life then the ones the Honey Badger ate!"

"Oh Terry, what a night that was, you the big game hunter with the safety catch on! What a good thing it wasn't a lion!" They both laughed, agreeing that they must relate the tale to George on his return from New Zealand.

Buster was leaping around having swallowed his meal of maize porridge and meat, gulping it down as usual, such a greedy dog; he was now ready for his walk and was outside jumping up and down trying to catch the flying insects. After his walk he was always taken to spend the night at the cattle yard where he was on guard duty with the night watchman, and would remain there until morning.

Ann, Terry and Buster set off on the walk around the boundary. Terry and his work force had made a dirt road around the inner side of the fence, which made a good place to walk, with the bush and cropping fields on one side and the fence on the other. They chatted away freely as they always seemed able to do, enjoying the walk and each other's company in the cool late afternoon air that gave such relief after the heat of the day. August was always a slightly cooler time with temperatures in the early to late twenty's. Terry seemed more relaxed, perhaps it was because it was Sunday, but never did he mention anything about what had been clearly bothering him and Ann did not like to keep asking, even when it really was all that she wanted to talk about, to get their feelings out in the open.

That evening they had both been invited to the Farmer's Training Centre where Peter and Ann Marks lived and worked. They too were from England. It was a Government run centre and Peter had become a good friend both to George and to Terry. They exchanged advice and borrowed machinery from each other as well as sharing many an evening together. It was lovely to go there and have other European company and, being only five miles away, it was easy to get to.

On their return at the unusually late hour of 11.30 pm they drove back in the landrover to the Leprosy Centre. There was a bright full moon; and they paused as they drove towards the dam over the lake to look out at the moon shining on the surface with its haunting light. Ann dared to hope that Terry was going to say something; she felt he wanted to as he pulled into the lakeside and parked the landrover. They sat looking out across the water in the silvery light of the moon: she was trembling, he was pensive, and it was a moment they never wanted to end. He sat there in silence absorbed in his thoughts but despite the concentrated focus on his face he seemed unable to tell her what she most wanted to hear.

Ann awoke early the next morning feeling very tired. She made her way to the unit at the hospital to start the day's activities; she had not slept very well with so much going around in her mind. She spent a lot of time that day getting the old man she was helping onto his feet and trying to get him to walk more; he did manage a few steps so at least she was making some progress she felt.

Terry awoke to remember it was Monday 1st August 1966, which was his Mum and his Uncle Arthur's 54th birthday. Being twins they shared the same birthday. He wished he could have spent the day with his mum and not stuck out here in the African bush. However, there was work to do and he had a busy day ahead as Yurum the foreman had taken the day off as it was the time for his two sons to be circumcised according to Wagogo custom.

Dawn and Guy had set off for a few days in Dar es Salaam to collect drugs for the hospital and to top up on various food items. They had all given them a list of their needs so they were going to be busy. The road to Dar was mainly dirt except for the last few miles, so it was a tough journey for them, hot and dusty too. This left just the three of them alone at Hombolo, Sister Win, Ann and Terry. At the end of the day Ann took herself home, made a meal, wrote some letters, had a bath and an early night. Terry had been kept busy the whole day, so much so that he was very late starting the engine for the electricity, it took all his energy to wind the fly wheel around to bring it into life, lighting up the whole centre as it did. He too was glad to return home, prepare his meal and retire early to bed.

The next few days were cloudy and served to add to the gloom that everyone seemed to be feeling. Terry and his men continued with the fencing of the north boundary and planting up the vegetable garden. Ann, too, was busy at the hospital with her work. It had been decided that Terry and his men would build a tennis court behind Dawn and Guy's house. Dawn, Terry and Ann all enjoyed a game of tennis; Dawn had told them she had some spare funds to finance the work. Dawn and Guy were to bring back a tennis net from Dar es Salaam and Terry said that he would be able to make and erect suitable posts to support the net and set about making the winding gear to tighten the net that he was to attach to the posts. Meanwhile suitable surface material was dug out of the ground a few miles away near Hombolo village, transported back and laid on the outlined tennis court.

Ann and Terry met up in the evenings, while Dawn & Guy were away, and went to their house to listen to some of their records. They had the luxury of a record player, which nobody else had. Ann and Terry both enjoyed "The Sound of Music" that was so popular at the time; it was also a good place to borrow books too, so they browsed through Dawn and Guy's collection. This seemed to cheer them up immensely but neither of them was really feeling fully themselves.

It was Saturday again so they only worked in the morning. Ann invited Terry to have morning coffee with her and Win at their house.
"Shall we go fishing today?" she asked him.
"I'd like to but I've two punctures to repair, so if you don't mind I think I'd better give it a miss."
"OK then. How about I come over to your house and make you some tea around five, does that sound alright?" Ann asked.
"Very kind thought," Terry replied. "That would be lovely and then after we can take Buster out for his walk again."
They enjoyed a lovely late afternoon tea of scones and jam in English style, sitting outside Terry's house on the rough grass that passed for a lawn. Ann had covered the little table with a beautiful white cloth and had even put a few flowers that she'd picked from the Bougainvillea in Win's garden in a jam pot on the table! They became fully absorbed in their surroundings, watching the

Wagtails, the Pied Crows and a Green Wood Hoopoe picking at seeds Terry had scattered for them earlier that morning only a few yards from where they were sitting, a rare treat to see them so close that they could almost touch them.

Neither Ann nor Terry could break the silence as they enjoyed their tea and scones together, sitting in the late afternoon sun watching the birds. Ann had really taken a lot of trouble to set the scene. Terry noticed, too, that she was wearing a new dress she had recently made on a local sewing machine. He could also detect the faint smell of her perfume as they sat there drinking in the cool evening air. There was no doubt the atmosphere was super charged; something had to give!

Then Buster came charging out of the house to lie at Terry's feet, this drove all the birds away and with it the excuse to remain silent.

They all sat there in the shade of the thorn tree. Terry looked across at Ann, and she looked back at him in silence. She was afraid that he would hear her wildly beating heart. He felt as if she was able to see into his very soul.

"Ann," he said, "this is so difficult, so very very difficult."

He gently took hold of her hand, looking into her eyes.

"You know, Ann, how I feel about you, don't you?"

"I had hoped," she responded shakily.

"We're so young and here we are in this place alone together most of the time. Are we not bound to feel something for each other? I'd hate for us to get into something that on our return home we had to unpick. That what we feel now was only due to the closeness of our living and working in this isolated place."

"I know," Ann replied in a hoarse whisper. "It's just what I feel too, or did do. But now I'm certain more than ever, that what we have is more than that and I can deny it no longer, to you, or to myself. I believe that when we return home we'll find that we have a unique bond between us, as we're both in love with Africa and want to make it our lives. We can and will do that, if we really want to, I know we can." They kissed each other for the first time as the sun slipped down behind the Baobab tree near where they were sitting and for the first time in many weeks they both felt at peace.

Ann didn't sleep that night; she was too excited and overwhelmed by the day's events, perhaps life was looking up at last she thought. She was up at 6am the following morning, Sunday, made some tea and took it back to bed and slept until 10am when she got up for breakfast. Today was the day that David Warren was due to arrive. The Bishop's secretary Mary Punt was bringing him out from Dodoma where he would arrive from Dar on the bus. So Ann guessed Terry would have to be ready to greet him, as David was to shadow Terry in his work for a great deal of his stay at Hombolo. Ann was pretty fed up about that, as it meant there would be little opportunity for her to spend time with Terry while David was around.

She took off to see if he was at home, and was delighted to see the landrover outside his house. She had to go and see that last night had really happened. She need not have worried as he greeted her at the door as she ran across from Win's house.
"How are you this morning?" she asked. "Was it all true last night or did I have a dream?"
"No," Terry replied joyfully, "it was certainly all true"
"No regrets then?" Ann asked him.
"No, none at all," Terry replied enthusiastically.
"I had to come and see you before you get busy with David. When does he arrive?"
"Not until five this evening and I'm off to Mass this afternoon at two at the community centre in Hombolo village. The priest only manages to get there on the first Sunday of the month, so it's my only chance."
"Are you walking there?" Ann enquired.
"Yes I am, as usual."
"Why do you do that? It's five miles to the village and there can be lions on that road. I saw some one day when out with Guy in the car. I don't want you eaten up after all we've just been through."
"Well," Terry replied. "I only earn a pound a week here as a volunteer and if I use the Landrover for personal use I've to pay

twenty four cents a mile, so I do it to keep costs down, can't afford otherwise! It's a nice walk and all on the level too. I'm always very careful, so don't worry."

"If you take your gun, don't forget the safety catch, will you?" she mocked.

"Ha ha, very funny," he replied.

Dawn and Guy arrived back from Dar es Salaam loaded to the roof and tired out from all their endeavours.

"Did you have a successful trip?" Ann enquired.

Dawn staggered out of the car after the long journey. "We managed to get most of the things we needed but some of the drugs were not available, so we will have to return again in a few weeks. How are things here then?"

"Everything is just fine, wonderful in fact," said Ann with a broad smile.

The next few weeks were full; everyone seemed to be so busy. David was with Terry from dawn to dusk, so he and Ann hardly had a minute together. But both were happy and content with the knowledge they had, and what they now knew they shared. They were wondering when to give their news to the others and how they would accept it.

David had a wonderful sense of humour and lifted all their spirits with the silly and sometimes frustrating things that he got up to. He was always breaking keys, causing Terry grief, but on the whole everyone enjoyed having him around. Dawn and Guy had David living in their house; it was not something they were used to, having a lively young man around the place. For Dawn it was particularly difficult as she liked everything in order, being 'The Duchess' that she was and was known for; with David around she had to put up with quite a lot!

One lunch time they had all been invited to Dawn and Guy's for a light lunch as they often did, just to make a change. Terry and David had been out in the bush fencing all morning in the heat so were glad to sit in the cool of the doctor's house sipping Orange Fanta at midday, chatting to Guy and listening to the World Service News.

"Lunch will soon be served," Dawn announced as she went along to the bathroom.

Then a scream went up, followed by Dawn walking through the sitting room from the bathroom clutching a pair of wooden clothes tongs with a flannel hanging from them.
"Who has used my flannel?" she challenged, holding it at arm's length and heading for the kitchen.
"It was me," David confessed. "I was all hot and sweaty."

Dawn could not remove the flannel fast enough and placed it in a bucket ready to go to the wash! Poor Dawn, she really was not used to David's rugged ways!

Ann was feeling good. She slept better and felt great. "Life is wonderful," she thought to herself, "Just wonderful. I'm so glad I came to Africa." Win noticed how much more relaxed Ann was and put it down to the fact that she was settling down now to life in the bush, after the excitement of living in Canada for the past four years. Win liked having Ann around and could see the excellent work she was doing and how well she got on with the children at the leprosy centre.

Sally, a missionary from Dodoma, came out for a few days to help with the work and often went around the place with David. This gave Ann and Terry the opportunity to be together, sometimes in the chicken house of an evening while Terry was grading the eggs, in the food store or on a walk with dear old Buster, when taking him to his night accommodation at the Cattle Boma. It was a matter of wherever they could steal time to chat and to just 'be' together.

On the 10th August Radio Tanzania came out to the Leprosy Centre to interview Terry to hear about the work on the farm and the contribution that the leprosy patients made to the running of the farm, to learn about the crops and livestock that Terry was farming out there in the middle of this semi-desert, and to ask him just why he had volunteered to come out from England to work and for no wages, apart from the pound a week of course. Ann was to make a recording of the interview with Guy's tape recorder, as he was out visiting a nearby clinic and would not get a reception. The interview was very good. Ann felt Terry did well and answered all their questions explaining everything clearly.

"I must say I thought you would be stumped when they asked you who Inter-Church Aid was that helped finance some of the projects," Ann later said to him.

"Me too!" said Terry. "I really had no idea, so had to guess and it seems my guess was correct. I told them it was a group of different churches sending in funds. Inspired or what? Perhaps my future is in radio?"

"OK. OK." said Ann, "You weren't that good!"

By mid August Ann was feeling time dragging. She was still restricted in her part-completed department building, when she really needed more space. She felt restless and unable to sit still for long. At least she and Terry were getting more time together and that was good. They would discuss many things, mainly in the evenings, for there was much for them both to learn of each other. For Terry his religious faith was important; Ann was learning that Catholics seem to have so many rules and regulations. There seemed to be a big rift and divide between the Anglicans and the Catholics and, by what Ann could see, a lot of mistrust for no real reason.

"It's surprising they let you come here at all, a Catholic on an Anglican Mission station. They do seem to treat you with a certain amount of suspicion I feel," she said to Terry. "But to be fair it seems your church, too, doesn't help by not allowing you to join in their services or go to their churches. Why is that? When surely you are all praying to the same God? I'm confused to say the least. I'm glad that I'm not really in either camp," Ann exclaimed.

All these questions made Terry wonder about the things he had been taught over the years, making him investigate all the questions that had been asked by George Hart, Ann and others. He decided he wanted to know the answers too, both for himself and to be able to answer others. He felt he should know these things and he wanted to make up his own mind about the Catholic Church, and what it was he himself believed. So in the last few months of his stay in Tanzania he spent a lot of time reading whatever books he could to crystallize his thoughts and his knowledge of the Catholic Church's teachings. He must know himself and he really should have some of the answers to the points he is often asked.

Terry and Ann decided to go public and in the middle of August they told Win, Guy and Dawn about their new relationship. Surprisingly nobody seemed to have much comment, perhaps they were not so surprised, but it was good to have it out in the open so at least everyone knew.

"I've written to my Mum and Dad to tell them about you," Ann told Terry.

"How do you think they'll take it then, Ann?" Terry asked her.

"I'm sure they'll be happy for me and will be pleased to meet you sometime. Perhaps when you go back home you could go to visit them. When do you return?"

"Well VSO have already booked my return flight for 17th November, that's just three months' time. They don't really give you much chance to think about it and were asking me in May when I wanted to return. I just went along with the original plan of being a volunteer for the one year. I would love to stay longer, but to be honest I don't have the funds and need to return to get started on my career and earn some money," Terry explained.

"Of course it's very different since I've met you, Ann, but I guess I do need the money. Also George is returning in early November, so I'll have completed my task here and I'm not sure George and I could really work along side each other, lovely as he is! He is such an untidy person and we work in different ways."

"Oh, Terry, I never even thought about you leaving so soon. I can't think of life here without you. How will I manage? I'm due to stay until May 67. I told the Diocese I'd stay for a year to set up the unit. That was before I met you!"

I can't even think about being here without you at the moment and just when we are getting to know each other too."

"Look," he said, "I'll go and see your parents when I get back. It would be good to meet them. I'll go and take them some slides, let them know that you are fine and have not been eaten by a lion!"

"Or a Honey Badger." Ann laughed.

"I can see I'll never be allowed to forget that, will I?" Terry replied grudgingly.

"No never! Can we now stop talking about you leaving? Do you mind? Let's try to just enjoy these days together. After all it's still only August."

As August progressed the heat of the day became more intense, by ten in the morning it was already twenty five degrees and the humidity was building up fast. Rain was not expected until the end of October and in any quantity not until November. These mounting conditions drained everyone's energy and each day had to be endured, together with the airless sleepless nights. It made their trips out onto the lake, viewing the birds and fishing at the weekends so much more necessary but always enjoyable. Terry was constantly on call and often called out to check on small bush fires, gathering his team of workmen and leprosy patients to beat out the flames before the fire took over in the dry desert-like conditions. The work of clearing the bush and cultivating it continued and visitors to the farm were impressed to see the bush turned to cultivated land ready for planting as soon as the rains arrived.

His continual confrontations with snakes worried Ann a great deal. Terry seemed to have nine lives and had shot many different specimens as he pushed back the bush and met the snakes whose habitat he was removing, pushing them further and further away in favour of growing crops.

One day as Terry was burning up a large pile of thorn trees and Guy was out exercising his dog 'Heinze', he asked, "How do you feel about clearing so much bush away like you are?"

"Well Guy, I guess it has to be done. There's plenty of bush and we have to grow food for the patients, but I don't do it easily or without thought for what I'm creating here. We do leave some of the natural trees for shade and never remove the giant Baobab trees."

"George says that when he returns he wants to start clearing the bush to build an airstrip to the north of the hospital and for that he will have to up root some of the largest trees. That's regrettable, but if it allows MAF to fly in here then it will have many advantages, which will be tremendous for the hospital. You see, Guy, when I watch the leprosy patients arrive here in a terrible condition, weak and sick most of them and then I see others leaving to return to life in their villages and being reunited with their families it makes it all worth it, as I'm sure it does for you too."

Win reported that the toilet blocks belonging to the leprosy patients were all backing up so this pushed another task onto Terry. For the next six days he and David had to suck out the contents of the soak away pits with a hand operated pump into a large tank and empty it out onto the fields that were to be ploughed. A most unsavoury task!

"I sometimes wonder what I will have to do next in this place," Terry said to Ann one afternoon when she went to see what he was doing. He sounded fed up, hardly surprising, with the smell and the heat and such a revolting task to do. She felt sorry for him and David and took them out a large bottle of cold squash that she had made from limes grown in Win's garden. Together he and David downed the contents of the bottle with gusto!

"What is it about this country?" Terry cried. "Nothing seems to work for very long?"

The following evening Terry was on his way to the electric generator to start the engine as he did every evening at around 6.45. Walking down through the thorn trees and on through to the area where the chicken houses were he was suddenly aware that something was in the trees looking down on him, watching him. He froze as he looked up in the fading light to see the eyes of a large cat: it was a leopard. Slowly Terry walked backwards keeping his eye on the leopard.

"He looked at me and I looked at him. I don't think he liked what he saw," Terry explained to Dawn, "because he turned the other way jumped down out of the tree and ran! I was shaking violently." He had rushed to the doctor's house, being the nearest for safety, hoping the leopard wouldn't follow. Poor Dawn clucked around like a mother hen, but no one was hurt and Terry still had to find the strength to go and turn the flywheel of the electric generator to bring life to it and the whole centre.

As August came towards its end Terry and Ann had been invited to stay with their English friends Margaret and Philip Cox at Bihawana Mission just twelve miles south of Dodoma. They left Hombolo at eleven in the morning and took a picnic lunch, which they enjoyed in a dried river bed en route. It was extremely hot as they strolled along the river bed after they had enjoyed their lunch together and it sapped all their energy.

They arrived in Bihawana at 2.30 that afternoon and sat and chatted awhile. Margaret and Philip seemed thrilled about their news which pleased them both as reaction at Hombolo to their relationship, had, they felt, been a little subdued.

The large church at Bihawana was the focus of the mission and stood majestically on a hill over looking the school buildings below. There was quite a large vineyard where the fathers had grown wine for many years and it was interesting to see around the fields where they were grown.

The Mission also had a tennis court that was just a few yards from their house, so they had a game of tennis in the cool of the evening, making a welcome change. Later they looked at some of Philip's slides and films and stayed up late chatting until the small hours. They remained at Bihawana until Monday morning. Margaret prepared them a cooked breakfast for a treat and they left at nine thirty to pick up shopping and post from Dodoma before returning once again to life at Hombolo.

Chapter Eight

It was September already; David and Terry were up inside the huge water tank cleaning out all the sludge, another difficult and unpleasant task, especially as they found a nest of African bees in there involving them in making a quick exit down the ladder! Ann was feeling low with the passing of another month and the thought of Terry leaving in less then twelve weeks. It was his twenty first birthday on 15th September so she was beginning to think what she could do to make it special for him. There was not really much choice of things, but she was sure she would come up with something for him. David had to return to U.K. on 9th September. They were all going to miss him. He had certainly cheered them all up during his stay and he seemed to have enjoyed it too. He took the train from Dodoma to Dar for his flight, everyone going to see him off at the station, a sad occasion for all.

It was Sunday 11th September; Ann had laid in feeling tired with the heat of the past few days, but had agreed to go to see Terry in the afternoon for tea together.

"Hodi," she called, as always as was the tradition. "Hodi." But there was no reply.

She opened the door onto the veranda to find Terry laying out flat in a chair as white as a sheet.

"Whatever is the matter with you?" she asked. He was half asleep and half awake but looked dreadful, almost drugged.

"Have you been bitten by a snake?" she asked, "or a scorpion or something?"

He just lay there moaning,

"No, No, I don't think so," he responded. "I just feel very weak and unwell."

"Right stay still and don't try to move. I'm going to get doctor Timmis."

Ann ran the couple of hundred meters to Dawn and Guy's house.

"Hodi, Hodi, Hodi. Guy you must come quickly. It's Terry. Please come quickly. He's at home and I don't like the colour of him. He looks really poorly."

Guy and Dawn jumped into the car while Ann was already half way back running to Terry's house. They arrived almost together.

Terry had got up from his chair and was sitting on his door step outside the house with his head in his hands looking pale and white. Please God, he is not going to die Ann thought. He looked so terrible.

"I told you to stay in your chair," she scolded him.

Dawn took hold of his hand while Ann went for some water to mop his brow.

Guy took his blood pressure and listened to his chest and asked him if he was in any pain.

"No I just feel so weak," Terry told him.

"Have you been near any snakes? If you have you must tell me now, it's vital."

"No, not seen a snake for days."

"Have you eaten today?" Guy asked.

"Yes, I had some of the fish we caught yesterday."

Guy examined him further and found that he had a lump on his neck, which he pointed out to Terry.

"How long have you had this?"

"Not sure," Terry replied.

"Well," said Guy, "I am going to take some blood and test it, as far as I can here, but if you are no better and I can't find a reason I'll have to take you to Dar es Salaam hospital. Are you sure that you have not been near any snakes?"

"No, I'm certain. I've been sitting here on the veranda most of the day."

Guy took the blood sample he needed and walked off to the hospital with it to test it himself.

"I'll make up the bed at our house and you're to come and stay with us," Dawn insisted.

Terry burst into tears and just looked so helpless. Ann and Dawn helped him to the car and drove him to Dawn and Guy's house.

They made up the bed, put on a fan and left him to rest and to sleep. Ann returned about eight o'clock that evening to see how he was. She slowly opened the bedroom door to find him just awake but still very pale.

"How do you feel?" she enquired.

"A little better" he replied weakly. "I'm so glad to be here. I felt very alone back there in my house. It was very frightening. It's a good job you came to see me."

Tears rolled down his cheeks and he looked so sad, so weak and run down; he was far from himself. She had never before seen him like that.

"Can I get you anything?"

"No thanks. I feel I just want to sleep and sleep, but please don't go away, will you?"

"Of course I won't," Ann replied. She kissed him and sat on the chair next to the bed holding his hand as he drifted in and out of sleep, tears streaming down her face.

Ann remained sitting by the bed until well after the lights had gone out at 10.30.

"I think you should go home," Dawn suggested to Ann. "There is nothing you can do. We'll sleep with our bedroom door open, but I'm sure that he'll be all right."

"I'll call in the morning, on my way to work. Will Guy know the results by then?"

"Yes he should do. Try not to worry Ann. We will be ready to take him to Dar es Salaam tomorrow, if need be."

It was nearly midnight when she left, feeling that he looked more comfortable and was at least sleeping. It was so unlike him to be sick and he looked very pale. She was terribly worried, partly because there was such little care available out there in the bush, apart from the limited help that Guy was able to give him.

Ann had a sleepless night and was up at six and over at the doctor's house before he had even had his breakfast. Guy always had a silver try laid up by Petro their houseboy the night before. Guy's routine was to get up for the seven o'clock news on the BBC World Service, and make the tea to take to Dawn: that was always how they started their day. However, Ann broke their routine by arriving at seven o'clock that morning to see how Terry was doing.

"He's looking happier this morning you'll be glad to hear," Guy told her.

"Can I go in to see him please?"

"Sure you can. He's drinking the tea I've just taken him."

Ann went in and there he was sitting up in bed. On the small table by the side of his bed was the silver tray, silver sugar bowl, silver jug and the best china.

"Look at you; you're a fraud sitting up there like a King! How are you today?"

"Not sure," Terry replied, looking pale and shaky, "better I think, but I'm sure the doctor will soon tell me."

"Well you're in good hands," Ann assured him. "You have to get better soon; it's your 21st birthday in three days' time. How can we have a party with you in bed?"

"Well you and I could," he said with a gleam in his eye.

"I don't think you are in any condition for that either," she laughed.

Terry dragged himself up later in the morning and into the sitting room. That action alone exhausted him and he slumped in the chair and fell asleep. Dawn later brought him some cereal, a rare item at Hombolo, with some fruit.

Petro, the houseboy passed Terry sitting in the chair. He paused, looked concerned and said, "Bwana is very sick. It needs medicine to take out his fever. He works too much hard every day on that tractor. Bwana Timmis must cut out the sick from his head."

Terry thanked him for the concern expressed in Petro's simple but sincere way.

Guy arrived back from the hospital to see Terry with the results of the tests at eleven thirty that morning, by which time Terry was back in bed again.

"Well, you'll be pleased to hear your blood count is a bit low, but the white count is fine. I think that you have 'infectious mononucleosis' otherwise known as glandular fever. In a few days the lump under your chin should start to shrink. It's a condition young fast growing people often do develop I'm afraid," Guy explained. "You'll have to rest and take it easy for a few weeks and drink plenty of liquid. You'll feel tired and have some pretty bad headaches, but you must rest and sleep as much as you can, and to aid that we insist you will stay here with us."

Dawn arrived in the room and was pleased to hear the news that it was nothing more serious. "You'll stay here with us until you are strong enough to look after yourself, do you hear me?"

"Yes, Mum," Terry mockingly replied. "And thank you, Dawn, you have both been very kind. I do really feel so weak and tired, so thanks for having me to stay."
Terry was so relieved that he did not have to go away anywhere for treatment and almost immediately fell asleep.

Ann was delighted to hear that it was not anything too serious, when she went to visit him that lunch time. Guy took her to one side. "Ann," he said, with a twinkle in his eye, "You do know that this is a real problem for you too."

"Why is that?" she asked somewhat alarmed.

"The virus that causes this is also spread by kissing!" he laughed.

She looked embarrassed and replied, "Well it's too late now!"

For the next few days Terry felt low, lacking in energy, and weak, spending most of his time in bed. Ann went in to see him three or four times a day sitting with him as he drifted in and out of sleep, feeling for him in his predicament, but happy that it was not more serious. She started to think about his

21st birthday that was on Thursday. It looked as if there would be no party and it was doubtful if he would even be out of bed by then. Oh dear!

When Terry's birthday arrived on Thursday 15th September 1966, there he was flat on his back with glandular fever. The gland on his neck had gone down somewhat, but he was still very weak and not himself at all. He managed to get up at lunchtime, but ate very little, taking just a slither of the birthday cake that Dawn and Ann had made with love and care. Ann had made a large and traditional key, six feet long, from cardboard and covered it with foil, tied on some balloons and presented him with it. There were also quite a few cards that had arrived from his family and friends in the UK. Dawn had hidden them away so it would be a nice surprise on the day. He sat slumped in a chair after lunch in the sitting room, opening his cards and gifts. Everyone then went out into the garden for Guy to take a photograph to record the happy event, before Terry returned to his bed to rest and sleep, exhausted by the efforts of the day!

"This really is not the way I imagined I'd be celebrating my 21st birthday," Terry said grudgingly to Ann.

"Well, it could have been far worse and you could have been on the dusty road to Dar es Salaam by now, so count your blessings!" she told him.

As the days passed Terry began to look and feel better, but remained quite weak. He was a poor patient and when he was feeling stronger did far too much and often became faint, which forced him to rest. After a week with Dawn and Guy he began to feel stronger so he returned to his house. The pace and routine of life began to return to normal, as he slowly picked up his load again, but still not quite at his usual pace.

The heat was growing more intense each day. Everyone was suffering from the increased humidity, with the hot air blowing in across the plains of the Wagogo region, as the rainy season drew closer.

"I feel so depressed some days," Ann confessed to Terry, one evening as they sat and chatted in his little sitting room. "Partly due to the fact that you are leaving in November I guess. I just feel sorry for myself remaining here alone, just when I've found you, someone that I want to be with. I wish I could return home with you. The time will drag so heavily when I'm here alone. Can't you stay on until I leave?"

Terry listened sympathetically, for he knew how it felt to be alone at Hombolo, the isolation you can feel.

"It'll soon pass, our time apart; nothing is forever. At least I can go and find a job and start to earn some badly needed funds. When I return to England after this year in Tanzania I'll have about five pounds to my name! Well, I know it's only my money that you're after," Terry laughed.

"Do you think you'll ever return to work in Africa again? You have often spoken of it and you do seem to have a special love for the life here?" Ann asked.

"I'd love to. It's really captured my heart in a big way, far more than I could ever have imagined. There are many things to consider of course, but I'm sure I will. I hope we'll both come back to Africa again one day to live," he said with a twinkle in his eye. Ann's heart missed a beat!

They instinctively knew they would return and hoped it would be together, to live and work somewhere in Africa. They would not rest until they did. This thought had begun to develop within them both, and would never stop until it was fulfilled. They felt they belonged there; this madness that was Africa grew daily within them.

They were attracted by so much that was Africa: the smiling faces of the African people, their bright and colourful dress, their traditional and simple life style, showing that contentment was not comprised of possessing much, but in wanting little.

The open landscape of the savannah with its vastness and beauty was captivating. The thorn trees and the wild grasses, the incredibly beautiful and exotic bird and animal life, the beauty of the wild and cultivated flowers that were in abundance, supported by an amazing variety of insects, all held them spellbound. The sudden red and purple sunsets that seemed to come from nowhere each evening, as the orange ball of the sun slipped down below the horizon with monotonous regularity, were contrasted only by the cool still morning air of dawn.

If the sights of the day captured their imagination, then the voices of the African nights, with distant drums mixed in with the whooping of the hyenas "laughing" and the occasional roar of a lion did too. All this was played out to the background of the musical whine of the mosquito as it carried out its deadly mission. Daily the country advanced in their esteem and affection as it slowly revealed itself to them, contributing to their deeply held love of Africa.

"Africa will give us no choice," Terry pronounced. "Hold that in your heart while we are apart."

On 23rd October, their friends, Margaret and Philip were staying with them for the weekend. For the first time in seven months there was rain, not much, just 0.24 inches, but it broke the humidity and settled the dust. It was very welcome, bringing with it that unique, unforgettable, evocative aroma that was Africa.

The following day Terry, Ann and Peter Marks from the Farmers' Training Centre near-by, attended a Government Auction in Kongwa to purchase new livestock to increase the herd size. The Diocese had been given money for the expansion of the farm from an overseas charity; it was agreed that the most effective use of the funds was to increase the cattle numbers, resulting in an increased production of milk for use by the patients.

They all set off at five in the morning to go to Ranch number three, at Kongwa, a sixty mile trip, arriving just in time for the start of the auction. Prices started high, at three hundred and fifty shillings for heifers, then the auctioneer surprisingly just left unannounced for some reason. The remaining animals were sold for an average of two hundred and thirty three shillings each. This allowed Terry and Peter to buy sixteen Zebu heifers that they selected from the stock that remained in the sale. They were planning to share these between the two of them. They employed a local man to sleep with the cows and to look after them, until Terry and Peter could arrange for a lorry to collect them the following day. The next day they sent out a lorry from Dodoma to Kongwa to collect the animals. Terry, Ann & Peter having returned to Hombolo, awaited the arrival of the new stock.

By six that evening there was no sign of the cattle. Terry went to see Peter at the Farmers' Training Centre to see what he felt they should do about the situation. By 8 o'clock that evening when there was still no sign of the cattle. Terry and Peter decided to drive to Kongwa again to find out what was going on.

First they went to tell Guy and Ann what they were planning to do, so they knew where they were and didn't worry too much.

"Be sure to let me know when you get back," Ann shouted after them.

"I will, I will," he replied as they roared off in a cloud of dust.

After the long bumpy journey back to Kongwa they located the man they had paid to guard the cattle. He informed them that when the cattle had been loaded onto the lorry the bottom had fallen out of it, therefore he was unable to send the cattle to them! So he just held them in an enclosure waiting to see what to do next. A quick inspection of the cows revealed that there were only fifteen; somehow one had gone missing!

Peter and Terry went off to find the manager, Frank Turner, at the Ranch Manager's house. They knocked and knocked. It was then 11pm so he was probably in bed. On trying the door they found it open and went inside to leave a note for him, telling him about the missing cow. They called and called and when they had no reply they opened the bedroom door to find Frank, the manager of the ranch, fast asleep. By the smell in the room it was not a normal sleep: he had clearly been drinking and despite shaking him they were unable to awaken him. They wrote a large note to him, attached it to the mirror by his bed and left him to sleep it off.

Going back to the guard who was caring for the cattle, they made sure he had some money to buy himself food for the next few days, with the incentive that he would receive further pay when the cattle arrived safely at Hombolo. They then set out on the return journey home through the African night.

Arriving back, tired and exhausted, Terry went to the window of Ann's bedroom as he had promised.
"Hello. Hello are you awake?" he shouted to her.
"Yes, sort of."
"What time is it?"
"It's 2.30, I'm whacked. It's been a long night."
"Did you find the cows?" Ann asked sleepily.
"Yes we did. I'll tell you all about it tomorrow, once I've had some sleep."
"Would you like me to come and make you a drink or something?"
"No thanks, I just need my bed." he replied wearily.
"Anyway glad you're back safely. I was getting quite concerned. Night night."
The following morning at 8 am Terry left for Dodoma, with Peter, to once more organise a lorry to go to Kongwa to collect the cattle. They managed to locate an Asian man who showed them his lorry and who agreed to go the following morning to pick up the cattle and take them to Hombolo. After a long negotiation with him regarding the cost, over two bottles of cola, while sitting in his hot

and dusty office, it was agreed he would have part payment then, and he would receive the balance of the agreed payment on safe delivery of the cattle to Hombolo.

He was as good as his word, and the following afternoon at 3 pm the fifteen heifers arrived looking in remarkably good condition considering the experiences they had endured over the past few days!

The new stock soon settled down to their surroundings, enjoying some of the irrigated Lucerne. They would have to wait for a while for the new season of grass, but since more of the bush had been cleared, there was going to be far more grass available to feed them all.

It was hard to believe, but the Hart family were due to arrive back from their leave in New Zealand on Thursday 3rd November. This meant Terry had to make sure all was in order on the farm and ready to hand back to George. The time seemed to have passed so quickly on reflection, and so much had happened.

He was sure that George would be pleased with the progress made since he departed for his seven months' leave: the bush clearance; the ploughing ready for the planting season; the cattle numbers and their good health; and the near completion of the boundary fence with the addition of a road used to patrol it. There had been no real disasters while he was away, apart of course from the loss of the hens to the honey badger. It just remained for Terry to prepare and write his report and handover notes for George.

A feeling of melancholy struck Terry as he realised that it was nearly time to leave Hombolo and Tanzania. He had grown to enjoy the challenges and the excitement of his job and had made many new friends, not least of these being Ann. He reflected on his decision to join V.S.O. and to come to Africa, after leaving Agricultural College. It had to be, he thought, the best decision he could have made: it had been a life changing experience, everyday learning something new. Africa indeed had so much to share.

Leaving Ann was going to be tough, both for her and for him; they didn't know how they were going to survive their six months apart. However, part of him did feel that perhaps it could be a good thing to see how they both felt after a period of separation. Terry had absolutely no doubt that he and Ann were meant to be together. But the next step was a big one, so it was important to get it right. But oh dear, how he was going to miss her and Africa!

On the morning of the Harts' return to Hombolo, Ann and Terry made a banner to tie across the road from the trees. Terry had found some white hessian sacks that had contained grain from America for the patients. He and Ann had cut these into lengths, sewn them together and painted on the words 'WELCOME HOME.'

At six o'clock the Harts arrived back after their long trip. They were so surprised to see the welcome home banner and so glad to be safely "Home." They all had dinner together, while going over the events of the past seven months, before taking to their beds.

The daytime temperature was in the region of thirty-five degrees most of the time, as the humidity increased with the clouds and the thunder rolling around overhead. There was always the threat of rain, something everyone longed to see and the soil cried out for with an unquenchable thirst.

Terry found the last ten days at Hombolo were desperate in so many ways. For some reason there was a big mix up with the Diocese over who would pay for taking him into Dodoma on Monday 14th November to catch the train to Dar es Salaam. From Dar he would fly on to London. They seemed to get very steamed up with little things like this, for no real reason. Terry was hurt, that after all he had done they should feel it necessary to have an upset over such trivialities as to who would pay for a bit of petrol. He said to the Bishop's secretary that if it were causing them such a problem then he would walk from Hombolo to Dodoma carrying his case!

This in turn upset Ann making her wonder how petty things may become when she was there alone without Terry's support. The stress of it all caused her to feel unwell and she took to her bed with a sore throat and she was in and out of bed for several days. She really wanted to spend as much time as possible with Terry before he left, but was feeling so tired, weak and a little depressed.

Terry started to teach Ann how to use the 16mm film projector before he left, so that she could carry on showing films to the patients. With that in mind they had two evenings when Ann was in charge of the projector while Terry stood by to give advice in case she needed help, but her heart was not really in it.

On Saturday 12th November a garden party was held on the lawn at Dawn and Guy's house to say farewell to Terry. All the staff had been invited to attend and some of the leprosy patients had also asked the doctor if they could be there to say farewell to Bwana Terry. Dawn, as she always did, had prepared a wonderful 'high tea.' There were speeches made and Terry was presented with two hand carved knobkerrie sticks (they signify a headman or leader): one made of black ebony carved by the Village Headman at Hombolo and another in black and white wood carved by a member of the farm staff, known as "Pungheartie," who looked after the cattle and lived at the cattle boma where Buster slept. Terry found the whole occasion very moving and humbling, underlining his sadness at having to leave. He'd never liked 'Goodbyes' very much.

Terry's last weekend at Hombolo was a mixture of normality and packing up his house and few belongings. Normality, in that on the Saturday evening they had a film show, where Ann proved she was going to be able to work the projector in the future by showing them all a film. It had the appropriate title of "Flight" and had been loaned to them by the British Council.

Terry cleaned his little house with a heavy heart: he had been very happy there, the first home of his own. Situated a few meters from the main water storage tank at the entrance to the Leprosy Centre, gave it open views of the landscape beyond. In the future it was to be used as a Guest House, so that anyone coming for a weekend to Hombolo would be able to stay there. There was also talk that one day they may extend it and use it as a school for the many children of the staff.

Ann awoke at daybreak, on Monday 14th November, the morning of Terry's departure. She just lay there dreading the hours ahead, what a long day it was going to be, how she wished that it were already over. She was just hoping that she didn't make too much of a fool of herself.

Dawn, Guy, Win, Ann and Terry all had a sombre last lunch together at Hombolo. Guy said an appropriate Grace before the meal, adding to everyone's feeling of melancholy. Even Dawn's houseboy Petro served the meal with a mournful face.

After lunch they sat and had coffee in a strained and sorrowful silence.

"Well," said Guy leaping up from his seat, "Anyone mind if I put on the World News as I'd like to hear how the cricket is going?"

Dawn gave him one of her 'Duchess' looks burst into tears and left the room.

Ann, immediately leapt-up and fled to her house, followed by Win, leaving Terry and Guy, who did not dare to turn on his radio!

"Terry," he said, "it seems we are all going to miss you around here you know. I've loved our little chats on the lawn in the afternoons, while having tea with you. Whatever am I going to do now? Thanks for everything, it's been great having you around and come back and see us, won't you?"

They all left Hombolo for Dodoma at 15.45 but on arrival at the station found that the train was delayed by an hour, which only served to cause a longer farewell. Terry wondered what the good was in goodbye and he hated them.

He was surprised at the number of people that had come out from the Diocesan office to say their goodbyes. Peter and Anne Marks were there from the Farmers' Training Centre at Hombolo, Dudley and Mrs Robinson, Project Manager for Hombolo, Philip and Margaret Cox from Bihawana Mission, Doctor and Mrs Kevin Engle, the Bishop's Secretary Mary Punt, the Diocesan Dentist, as well, of course, as George and Joan, Win, Dawn and Guy. Ann was very resolute and was taken under the wing of Margaret and Philip who invited her to join them for the weekend after Terry had left, which was well received.

As they stood on the platform of Dodoma Station saying their goodbyes, Ann passed Terry a small envelope.
On it she had written,

'Terry,' "To be opened <u>after</u> train leaves Dodoma!"

He kissed her goodbye, assuring her he would write as soon as he arrived home. He held on long and hard to her hand not wanting to let her go.

With all the goodbyes and hand shaking done, Terry climbed aboard the dusty train and found a carriage with an upper bunk. He felt if he slept up there he would be out of the way of anyone else coming in and out. He returned to the window to await the guard's whistle and wave his final goodbye to the assembled body of friends. He had a lump in his throat and tears in his eyes. The shrill sound of the whistle sent the huge steam engine slowly and laboriously on its long journey to Dar es Salaam, as it pulled the carriages out of Dodoma Station. Everyone standing on the platform was waving and shouting messages. Terry waved back until they all become just dots in the distance on that flat and dusty township.

Tears streaming down his face he went and sat on the lower bunk. Fortunately he had the compartment to himself, so far. He was still clutching the envelope that Ann had given him and sat there staring at it. He had an urge to jump off the train and return to them all, as this really was not what he wanted to be doing.

He sat with the envelope in his hands, just staring at it. After a while he found the courage with his tear-wet fingers to open and read the contents.

My Dear Terry,   Monday 14th Nov 1966

When you open this you will at last be on your way with, I know, very mixed feelings. However, I am quite sure that once you are safely at home in Weymouth and with family and friends again you will soon feel you've never been away. It's a great thing 'going home,' its worth going away just so that you can go home again!

The last few days have been an ordeal in more ways than one and I think probably you feel quite relieved to be 'en route'! I honestly think and know that you can go, feeling you've accomplished a great deal at Hombolo – it has all been appreciated – I've heard the comments you know and they won't forget you in a hurry.

For myself Terry, I almost feel that part of me is going with you and I hate to see you go yet I know that it is just as well, - after all, I suppose 26 weeks isn't a long time when one puts it in relation to a lifetime (or even 26 long years!!)

I shall be thinking of you tonight on the train and in the days ahead. I hope your travel plans <u>all</u> go without hitch and you can even enjoy the journey. I'll be pleased to hear of your safe arrival in England and reports of the 'chilly' or 'warm' reception! Please give my best wishes and 'Jambo's as Skippy (David) would say, to your parents and Sister and family – I look forward to meeting them next year too.

Well Terry, I haven't been able to tell you, all in person, what I wanted to say always but please know, above all else, whatever you may be doing and wherever you are, that 'I love you' – in case you missed it 'I LOVE YOU'!! Am going to miss you terribly but am looking forward to receiving and of course writing letters – especially the carbon copies – don't forget to vary them will you?

You'd better have a sandwich now and then try to get some beauty sleep! Look after yourself Terry, have a good rest and relaxation, enjoy your party and please write soon! Thinking of you always.
With all my love
Ann xxxxxx

The tears flowed and his heart sank, upset at leaving Ann and his friends. It was such a sorrowful parting and he was so sad leaving Hombolo, which would always hold a very special place in his heart. The hot dry Africa slowly passed the window of the train, as it sluggishly made its way, journeying on towards Dar es Salaam; the long hot sultry night lay ahead.

Chapter Nine

At 9.45 the following morning, the train finally pulled into the station at Dar es Salaam. The night had been long, very uncomfortable, and the train noisy with chatter going on throughout the night. The train seemed to have stopped everywhere on route, Kikombo, Gulwe, Kilosa, Kimamba, Morogoro, Musua and Pugu to name but a few. Terry was shattered and made his way to Luther House on Kivukoni Front, near the Old Yacht Club overlooking the sea. Many of the Missionaries had overnight stays there; it was basic, but clean and well cared for, providing reasonable meals. All he wanted in the next two days was to rest and sleep, before setting off back to London.

On Thursday 17th November 1966, at 20.00 Terry stepped aboard the 'Super VC10' Flight B.A. 165 stopping off at Nairobi and Rome, arriving at Heathrow 7.15 the following morning.

It was a dark and dreary scene that greeted him, which seemed to match his spirits. Everyone seemed to be rushing around so. What was their hurry? He made his way to Waterloo on the underground, and sent a telegram home to inform them he would be on the 8.30 train from Waterloo, arriving 11.50 in Weymouth.

It was so strange being back in England again, down to earth with a real bump. Things had changed so much in the short time he had been away. No longer did a steam train use the Waterloo – Weymouth line; it was now diesel, which always looked to him, like carriages without an engine. On the journey to Weymouth he went to buy some coffee and a packet of crisps. To his surprise he was asked which of about ten different flavours he would like to have. Previously there had only ever been one flavour! This confused him; after all in Africa any sort of crisp would have been most welcome. Was it really necessary to have so much choice? There were many things to adjust to and although it was nice to be going home to see everyone again, he felt that not only had he changed so much, so had the world he had previously known.

At a few minutes before twelve the train pulled into Weymouth Station. It all felt so familiar, while at the same time peculiar. He arrived back feeling a very different person, with a wider vision of life and restlessness unknown to him before. He stepped out of the train with all his worldly goods in a small case. There, coming towards him, was his mum, Auntie Potton and mum's friend, Joan Cotton.

Over the address system he heard a voice say,

"We would like to welcome home Terry Reeves from Hombolo Leprosy Centre in Tanzania, where he has been working with VSO – Welcome Home!"

This was repeated several times!

It was good to see Mum and the Aunties again, after so long away. He rushed up and gave them all a hug and a kiss.

"What's all that about on the loud speaker then?" he asked.

"That's your dad," his mother replied, "He couldn't be here because of work, but he knew the stationmaster and arranged it with him."

"How embarrassing," Terry responded. "But nice thought"

They took the taxi back home to 1 Tennyson Road, where they had lunch and sat around chatting. It was not long before they were all going on about the lorry drivers' and dockers' strike, how they wanted their pay increased to £100 a week. How ridiculous, Terry thought; how anyone could ever be worth that amount of money for a week's work he had no idea. As the chatter continued, Terry's mind drifted back to Africa, slowly losing touch with what was being said around him.

Within an hour of his arrival at Tennyson Road he was wishing that he was back in Africa. It was great to be home and to see everyone, but now he was ready to return!

The next few weeks were so alien, he felt like a fish out of water, wishing he were back in Tanzania with Ann, with the excitement and challenge of life there. He had to really work hard to pull himself together and to accept his situation, difficult as it was going to be.

There were things that he had to do; he wanted to go to see Ann's parents as he had promised and he needed to make an appointment to visit the V.S.O.'s office at Hanover Street in London for his debriefing. This was his chance to tell them all about the work he had been doing, his life and problems in Tanzania, to help V.S.O. when sending other volunteers out to the country in the future and for them to assess how well Terry had been selected by VSO for the task that he had been asked to do.

On the day of his trip to London he felt excited to be going back to V.S.O.'s office. It was like starting out all over again. As he sat on the train to Waterloo, he looked back to that day, just over a year ago, in 1965, when he had last made the journey, reflecting on how it had all turned out for him, changing his life far beyond expectations.

On arrival at the V.S.O.'s office on Hanover Street there was chaos. Apparently a volunteer Alison Smith, had been involved in an accident in Nairobi and died. Everyone was running around like headless chickens trying to find out just what was going on and what had happened to her.
Terry just had a few minutes with John Isherwood, on behalf of the directors, who apologised profusely for not being able to spend time with him. Terry understood totally and left them to get on with their sad and distressing task. He had never known or met Alison Smith, but he thought how that could so easily have been him and how distressed his family would have been.
V.S.O. later wrote telling Terry of the confidential reports they had received about his year's work in Tanzania, that both were first class, which he was delighted to hear.
As he was in London he decided to spend the day looking around the city. While in Tanzania he had read a lot about David Livingstone the Victorian explorer and was fascinated by his life, admiring his courage and work. He remembered that David Livingstone had been buried in Westminster Abbey, and felt drawn

to go and seek out his burial place, now that he had time to spare while in London.

He went into the historic and magnificent abbey. There in the centre nave, near the tomb of the Unknown Warrior, just up from the main door, was Livingstone's final resting place. Set in the floor there was a large black marble tombstone over the grave of the great explorer. Terry sat on a chair at the side, looking at the tombstone, contemplating the great man's life.

He felt a strange union with Livingstone, having just come from the very place that he had walked, all those years ago. Livingstone's book spoke of him walking through "Wagogo" country, which would have taken him straight through Hombolo itself.

Terry sat there reading the inscription in gold letters on Livingstone's tombstone:

'Brought by faithful hands over land and sea,
here rests
David Livingstone,
Missionary, Traveller, Philanthropist,
Born March 19, 1813
At Blantyre, Lanarkshire,
Died May 1st 1873
at Chitambo's Village Ilala.

For thirty years his life was spent in an unwearied effort to Evangelize the Native Races, to explore the undiscovered secrets, to abolish the desolating slave trade of
Central Africa.
Where with his last words he wrote,

"All I can add in my solitude is may heavens rich blessings come down on everyone - American, English or Turk - who will help to heal this open sore of the world."

Terry sat there for some time, as people passed by stopping to read the words. How much he wondered, did any of them really know about this man and the places he had travelled; how many had walked along the same path, as Terry had done just days before.

Christmas approached, not that Terry had much feel for it, as all he could think of was the previous Christmas spent at Hombolo and he longed to be able to spend it with Ann.

On 21st December he had arranged to go and stay for two days with Ann's parents at Pucklechurch, near Bristol. He wanted to show them some slides of Hombolo, so they might see something of Ann's work, to reassure them that all was well. They didn't have a slide projector, so Terry took his newly purchased Boots' model, together with his screen, on the train to Bristol Temple Mead station and then on the bus to the suburb of Staple Hill. There Mr and Mrs Bangham had agreed to meet him in their car. Although they did not know Terry, it was clear who he was. How many people do you see getting off a bus with a long rolled up screen?

"Hello, you must be Terry," Mr Bangham said as Terry stepped off the bus at Staple Hill.

"Yes," he laughed. "I wonder how you knew that!"

"It's good to meet you and thanks for coming to see us. My wife Margaret is over there in the car park behind the Co-op. Come over and meet her."

Terry shook hands with Ann's mother and they got into a very smart white Triumph Herald, which impressed Terry.

They zoomed off to the village of Pucklechurch a few miles from Staple Hill, chatting as they went along. The house was named "Meadowland Cottage," so Terry had thought it would just be a small country cottage. They travelled through the village and up a long narrow lane and there at a junction was a modern house set in a large garden on the crest of a hill. Mrs Bangham opened the gates and they drove in along the curved gravel drive. Wow! Terry thought, what a beautiful place and with such fantastic views of the countryside from the garden in front of the house, a real dream house, built with style.

Cecil and Margaret made Terry feel very welcome and 'at home'. They spent many hours chatting around the kitchen table, until Terry felt that he had known them forever.

He showed them the slides and related many of the tales of life at Hombolo, explaining some of the day-to-day problems that Ann faced.

Cecil, now a teacher, as Margaret was, had served in the army during the war years and he related some of the events of that time. Clearly, he did not have an easy war, spending a long spell lost in the Desert of North Africa with fascinating and horrific tales of his time spent there. He had recently gone out to Sarawak to teach, but the conditions were so bad that Margaret did not go out to join him and he returned after a year. His experiences helped him understand something of the life that both Terry and Ann had shared in Tanzania.

The first letters were now coming through from Ann. It always took ten to fourteen days, she had been wondering how his meeting had gone with her parents. How good it was to hear from her and to learn all that was going on at Hombolo since he had left.

She wrote, "I've been hanging on almost hourly for your letters to arrive. I'm missing you so much. Everything here is a reminder of you, your house, Buster, the Land Rover, the tractor etc. I'm slowly getting used to the idea that you won't appear round the corner and just look forward to your next letter, while trying to keep busy; you know how life is here."

Ann was missing Terry every bit as much as he was missing her. She was expected to return to UK in May at the earliest, still months away. It was to be a difficult time of waiting and separation for them both.

Terry loved to hear all about the farm, the crops he had planted and later to see the slides Ann sent him, showing the progress in the work that he had started. It was somehow rewarding to see the crops now growing in places where there had previously only been bush. He had organised the clearing of the land and ploughed it for the very first time in its history. It made him miss the life he had enjoyed there and the challenge of Africa in general, where he yearned to return.

However, he had his own challenges at this time; the first one was to seek a new job and he busied himself with the task. He found quite a few suitable looking jobs he could apply for in the Farmers'

Weekly, but was really looking to break into Management and not do the usual stockman type jobs; they would bore him silly after the excitement of Tanzania.

He replied to an advert for an Assistant Farm Manager at West Stoke Farm, Stoke Charity, near Winchester. The salary wasn't much at £750 a year, but it would be his first step into Farm Management, that was the important thing and a step onto the management ladder.

On a cold wet day in early January 1967, Terry took the train to Winchester where he had been invited to attend an interview with John Rowsell, the owner of the farm. Vic Williams, the farm manager, met him at the railway station. He drove him to the farm, situated a few miles from the city. It had quite a grand entrance with a long drive to where the main farm office was situated. Vic was the old style manager; he clearly had some rough edges, but seemed a kindly man, if a bit of a rough diamond. Terry took to him immediately. They had a good chat and he felt that he and Vic could work together, given the chance.

At the farm he was interviewed by John Rowsell, who was intrigued by Terry's time in Africa, most of the interview was about his experiences there and the condition of leprosy.

It was a large diverse farm of some 2,000 acres. They grew so many different crops: beans, oilseed rape, barley, wheat, oats and grass seed. They had a large flock of laying poultry and an egg-marketing unit. There was a pig manager who looked after large numbers of breeding and fattening Landrace pigs, a farm machinery workshop, a full time carpenter and lorry driver, three tractor drivers with other workers, as well as a huge mill that produced all the animal feed that was required on the farm.

It was just the place for Terry to learn about the many different aspects of agriculture, from the management viewpoint and to bring him up to date after his time away. He did hope that one day he would be able to move on to become a farm manager himself, as impossible as that seemed and perhaps a bit over ambitious he thought.

It was explained that there was a widow lady on the farm, a Mrs Griffin, who could provide him with good lodgings in her thatched house, the cost of which would be deducted from his salary. No overtime was payable and he would be expected to work whatever hours were necessary to do the job. There was a bonus after harvest, but how this was arrived at no information was ever given. He would always be responsible to Vic Williams, the farm manager, and would be expected to take over his work when Vic was on leave. It was clear that Terry was going to have to work hard, for little reward, but he could see that he would learn a great deal too. At least the pay was far better then the one-pound a week he received while in Africa.

Three days later on 17th January 1967 Terry received the following letter from John Rowsell:-

"Dear Reeves,

Further to my hurried note on Friday, I am pleased to inform you that I am prepared to offer you the position of 'Assistant' to Vic Williams, the Farm Manager at West Stoke Farm at a salary of £750 p.a. from which will be deducted the cost of your billet.."

Terry was delighted and accepted the offer, which would give him his first step onto the farm management ladder. It was to become for him, the beginning of nearly two intensive and hard working years, when he would be learning and involved with almost every aspect of running a mixed farm, and having to physically do the work, when he stood in for anyone taking their leave. He learnt much about the management of men from Vic and the two of them worked well together, becoming good friends.

Ann was thrilled with the news about the job and was now more then ever ready to return to England and to be working near to Terry, if she were able to find a suitable position.
She had just returned from a two-week break in northern Tanzania and Mombasa, Kenya, having driven there with Marj. and John, friends from Dodoma. They had all spent Christmas Day at Moshi in a pretty dreadful hotel, but it was in a lovely area with views of Kilimanjaro.

On the Boxing Day Ann took the bus to Mombasa where she had arranged to meet another friend Gwyneth, who she had originally met when Gwyneth had visited Hombolo.

They had agreed to meet at the YWCA in Mombasa. That entailed an eight hour journey on the dusty dirt roads. Ann had a long wait for Gwyneth, and wondered if she was going to turn up, as arrangements had been made so long ago. However, she did finally arrive, if several hours late and they went off to stay at the private cottage of a friend of Gwyneth's, at Likoni, on the beach overlooking the Indian Ocean. Ann loved it there, the most beautiful beach ever with white sands and palm trees, looking out over the rolling surf, Paradise! "It all worked out wonderfully in the end." She told Terry in a letter, making him green with envy.

Terry moved into his new lodgings with Mrs Griffin, a pleasant lady well into her seventies. He had a small bedroom at the back of her thatched cottage at the entrance to the farm and also the use of her front room, where he had his meals and sat in the evenings, if he was not out or working. It was comfortable enough and she took good care of him providing all his main meals.

As January turned to spring the waiting was beginning to get them both down. Letters become more frequent and urgent, the separation was certainly not making any difference to the way they felt for each other. Terry joined one or two groups like Young Farmers' Clubs that he had always played a big part in when he was serving his apprenticeship in Dorset. But he didn't feel like taking part and getting involved; all he could think about was the excitement of his past year in Africa and how Ann had come so dramatically and unexpectedly into his life. He was as certain as he could be, that he and Ann were for life, there was that special bond between them, as indeed she had predicted and there was no changing that. He just longed for them to be together again, but that wouldn't be until May, which seemed a lifetime away. He had already booked two weeks' holiday, which fortunately worked in well with farm work.

As he began to think more and more of Ann's return, he decided that it was time to start to look for a car. Living out in the country at Stoke Charity meant that it was difficult to get around without your own transport, although he was able to borrow a car from time to time.

He and Bill, one of the men from the farm, had a look around the garages in Winchester to see what was on offer. Terry fell for a lovely looking Morris 1100, a light shade of blue, with the registration number '138 LOT'. They took it for a test run and after going through the monthly repayment costs, to purchase it over two years, Terry signed up for it. He proudly drove it out of the garage a few days later with the first trip being to Weymouth, to show his parents and take them out for a ride. The car was a great success, except it always made a clonking noise at the rear, every time it passed over a bump in the road! He found out later that this was a common fault of the model.

Ann wrote to say that her return trip had now been finalised, that she would arrive at Gatwick on 16th May at 07.20am. How excited they both were and ticked off the days, as month followed long month of waiting.

A few days before Ann was due to leave Hombolo, Dawn gave one of her splendid farewell parties on the lawn. George and Joan and their two daughters Anne and Margy were there. Ann had made many dresses for them both and for their dolls, which the girls loved. Margaret brought along a photograph of her with a dead porcupine shot in the maize field. Guy had taken the picture and Margy asked Ann to give it to Terry who she remembered well from his many visits to their house. There was a number of the African hospital staff at the farewell party. Ann had worked with them and taught them, during her short time at Hombolo. She always made friends wherever she went and was loved by them all.

During the party while sitting on the lawn, Ann noticed one of the blind men, Dixon, a discharged patient at Hombolo. Dixon was with another man sitting on the ground by a tree, just off the roadside. Out of respect, as he saw it, he remained at the entrance of the garden on the drive. Ann saw him there and wondered what he was doing; thinking he might be lost she went to greet him.

"Jambo, Dixon. Can I help you?"

"Madam Ann," he said. "I have come, with my friend, who has some English in him, to see you from my village many miles from here. Through leprosy my legs died, but you gave them back to me by showing me how to use them again. You made me do many hard and difficult exercises. I complained and cursed you for making me work hard to do impossible things. I shouted and screamed at you but you did not listen to my complaints or how much I swore at you. You made it possible for me to walk. You see I have walking still in my legs," Dixon said.

"Then before you sent me back to my village, you showed me how, even with my dead eyes, to make rope out of the Baobab tree bark. Now, because of you, I make some shillings with this work, for my family, and myself; you give me life again. I'm a proud man, but I was ignorant too and a fool. I asked you for forgiveness. I come from my village to thank you for everything. I hear that you are going to leave us to return to England to be with the Bwana who was here and came to plough so much on his tractor to give us food. I cannot come with you as my eyes are dead, but I never will forget you."

Ann, stood in silence, feeling so humble, so small, somewhat shocked by Dixon's words. "Please wait there," she told him as she went to rejoin the party on the lawn. She quickly took some sandwiches and cake from the table, wrapped them in a napkin and gave them to Dixon and his friend who had translated for him.

"Please take these for your journey," she said. "I'm honoured that you come to say goodbye and of course I forgive you. I'll tell Bwana Terry that you came to see me; he will be very happy too." She shook their hands; Dixon's hands were hard with the labour of rope making.

"May God bless you both."

Ann was very struck by this experience, underlining for her why she loved the people and country so much. They have so little yet will give you all they have, just to say thank you, she thought. The young girls, who were leprosy patients that she had worked with, training them to sew and to knit then arrived to say goodbye.

They too were sorry to see Ann go, but did so with a cheery but very tearful farewell.

Ann was ready to leave Hombolo in many ways, but loved the work and the people of Tanzania and would certainly miss it, as did Terry. But, everything was now focused on them getting back together after their long and forced separation.

Sadly, but unknown to them, separation was always going to haunt them and be a feature of their lives.

The excitement and expectation grew as May approached. Ann and Terry had agreed that after they had met at Gatwick Airport, they would drive to Pucklechurch and stay there with her parents for the week of Terry's holiday.

The week before Ann's arrival, Terry had arranged to take his parents up to Norwich to stay with his sister at Olive Road, New Costessey. Anna-Marie was now nearly four years seven months old and Craig nearly eighteen months, so Mum and Dad were keen to see them both again. Terry with his newly acquired car was happy to drive them up to Norwich on this trip, taking his very first trip on a motorway. He stayed overnight with his sister then the next day drove down to London to meet Ann.

Early on the morning of Tuesday 16th May 1967, after the long drive from Norfolk, Terry arrived at Gatwick Airport just after 06.30 ready to meet Ann's flight, due in at 7.20. His heart was in his mouth as he waited, eyes fixed on the arrival board. It was the moment they had both waited for since the sorrowful parting when Terry left Dodoma Station the previous November. Everything they had both been through in their relationship at Hombolo, raced through his mind as he waited for the flight to arrive.

At the same time as the report on the arrival board announced that the flight had landed, Ann suddenly appeared, as if by magic; she must have raced through the customs and was the first person out. They ran towards each other, throwing themselves together in a long embrace; they could not let go, as all the stress from the time of separation drained away. They just stood there speechlessly wrapped in each other, smiling and crying and holding on to each other, fearing to let go and not quite knowing what to do or say next.

They eventually prised themselves apart for Ann to telephone her parents to report her arrival. Terry just stood gazing at her and could not believe that they were again together, even if in somewhat different surroundings. She stood there chatting to her mum on the phone in the airport arrival lounge, wearing an African print dress she had made. He noticed her long slim legs and how very happy she looked.

Together they drove out of Gatwick and on to the M4 motorway, which would take them to Pucklechurch. They hardly knew where to start, both firing questions at each other, enquiring about this and that. Terry wanted to know all about Hombolo and the people he and Ann had left behind. Ann wanted to know all about Terry's new job in Winchester and if he enjoyed it. Then there was the question of where Ann might look for work and in both their minds, linked to this, there was the question that neither of them dare speak of. Did they, would they, both feel towards each other as they had done in the surroundings of Hombolo?

Ann's mother and father were so delighted to see Ann; they of course had not seen her for over three years, so the excitement was high. They made Terry very welcome again in their lovely home, and he was delighted to be spending a week with them and with Ann in these beautiful surroundings.

Their week together, after so long apart was full of chat and catching up on so many people and events. They went on long walks in the fields and countryside around "Meadowland Cottage" that was hidden away up a narrow lane in that rural haven. They had no ambition to go anywhere, or do anything, except to be together, which they delighted in.

They spoke much of Africa, clearly they both loved and missed it very much, together sharing a dream to return one day to work there.

The week quickly passed, and decisions were made; Ann said that she would start to look for work as an occupational therapist near to Winchester; in the meantime Terry would come to Pucklechurch whenever he was able to get away for a weekend, for he had to work some of the weekends. It was going to mean more separation for them, but hopefully not for too long.

"I just long to be with you and never have to say goodbye again," Ann said when the time came for him to leave. "I could always take any job and move to a better one later if I wished. I really want us to spend our time together more after the months apart, it's hopeless like this." Ann tearfully said to Terry as he left to return to Winchester that afternoon.

Terry drove off back to West Stoke Farm with a heavy heart, wondering if the separations they were always having to endure would ever end. He was really finding it all so hard to cope with, realising that he must quickly bring it to an end by asking Ann to marry him. He did not want to rush her, but he was sure she felt the same about their situation.

Ann was unhappy at being left behind at Pucklechurch; as good as it was to be there with her parents, she wanted to be with Terry and the continued separation was more than they both could bear.

It was soon the weekend again, time for Terry to make the return journey from Winchester to Pucklechurch to be with Ann. They both just lived for the weekends when they could be together. However, this weekend was to be special, as he just knew he had to sort out the present situation, which couldn't go on any longer.

When Terry arrived at Meadowland Cottage the gates were open, signalling his arrival was expected.

"The man in your life is here." Ann's father called out from his ladder, where he was painting, as Terry drove in. Mr Bangham carried out all the maintenance and painting to their house, spending nearly all his school holidays around the house and garden and was happy doing it.

Ann rushed out to greet him laughing at her father's remarks.

"How was the trip? How did you manage to get away so early? When do you have to go back? Come in and tell me all. I've missed you so much, this separation is terrible, and the week drags by, but the weekends fly."

Terry took his bag into the house, greeted Mrs Bangham who was making some tea while Ann took his bag up to his room. Terry followed and they sat on the bed to have a few minutes together before they joined her parents. "Now, don't worry," Terry told Ann. "I've been thinking about things while away and I've a plan."

"How exciting! What is this great plan of yours then?" she asked laughing at him.

"I can't tell you now as they're waiting for us downstairs. Come on let's have some tea!"

"You can't say that and then go for tea, at least give me a clue. Please!"

"Later, later. Come on now tea time!"

That evening Terry and Ann walked up the lane across the field and back again to sit on the hill that looked out across the fields towards the old railway line and looking at the view towards Bristol. They enjoyed the late evening sunshine and just being together again, such a luxury.

"Come on then what's this great plan of yours, mastermind? Tell me what it is. Are you going to move Pucklechurch nearer to Winchester? Is that your plan? I just wish you could. I'm doing all I can to find a job in your area but it takes time and in the meantime we just have to go through this separation each week and it's killing me."

"Well if you'll let me get a word in I'll tell you!" Terry responded smiling at her.

It'll not really help with the immediate problem of us having to part each week I'm afraid, but it will ……………"

Before he could go on, Ann interrupted. "Well what sort of plan is that then? I'm going crazy here without you. You said you had a plan; it doesn't sound much like it if it's not going to help. I hate this separation, especially on top of the six months while I was in Tanzania. It's hopeless."

Ann raged on at him, letting out all the aggression she felt towards the situation.

"Ann, will you marry me?"

Finally he had silenced her – she stopped stunned at what he had asked. Her face lit up.

"Of course I will, it's what I've always wanted, of course I will. Yes! Yes! Yes! That's the best plan in the world. It's wonderful; you've made me so happy, as I will you."

They sat there as the sun went down, just holding on to each other, dreaming and absorbing the moment.

"When will we tell Mum & Dad?" Ann asked. "I suppose you'll have to ask Dad. He would like that."

"Yes, I'll have to pluck up courage and see him tomorrow."

The next day, Saturday, Terry tried to get to see Mr Bangham on his own, but it was not easy. First he was in his study doing some schoolwork, and then he was out with the dog. Before Terry could catch him he was off down to tend his vegetable garden.

"What can I do?" Terry said to Ann while they sat in the lounge having their morning coffee. "There is nothing for it. I'll have to go down and ask him while he is in the garden."

"OK. Good plan, go now. I'll go and tell Mum at the same time. She's in the kitchen."

Nervously, Terry set off down the garden where Mr Bangham was forking up his potatoes.

"I'm glad I've caught you," Terry stammered. "There's something I need to ask you. I realise it's not the best place, but Ann and I wish to marry and I wanted to ask for your permission. We've known each other over a year now and in very close circumstances; we've decided that this really is what we both want. We wouldn't be able to marry for about a year, as we need to save up, but we're sure we can do it."

Mr Bangham, looked a bit startled, nearly putting the fork through his foot as he thrust it into the ground before making his response. He then took a deep breath and said, "Yes of course that's fine, very nice, Margaret and I will be very happy for you to marry Ann. Yes, delighted in fact.

Next May or June will be splendid, you just let us know and we'll fix a date that suits us all. That's wonderful news."

Terry later heard how Mr Bangham had not been surprised at the question, only at the venue! He had remembered how he had felt when he had to go and ask Margaret's father if he could marry her.

Terry rushed back to tell Ann that her father had given his blessing.

"I've just told Mum that you were speaking to Dad. She's delighted too. They both like you very much. I know it's not them that has to like you, but it does make everything much easier and happier this way."

"It sure does. I'm so pleased. Looks as if things are looking up, doesn't it?" Terry said happily.

"It's wonderful, everything is taking shape and I've only been back a short while. All I've to do now is find a job," said Ann.

"So you don't want an engagement ring then? Ha ha" Terry laughed.

"Of course I do, when can we go and look? I don't need anything expensive but I would love an antique ring, if it were possible. Let's have a look in Bath and see what we can find there."

Over the course of the next few weeks Ann applied for any jobs that looked as if they might suit her. She also went up to Scotland to see her grandmother in Peterhead for three days, to share the good news of her forthcoming marriage. Ann had not seen her grandmother for many years, having been away in Canada working and then of course in Africa. She always had such happy memories of holidays spent in Peterhead with her grandmother as a young girl and was keen to see her again. Her gran lived with her Auntie Belle, who was a milliner and had a shop in the town. They had lived together ever since her husband, Ann's grandfather, had died. Ann told her gran that as soon as she had sorted out a new job and settled in she would bring Terry to meet her, probably in the New Year.

On 26th June Ann was invited to attend an interview for a job as an occupational therapist at Basing Hospital, near Basingstoke. It was really very near to Winchester, which she was delighted about, for she hated so much the continual distance between them, as Terry did. It was a few miles from Winchester and not as near as she would have liked, but it was better than being stuck on the other side of the country at Pucklechurch.

The interview was a great success and Ann started in her new job on Monday 10th July, having found lodgings with a Mrs Dewsbury, at 22 Eastrop Lane in Basingstoke. She agreed to let Ann a room, with use of a sitting room. Terry was about twenty miles away, so he was able to drive over in the evenings when they'd both finished work. This was a tremendous improvement and enabled them to spend time together, make new friends and make plans, both for their wedding and for their future life together.

Life fell into a new pattern. Terry drove up to see Ann most evenings and weekends, if they were not working, and they made frequent trips to Pucklechurch to see Ann's parents and to Weymouth to see Terry's. Their relationship grew stronger, bonded always by that African experience. They spoke often of their desire to return to work in Africa one day, as that was and always would be the centre of their lives.

In the meantime Ann enjoyed her work at Basing Hospital, and made new friends, as she readily did wherever she went. They enjoyed this time, both learning new things in their work, even if it required long hours. During harvest time Terry was driving one of three huge twelve foot Massey Ferguson Combine Harvesters on the farm, harvesting crops from June until October. He had to put in long hours, always looking forward to rain so that he could take time off to go and see Ann.

John Rowsell, Terry's boss, offered to do up a flat above the stable block on the farm for Terry and Ann to live in, once they were married: it had two bedrooms and a lovely sitting area. They were delighted with the kind gesture and were given some say in how it was decorated.

The Catholic Church said it was necessary that anyone that married a non- Catholic, that person must receive instruction about the duties and obligations of their partner in the church. So Terry made an appointment with his parish priest Fr. Roy Bennett, at St

Peter's Catholic Church in Winchester, to attend such instructions with Ann.

This was done in order that Ann would know more of Terry's religious faith and its demands. Every week, for about six weeks they both went to see Fr Bennett. He was a lovely, happy and worldly man with whom they discussed everything, from what the Church stood for, what it meant to be a Catholic, and what was expected of them should they go on to have children. It was always an open and honest discussion and they came to enjoy it, with all it taught them both. Fr. Roy Bennett was a sincere and caring man with a good sense of humour who went on to become a good friend, following their lives and fortunes with great interest.

1967 ended with Terry and Ann planning all the details of their wedding, now set for Saturday 8th June 1968 at St Peter's Catholic Church Winchester. They had considered marrying in Bath, it being nearer to Ann's parents' home. However, since Terry had always attended the church in Winchester and they both were living in that area, they chose the beautiful Church of St Peter's. Ann, who had a strong faith in a God, had never really followed a particular religious belief, so was very happy with the plan. Full of excitement and joy and with the blessing and help of both sets of parents the preparations progressed.

The other side of happiness is so often sadness and the New Year began with the sad news of the death of Ann's grandmother at Peterhead in Scotland.

"I'm so pleased that I went up to Scotland to see gran in June. She had been happy for me and was looking forward to meeting you," she tearfully explained to Terry as he comforted her. "I'll always have happy memories of her and my aunt who she lived with in Peterhead. Poor Aunty will miss her so much, as we all will."

The blighted year seemed to take off with so much to do and think about. Ann was making her own dress and was often in touch with her old school friend Mary who agreed to be bridesmaid; they had always kept in touch so were good friends. It was a special treat to have Anna Marie, nearly five years old, join Mary as bridesmaid.

Craig, Terry's nephew, was now two and a half years old, but was a bit young to be pageboy; instead he was going to present Ann with a silver horseshoe on the day.

Terry's family planned to hire a minibus to take them to Winchester for the wedding. They were all now busy looking for suitable outfits, finally settling for a crimplene fabric, in order that it did not crease while they were travelling.

But on the day of the wedding they all piled into the minibus, carrying their outfits, planning to change into them on arrival! They stopped on the way near to Shaftsbury for coffee. The total cost of the coffee for the six of them on the bus came to seventeen shillings and six pence, a fact that Terry's father could not get over. He spent the whole of the Wedding Day telling everyone he met of this event and the cost of it; he was so overcome by the extortionate charge for the coffee.

On arrival in Winchester, Terry's family took over the female public toilets opposite the church as their private dressing room to change their clothes, much to the surprise and concern of other people wishing to use it! The Reeves family had arrived in town!

It was a beautiful day for the wedding and Terry sat with his bestman Patrick some fifteen minutes before the start, in the first row, on the right of the aisle awaiting Ann's arrival. As they sat waiting there was an almighty crash. Looking around they saw Ann's mother lying in the central nave, having slipped with her new shiny-soled shoes. She quickly picked herself up and sat in her place awaiting Ann's arrival, apparently none the worse for her experience!

Their Wedding Day was perfect. Terry and Ann were at last together in every sense of the word, safe in the knowledge that now all the days of separation they had both hated so much, but had endured, were finally over.

Chapter Ten

After their ten day honeymoon on the beautiful island of Guernsey in the Channel Islands, Ann and Terry were excited and ready to start their new way of life. It had been a wonderfully warm summer and the little Stable Flat above the horses in the courtyard of the house, was just perfect for their first home. They could lie in bed early in the morning and hear the clip-clop of the horses below. Terry's boss had given them use of his swimming pool in the adjoining garden, which in the heat was a real treat. Ann, a keen swimmer, took full advantage of it when returning from work on those long hot days of 1968's summer months.

On return from their honeymoon Terry was straight into the harvesting of grass seed that began about that time, while Ann was back to work at Basing Hospital as the new Mrs. Reeves. There was a lot of visiting to do of family and friends, with trips to Pucklechurch and Weymouth, a fairly regular occurrence. Slowly they began to make new friends and when work allowed they enjoyed their new surroundings and the Winchester area, rich in history.

As the year moved on towards autumn they began to consider their long-term plans, and to think about the future. Both agreed that they would love to have children one day; Ann was a little more concerned, as her body clock was five years ahead of Terry's. However, they really wanted to have a couple of years enjoying their life together first, following all those days of living apart in separate countries and then in different parts of England, it was time to enjoy just being together as a couple, a time of healing and to have fun.

Terry began to feel at a point in his career when he should consider moving into farm management and began to look out for appropriate vacancies, scouring the Farmers' Weekly to see what was available. The urge to return to Africa was uppermost in both their minds, but at the same time they felt it was important for Terry to get into a management post in England, to gain experience before applying again overseas.

"Where do you fancy living?" Terry asked Ann as they sat at the side of the pool after work one evening at West Stoke Farm.

"Do we have a choice?" she asked.

"There are quite a few management jobs advertised now, being the end of the farming year, a time when managers often move on for one reason or another. We need to focus my applications, but I suppose it'll depend on the type of job, what's expected of me and if I feel able to do it, rather than where it is. I've always had a mixed farm background so that'll help as it's given me a wider knowledge."

"So you know a little about a lot!" Ann jeered.

"Well you could say that, especially if you want to be pushed back into that pool," he laughed.

"I don't of course have very much management experience; my apprenticeship in Dorset was good, but not aimed at management skills. My only management experience before this was at Hombolo, hardly high powered." Terry explained. "But it did open the door to my position here as Assistant Farm Manager. I'll just have to try and trade off that I suppose. My National Certificate in Agriculture will help, but it's not a degree, which can sometimes open more doors in this type of employment."

"Could you take time out and study for a degree?" Ann suggested.

"Well I suppose I could, but it would be expensive to finance and we'd have to find somewhere to live and on just one wage. I'm not sure I would be very happy with an academic style of life either, being a more practical, hands-on sort of person," he explained. "A degree would certainly help in finding an overseas post when the time comes, but I really don't think that it's a lifestyle for me somehow."

"There is a good management job I noticed in the Farmers' Weekly this week in Wiltshire, a mixed farm with a large acreage of corn. Think I'll send off for that. It's in a lovely part of the world, with a huge farmhouse."

"Sounds good, why not? You have nothing to lose. Do they always provide you with a house," Ann asked, thinking about where they might live.

"Yes, always, you have to be on the farm you see, especially if there is livestock around. It's usually a very nice farmhouse, far better then anything we could afford to take on, if we were buying. A large house will be useful too for when we have children, and no mortgage to worry about at that expensive time. I'm planning to stay in agriculture, either here or in Africa, so a good house would be a great asset. Looking ahead to when we retire we should then have saved enough to buy a place of our own."

"Wow, you are planning ahead. You'll have us in our dotage before long." Ann laughed.

The application for the post of farm manager in Wiltshire was sent off, but a week later a letter arrived, thanking Terry for his interest, informing him that on this occasion he had not been successful. It was disappointing for them, but there were others he could and did apply for.

"How do you fancy me working for a Lord?" Terry joked one day.

"Do I get to have a title if you do?" Ann asked.

"No afraid not, it doesn't work quite like that!"

"There is a job advertised as farm manager in Beaconsfield, Buckinghamshire. It's a bit further north than we would like to live, but it sounds interesting and looks my sort of job. I think I'd be in with a chance. I have to apply through Lynch and Sayers a firm of management consultants who are handling the appointment for Lord Burnham. I think I'll have a go."

Within days of his application Terry was invited to attend the office of Lynch and Sayers in Warwick. There are sure to be others invited to the interviews, so can't get too excited," he said, "but it's a good start and good experience to have at least an interview."

The interview went well for Terry; the consultant seemed very interested in his Tanzanian experience, which created much discussion and always seemed to open doors for him. He hoped it would be something they would remember him by, making him stand out in their memory, compared to the others they were to interview. They must have been impressed, as two days later he received a letter asking him to attend an interview with Lt. Col. The Rt. Hon. Lord Burnham, his Land Agent Major Rimmer and the consultants Lynch and Sayers on Monday 7th October at the office of Hall Barn Estate in Beaconsfield.

"Wow! Great news," Terry exclaimed.

There were two others at the interview and the three of them looked around the estate as a group, but were interviewed individually as well. Terry did not care for that format. It was one thing knowing that others were in line for the job, but another to actually see them and have to share the day with them.

First all the candidates were taken around the farm by the consultant: Hall Barn Estate was situated on the edge of Beaconsfield. There they met Lord Burnham's resident Land Agent, Major Rimmer, who was responsible for the whole estate, which included many houses, tenanted farms and properties, all of which seemed to be in a pretty poor condition. Apparently the present Lord Burnham had only recently taken over after his father's death and was seeking to improve the estate, consisting of tenanted farms and the "Home Farm," slowly taking back tenanted farms as they became vacant and adding them to his own Home Farm. There were also many houses and shops around Beaconsfield owned by Lord Burnham all in a similar state of disrepair.

The estate had a large area of woodland looked after by two foresters, who were responsible for maintaining it. They were also gamekeepers for the shoot, something very dear to Lord Burnham. The Estate held the Guinness Book of Records award for the largest bag of birds shot in one stand, a shoot at which King George V attended in December 1913, when 3,937 birds were shot.

Both the current Lord Burnham and his father had been forced to sell off a great deal of the original land ownership to pay death duties, so they were in a poor financial state.

While going around the estate, Terry chatted a lot to Major Rimmer, as it would be him he would be working alongside. He seemed a kindly man carrying the usual Army air about him. Terry thought that as the Major would have the ear of Lord Burnham, it might help his case if he could leave a favorable impression with him, without being too forward or over bearing.

At the end of the day's tour all three candidates returned to the office of Hall Barn Estate in the old town of Beaconsfield, sitting with half smiles on their faces and fear in their hearts, awaiting the decision of the interview team. It was a strange situation, they all hoped they would get the job, but knew that there was only a one in three chance. The tension was high as they sat there awaiting the outcome, wondering who would be the lucky one!

After the three candidates had waited some fifteen minutes, footsteps were heard from the office above, where they had all been locked in discussion, this was followed by heavy footsteps down the wooden staircase to the room where the tense candidates awaited their fate.

"Mr Reeves," the consultant called, "would you come up stairs please?"

He froze for a second, looked around at his fellow interviewees and made his way up the long staircase with excitement and a broad smile.

There in the large office at the top of the stairs, sitting behind a long table was Lt. Col. William Edward Harry Lawson. 5th Baron Burnham, otherwise referred to as 'Lord Burnham'. A large man, he looked a Henry V111 type of character, as he sat there with his white beard, pulling on a cigarette as if his life depended on it. Surprisingly, he was the one that looked the most nervous.

"Come in, Reeves," he commanded.

Next to him was the smiling face of Major Rimmer, now familiar from the tour of the estate earlier in the day.

"We would like to make you an offer," the consultant said in his businesslike tone.

"Lord Burnham would like to offer you the position of Farm Manager at a salary of £1,100 per annum. You will be fully responsible to him for all your duties through Major Rimmer, but you will report to us the management consultants; we are retained to provide Lord Burnham with a quarterly report on the farm with a financial statement.

Part of your package, of course, will be a house, Oak Lodge, at the entrance of the estate that you saw earlier today. You will also have free firewood, free rental on the telephone and use of the landrover.

We understand that you could take up your duties on Wednesday 30th October 1968; this will be for a six-month trial period.

We will confirm all this to you in writing, but if you can tell us if this is acceptable, then we will inform the other candidates waiting downstairs and dismiss them."

Of course Terry did not hesitate to accept, he realised that this was the step into management that he'd been looking for, accepting the offer made with pride. He shook Lord Burnham's hand, then Major Rimmer's and the consultant's thanking them all.

"I shall look forward to joining you at the end of October and getting started on the challenges ahead of bringing the estate into profitability."

"We will be decorating the house inside for you," Lord Burnham informed him.

"Will you keep in touch with Major Rimmer regarding your move to us here and the progress?"

"Yes, certainly I will," Terry agreed.

The Major smiled at Terry, "I'll be in touch," he said in his military way.

Terry left the office on a high and drove back to Stoke Charity. He couldn't wait to tell Ann. How pleased she would be he thought, as the next stage of their new life together fell into place.

On his arrival at their flat Ann was making a cake in the small kitchen, she looked very much at home doing it, always being such a creative person.

Terry walked past her with a long face and slumped into the chair in the sitting room.

"Oh dear," Ann said looking at his sad face, "well, never mind, there will be others and at least you've experienced an interview which is a good thing to do.

Tell me what happened. What was 'The Lord' like? What did you have to do?" she asked.

"Well, there were three of us at the interviews, we all met Lord Burnham, his Agent and the consultants," Terry explained.

"What was Lord Burnham like then?" Ann asked again with interest. "Don't think I've ever met a real live Lord."

Terry, unable to keep up the pretence any longer, had to put Ann out of her misery, as she looked so sad for him, knowing all the effort that he'd put into the interview.

"Well, Lord Burnham said that as I was the best looking chap there he would offer me the job!"

Terry sat there waiting for this to register with Ann and laughing at her puzzled face.

"You mean you have the job?" she screamed at him questioningly.

"Got it in one."

"You rotter! I really thought someone else had been given the job. Fancy coming in here like that. You're a tease," she said as she punched him on the shoulder, planting a kiss on him. "That's fantastic news, well done, brilliant."

"When do you start? What's the house like? Where is it situated? What is the garden like? What's the salary? When will I have to give my notice at work?"

Steady on, I'm exhausted. Would you like a cup of tea?" he asked her.

"Yes please," she replied.

"Thank you, so would I," he laughed, so off she went to make some tea for them both. He then filled her in on the tense day of events and answered all her questions.

Terry and Ann both gave two weeks' notice to their respective employers and prepared to pack up their few belongings at the Stable Flat and make preparations to move to Beaconsfield.

At times, life had seemed to remain static they felt, with nothing much happening, but on looking back they both could see that since their first meeting in Africa life had not really stood still for very long at all. Nothing is forever.

The move to their new home in Beaconsfield went well and as they had little in the way of possessions, there was not that much to do to pack things up. They never realised just how little they had until they moved to Oak Lodge. It had been the gatehouse to Hall Barn Estate. It was rather unique as the exterior of the house was covered in woodcarvings that a previous Lord Burnham had brought back with him from overseas; those who passed by often stopped to gaze at it and some took to looking in the windows!

It was only a fairly small house with two bedrooms. Their few things looked very sparse, and they certainly needed more furniture as soon as they could afford it. They had only kitchen stools, no easy chairs, or indeed a table and chairs to sit at to eat. They soon purchased a few things and Ann made curtains for the windows.

They went to a furniture auction in Amersham, nearby, where they purchased a second hand oak draw leaf table for a £1. It needed a lot of work on it, but after spending many hours scraping it down and varnishing, it was a table to be proud of, something they had created together.

The home making extended into the garden, which was a mixture of grass lawn, a vegetable area, a small lean-to green house of dubious quality and a coal shed, with flower beds at the front. They enjoyed working together on this and making it all look homely.

Money was in short supply, but Ann soon found a new job as an occupational therapist at Wexham Park Hospital, near Slough, so that was a great help. Slowly they were able to purchase their needs for the house and even had enough to rent a black and white television. Terry loved to watch all the space mission programmes and to follow the Apollo mission to the moon. It all fascinated him and proved what Sister Magdalen, his old school teacher had always said. "There are more things in heaven and earth than this world dreams of." She, he felt, was absolutely right, we were just specks of dust in the overall universe.

As far as his work was concerned Terry soon found that he had taken on a huge challenge with the management of Hall Barn Estate. The farm was run down and overgrown, weeds and grass grew wild everywhere, fences were broken down or non-existent and a few scruffy beef cows seemed to wander freely everywhere, even onto the roads at times, causing considerable danger to traffic on the A40 that ran along one edge of the farm and through Beaconsfield.

The farm machinery was poor at best and tractors were underpowered for the work involved. There were hardly any useful buildings and those that existed were from a by-gone day. There was a farmyard with derelict dairy buildings on Hedgerley Lane and the same at Woodlands Farm just south of the town where Lord Burnham's brother, Hugh and his family lived.

There was a derelict poultry farm at the back of Lord Burnham's mother's house that was little use except for firewood, consisting of two long wooden deep litter type houses, which seemed to have been used by cattle, for which they were not at all suitable.

The stable yard at Hall Barn House was the centre of the Home Farm, consisting of an old courtyard that had, in its glorious past, been a stable block and garages for the house. It was divided up into stables, storage and garages, that were now used to house the tractors and odd bits of machinery. It had in the past been a very smart and busy centre for the estate, providing all the major services. There were two cottages attached to the yard; one occupied by Arthur Tew and his wife, he had been the chauffeur and was now the caretaker of Hall Barn house. The retired groom Mr Wooler and his son lived in the other.

The Farm Manager's office was a small room next to the Wooler's house, containing a table, one easy and one hard chair, with a one bar electric fire. Apparently the previous Farm Manager had often been found asleep there in the easy chair, after a liquid lunch! There were no farm records and only a very old plan of the estate and a cropping plan some four years old.

Terry could see there was so much to sort out, before he could even start to make a plan for the farm and its future.

It was time to be introduced to the work force! Major Rimmer had arranged to meet Terry on his first day to introduce him to the staff. First up was Paddy, a short stocky Irishman who had a strong thick Irish accent; Terry could hardly understand what he was saying. It was beginning to look as if Paddy was the only one that had ever done any work on the farm. He seemed to spend his time driving a white 'David Brown' tractor, aimlessly around the farm, pretty well as he pleased, enjoying the country air, clearly needing some guidance for his day to day operations.

"It's a grand day for yeh," he said, when he was introduced to Terry, wearing a look on his face that said, "I've seen it all before, you'll not stay for long and I'll make sure you don't."

It seemed he had enjoyed a comfortable unchallenged life, retiring to his comfortable cottage in Beaconsfield by night and that is how he wanted it to stay. Terry was not impressed!

There were two foresters, Charlie and Dick, whose sole task was to keep the woodlands in order, to ensure the rides through the woods were kept clear for the shooting season and to feed the pheasants. They also cut firewood for the house and all the staff who were supplied free. Charlie and Dick were brothers, but neither could drive a tractor, so Paddy seemed to act as their personal chauffeur to and from their work in the woods!

Charlie and Dick were a lovely old fashioned couple of chaps, with very likeable personalities, but so unworldly. Charlie had served in the army during the war, so was a little more worldly wise; he kept racing pigeons and loved his garden. Dick had always lived with his mother, making few demands on life. He had been used to her running around behind him caring for his every need.

The one useful thing was that they both could and did ride a bike and would often be seen around the roads and tracks on the estate. The estate had been well laid out and planned at some stage in its illustrious past, as there were various stone obelisks and statues dotted around, often in the most unlikely places. Terry would laugh to himself, as when he was out in some far off corner of the estate in the woodlands, he would see a statue with Charlie or Dick's lunch bag hanging from its arm, indicating that they were around somewhere having their lunch or working.

Temples and mazes were dotted around the estate indicating something of its past history. The house itself had been built in c1651 for Edmund Waller on his return from France; he was a poet and Poet Laureate. He died in 1687. Sir Edward Levy-Lawson, creator of the Sunday Times and the Daily Telegraph, later Lord Burnham, bought the house in 1832.

Fortunately the tenanted farms on the estate, were not Terry's responsibility, Major Rimmer managed those. The "Home Farm" was, he could see, going to be more than enough to keep him busy. Where did one start Terry thought!

Well first it was necessary to get the place tidied up and get rid of the rubbish, such as old machinery. Then he managed to get Paddy to go around the whole farm with a "Bush Whacker" on the rear of the tractor, cutting back the long grass along tracks and in fields. This was a new experience for Paddy, he didn't seem to like to be given instruction on what to do, always putting up some objection or pointing out a reason why he could not do as he had been asked. It was necessary for Terry to push ahead with a firm hand and not listen too much to his objections, telling him to just get on with it. Paddy was going to be hard work and difficult to control, but Terry was determined that Paddy would not rule the roost.

Charlie and Dick said to Terry one day, regarding Paddy. "You just wait until its full moon; he goes mad then and nobody can do anything with him!"

It turned out they were right, as when ever there was a big problem with Paddy, it nearly always coincided with a full moon.

An additional tractor driver Chris was employed to boost the manpower. Lord Burnham was not easily persuaded that it was necessary, as he was always under the impression that Paddy could do all, when in effect it was not possible. Chris was a keen young man and in a way was a good antidote to Paddy.

Chris worked hard, and long hours and was able to see and understand what Terry was planning for the farm's future, helping him, with Paddy to achieve it. He was prepared to put up with the poor conditions and the second rate machinery available, being able to see that progress would bring success. Paddy felt that he had to keep up with Chris, so from that day was slightly less painful to work with, until 'full moon' of course!

Having got rid of so much rubbish and junk, Terry was now able to see things more clearly. The next stage was to see what condition the land was in. Fortunately into the yard one autumn day drove a wily Welshman by the unusual name of John John. He seem to have the gift of the gab and Terry was at first a little suspicious of him, thinking that he was little more than another salesman. Not so, as this little man, not much more then five foot tall, was to prove to be the salvation of the farm and went on to influence its success and future.

John sold agricultural lime and the land at Hall Barn seriously needed large quantities of it. Terry and John went around the whole farm taking samples of the soil with a soil auger. Each sample, from various positions in every field was put into a test tube; chemicals were added with the reading telling them if the soil was acid and to what extent. The whole farm was so acid it was a wonder anything grew. Sample after sample proved the same, so much so that Terry wondered if this John was having him on, in order to sell the lime.

Unintentionally there was a check, as Terry also sent out soil samples to the Ministry of Agriculture for a more general test of the soils condition, to establish if there were other needs and fertilizers required. These only confirmed the accuracy of John's test. Slowly Terry and John tested the whole farm and it was not long before the lime wagons arrived and covered the whole of the farm with lime to lower the acidity, allowing the crops to produce their best, a process that was necessary to repeat every three years, in order to keep the acidity under control and the crops growing well.

John and Terry became lifelong friends over the years, by spending so much of their time together on this task. In the heat of summer and the cold of winter the ritual was carried out to establish the amount of lime required, there being years of neglect to catch up on. A great deal of lime and money was needed to put fertility back in the soil, which in the end was achieved.

Ploughing and the planting of winter crops followed and by spring the whole farm looked a totally different place. Everyone would comment on the improvements, which was both heartening and encouraging. Terry had taught the woodmen Charlie and Dick to drive, so they were happy to go off each morning with their own tractor and trailer, to go about their work in the various woods on the estate. While Paddy, with the exception of the times when it was 'full moon' was kept under reasonable control, but was always a tricky chap to deal with. Chris, on the other hand was a tremendous asset and a skilled tractor man with great ploughing abilities; he and Paddy took their turn at the weekends to feed the cattle and became a general good all rounder with Paddy becoming an excellent stockman.

Terry and Ann took a well earned holiday in the Lake District in July 1969. On the way they went to call on their friends Margaret and Philip from Tanzanian days, who, having returned from their teaching posts at Bihawana, were now back and living in their home town of Grimsby, where they were both teaching. It was good to see old friends, and they delighted in being able to reminisce about their days in Africa. It was somehow strange to see them in an English environment for the first time.

Ann and Terry had a wonderfully restful holiday in the Lake District, staying in and around Keswick at various B&B farmhouses. They toured around in their newly acquired, second-hand, grey, Triumph Herald, a wonderful car that had the ability to turn around on a sixpence, something no other car has since achieved.

They enjoyed a time of rest, walking, laying in fields in the warm sunshine, enjoying an endless amount of strawberries and generally unwinding after their recent endeavours.

They had settled well into Oak Lodge, which had a real country cottage feel to it. Ann enjoyed her job, working as an occupational therapist, even if it was not quite as fulfilling as her work at Hombolo had been. The same applied to Terry's work too, but it was challenging and gave him good experience.

Never far from their thoughts was the question of when would be the right time to return to their main love and ambition, to work and live in Africa, where they had met. But as often happens in life, something came along to divert their attention.

Just before Terry's 24th birthday in September 1969, Ann broke the news that she was pregnant; they were both delighted at the thought of the baby's arrival to share their lives. They quickly spread the news to the rest of the family and began to look forward to April when the baby was due to arrive.

Hall Barn House was to undergo some changes too. It had been decided to reduce the house in size by removing a large Victorian extension, making the house more economical to run, while at the same time returning it to its original size, when first built for Edmund Waller in 1651. Christies were brought in to list and auction the contents of the house. A collection of French Literature, fine old English and Continental clocks, furniture and works of art, tapestries, rugs, carpets, books, porcelain, silver and household effects were all sold off at a fascinating auction held on the premises on Monday 29th September 1969. Times were indeed changing for Hall Barn Estate.

The harvest for 1969 was larger then it had ever been, but that was not difficult, and with Terry's competitive advanced selling of the corn crops, there was considerable improvement to the farm finances. There was still plenty to be done before a profit could be expected, but they were going in the right direction.

"Jolly good, Reeves, well done. Great improvements all around." Lord Burnham exclaimed heartily, when they met in the stable yard one afternoon.

"Are you going to join me for the shoot at the weekend? We have some very influential people coming along; I hope there's going to be a good show of birds."

"Yes, I'll be there, looking forward to it. There are plenty of birds this year. The difference now is that you'll be able to see to shoot them, as we've cleared all the rides that were so overgrown. Be sure to tell your shooting friends about the golden pheasant that still roams around: they mustn't shoot it."

"I'll tell them. Well done, Reeves. See you on Saturday, thank you, and keep up the good work." His black Labrador scampered off towards the house, followed by Lord Burnham. The cool autumn nights that were setting in pushed everyone towards their log fires earlier.

Lord Burnham was pleased to see the visual improvements to the Estate, but due to the cost in achieving this, the improvements did not hit the bottom line, so financially the estate was even worse off.

He did make a lovely gesture when told they were expecting a baby. He explained that Mr and Mrs Jackson, tenants at Lillyfee Farm on the estate, were going to retire. This meant that the land from that holding would be added to the Home Farm, making extra work and responsibility for Terry. Lord Burnham offered them the farmhouse at Lillyfee Farm to move into as soon as it had been redecorated.

Ann and Terry were so excited and arranged to go and see it, just before the Jacksons left to retire in Cornwall. The farmhouse stood in a large graveled yard overlooking open fields, with a huge eighteenth century wood barn on one side of the yard, with other smaller farm buildings around. The house was fenced off and surrounded by an acre of garden, consisting of a large lawn that went down to a small pond at the front, with apple and nut trees and a large fruit and vegetable plot at the rear. There were four bedrooms and two bathrooms, as well as a large farmhouse kitchen, utility room, dining room and lounge. It was perfect, such a wonderful spot to bring up a family too, with country lanes to walk down on each side of the entrance. They moved in to the house on 14thFebruary 1970, St Valentine's Day, with the help of their friends Patrick and Mary. What an exciting day it was and the beginning of a new and very happy phase in their lives.

The large parklands surrounding Hall Barn House were good for grazing and around twenty single suckled cows grazed there.

"Reeves." Lord Burnham called out, as he was passing on the road to the woods one afternoon, while walking his black Labrador. "What do you think about us having some Sussex Cattle? I've always liked the look of them." We do have to try and make some money from the damn cows you know."

Terry agreed. "Yes, why not? They're a very good breed, and would cross well with the Herefords we have. We could purchase a Sussex bull and a few more Hereford heifers, increasing the size of the herd to around say 100 cows. Then we could rear the progeny and sell them for beef. There's a good market and we might even sell them straight to a butcher to get the best return."

"Would you do me some figures, Reeves, and let me know where you might find such stock and how much it's likely to cost. We need to do something to increase returns and I love Sussex cattle."

"It doesn't stop there, Lord Burnham," Terry replied. "We'll need new buildings or at least improve the ones we have, better machinery for hay making will also be necessary. However, I'll draw up a plan and we can go over it together."

Terry set to and in a few weeks agreed a plan with Lord Burnham to develop the Single Suckled Herd to one hundred cows, using a Sussex bull and to fatten the progeny on the Home Farm, selling them for beef to the local butcher, Weeks.

There were other exciting events taking place in the world at this time. On 11th April 1970, Terry's eyes were looking to the heavens; he always had a keen interest in the Apollo mission to land a man on the moon and followed every move on television. But on that day Apollo 13 was making its 3rd mission to land on the moon. James Lovell the captain, and his team were sitting on top of a Saturn V rocket at the Kennedy Space Centre in Florida, all ready to set off at around 9am that morning. Terry made sure he was near a TV to watch this historic moment; the excitement was everywhere, everyone being amazed by this incredible event.

However, at Upton Hospital, Taplow, near to Slough, other things were going on that were equally as fascinating and every bit as exciting. Paul Edwin Reeves was somewhat reluctant to come into this world. Terry was hoping that he would hang on a bit longer, so that he would be able to see the moon launch take off. He need not have worried, as it was 22.04 before Paul showed his face. He came into the world smiling, as he has done ever since. How delighted and proud Ann and Terry both were to have a son as their first born, even if he caused his mother plenty of grief while making his entry at over nine pounds!

Like Paul's arrival the Apollo mission was slow to get going and although it took off early that morning with the intention of landing on the moon, due to a malfunction later in the day, it had to limp back to earth on 17th April.

After a few days monitoring at the hospital Paul was welcomed home to the wonderful environment of Lillyfee Farm. Ann and Terry had the usual disturbed nights and took it in turns, as far as they could, to provide the love and care Paul needed in those early days. He soon took to laying in his pram under the nut trees in the warm summer sun, where their dog Prince a beautiful golden retriever, took to laying by his pram to protect him, as together they grew up and became friends.

A few days before Paul's christening at Our Lady of Peace Catholic Church in Burnham, Terry met Enid Lady Burnham as he often did when she was out with her dogs. She was the mother of Lord Burnham and was often seen around the estate exercising her black Labrador dogs and loved to stop for a chat.

"How's your new son?" she asked Terry, as she walked near the old poultry farm.

"Very well indeed, Lady Enid thanks."

"So when are you having him christened?" she asked.

"It's next Sunday. We've decided to call him Paul, his second name will be Edwin, after Ann's Grandfather."

"What a lovely combination," she said. "I do hope that he cries at the christening."

"Why do you say that?" Terry asked her curiously.

"Because, they say, that when they do, the devil is going out of them!"

In the next breath she leaned forward and said, "None of mine cried!"

Then off she went with her dogs with a big smile on her face, waving as she went.

There were no worries on that score. Paul did have a little cry as Fr. David Woodard poured the water over his head the following Sunday afternoon, with his proud parents, grandparents and godparents, Margaret and Philip Cox. They all wondered just what sort of world this beautiful child would have to grow up in and what he would do with his life!

It was an excellent summer and Hall Barn Estate Farm began to look much improved. John John, the lime man, had a big interest in and involvement with the local agricultural show; he suggested to Terry that the farm was so improved that he should consider entering it into the Royal South Bucks Show. Farmers competed for cups and awards that were then given out at the annual ploughing match and dinner. "There were," he said, "several classes that they could enter the farm into, such as the "Best Crops," "Best All Round Farm," "Best Livestock" etc." Terry discussed this with Lord Burnham who was keen to have a go and thereby to gain from the additional PR that it would give, if they were to win something. So Terry set the wheels in motion and made a few entries for the next show that was to take place, as it did every year, in October.

Development of the beef herd went ahead; Terry attended an auction in Sussex to buy a young Sussex bull, together with some in-calf Hereford heifers. It was a very different experience from the last time that he went to purchase livestock, in Tanzania! Over the summer, work was carried out to improve buildings to house the cattle during the winter, so that by autumn everything was ready for the arrival of the newly born beef calves.

The consultants were proving to be a bit of a pain in Terry's side; they would come to the farm each quarter and glean from him all that had taken place on the farm since their last report. They would then go away, write up a report and present a glossy brochure at great expense to Lord Burnham with all this information on it.

"Why do you feel it's necessary to have consultants to do this task for you? They really do very little for the amount you pay to them. It's only information that I've given them in the first place." Terry asked Lord Burnham, when he was in the office with him one day.

"Well, Reeves, they are really very expert in what they do and I need their guidance and help."

"Well I could do that at nil cost to the business. They really don't do that much," Terry explained.

Lord Burnham looked on in disbelief. "I think you will find that they do a first class job," he said.

Terry decided to show Lord Burnham just how little the consultants did in fact do and at the next quarter's report set them a trap.

When they came to the farm office as usual, to gather all the information from Terry, he decided to give them completely false data, knowing that they never checked anything as they were expected to and never put a foot onto the farm, as they should have. He did this to prove to Lord Burnham that they didn't really do the job he was asking and expecting of them, that they only copied the information Terry gave to them, presenting it as if it was their own work.

Terry always received a copy of the Consultants' report direct from them. When it arrived he checked to see if they had, as usual, just copied the information given to them, without undertaking any sort of check. Sure enough all the figures were just as Terry had given them and completely wrong.

Terry rang and made an appointment to see Lord Burnham in his office at Hall Barn.

"Come in, Reeves" he said crisply in his usual army manner. "What can I do for you?"

Terry was holding the consultants' report. "Have you read the latest report from Lynch and Sayers?" he asked Lord Burnham.

"No, it's only just come in. Why?"

"Well if you study the figures you'll see that the information I gave to them was all false. I did this to prove to you that they're not doing the job that we pay them to do. I'm sorry to do this, but it was the only way I could get my message across. We are paying over £2,000 a year for a service that they are not providing."

He quickly read the report and without a word picked up the phone to Lynch and Sayers's office in Warwick.

"This is Lord Burnham here, from Hall Barn Estate in Beaconsfield. I've just received your latest quarterly report and from its information I can see that you clearly have no knowledge of what is going on around my estate farms. You've not inspected the farms nor do you have any idea of the stock numbers, crops or the new acreage that we now have. You're not, and have not been carrying out the task set you. Your contract with me is therefore now terminated. There's no point in your sending an invoice for this work, and, if you do I'll take you to court for breach of contract. Goodbye."

"I'm sorry Reeves, that I didn't listen to your advice. Do you think you can provide a report for me each quarter? We can then sit down with Major Rimmer and go through it together at our monthly meetings."

"Certainly I can," Terry gleefully replied. "With some help from our accountants with the figures, that's all I'll need."

"Reeves, well done, you have just saved me from paying a very large fee!"

Chapter Eleven

Ann very much enjoyed her new life as a mother, loving to be with baby Paul and caring for his every need, always busying herself in making the home at Lillyfee Farm, as well as looking after the lovely garden. She was so happy and content with her lifestyle, which reflected on everyone that came to visit and stay with them. She still, despite this, thought often of Africa, especially when old friends from those days came to stay. The slides would come out and they would chat deep into the night about old times and the excitement of those days. But at that moment she was in heaven and they were already thinking of extending the family. In August they were able to announce that a brother or sister was on the way for Paul and due at the end of March 1972. They were both absolutely delighted, looking forward to their new arrival in the spring.

"Let's hope there's not another Moon launch when the baby arrives; I can't guarantee to give birth so conveniently this time," Ann laughed.

When the estate took back Lillyfee Farm into the Home Farm, they also took over an old loyal worker by the name of Jimmy. He was of the old school and with the extra work Terry was pleased to have a reliable and trusted old hand.

Jimmy was able to do a lot of the tractor work and knew Lillyfee well.

There was just one thing: Jimmy would never send in his time sheet on time and so each week Terry had to ask him several times for it. One week all the deadlines had been passed, so Terry called Jimmy into the farm office for an explanation.

"Now, Jimmy, you know I must give in your hours to the main office each Thursday if you're to receive your pay on time and the overtime due to you. Every week you're late. Why's that?"

"Sorry," said Jimmy, "I forget and leave it at home."

"Ok," said Terry. "It's Friday now and I don't have your hours, so here is a time sheet. Fill it in now please, sign it and I'll make sure it gets through, so you receive your pay on Saturday as usual, but this is the last time. You must hand it in by Thursdays in future, is that clear?"

Jimmy looked confused, his face reddening.

"What's the problem Jimmy? Just fill it in and I'll take it to the office for you."

"I want to see his Lordship." Jimmy demanded.

"You do?"

"Yes, I do." said Jimmy.

"OK, but he'll only refer you back to me you know!"

"I want to see his Lordship."

Terry picked up the phone on his desk and rang Lord Burnham's office and arranged for Jimmy to go and see him straight away.
"Right, Jimmy, you can go across now and see him as he's there for the next fifteen minutes."

Jimmy sheepishly went off to see Lord Burnham, still clutching his timesheet in his hand.

Terry wondered whatever the matter was with the man. He had always been slightly odd, he thought, but harmless. In twenty minutes Jimmy returned to Terry's office, put the completed time sheet on the desk and left without a word.
Terry picked it up and read the attached note.

"Reeves, this man cannot read or write!"

Suddenly Terry understood. Jimmy's wife must always have filled in his time sheet for him and he must have been too shy to tell Terry! Well, Well.

At the Royal South Bucks Show in 1971 Terry won awards for the "Best Winter Barley", the "Best Spring Barley" and "Best Grassland," as well as second prize for the "Best Stock Farm in South Bucks" for which he was presented with the silver "Festival Challenge Bowl." Lord Burnham was delighted, farm profits were still elusive, and it would take time, but things were getting better on the financial front, as well as visually.

However, Terry was very aware that his own personal finances were in a poor state. His pay had never increased in two years and things were getting very difficult, especially with a new baby on the way. They missed Ann's salary and of course they had a large Farmhouse to keep going. But somehow they managed to balance the books each month and felt that a rise would soon be offered as the farm finances began to improve.

Ann's parents came to spend Christmas 1971 with them at Lillyfee, for the first time ever; they had such an enjoyable celebration together. Then on 5th January 1972, Margaret and Philip, friends from Tanzanian days were home from their new teaching post at Malole, near Kasama in Zambia so came to spend a night with them while in the country. Of course, that once again opened their hearts and minds to Africa, their first love, hearing the stories and feeling the excitement of travel again made them both a little restless.

However, they had their very own excitement: at 02.15 on the 28th March 1972, Lynda Mary Reeves made her fairly effortless entry into the world at 7lbs 13ozs at the Red Cross Memorial Hospital, Taplow, near Slough. Terry rushed along early the following morning to go and greet Baby Lynda and to see how Ann was after the birth. There was absolutely no problem in finding Ann in the ward, as hers was the only white face! - Well it was Slough! What joy and excitement it was. After two days, Ann and baby Lynda were allowed to come home. They were proud parents again, with the perfect family of an elder son and younger daughter.

In the following months family and friends came to stay keeping Ann and Terry very busy. The farm continued to improve and the workload increased. This year the annual Royal South Bucks Show was to be held at Hall Barn Estate, an honour indeed, with Lord Burnham as the host. They were again awarded the 'Festival Challenge Bowl' for the 'Best Stock Farm' in South Bucks, as well as the 'Best Kept and Cultivated Farm.' Dick and Charlie the woodmen, were both awarded cups for long service to Hall Barn Estate, which pleased them greatly.

The shooting season was upon them again, another busy time, as more of Lord Burnham's family and friends gathered for the Saturday shoot. Terry's mind was more often focused on another important issue, the urgent state of their personal finances. This concerned him greatly wondering what to do about the situation. As far as Terry was concerned, the shooting season meant he was at least able to shoot game to help feed his family.

There was still no sign of an increase in pay and they were now really struggling to keep the large farmhouse at Lillyfee warm, as well as themselves fed. The nursery was fine as there was a storage heater in the room; their main concern was for the children that they should keep warm enough.

Terry was prepared to do anything to make sure that Paul and Lynda did not suffer in anyway. He even considered taking a second evening job such was his concern. He and Ann could easily add another jumper to keep warm and frequently had to, but this was not really practical for the children. Ann made all their jumpers, acquiring cobs of wool from mills in Scotland through a contact of her Aunty at Peterhead, and sold some of these jumpers.

There was a wood fire Rayburn in the kitchen, so that kept at least one room warm with some of the heat helping to raise the temperature in the rest of the house. The Rayburn was also used for cooking, reducing the electricity costs.

Even so, £83 a month didn't go very far and they had many sleepless nights wondering what they could do to improve things. Ann was an excellent housekeeper, but Terry felt he couldn't go on expecting her to stretch things further and further every day. The children needed new clothes as they grew up, as well as so many other things.

They had a paraffin heater they carried to their own bedroom at night and stood it on the landing by day. This consumed a gallon of paraffin a week. Terry collected it each Saturday morning on his way to High Wycombe, from a small pump at the filling station at a cost of 10 pence for the gallon. One weekend they could not find the 10p between them to go and buy the paraffin, it had got so bad near the end of the month. Terry had a few pence in his pocket and Ann had a few in her purse, but still not enough. Then they remembered that the green swivel chair in the lounge often jingled with coins that must have fallen out of people's pockets. Sure enough, there they found a few coins and Terry was able to go off to the garage to get the gallon of paraffin.

"This is madness," he said to Ann. "It's got to stop and somehow I have to improve things for us all. We cannot go on like this."

By some means they got through that winter of 1972, but both realized they could not face another winter without more money: something had to give.

Ann was disappointed for Terry. "You've worked so hard for Hall Barn Estate and yet they have never offered you more money, in spite of the cups and awards you have won for them and turned their grotty run down farm into a proper business. What are we going to do?" she asked Terry as they sat down to discuss their plight after the children had gone to bed, one evening in the spring of 1973.

"The first beef calves will be ready for sale this coming autumn from the new Sussex cattle. When those are sold, we should be in profit for the first time," Terry explained. "Then Lord Burnham is sure to consider a rise for me. At least in the summer we can live from the garden crops and the pheasants and rabbits in the freezer."

The Royal South Bucks Show took place early in October 1973, this time at Pennlands Farm, Farnham Common. Paddy had developed his stockmanship skills caring for the bullocks and putting in a great deal of effort. At the show he walked off with champion of the baby beef class with his well groomed, twenty month old, Sussex cross Hereford bullock, much to Lord Burnham's delight and satisfaction. The farm again winning the award for the best stock farm and the best kept and cultivated land, with fourth prize awarded for their winter oats.

As autumn set in, Lord Burnham was getting very excited at having the first Sussex cross animals ready for slaughter and was keen to have some on the table for himself.

"Reeves, will you see that the first animal that goes to the butcher is jointed up and taken to Hall Barn kitchen for Lady Burnham? We're both really looking forward to tasting the first meat from these beasts."

"Of course I will. I'll go to the butchers when the cattle are ready for slaughter and make sure that they're jointed and labelled for Lady Burnham, then bring them myself to the house."

Terry, too, was looking forward to tasting some of the steak, after having looked after and cared for the stock for three years. He felt sure that Lord Burnham would see he had some of the first meat, for him and the family to enjoy.

On the appointed day Terry went to the butcher's premises near Slough and loaded the trays of meat all neatly labelled into his Landrover. He drove to the rear of Hall Barn House and carried the trays up to the kitchen, where Lady Burnham was waiting for him to load them into her fridge and freezer, tray after tray until the job was complete. She was delighted with it all.

"What a splendid job, Reeves. Well done. It all looks very nice indeed."

Terry thought she must have put a pack of the meat to one side for him to take home, but none was forth coming. He turned to leave the kitchen, and as he approached the door, Lady Burnham, holding a packet of bones, shouted to him.

"Reeves, would your wife like some bones for soup?"

Terry turned around with a look of utter disgust on his face and said,

"No thank you, Lady Burnham!" and walked out.

That he thought is the end, the absolute end.

He went home and relayed the event to Ann, who could hardly believe it.

"I'm going to go and see Lord Burnham and ask him for a rise," he told Ann.

"I don't like having to do it, but there's no alternative. That was just the last straw. I have to do it."

True to his word, the next morning, he rang Lord Burnham for an appointment. It was one of those bright October days when everything is covered with that special autumn light. He drove down through the woods to see Lord Burnham in his office at Hall Barn House.

It was the day for being bold Terry felt, so he drove up to the front door of Hall Barn and parked the Landrover. Normally he would park in the yard at the rear of the house. He was feeling a little apprehensive, as he did not like having to ask for more pay. He always thought that if he did a good job he would not have to ask, that it would be offered to him. But need overcame his fear, as he thought back to the last winter and the trouble they had had finding enough money to live on. He considered all the things that they were going to need in the coming year for Paul and Lynda as they grew up, together with the needs of Ann. It would be a while before she could even consider returning to work again.

He went in the front door of the house, turned right in the large hallway and knocked on the door of Lord Burnham's office in the corner of the hall.

"Come in!" he boomed. "Oh! It's you, Reeves. Come in and sit down."

"Good Morning, Lord Burnham, thank you I will."

"Now what can I do for you this morning? You rang asking to speak to me urgently." Lord Burnham said, as he played with his moustache.

"Well, you see Lord Burnham, I have worked here now for nearly five years. When I first came here the farm was very run down and overgrown. I've improved the farm considerably, taken on more land, cleared the wild areas of the woodland and improved the shooting. As you know, we have won a number of awards in the Royal South Bucks Show year upon year, and we even felt ourselves in a position to host the show here last year. The number of cattle has increased and we've developed the buildings the best we could. I've also taken on the work the consultants had previously been paid to do that saved at least two thousand pounds a year."

"Yes, yes," Lord Burnham responded. "I do know, why are you telling me all this?"

"Well, Lord Burnham, you see, since I came here I've never had any increase in my salary. You did kindly let me move to Lillyfee Farm in 1970 and had it redecorated for us. We are very happy and grateful to you for providing such a lovely home. But we're finding it extremely hard to manage on the salary we have, especially in the winter, with heating costs as they are. So I've come to ask if you'll consider increasing my pay, in view of all the improvements and the work that I've carried out to date."

Lord Burnham, playing thoughtfully with his moustache, stared across at Terry and said, "Reeves, do you know what the family motto is?"

"Yes, Lord Burnham, I do. It's all over the estate, on walls and badges and buildings."

"Well, what is it?" he growled.

"It says, 'Of Old I Hold,' " Terry responded.

"Well Reeves, that applies to your salary!"

The blood drained from Terry's face. He could not believe what he was hearing and just sat there in disbelief with a deep sinking feeling.

"Well, was there something else, Reeves?" Lord Burnham asked Terry.

"No, Lord Burnham, absolutely not, nothing else, nothing at all."

He drove straight back home through the woods to Lillyfee in tears.

He loved working on the estate; it gave him a feeling of belonging and all the history of it gave a certain pleasure. He enjoyed improving things, making them better, restoring things and he took pride in what had been achieved, in all the improvements, getting the right labour force, even with the likes of dear Paddy to put up with. But he had to be able to pay his way and to build a future for himself and the family. There was nothing for it; as much as he did not want to, he had to look for another job.

Ann was equally upset by Lord Burnham's behaviour and attitude.

"You're right. There's nothing more that you can do; he doesn't deserve you. It's so sad after all that you've done and achieved, but he has left us with no option."

"What do you think about us returning to Africa?" Ann asked. "Maybe this is the push we needed, before we get too comfortable here."

Terry was thoughtful; he still could not believe that all he'd done had been for nothing. "I'll have a word with Major Rimmer first, to see if he can help, before I finally throw in the towel."

The Major had become a friend as well as a working colleague, although he just got on with his work of improving the domestic buildings on the estate and attending monthly meetings with Terry and Lord Burnham. But Terry thought it was worth having his view, as he had known and worked with Lord Burnham for a long while.

The Major reported back after his discussions with Lord Burnham, that the estate was not in a healthy way financially, due to years of poor management, he would have liked to have been able to increase Terry's pay, but it was not possible at that time. There were explorations going on to establish if the seams of gravel at Woburn Common might be worth mining and selling to a gravel company, but that was in the future and by no means certain.

"That's it," Terry said to Ann after reporting on his discussions with the Major. "I'm going to start looking around to see what jobs are on offer."

The following week in the Farmers' Weekly of 2nd November 1973, Terry spotted an advert in the jobs' section.

'Seychelles'
'Livestock Manager'

'Our clients, farming on Mahe Island in the Seychelles Group are developing a new livestock unit to supply the rapidly expanding local and hotel trade. This provides a unique and challenging opportunity for a man to be responsible to the resident Director for managing and developing an exciting project in a superb tropical environment. Practical unit management experience including familiarity with budgetary controls is desirable. In addition to proven organisational and administrative skills, the successful candidate must have, above all, the enthusiasm and drive to exploit the potential of a developing situation. The salary is competitive and negotiable with a bonus or gratuity. The contract will be for a minimum of 2 years and conditions include generous home leave, free passages and accommodation."

That sounds exciting he thought. I think I'll have a go. Off went the application to the consultants and he waited.

"Where are the Seychelles?" he asked Ann.

"Not sure. Let's get the atlas out."

Together they looked to find where it was and found it off the coast of their beloved Africa in the Indian Ocean.

"Well, I know we always said we wanted to return to Africa." Terry said. "This is not quite there, but it does look very close and the job does sound suitable, exciting too."

"What about Paul and Lynda? If we settle in the Seychelles or move to Africa there are bound to be schools for them. I imagine we might even in later years be able to send them to private school, as often fees are paid by the employer, aren't they?" Ann suggested.

"Steady on let's get an interview first! You're running way ahead.

You know this might just be the very thing for us and could lead us back to Africa. The Seychelles sound stunning."

The following week on Thursday 14thNovember, Princess Anne's Wedding Day, Terry was invited to the consultants' offices at Warwick, where they interviewed him. They were able to tell him more about the job and the owner of the farm business.

To Terry's surprise they asked him to attend an interview with Mr. Brooks, the owner's son, who was due to arrive in London at the weekend to recruit for the post and would Terry attend at their offices on Monday 19th November to meet him. That was unusual he felt, but at the same time Mr. Brooks jnr. was only here for a short time and by the sound of it wanted to make the appointment as soon as he could.

Terry wondered if the other applicants would be at the interview, as they had been the last time for the Hall Barn job. He hoped not.

He need not have worried, as when he was called in for the interview, he found to his relief, just the consultant and a very tall, sun burnt, fair haired man, Mr Philip Brooks Jnr.

They discussed the Seychelles Islands, the climate, schools, shopping, what other expatriates were working on the islands and all about the farm, when it was started, who owned it, and how well established it was. It all sounded very exciting indeed.

Terry was surprised how little they asked about him. The work he had done in Tanzania, seemed to be the main source of interest, other then that, it was just a case of if your face fitted! It soon became clear that Terry's did, as at the end of the interview they told him that they did have others keen to take the job, but would like to offer it to him first. He was surprised and somewhat taken aback at the speed with which it was all moving and asked if he could first consult with his wife, which they agreed to and took Terry to another room to make his call in private.

"Hello Ann, I'm in the consultants' offices here in Warwick. Guess what? They've offered me the job in the Seychelles. What do you think?

We would go out in February next year on a two-year contract. The salary is £2,750 a year, plus a fifteen percent gratuity tax free. I get two weeks' local holiday a year and four weeks' home leave per year of service. We are also provided with a three bed furnished bungalow, rate and rent free, as well as a maidservant, all airfares of course, and a good baggage allowance. There are playgroups for the children on the island, as well as an International School as there's a lot of Americans working at the tracking station. We would have to pay fees for that, but he told me they were inexpensive."

There was a silence with no comment from Ann.

"Are you there? Did you hear that?" Terry asked anxiously. "Have you fainted?"

"Yes, yes I'm here, just a bit shocked. Do we have to say yes or no right now?" She asked.

"They may wait, but there are other interested parties and we might lose it if we delay. Do you have any doubts about taking it then? If so we'll not accept and discuss it more when I get back? After all there will be other jobs to go for should we lose this one."

More silence!

"No, no, don't do that. Go for it. I was just thinking it over. It seems a fantastic opportunity; we would be mad not to take it. Do you realise it's almost three times your present salary alone, without all the holidays etc. and the chance to live in such a beautiful place, as we saw from the book we acquired last week."

"So that's a 'Yes' is it?" he asked.

"Are you happy about the job? Do you think you can manage to do it?"
"Yeh, no problem, once I get into it," Terry confidently replied.

"One thing for sure, we won't need any paraffin for heating! Temperatures are in the 70 – 90 degree range, with high humidity and heavy rainfall in December to February. At least we wouldn't have a problem finding the 10p for the paraffin."

"Yes, then go for it," an excited Ann exclaimed. "Go for it."
"And by the way 'Congratulations'. You've done very well!"

"OK, I'll tell them I accept the offer. It has to be right, doesn't it? What an incredible opportunity it is. I'll go now. See you later this evening."

Terry arrived back at Lillyfee late that evening, due to long train delays, but it gave him chance to think things over and take in the happenings of the day; things had moved so fast. It was one thing applying for new jobs, quite another deciding whether or not to accept one. This move would mean very big changes in all their lives, not least giving up Lillyfee, which they had both grown to love.

Then there was the fact that they would be leaving parents, grandparents and friends, so much to consider this time around. At least they would have long holidays at the end of their contracts and be in UK for two months at a time, fully paid. He felt confident that it was the right thing to do, perhaps wishing it had been in Africa, but that could well come from this move. It would be lovely for Paul and Lynda to have the sea on their doorstep, with the swimming too and should be good for the children in the long term.

Ann was so excited on his return, as he related the events of the day to her, going over every detail. He, as always, went first to see Paul and Lynda who were in bed and asleep. As he looked at them and kissed them both goodnight, he just hoped that what they were about to do, would bring only happiness for them in their young lives.

Terry and Ann sat and chatted into the small hours, making plans for the future. They decided that as soon as the offer came in writing, from the consultants, that Terry would give in his notice to Lord Burnham.

The country was in a bit of a mess at that moment too. The miners' strikes had been going on and off for months, they were fed up with hearing about all that. With the miners having now put a ban on overtime, there were electric power cuts as a result. Who knew where it was going to finish up?

The next morning the consultants rang and spoke to Ann, to inform them that they were gathering the details together and would soon send the job specification and letter of agreement out, that if they had anything that they wished to ask in the meantime, then not to hesitate to contact them.

They could hardly keep it all to themselves, but had to say nothing until it was offered in writing.

On 4th December 1973 the letter confirming the new position as "Livestock Manager" in the Seychelles arrived. Terry had come home for breakfast at nine as he usually did, after seeing to the men and the cattle following their 7.30 start.

"It's arrived," she called as he came in the back door carrying logs for the rayburn.

He quickly read the letter and glanced at the formal agreement from the consultants.

"Wow," was all he could say as he sat in silence. "Wow."

"So it's really happening. I can't believe it, can you?" he enquired of Ann.

"We're off to the Seychelles eh?" Ann said. "A few weeks ago we had never even heard of it and now we are going to live there on Mahe, four degrees south of the Equator, a tropical island four miles by about seven. What a dream."

"Yeh, you're quite right, Woweeeeee!"

"So when will you give Lord Burnham his Christmas present?" Ann asked, meaning Terry's notice.

"How about if we sleep on it and post the signed agreement back to the consultants tomorrow and then I'll get a meeting fixed up with Lord B."

"It's so fitting that Mum and Dad are coming for Christmas, don't you think?" Ann commented. "I'm really pleased that we asked them. It's worked out well and we can break the news to them then. I don't look forward to that, but I'm sure they'll be pleased for us once we explain how difficult it's been for us this last year."

The next day Terry rang Lord Burnham's office to arrange an appointment for that afternoon.

"Reeves, I think we do need to speak about arrangements for the Christmas shoot on Boxing Day. You're going to be here I hope?"

"Yes I'll be there, Lord Burnham," he replied. But not for very long after he thought to himself! "There is another important matter that we need to discuss first."

"Right you are. See you at 2.30 then Reeves in my office."

Terry had always thought that to give in his notice to Lord Burnham after the poor response he had to his request for more pay would be easy to do. But when it came to it he felt rather sad and melancholic.

He had put a lot of himself into the place since his arrival in October 1968, shortly after his arrival back from Africa, as well as being newly married. He had really enjoyed it and loved the place, the flowing parklands, the gardens of the house and the beautiful woodlands. Lillyfee, too, was a joy and he knew it would never be easy to find such a place to live again.

He pulled the landrover in to the side and paused on the verge by Dipple Wood, on the track running down towards Hall Barn House. He looked out across the now familiar parkland, suddenly being very aware that what he was about to do would have far reaching effects, both for him and the wider family. He was not really having second thoughts, but deep thoughts nevertheless. He was the one responsible for the changes that were about to take place; he was at the point where he could make them, or not, and when made, there was no going back.

There is never any sure way of knowing if you are making the right decision with anything in life; you just have to do it with the knowledge and information that is before you, and trust.

There was no way they could go through another winter like the last one, he thought. He would not subject Ann, Paul or Lynda to that again and it would only get worse. To go and live and work on a tropical island in the middle of the Indian Ocean, well what was he thinking about? It had to be the most wonderful opportunity ever.

Lord Burnham looked stunned when Terry broke the news to him, remaining silent for quite a few minutes. Terry almost felt sorry for him, but he remembered it had all been in his hands, so how could he be surprised? However, they had come through a great deal together and he was genuinely sad that Terry was handing in his resignation, for despite all, and the fact that they had both come from very different backgrounds, they had got along well together and held each other in great respect.

Chapter Twelve

As word got around that Terry had resigned his post as Farm Manager and was going to live in the Seychelles, the excitement grew and with it the cold fear of what they were about to embark on. As far as they were able, they explained to Paul and Lynda the situation and how they were going to live by the sea in a warm place. Terry and Ann's main consideration was always for them and the effect the move would have on their young lives.

Most people they told would say, "How wonderful to be going to live in the Seychelles." This was true, and they were both happy and excited to be entering into this new phase of life.

There were of course many things they would be leaving behind when taking up their new life. It takes a lot of courage and nerve to carry the plan from dream to reality and there were times when they wondered, "Are we doing the right thing?" A natural reaction when everything that is normal and everyday is about to be turned on its head, with so many new things to learn and to get used to, not least the hot climate of the Seychelles, coupled with the ninety percent humidity.

The excitement of it all carried them through the times of doubt, with events rapidly sweeping them along. There was much to do, the shipping of their household goods to organise, as well as storage and clearance of the contents of Lillyfee Farm house. Terry was in touch with Eastern Lines Services Ltd. to arrange the collection of their trunks and boxes for shipping to the Seychelles. Vessels ran about once a month and it took about a month for them to get there. The next departure that most suited them was mid January 1974, so they were aiming to hit that date. Otherwise they would wait too long for their things, once they had arrived in the Seychelles.

The saddest thing they had to do was to find a new home for their beloved dog Prince; it was the biggest sacrifice in all of this. He had grown up with Paul and Lynda and spent most of his time with them, as well as with Terry where he loved to ride in the back of the landrover, leap out and run down through the woods. It was like leaving a member of the family behind and was the cause of much heartache for them all; to such an extent that Terry felt he could hardly look Prince in the eye. They did find a lovely couple that loved and cared for him and who wrote to them for years sending photographs of Prince, until he finally died in doggy old age. He had been a very special companion and friend. Ann and Terry just hated doing what they had to do, but there was no way he could have gone to the Seychelles with them or have enjoyed it if he had.

Christmas was soon upon them and Ann's parents came to stay for a few days, which was rather nice, giving them the chance to hear all about the new venture. It was one of those Christmases that you remember each year, when again the time to celebrate comes around again.

Once the New Year arrived it was time to begin the adventure, to leave all the old things behind and to go blindly in faith into the future. It was all systems go to get everything organised, packed, distributed and cases ready for the off on 28th February 1974.

The coal miners were still causing problems for the country with their strikes, and there was no sign of a breakthrough in the talks. The Prime Minister, Mr Heath, decided to call a general election, so the people could decide just who ran the country. The election was called for Thursday 28th March, the very day that Terry and Ann were due to fly out to the Seychelles

The British Airways flight from Gatwick Airport was to take them direct to Mahe, the main island of the group in the Seychelles. The flight stopped in Nairobi for a few hours, which was the nearest they were going to get to their beloved Africa on this occasion.

As the plane flew near to the Seychelles they could just make out the small green cluster of islands, specks in the deep blue sea; they could see Mahe rising steeply and majestically out of the sea. It was a beautiful island, surrounded by so many others of a smaller size, with a high mountain backbone running most of its length, green and lush with vegetation, surrounded by a fringe of white coral sands. It looked a real tropical paradise, at least scenically. They felt so excited; the adventure was about to start and they looked forward to their new life, living and working on this beautiful island.

"Is that really where we are going to live?" Ann said as they all peered out the window. "It looks as if the islands could easily sink. What a fantastic scene. It's bewitching, unbelievable, magic."

Terry was busy trying to keep Lynda calm as her ears were giving her a few problems after the long flight and the rapid descent, as were his own. The plane dropped lower and lower: it felt as if they would land in the sea as it hovered over the surface approaching the runway. The airport was quite new, having been completed by Costains Group in 1971. On the 4th July that year, the first ever passenger jet a BOAC-VC-10 landed on the 3,000 metre long concrete runway and now they were about to do the same.

The terminal buildings looked small compared to many airports they had used. It all felt a little unreal, set as it was in the dazzling whiteness of the coral sands. The whole place looked and felt magical, glinting in the sun. The plane drew to a halt. A man entered the cabin and told them they could not get off until he had walked through the plane with an insecticide, in order to kill off any malaria carrying mosquitoes that may be on board. So far, the islands were free of the disease and they wanted to keep it that way. While they all sat there waiting, the pilot informed them that there was no clear result in the UK election and it looked as if Ted Heath was going to have to resign after negotiations with the Liberals had failed and it would be necessary to hand over to Harold Wilson. That in itself seemed unimportant from this distance, there were more pressing things before them at that precise moment.

As they stepped out of the aircraft the heat and humidity was overwhelming. The balmy breeze, coming straight off the sea gently fanned them; it was like stepping into a hot steamy bathroom. They walked across the concrete runway to the airport buildings and quickly through customs. It was strange to see pictures of the

Queen and the familiar Union Jack, as of course it was still a British colony.

The rugged, lofty peak of Morne Seychellellois towered above them in the airport, forest–clad for most of its nine hundred and eleven metre height. Alongside were the triple-peaked mountains of Les Trois Freres at seven hundred and sixty seven metres that loomed over the capital of Victoria, a truly picturesque scene into which they had now become swallowed up.

Archbishop Makarios of Cyprus, who was banished to Mahe by the British in 1956, spending a year there in exile, wrote: "I've visited many places all over the world and it is no exaggeration to say that the Seychelles Islands contain the most beautiful places I've ever seen." It certainly was looking that way, very impressive.

Suddenly, to their relief, they spotted Philip Brooks who had interviewed Terry the previous November, standing in the arrival lounge. He welcomed them and helped with their cases.

They followed him out to the waiting transport. It was not a car, but an open back van, which was something of a surprise and they wondered how they were all going to fit in. They were so tired, that all they wanted to do was to get to their new home, settle the children and to rest after the long journey. Philip placed their cases in the back of the dusty pick-up and the four of them squeezed into the front cab along side him. He was very quiet and did not have much conversation, apart from enquiring about their journey.

He drove south along the road to 'Anse ux Pins' for about two miles to Sawa Sawa Farm which was set alongside the main road and up the hillside on the right. There were palm-thatched dwellings everywhere along the road. Terry noticed a structure that looked like a large golf ball, high up on the mountain top. It was apparently one of Mahe's best known landmarks, the United States Satellite Tracking station. They continued on past the Reef Hotel, the golf course and other houses scattered amongst the palm trees and shortly after pulled in to a small track that took them to a wooden colonial style house, surrounded by vegetation. There they stopped and all piled out with great relief. The heat was intense in the afternoon sun; Lynda was uncomfortable and difficult to keep happy, while Paul looked very weary and tired, but still hanging on to his teddy bear. But at last they had arrived. They all went up the steps to the veranda of the house and sat on the wicker chairs looking out towards the sea. A young woman appeared and introduced herself as Pauline, Philip's wife.

"Welcome to the Seychelles," she said. "How was the trip? I know it's a hard journey with children. We have two and I go home to see my Mother in Bath from time to time, often alone. It's not easy! This is the house of my father and mother-in-law; they're out at the moment. Philip has gone up to prepare your house, which is on up the hill further, above our house. Would you like a drink? Silly question I know. I'll bring a jug of squash for you all. You will find you can never drink enough here, it's so hot."

Pauline left to get the drinks, leaving Terry and Ann with the children on the veranda of this colonial style house. The scene was truly tropical, looking out to the Indian Ocean surrounded by palm trees and frangipani branches amongst the giant granite boulders that were strewn around. The humidity was intense, energy sapping. Every item of clothing stuck to them; they longed to feel a breeze on their faces. They noticed instead a faint smell of pigs, which they didn't associate with the scene stretched out before them.

It seemed ages since Pauline had gone for the drinks and Terry, for some reason, began to feel just slightly uneasy about the situation. However, she arrived after some fifteen minutes with the tray of drinks and was almost jumped on, as they were all very hot, dry and thirsty.

"Here you are," she said. "Philip will be along shortly to take you up to your house. We used to live in it, but moved to a new one that we'd built just below yours. I'm afraid your house is a bit basic. I've put a few items in the fridge for you, but if there's anything else you need please ask us." With that Pauline disappeared into the house.

They sat there having their fill of drinks, with Ann trying to keep the children happy; they were so tired and hungry and just wanting to settle. They had been very good on the long flight from

Gatwick, but they had their limits and were not familiar with the heat having just left an English February behind them. They had all been through so much and were exhausted. The adrenalin was keeping them all going, but at this stage it was wearing thin.

The pick-up shortly pulled up outside again and Philip called them to get in and to go up the hill to their new house. Another wave of excitement helped lift their spirits as they drove off up the very steep hillside, along a track made from two strips of concrete. Up and up they went, as it became steeper and steeper, higher and higher around sharp bends until they drew up alongside a concrete block shed.

"Your house is just around here, but this is as far as you can go with a car!" Philip explained to them.

They followed him along a dirt path and there by the side of a huge rock was a tiny bungalow with a flat tin roof and small louvred windows. There was an open sided veranda with two cane chairs and a single bed against the wall that was used like a sofa. The whole area of the veranda was about eight feet square and, because it was open sided, would not be usable when it rained and the Seychelles had plenty of that in season.

Philip took them into the small house: there was a galley kitchen on the right, with sink at one end. It would certainly be difficult for two people to be in there at the same time, Ann thought.

Next to that was a narrow toilet and shower area – no bath! Opposite was a small room with a table and four chairs that only just fitted in. Adjoining was the main bedroom, containing a four foot six bed, a small dressing table that had two small side mirrors, but no central mirror! It contained a very small narrow cupboard that was used as a wardrobe, but due to the confined space was impossible to open the doors! Surely they would die of the heat in there they thought!

Off the veranda was another bedroom with two small single beds and a chest of drawers that was to be used by Paul and Lynda. That was it!

Philip looked very sheepish and said, "I'll leave you to settle in and by the way don't worry about all the building materials around the house. We'll get it moved shortly!" He jumped in his van as fast as he could and shot off, leaving them to absorb what was before them.

Terry looked at Ann, the first time that he had dared to do so since they arrived at their new home!

"What have we done?" he asked. "What have we done?"

The house in itself was a big enough shock, but the fact that it looked out onto the long thatched roof of the piggery below and onto the area where the cooking of all the chicken offal took place, well that was the limit! On the other side where three large deep litter houses full of chickens, or would be once they were completed. Behind the house were more chicken houses and a food store!

On raising their eyes above the piggery there was an amazing view of the Indian Ocean, the palm trees and Mr and Mrs Brooks' house below with their garden stretching down to the main road. The smell of pigs was in the air the whole time, not to mention the offal cooking below and the smoke from the fire, all this in the heat of the sun.

They didn't know what to do. The first thing was to care for Paul and Lynda and settle them down for the night, as they were so tired. In the kitchen they found a few small items in the fridge, cheese, milk, bread etc. Much to their surprise on the worktop was a bill for the few things purchased on their behalf by the Brooks for the sum of twenty-four rupees.

They unpacked their cases, looked around at what had been put in the house and felt totally depressed. Ann somehow managed to put together a meal from the few ingredients she found. They made up beds and soon Paul and Lynda were ready to sleep. Their room was very, very hot, so they only needed a sheet to cover them. Tiredness soon overcame them and they eventually went to sleep.

"Well, just what are we going to do?" Ann was anxious.

"First things first," Terry replied. "Where is that bottle of brandy we purchased in duty free? I really think we need it, don't you?" he said, going off to find it.

"I don't believe it," he exclaimed, "there are no bloody glasses in the place, no glasses at all. No cups, only mugs, three plates, two bowls, two bent and buckled saucepans with a handful of knives and forks. I can't believe that anyone would prepare a house for guests like this. It's too bad."

Ann was almost in tears. "I'm tired. I don't need this. It's terrible, terrible for me, the children and for you. They should be ashamed to present the accommodation in this way. In fact, I don't think they were even ready for us and it's why they kept us waiting so long when we arrived."

"Hang on," Terry shouted from the kitchen. "I've found some egg cups, they'll do."

He poured some brandy into each of the egg cups and they sat in the wicker chairs on the veranda, sipping from them, looking out at the now fading light as the waves crashed in on the shore line below, both feeling very sorry for themselves.

"I think we have just jumped out of the frying pan into the fire. Where do we go from here?" Terry said, expressing his thoughts out loud.

"I really have no idea," Ann replied tearfully. "It's a nightmare, isn't it? What can we possibly do?"

"We can't return to England. We have no house, no job and no money. It would be impossible. Our contract is for two years. We can't break that, as they'll not pay our return fares, even if we appealed to the agents who appointed us, and that would take forever."

"There is only one thing we can do," Terry suggested. "We have to sit it out and stay the shortest length of time we can get away with. I'll go and see the Brooks tomorrow and tell them we need more things in the house, until the ship arrives with our boxes, and that could be weeks away yet."

"Then how about if we try to make the best of it and see how things work out? It's a beautiful island, that's for sure, from what little we've seen so far. Once we get a car we can go out and enjoy the beaches and take picnics and just make the best of the good bits. Goodness knows what I'll find when I start work, if this is a sample of their organisation abilities, but I'll just have to face that the best I can."

"What do you think?" he asked Ann.

"We don't really have a lot of choice, do we? It all sounded so perfect, too."

"Yes, let's do that then; there's no way that we can do a 'moon light flit' and leave the country. Suddenly, Lillyfee Farm and Lord Burnham don't seem as bad as they did, do they?" she remarked.

"Come on now," Terry replied. "Have you already forgotten how last winter we had to scratch around to find ten pence for some paraffin? We'll not be doing that here in this heat and, if we really hate it, after a year we should have saved enough to go home."

"You're right of course, there really is no other way around our situation is there? Maybe we'll all feel better about it tomorrow," Ann said as she made her way to bed.

The long hot airless night seemed to go on forever, as they tossed and turned in the heat that was followed by a hotter and steamier morning. They must have slept, but neither of them felt as if they had, as they crawled out of their box like bedroom to face their first day in the Seychelles.

Some fruit had been left on the wall of the veranda, so it seemed someone cared if they lived or died. Ann cut up the pawpaw and mixed it with banana for their breakfast. Terry went down to the farm to see Philip Brooks to try and sort out things with him. He had been in a terrible state and could not sleep or eat feeling so furious about the way they had been treated. An hour later two men arrived with large boxes of household items. Ann felt it was like Christmas as the basic requirements of a kitchen appeared out of the boxes. Terry must have really pulled out the stops, as a little while later two more men arrived with boxes of groceries, cups and plates and, yes, some glasses too.

A hot and exhausted Terry arrived back mid morning, looking grave, as he could do when he was upset.
"You'll never believe what I have found out, this family is totally crazy!" he exclaimed.
"Well sit down, have a drink and calm down. I've received a stream of boxes with everything in but the kitchen sink." Ann explained. "So we have a lot more than we did and, look, we have glasses!"
"But will the brandy last?" Terry enquired. "I think I need one now!"

He ate some late breakfast and looked a little more relaxed, much to Ann's relief. Paul sat on his knee clutching his teddy, as Terry explained to Ann what he had found out about everything and why their arrival had been so poorly prepared for.
"Apparently Philip and his father 'Carly' Brooks had had a big row. They were not able to agree how the farm should be run and by whom. As a result Philip had stormed off to U.K. earlier last year to find a Farm Manager to help run the place, against his father's wishes. Carly wanted nothing to do with it, even when Philip explained that he had appointed me and that we were due to arrive to start work.
Carly took himself off for the weekend and closed his house up. He didn't want to see us or have anything to do with the situation." Terry explained. "Being the dictator that he sounds like he is, he didn't like Philip going over his head and just ran off. Philip and Pauline had to find a way to open up his house to welcome us, as their own house is only part finished so they couldn't receive us there. That all took time, and they hadn't prepared our house which Philip and Pauline had only just moved out of hours before he picked us up at the airport yesterday. What a carry on!"

"So where does that leave you?" Ann enquired.

"Looks like I'm the meat in the sandwich. Not sure what Carly will do when he meets me. I spoke with two young Kenyan men that Carly employs. He'd brought them over from Kenya, a carpenter and a plumber. Carly, apparently had an Agricultural Lime producing business when he lived at Nakuru in Kenya and sold it to return to the Seychelles to buy Sawa Sawa Farm. His plan was to produce meat for all the new hotels springing up on the island, as well as for the local people and the supermarkets. He is a Seychellois, born here and went to live and work in Kenya years ago, now he has returned here in his retirement. As I said he had a big bust-up with Philip about the running of the new farm. The two Kenyans told me that Carly has a very low opinion of his son Philip, who they say is a bit of a psychopath! So it all sounds a bit of a mix up, to say the least."

"You're right," Ann agreed. "Let's hope that Carly is not as fierce as his name. You do remember that in Swahili 'Kali' means 'Savage!'

"Interesting as all this is," Ann interrupted, "just at the moment we have a more urgent problem. The water won't empty out of the shower or the sink, the toilet doesn't flush very well and there is a bad smell around, apart that is from the smell of the piggery just below our window that's always there."

Terry went to take a look. He wondered if there was an outside drain blocked. He searched around to see if he could see any sign of a manhole or inspection culvert, where he might investigate the problem. He walked round the house but found nothing; there was, however, a very strong drain smell. He stood outside the kitchen window a few feet from the house and called up to Ann to tell her that he couldn't see anything and to enquire if it was still blocked. As he did so he suddenly become aware that he was sinking and before he could do anything the ground just seem to give way and swallow him like quicksand. In seconds he was up to his chest in an evil smelling black liquid in a large deep hole in the ground. Ann looked out of the window and wondered what on earth was going on. She raced out to where he was standing in this black fluid that was now up to his shoulders. She grabbed his hand to try and help him out. He managed to struggle to the lower side and with Ann's help scrabble out of the hole. He looked like a beached whale!

"You stink," she screamed at him. "What is it? What has happened?"

"I'm not sure, but get away from here, get the hose pipe," he shouted as he dragged himself away from the hole onto firmer ground.

Ann came running with the hosepipe and helped him wash the sludge from his face, now covered in a black film.

"You're lucky that you didn't drown in there. Tell me it's not what I think it is," she said laughing, almost in hysterics.

"Stop laughing and wash me down. The stinks overwhelming and I've lost a shoe in there somewhere too."

Ann continued to spray him with water hardly able to bare the smell, while at the same time laughing uncontrollably at the state he was in!

"It's no good you'll have to take everything off. You can't keep or wear those things again. It's a good job it's so hot here," she laughed. "Not many places in March where you can stand outside being hosed down with cold water! Come on now, take everything off and I'll try and get the worst of it off for you, before you go in the shower."

Slowly, Terry removed his clothes that were stuck to him, leaving them in a wet heap by the side of the hole. Ann worked away at getting the worst off him with soap and water, while he was standing on the small lawn by the side of the veranda. She was still in a state of uncontrollable laughter.

"I've had to do many unusual things in my time," she said, "but never anything like this. Ah well, for better or worse I seem to remember we agreed."

"Just shut up and get on with it," Terry replied.

With that a young Seychellois lady appeared over the horizon, carrying some fish and bananas, sent up for Ann and Terry by Pauline. At first she didn't notice what was going on. Suddenly she screamed, dropped the fish and bananas and fled down the hill, back to the farm in fear and terror!

Terry fled to the house where he continued to wash off the slime in the shower which was still not draining away very fast.

Later, after further investigation, they found that the drainage system was a very primitive septic tank. A hole had been dug out and lined with concrete blocks, but the top had been constructed from coconut tree trunks that had been laid on the top and covered with soil. Over the years they had rotted and when Terry stood on it, the palm trunks just couldn't hold his weight and so collapsed, dropping him into the void below.

It was rather symbolic of the way things went in the early days of their time in the Seychelles, but slowly they did settle into an acceptable routine, as difficult as life was for them. Knowing that it would not be forever did help somehow.

Next day Terry went down to the little hut near to Carly's house where they sold vegetables. He wanted to buy a fresh lettuce. There sitting on a chair was the man himself, Carly Brooks.

Terry paused, unsure how to play the situation.

"Good morning. You must be Mr Brooks?" Terry enquired. "I'm Terry Reeves. We arrived on friday from UK."

"Oh! Yes of course. Hello," replied Mr Brooks looking very uncomfortable.

"What a beautiful old house you have. I would love to know all about it sometime," Terry said trying to break the ice.

"Yes, it's very old. I knew it as a child," Carly informed him.

"I was hoping to buy a lettuce from you, if you have one. Our children love salad when it's hot like this."

"It's always hot here you'll find," Carly remarked sharply.

"So I understand," Terry replied

"You want just one?"

"Yes, please."

"I suppose you'll want tomatoes as well, for this salad," Carly suggested.

"That would be very nice. Do you grow those here? We only had aeroplane food yesterday."

"Yes, everything is grown by me; it's not easy here you know. Some people think we are on a permanent holiday. Let me tell you we're not, its damn hard graft, long hours and determination that produces anything on this island. Nothing grows in the trees, except the coconuts," he grinned.

Terry was pleased to see a crack appear, perhaps there was some humour in the man as he did have a bit of a glint in his eye as he made that comment. Terry actually finished up getting on very well with Carly, after the first few weeks. They found that they had similar views on how the business might develop. In fact they both agreed that the best thing would have been to turn all the chicken houses and piggeries into holiday accommodation and then build a restaurant where Carly could run a bar and enjoy entertaining the people. But it was just an idea that Terry felt quite amused Carly. He was a very social person and loved to chat with people: it would have suited him, but he didn't have the courage to change things at that stage.

Terry found the business in poor shape with many problems. A lot of the poultry houses were not yet complete and were still in the process of being built. All the animal feed had to be imported from South Africa, so they were dependent on the ships arriving on schedule, which they often failed to do. The chicks too were imported from South Africa and flown in by plane on a Sunday afternoon, two thousand or more at a time. It was difficult to find staff that stayed sober and were reliable. Most of the men had access to palm trees and extracted the sap from the tip of the palms to make beer. It was a powerful substance and knocked them out by midday if they were allowed to drink it. Not good if you are relying on them to look after hundreds of pigs and thousands of chickens.

Carly was right about his son Philip, who really had absolutely no idea about life and was only carried through by Pauline his wife. The butchery was being developed where they made wonderful hams and sausages, and also the meat was cut up and packaged.

Carly's wife, who worked from dawn to dusk and was a real expert in such matters, ran that side of the business. The products were in great demand; it became necessary for them to set up a shop in the main town of Victoria to distribute their goods. Carly had a small market garden and tried to grow some lettuce and vegetables to add to the sales in the shop. Not an easy thing to do in the heat of the Seychelles.

Terry and Ann's life settled into a pattern. Paul and Lynda enjoyed the sea so much and soon settled into their new way of life. Every weekend Ann would prepare a picnic, which they would take to a beach around lunchtime. If the beach they chose had another person on it, then they would drive on to the next one, such was the choice they had of people-free beaches. Some of them like Takamaka Bay, Intendance Bay and Grand Anse were vast; they felt at times as if they were the only people on the island, often having the whole area to themselves, with not a soul in sight.

Ann slowly got to know others living and working in the Seychelles while she was out and about with shopping and the children, especially as Paul had started at 'Miss Grace's Pre-tending School' in Victoria, where he too made many new friends.

There were all types and all nationalities on the islands, a very mixed bag. It was easy to imagine an unchanging habitation, but they soon came to realise that there was a steady flow of people coming and going the whole time, some leaving at the end of their contracts, while some, like Terry and Ann arrived to start a new life. One day Ann came home to tell Terry that she had met this lovely lady from Wolverhampton named Pat. Her husband David was a lecturer at the local college. They had arrived recently and did not live far from them in flats at Turtle Bay Court, near the Reef Hotel. As so often happens when living in far away places, where you share experiences, Pat and Dave went on to become life long friends.

Terry and Ann threw themselves into playing tennis which they had both always enjoyed; they were able to use the courts at the

Reef Hotel, just a couple of miles down the road. It was in a beautiful setting on the edge of the beach. The housemaid that was provided with the job, Bertha, looked after Paul and Lynda and gave them their tea on the evening when they went to play tennis. They would go about twice a week and really become quite expert. They used the occasion to get away from the farm and to spend time together. After their tennis they would sit at the Hotel in its dream-like setting and enjoy a long cold drink after the energy sapping game, although it was usually a little cooler around five in the evening. They enjoyed these times so much.

Carly Brooks was a great one for giving dinner parties, partly because he felt it would attract people to the business, but he was also a very social person. One Saturday Terry and Ann had been invited to such a lunch party at Carly's house. They never really knew many of those that had been invited, but they enjoyed chatting to the different people. It was always interesting to hear how people came to be in the Seychelles, how they found it and what they did. Most were in large government houses and seemed to have everything found for them; you were left wondering just what useful thing some of them could possible be doing on the island.

At one of these lunch parties, Terry found himself sitting next to a very interesting old man who seem to know a great deal about the islands and had travelled to many of the other eighty eight islands that form the Seychelles group, the total number is the subject of much dispute. It was interesting to hear all about the background, and the changes that had taken place, in particular how the French and English seemed to have exchanged control of the islands at regular intervals. He also spoke a great deal about Africa for which he shared Terry's love. Terry told him all about his own experiences in Tanzania as a volunteer. They discussed David Livingstone, one of Terry's great heroes, who was also the hero of this old man who seem to have a deep knowledge of and admiration for him and his work and like Terry had been to Livingstone's museum in Blantyre, Scotland.

Terry went to get the old man another drink. All the talking he said made him thirsty. He was quite well dressed and Terry was beginning to wonder just what the old man did on the island. He was about to ask him this question, when a large Rolls Royce with the Union Jack on the bonnet, arrived in front of the house. The old man got up out of his seat, shook Terry by the hand, said goodbye to his hosts, stepped into the Rolls Royce and was driven away by his chauffeur.

Terry stood there with his mouth open. "Who was that?" he asked Carly.

"That's the Governor of the Seychelles Islands. Didn't you know?"

Ann and Terry's finances were starting to recover: the salary of £233 (rupees 2830 a month) was helping that. But prices were much higher than the U.K. largely because everything had to be imported. Electricity prices were very high as were school fees. Paul had started out in nursery school and then moved on to the International School, which became a bit of a drain on the finances. They didn't want him to go to local schools, but to get as good a start in life as possible. They were fast getting back to the situation they were in with Lord Burnham, but thankfully not quite that bad yet.

Saturday afternoons were often spent with Paul and Lynda, watching the planes arrive at the airport. They loved that. They were able to stand within a few metres of the landing strip, something impossible to do anywhere else. It was amazing to be so close to the aircraft as their wheels touched down on the concrete landing strip. Watching the planes always made them feel close to home somehow, as well as a little home sick.

They were fast becoming close friends with Pat and David Cocks spending a lot of time together. They enjoyed each other's company, exchanged meals, went out on picnics and days out, making the Seychelles' experience that much more bearable. David had a small boat that he kept on the shore line and enjoyed spending his time doing it up, turning it into a very nice craft, painting on it a picture of an Osprey, the name he had given to the boat. Pat found a lovely tasty little shellfish that was hidden under the sand on the shore line and together they would often be seen digging them out of the sand, putting them in a bucket and carrying them home to cook and eat. It was known as the 'Tek Tek' and became a favourite. It was rather like a cockle to eat. They enjoyed the simple things together and David's dry humour and his being slightly prone to accidents kept them all going.

One evening when Pat was heavily pregnant, she appeared at the ridge by Terry and Ann's house puffing and panting, having somehow climbed up the very steep hill. Terry wondered if she was about to give birth and rushed out to meet her.
"Whatever is the matter, Pat?" he asked her.
"It's David. He was fishing in the boat and when throwing out the line caught the hook in his arm. I managed to get him back to shore and then into the car and drove half way here, but then went off the road on the steep curve below."
She was in a terrible state and Terry wondered if she might start giving birth at any minute. He tried to calm her down and called Ann to help her. He then shot off to try and find his friend Dave. Dave was sitting in the car, that was half on and half off the road at the bottom of the hill below their house. After establishing that Dave was reasonably comfortable, as comfortable as you could be with a large fish hook stuck in your upper arm, Terry ran back for his car, bundled Dave in and took him off to the hospital in Victoria. There they cleaned the wound, while Dave was left looking up at the grubby hospital ceiling making his usual comic comments. After much difficulty they managed to remove the hook from his arm, much to his relief. Pat was reassured to see him back, minus the hook and Dave was pleased to see that Pat had calmed down after the excitement he'd caused her.
For Terry it was the first of his visits to the Seychelles' hospital, a place that would go on to have a great significance in his life in the Seychelles and ever after.

Chapter Thirteen

On one memorable occasion Philip Brooks had heard that there were some local pigs for sale on a small island nearby and as the shop was low on pork and orders flooding in, he decided to go and see the pigs and bring one back to the farm. He suggested that Terry might like to go along with him. The island was one of the very small inhabited islands about three miles from Mahe. Arrangements were made with a local fisherman to go with his boat and take them out to the island. Setting out early in the morning, the fisherman, William, told them that the island they were to collect the pig from had so much coral around it that it was difficult to get a boat in if it was very heavy. He suggested that they drop one person at another island on the way, to make the boat lighter and easier to gain access.

Philip suggested this should be Terry and they dropped him off onto a totally uninhabited island about a mile from where the pig was to be collected. He had no problems with this, until he saw the little boat that had dropped him off disappear out of sight on its mission to collect the pig. They told Terry that once the pig had been loaded they would return to pick him up and then all return together to Mahe.

Sitting quietly on the beach he suddenly had a nasty thought. What if they didn't come back? Who would know that he was there? He tried hard not to think about it and went off for a walk along the sandy coral beach. It was beautiful, so quiet and so peaceful. What a wonderful experience he thought, alone on an island in the middle of the Indian Ocean and only two other living people knew he was there. Well at least he hoped they were living!

He had a bottle of warmish drinking water, but that was all he took with him. He put it in a pool amongst some rocks to keep it cool. 'Desert Island Discs,' a radio programme at home, kept flashing into his mind. What records would he like? Well just now he would settle for some shelter, so he moved off into the nearby trees on the shore line. As he did so a crab ran out of the shrubs and off towards the sea. Ah, Terry thought, at least I'm not totally alone here!

He decided to take a look around and walk to the other side of the island, which must have been about a hundred meters long and sixty wide. In no time he had nearly walked around the whole island, looking into bushes for signs of life or for anything that indicated someone had been there before him. What a thrilling experience it was, exhilarating and exciting, tinged with some fear because of the extraordinary situation in which he found himself.

He laid in the shade of a large takamaka tree that fringed the shore; it was a handsome specimen with branches that spread its generous shade on that hot day. The wood from that tree, he remembered the Governor from the party telling him, was a hardy timber, which made excellent boats and furniture. Could be useful, he made a mental note! Otherwise the island seemed to be covered in palm trees with plenty of coconuts around. This gave him some comfort, and at least he would not die of hunger! Suddenly there was a rustling in the trees, followed by a noise like the laughing of a witch, then out flew a large white bird. It looked like a White Tern, not that Terry was that well up on birds of the Seychelles. It certainly made him jump.

He got up and completed his walk around the island arriving back where he had started. The sun was up high in the sky now and he was beginning to feel the heat. He went off to get his bottle of water from the pool that he had placed it in earlier to keep cool. Alarm bells rang in Terry's head: the pool was no more and the bottle had disappeared. The tide had come in and swallowed up the pool and Terry's bottle with it! Suddenly eight gramophone records had no significance. Where would he find water?

He retreated to the shade of the takamaka trees, his throat feeling very dry. The temptation to drink the sea water is great at such times, but of course he realised that he couldn't and had to keep in the shade and out of the noon sun. Noon became two o'clock; he was not only very thirsty by this time, but feeling very concerned. He should have a plan he thought, in case they didn't return. Philip wasn't the most reliable man he had met. What if they forgot? Surely William would remind him.

So many thoughts started to race around in his head. What if they had sunk, drowned even, who would know he was there? Fear was growing within him. What could he do he kept asking himself. How do you make a fire in that circumstance? He tried to remember. Could he collect water? How does he collect water? What did he see on his walk around the island that could be useful to him? Was there a bottle? Any plastic that might be useful? His whole mind was taken over with thoughts of survival and what he should do. First of all he thought, he should pray: come on he was supposed to be a Christian; pray, for goodness' sake pray.

Just as that thought had passed through his mind, he heard the distant humming of a motor. Was it like a mirage he wondered, people did have them in desert conditions? There on the horizon he could see the little boat. What relief he felt but was not totally convinced until Philip paddled onto the shore from the boat to greet him.

"Sorry we've been so long," he said. "We decided it was best to take the pig back to Mahe as it was so big and then return for you, except we had to get some more petrol which delayed us. Have you been all right here?"

Terry could hardly speak his throat was so dry. "Yes," he croaked. "I'm all right. Do you have any more water?"

"There are plenty of bottles on the boat. Come on, the pig is waiting for us on Mahe," Philip replied as they both waded out to the little boat that was to take them off the island. "Did you enjoy your day on an uninhabited tropical island?"

"Yes," Terry replied smiling to himself, as he thought of what might have been.

One of the strange things about life in the Seychelles is there is no feeling of seasons. Spring, summer, autumn, winter, seem all to blend into one. The trees remained pretty much the same the whole year round. They didn't really shed their leaves as they did at home in the autumn. There was a cool or cooler season with a slight variation in temperature of about eight degrees from June to September, when the southeast monsoon blew.

The hot season ran from November to May when there was also plenty of rain, in fact two-thirds of it occurred then. At Christmas tourists often came expecting to find hot and sunny weather; more often it was continuous rain at that time which could go on for weeks. The climate is often described as 'hot and moist' with an average humidity of seventy five per cent for the year; that was certainly how Terry and Ann found it.

With few seasonal changes such as they were used to, time could easily slip past. Terry and Ann couldn't wait for the arrival of their crates with all their belongings, having lived from the contents of their cases since their arrival. Paul and Lynda, too, were looking forward to being reunited with their toys once more. Shipping expected to arrive in Mahe was listed on the back of the 'Seychelles Bulletin' published each day at the price of twenty cents, a bit like a daily newspaper. On the copy of Thursday May 23rd 1974 it showed that the 'Donegal' was due in port on 25th May. That was the ship they had been informed that would be bringing their crates with all their personal effects. Excitement grew as the day approached. Everyone had something they had been waiting for and when the lorry delivered the crates it was like Christmas as they all found some item they had forgotten, as well as others they wondered why they had packed.

Having a full house of contents made the bungalow more homely, but very cramped. They were still not feeling settled in the Seychelles, but put up with it all and made the best of the good things. Being surrounded by pig and chicken houses and the associated smells, plus living in a cramped house was always going to be less than ideal. It was good to have a record player again and to be able to sit on the veranda at night looking out to sea with the music playing. They had wisely sent out a fifteen cubic foot deep freeze, packed with sheets and clothes. The deep freeze was a welcome addition to making life a little easier and it could be sold for twice the price when the day came for them to leave the islands.

As the year rolled on the challenges became greater. For Terry work became busier and all consuming, as the size of the enterprise grew. He had imported two Landrace Boars from South Africa to cross with the Wessex Saddleback sows they already had on the farm. The pig numbers increased rapidly, with the sows now producing an average of twelve to fifteen pigs a litter and over two litters a year, with the improved survival rate of the piglets since Terry had redesigned the buildings carrying out substantial alterations.

The pigs were fattened on the farm and at about six months of age slaughtered for ham, chops, joints and sausages as fast as they could be produced. That and the now three thousand day old chicks that were being flown in each week from South Africa to produce chicken meat, kept the whole place buzzing.

Hotels were developing fast on the island, every week there seemed to be news of yet another that was going to be built. All this, plus the people of the support team necessary for the building work, together with the already well staffed American tracking station, colleges and financial institutions, contributed to a heavy demand for meat and vegetables of every type from the population of the island.

Demand was high, but so were the costs. High grade animal feed from South Africa had to be shipped in, for there was nothing available on the island. With total reliance on shipping it was difficult to manage the stocks of animal food required and kept in store. The food had a shelf life of course, but if the farm ran out of stock feed the situation would be very serious indeed. Capital costs for buildings and machinery were very high with everything having to be imported. Labour was a major problem: the basic instinct of the Seychellois was not to work. They had coconuts in the trees and fish in the sea, why would they need to? At least that was the general attitude and difficult to change. So against this background, with father and son forever at each other's throats, it was not difficult to see that the business they were developing did not have a great future.

Ann was kept busy trying to find their household needs to keep them alive and healthy. There were shortages for long periods, sometimes no flour, no bread, no sugar or no rice, then no potatoes and so it went on.

Shopping took hours, as you searched around to find what you were looking for, digging around in the many shops, some like "Sham Peng Tong" who advertised themselves as General Merchants and sold anything from coffee to motorbikes. If that failed there was "Kimkoon and Co. Ltd," Chinese owned, who promised to find anything for you. The reliance on shipping was evident everywhere and in every business. After months of being without a certain item like, say, potatoes, a great cry of joy would go up when a ship arrived with new stock that was quickly snatched up.

Taking Paul to school, four miles away in Victoria was a daily task. They managed to get a group of mothers together to take it in turns to ferry the children from their area to the school and back, so that helped. However, it had to be monitored well. All this in the daily heat and humidity was hard, tiring and often very stressful.

It was good to relax on the beaches at the weekends, to go for a swim or to walk along the shore in the evenings where they would watch the setting of the sun in those idyllic surroundings of blue seas, white beaches and palm-fringed shores, far - very far - from the madding crowd. This was often followed by the wonderful spectacle of the moon rising into the evening sky, casting its shiny path like a walkway across the sea.

Having been introduced by Pat and Dave Cocks to the little known shellfish the Tek Tek, they spent many hours collecting them to take home to cook. With salt and vinegar they were delicious. Tek Teks were very similar to a cockle and were found living at the edge of the water just under the sand. On 15th September, Terry's 29th birthday, Pat and Dave had produced a card with a verse they had made up about the Tek Tek:

TEK TEK

He lives amongst the gravely sand,
He's easily found by the turn of a hand.

Except when the tide is strong and high,
He then disappears in deep beds to lie.

Here at Anse-aux-Pins he's not at all classy,
It's in his pin stripes at Grand Anse he's flashy.

How long he has been there no-one is sure,
But let's hope this isn't his final tour.

He's nice in soup; he's also nice cold,
But best of all he's left to grow old.

With locals and ex-patriots he sees plenty of action,
He's even become a great tourist attraction.

So remember T. Reeves, next time you go Tek Teking,
It may be the future of Seychelles you're wrecking.

And when you're back home, round the fire all cuddly,
You will think of Tek Teks and say weren't they luv'ly.

So it was with their new life long friends they spent many happy hours.

That, other friends, the children, and tennis, seemed to keep them occupied and mostly happy in their day to day lives.

As December came along, it seemed very unlike Christmas. The days were getting hotter and more humid. The rain arrived in huge downpours. Terry measured these with a rain gauge outside their house. It was nothing to get five or six inches of rain in a day.

They had met a newly arrived young couple Jane and Billy who worked at the privately owned bakery known as 'Seybake' owned by a couple from Bristol. They were a bit lost, just as Terry and Ann had been in the early days, so they took them under their wing becoming good friends.

"If you'd like to come and have Christmas dinner with us that would be fun," Ann suggested to them. "It would be far better than you going to a hotel especially as your crates have not yet arrived from UK. It's a steep climb up to our house, but if you can ignore the piggeries and the smell, the views are amazing. Come anytime, late morning onwards. We'll have been to the midnight Mass on Christmas Eve so probably up a bit late."

Jane and Billy were so delighted and looked forward to spending Christmas together with their new friends. It was the first Christmas for both couples in the Seychelles and so would be different.

On Christmas morning it was pouring with rain, something they could have done without, as it meant they could not sit on the open sided verandah as the rain would blow in. It was normally used like a sitting room so it would really cause problems with them having guests. Terry had to carry out various duties on the farm: Christmas morning or not, the livestock had to be cared for and he knew he could not rely on the staff doing all they should. As the morning passed, the rain increased. By 11 am it was a continuous tropical downpour. Terry read the rain gauge. It measured six inches already for the day and it was still pouring down.

"How's the turkey?" he asked Ann as she busied herself in the small kitchen.

"I think it's the only dry thing in the house," she replied.

"It's going to be ready by 12.30, but I'll keep it warm until Jane and Billy arrive. Paul and Lynda are happy playing in their room with their new toys; I think they have the best place, as the rain seems to drive in everywhere else."

By 2.30 there was no sign of their guests and still the rain fell.

"I don't think they're going to make it, maybe they are flooded. We better have our dinner don't you think. What a shame as they were really looking forward to coming here and we'd all have enjoyed it. This rain has certainly put a dampener on the day, a Christmas that we'll always remember for sure."

The total rainfall on Christmas Day was thirteen inches, something of a record; it had created a brown ring around the island where the soil had been washed into the sea. Days later Terry heard that Jane and Billy had set out to come to them for lunch but found the roads blocked with flood water, and were forced to go to the Reef Hotel instead for their dinner.

The New Year of 1975 arrived quietly; the rain had finally stopped, but everywhere was soaked. Large brown palm leaves were scattered around everywhere, dragged down by the heavy rain. When the sun did shine the humidity was incredible, making it very uncomfortable, with the least exertion sapping all their energy. As the farm was built in tiers on the hillside, Terry had to go up and down the whole time as he managed the various activities. It was a very hard climate to work in, designed more for lying on the beach under a tree!

The developing news in the Seychelles over the New Year was the talk of gaining independence from Britain. Not so long ago the Seychelles were almost as keen as the Gibraltarians to remain under the British flag and enjoy its protection. Now they were well on the road to independence, which would no doubt be claimed as a victory over colonialism.

In fact it was almost entirely the result of a British decision to cast them off, part of a policy to get rid of the last vestiges of colonial responsibilities. Mr James Mancham, the Seychellois Chief Minister, had recently agreed with Mrs Hart, the British Minister, that the Seychelles would not become an "associated state" once they gained independence. Britain had prepared the Seychelles for independence the best it could, but the islands had few resources other than beauty to exploit. Clearly its destiny was in developing the tourist trade.

The other apparently vital news of the year was that the 'King Neptune Fish n Chip Shop' in Victoria would now remain open from 5pm – 9pm. Whoopee!

The importance of receiving letters could never be underestimated; it was their very life blood and they yearned as much for them while in the Seychelles, as they had done in Africa, every letter read and re-read. As they devoured the latest batch, most of the New Year letters were on the subject of the Christmas that had just passed, except that is for one!

"Guess who is coming to visit us," Ann proclaimed reading her way through one of the letters.

"Visiting us? I can't imagine. Oh just a minute, it's not is it? Yes I can," he said having thought about it and with trepidation in his voice.

"Yes, it is, I'm afraid," she said smiling.

"Oh no! Surely not? There's no way we can have her stay here, there's hardly space for us and she takes the space of three people. Love and respect her as we do, it's just not possible," Terry replied.

"There are three things that always seem to follow us around, wherever we go, blocked septic tanks, smoking chimneys and Auntie Lesley. Well, the third one sounds as if it's on its way."

Ann read out part of Lesley's letter.

"You will meet me at Mahe Airport on Saturday 31st May 1975. I will arrive at 2.30pm. I'm looking forward to seeing you all in your new home. As it's such a long way to travel to see you, I'll stay for three weeks, leaving on Saturday 21st June."

"Oh will you?" Terry remarked. "Why does she always demand and never ask I wonder?"

"It's what she has been used to in Africa, always telling people what to do; I guess it's how she got things done," Ann explained.

"Well, there's no way she can stay here, there is hardly space for us. We'll have to look around and see if we can find somewhere where she might stay, a B&B or something."

"I'll have a chat with Pat Cocks in the morning and see if she knows anywhere," Ann suggested. "It'll be nice to see Lesley, just the same, won't it?"

"Of course it will, but she's just such a handful. I can't imagine what your Mum and Dad will think when they hear she's coming to see us. They will laugh!"

Terry and Ann both had the greatest respect for Lesley and all that she had done in her life; she was one of life's real celebrities. She had worked in Tanzania for nearly thirty years as a missionary with the Christian Mission Society (CMS). Having worked mainly on her own, miles from other white people, just north of Kigoma, in the west of Tanzania at a place known as Kilinzi. She had built a new hospital there that was the only medical treatment centre around. People would walk miles to receive treatment and some would bring their animals for her to treat when they were sick. Lesley was a female Dr. Livingstone, a woman of character and determination, never accepting no for an answer.

Ann went along to see Pat at their flat the following day and established that there was a small privately run, beach-side B&B near by. Together they went to check it out. The "Casuarina Beach" Guest House was very suitable and Lesley was booked in to arrive on 31st May. Pat and Dave were intrigued to meet Lesley and looked forward to that day. Ann explained all about her, the life she had in Tanzania and how Lesley had taken Ann to Hombolo in 1966, where Ann and Terry first met, and he met Lesley, formidable lady that she was! They chatted along like old friends as Pat and Ann became very close in their new friendship, while enjoying a long cool drink and sheltering from the heat of the day.

Dave wondered if Terry would like to go with him on a deep sea fishing trip that weekend. It was a competition that started at 1am for two hours, to see who caught the most fish. "Do you think he would be interested?" Pat asked.

"I'm sure he would. It'll do him good to get away from the farm for a few hours," Ann replied. "We'll let you know."

Ann put the proposal to Terry who was delighted to be invited, despite having to lose a night's sleep while fishing.

Dave and Terry prepared for the trip on the Friday evening. Pat and Ann drove them both over to Anse a la Mouche Bay, on the south west coast of the island, from where the boat was due to depart at 11pm, returning the following morning around four. Fortunately, Terry and Ann had Bertha, their housemaid, who would be able to take care of Paul and Lynda, so they made arrangements for her to be in charge that night. They set off in high spirits; Terry had been unable to resist a few bags of the new batch of pork scratchings, which Mrs Brooks had just removed from the hot fat, to take with him. She made pounds of them to sell at a few rupees a bag. They were so delicious, especially when warm, and very popular. It was only a few minutes drive to the beach. They found there the other four men, Martin, John, Clive and Mark who were to join them on the trip.

"Bring back lots of fish," Ann and Pat shouted, as the six men climbed into the local fisherman's boat.

"Yes, we hope so," they shouted back.

Dave was wearing a very large brimmed hat made from the leaves of a banana tree, not that they would need shelter from the sun as it was an all night event.

"I feel like one of the apostles in this little old local boat, and we have a John and a Mark on board," Terry said as they started off on the trip.

"What a beautiful starlit night, so clear; I've never seen so many stars stretching out so far, and the water so calm; it's like glass. Looks like it's a good night for the fish," he suggested to the others. "What's the plan for this competition? Does anyone know?"

"We go out about an hour in distance from the island, as the other boats taking part around Mahe will do, then we all commence fishing at 1am for ninety minutes. The boat that has collectively the most fish in weight being the winner," John explained.

"Sounds pretty straight forward: all we have to do then is to catch the fish!"

Terry sat at the front of the small boat, the others on either side; the onboard motor purred away gently taking them further out to sea. They laughed and chatted while enjoying a drink either of water, Seybrew beer or cola, while tucking into the pork scratchings that Terry had brought along from Sawa Sawa Farm. It was a glorious evening and they could see the lights of Mahe twinkling in the distance as they moved deeper out into the Indian Ocean.

"I think we should get our fishing lines ready," Dave said, "then we'll be ready to drop them over the side at 1am."

"What type of fish are we likely to catch?" Terry enquired. "Nothing too big I trust in this boat and with all of us on board."

"Red Snappers, we hope," replied Dave. "They're big so would boost our catch weight. I think there are Parrot Fish, King Fish, Cordonnier and Mackerel in the area. Just have to drop the line over the side and wait and see what comes along."

The boat purred on its way under the guidance of James, the Seychellois fisherman. He seemed to know what he was doing and everyone sort of relaxed into a doze after all the chat and excitement. An hour on into the journey they stirred as the engine changed tone. They had arrived at the given spot, exactly one hour from shore. The engine ticked over holding the boat in a stationary position, everyone making sure that their lines were ready and at 1am they started to fish.

Then suddenly they become aware of changing conditions. They could no longer see the lights of Mahe and the sea was not as calm as it had been.

The boat seemed to be rising and falling at an alarming rate. One minute they were on the top of a wave and looking down into a valley of water. The next, they were in the valley and looking up at a wall of water above them.

This roller coaster ride continued, a violent swing sending them up and down in a fifty foot swell. The speed of the change was terrifying, the turbulence and ferocity of the storm and the sudden vulnerability they all felt.

"I wish I'd not eaten so many pork scratchings," Terry said.

"I wish you hadn't been so generous with them too," Dave replied with a groan.

Any thoughts of fishing stopped; one by one their heads were over the side of the boat being horribly sick, trying to hold on to the side of the boat as it tossed them around like rag dolls. They all looked green and pale; Dave's hat had shrunk in size having been soaked by the rain. It had moulded itself to his head, outlining his green face.

Martin the taxman looked as if he was going over the side as he leaned over so far to be sick. John, Clive and Mark were little better, all looking shocked and very sickly, with everyone soaked to the skin by this sudden downpour, there being no shelter on the boat. There were of course no toilets, so in turn they had to pass a can around and try in the motion of the boat to do what they all suddenly felt they had to do!

It was quickly agreed they should head back to Mahe: conditions were dangerous and volatile. The only question was in which direction were they to go? There were no navigational aids, of course, and because of the storm they were no longer able to see the direction they should take. They had been spun around so much they had no idea where they were, and still the storm raged on; they all felt so ill that to die would have been a great relief.

A controlled panic set in. What were they going to do? If they set off in the wrong direction they could miss Mahe. The next land in this big ocean was India! The Seychellois owner and pilot of the boat, James, was the only one that seemed less concerned. Perhaps, as a fisherman he was well used to these waters and the changing moods. He fought strenuously with the engine and the controls to keep it all going and heading in the direction he thought would get them all home.

They had no alternative but to trust him and assist him in anyway they could, trying to keep the rain out of the engine compartment and keeping the water bailed out, faster than the sea was tossing it in.

After two hours they were losing heart, plus strength and faith in their leader James, as they became weaker, more tired and exhausted. He might be local and understand the waters, but had not got them back home.

The storm seemed to be easing except for the high winds. It was increasingly difficult to keep the water in the boat down to an acceptable level. They bailed it out furiously with anything they could lay their hands on, tins, hats, hands, anything: their lives depended on it. Water was flying everywhere as they worked tirelessly to keep afloat. Everyone's stomach was completely empty and they felt a coldness inside them and very, very weak.

"Land Ahoy!" someone suddenly shouted. Through the cloud they were able to see a grey outline of palm trees and a beach.

"We've made it! "they all shouted." Well done, James, our captain and pilot. Fantastic, never thought we would see Mahe again. Hooray! Hooray!"

Incredibly, James had returned them to Anse a la Mouche beach, the very spot from which they had departed in such high spirits the previous evening.

They beached the boat and one by one the bedraggled bunch staggered off and paddled to the beach. Their legs were shaking as they got used to being on firm land again. The speed at which they lost the feeling of sickness was truly amazing and for that reason alone they felt slightly better. They lay on the sand for a few minutes to try and recover. By this time the hat on Dave's head had shrunk to the size of a tea cup, making him look so funny.

"Hello there," they heard someone shout. It was Ann, Pat and the other wives running to greet them. They had been waiting for them and were so relieved to see them all alive. The rain continued to sheet down as they all dragged themselves into their cars, the first shelter they had enjoyed throughout the whole terrible ordeal.

Terry slept until mid afternoon, having decided not to go to the farm that Saturday morning, as he would normally have done. He took the day off to recover from the aborted fishing trip.

"You're lucky to be alive, you know," Ann said to him. "What would we have done if you'd never come back? You don't swim and you had no life jacket. You really are an idiot sometimes. We all feared the worst as we waited on the beach; and saw the size of the waves and the violence of the storm. Poor Pat, she was beside herself. We didn't know what to do next. By the way, where is all the lovely fish you promised us?"

"Sorry, looking back it was a bit careless, but it started out so clear and calm that we never imagined it would turn out as it did.

Believe me, it was not much fun for us either, fighting with the elements. Sorry about the fish. We had our minds taken off fishing. It was that or we certainly wouldn't have made it back. Don't worry, I won't be doing it again in a hurry."

Food suddenly took on a special meaning and taste; he just couldn't get enough of it having been so sick, totally emptying the contents of his stomach into the Indian Ocean. Slowly he recovered his strength and by Sunday was ready to go off to church with Paul for the 5pm Mass in Victoria and then on to the airport in the Volkswagen Van to collect the 3,000 day old chicks that arrived on the 18.30 flight from South Africa. It was the usual Sunday evening task. Paul loved to help his Dad count them out once back at the farm, and Ann would bring Lynda to see them before she went to bed.

Life got back to normal, and work, shopping and ferrying children around to different events took over. Ann had met Denise a lovely Seychellois lady at Anse Royale, just down the road from them. She had multiple sclerosis. Ann spent a couple of hours twice a week giving her some exercise treatment, using her occupational therapy knowledge. Denise was so grateful and made quite a marked improvement with Ann's help. There was little care of that sort on the island, so Denise was so pleased to have met Ann and insisted that she pay her a proper fee. Ann always loved to help others in her life and took great joy at being able to help Denise, leaving her better able to cope with her disability; they also became great friends.

Terry and Ann continued to go to the Reef Hotel tennis courts, near-by, where they would enjoy a vigorous game of tennis in the early evening. They had both improved their game and enjoyed these matches in the shade of the palm trees at the front of the hotel, then relaxing with a cool drink, looking out over the sea to the coral reef at the rear of the hotel, before setting off back on the mile drive to Sawa Sawa Farm at Anse aux Pins, treasured moments indeed.

On return from tennis one evening, Bertha, their sixty-year old children's maid who had been looking after Paul and Lynda while they were out, gave them a letter.

"Mr Rebuck, came to see Mr Terry while you were out and left this letter for him. Mr Rebuck says it was urgent!" Bertha explained.

"Who is Mr Rebuck?" Ann asked

"No idea," Terry replied. "There is one sure way of finding out and that's to open it!"

Mahe
5.3.75

Dear Sir,
Sorry to interup you, of asking if you can help me by 5 Rhodes Islands chickens mothers to obtain source, I already had a cock standing alone. And a young pair of "Derrace Chickens," I don't know the English name of them, but they had long legged, long necked, long and flat tail, short and big beak short and large crest.

Please have conscience to help others, I shall be great for your kindness.

    Yours faithfully
    Lewis Rebuck.

Gladly, Terry was able to provide Mr Rebuck with what he required. The letter had been typed out well and was typical of the many funny and sincere letters that he received.

Lynda and Paul began to look forward to their birthdays as they always did. It was Lynda's third birthday on 28th March and Paul's fifth on 11th April. They were no longer babies and their growing into young children marked the passage of time.

"It always seems such a shame that they will never really remember anything of the Seychelles and the beauty of the place in which they've lived. Maybe when they're older they will return to visit their old home. Who knows?" Ann wondered.

"Yes," Terry replied. "Perhaps we will too in our old age!"

A meeting at the International School in Victoria on 8th May confirmed that Paul was doing well with most of his lessons, which was pleasing even in one so young. With the heat and humidity it must have been difficult for him to concentrate and work. They were reminded that Sports' Day was to take place on 5th June.

"Can't imagine what they will do in this heat," Ann said. "Let's hope there's no parents' race."

They began to look forward to the arrival of Auntie Lesley. They had warned 'Casuarina Beach Guest House' that Lesley was quite a forthright lady; they were very kind and offered her a place on their veranda where she could sit and read or write as she wished.

Lesley duly arrived on Saturday 31st May 1975 and was so pleased to see them all. It was in fact her second visit to the Seychelles; the last had been by sea in 1953 on her way to visit Bombay. She had little in the way of family, had never married and as she said, nobody else seemed to understand her as Terry and Ann did! Their understanding of her was in part due to the fact that they had both lived in Africa and so understood her ways. She had a heart of gold and had done such wonderful work in her thirty years as a missionary, where she was affectionately known as "Warrior." They shared that great love of Africa, its people and of her.

She enjoyed helping to unpack the day old chicks when they arrived and looking around the farm. She agreed living next to 'the porkers' as she called them, was not so nice!

They delighted in showing her around the island to see some of the sights, like the superb views from the tea estate around Morne Blanc, where you could sit and enjoy a pot of their tea in the cool mountain air, such a relief on a hot and humid day. She enjoyed the wonderful beaches with their peacefulness, the exotic park that makes up the Botanical Gardens with some of the finest specimens in the world of flora and fauna: the world famous Coco de Mer tree, palms and specimens like the Breadfruit tree, the Betel palm and fine ornamental flamboyant Bougainvilleas, Hibiscus and so many colourful shrubs. Her flat in Cranbrook was full of plants so these gave her great pleasure.

The Seychelles was of course famous for the Giant Land Tortoises that drag their heavy shells around in a prehistoric way. Lesley loved those and perhaps identified with them: they travelled at less than 30 yards per hour, only a little slower than she did those days.

Just the same, everyone admired her courage, faith, and endurance to travel the world alone to far away places as she did, right to her last year, showing the same lack of fear she had when she first set foot in Africa in 1946.

She was a woman of outstanding faith and spirit.

Her departure on Saturday 21st June left them feeling empty, for, as maddening as Lesley could sometimes be, they loved and missed her amongst them. However, as so often happens, life went on to take control in its own forceful way.

The following Monday Ann said she thought she would go and visit the doctor to see if he could do anything about a mole on her toe that had become slightly enlarged and was rubbing when she wore her tennis shoes.

"If that's your excuse for playing so badly, well it won't wash, you know!" Terry laughed.

"I've beaten you the last five matches, don't forget!" Ann responded.

"We're booked to play again on Wednesday, so look out, cheeky."

"Ok. I'm ready for it. Must be my turn to win but if you have an injury I'd better let you win, like I did last time!"

The doctor said that the best thing he could suggest was to have the mole removed, and then there would be no further problem with it rubbing on her shoe. He said he would make an appointment with the hospital for her to go in for the day to have the operation, and would get in touch with her once he had fixed a date.

Chapter Fourteen

Six weeks passed and nothing was heard from the doctor. They knew it was not really very urgent and being in a foreign country did not like to push themselves forward or try to jump the queue. There were many more important things for the one and only hospital in the Seychelles to concentrate on, and the hospital resources were very limited. It always worried them to see the capacity of the hospital. As aeroplanes with three hundred people came into the airport, they always thought, what if……?

One of the favourite places where all the expatriates gathered at weekends was the Friday night Fish-n-Chip night, a real feast that took place at the Northolme Hotel. It was a colonial style building in a unique setting, situated in gardens and overlooking the sea on the North West coast of Mahe. Everyone seemed to enjoy the setting, watching the flying foxes in the garden whilst enjoying the fish and chips that were cooked on the veranda overlooking the sea.

While they were enjoying their meal, Ann's doctor, who had been sitting with his wife, must have noticed her and he came over to their table.

"Mrs Reeves?" he said rather anxiously.

"Yes it is. Hello Doctor."

"Mrs Reeves, I'm so sorry, I thought it was you, and remembered that I was going to make you an appointment to see the surgeon and I haven't done it. Can you be at the hospital for ten o'clock on Monday morning and I'll make sure the surgeon is there. It should only take about an hour or so. If your husband can come as well, he will need to drive you home, as the toe will be a bit sore afterwards. I'll be there too. Please forgive me, but I completely forgot until I saw you now. I'm so sorry to interrupt your meal."

"That's fine. We can be there, can't we?" she asked Terry.

"Yes, I'll be able to get away," he replied.

"Thank you, Doctor, we will see you on Monday then."

"That was nice of him," Ann said. "He seems very keen to help me get in and to do the operation. How kind of him."

"Mmm," Terry said thoughtfully, "he certainly was."

On Monday 4th August Ann attended the hospital and had surgery on her toe. Terry sat in the open-sided waiting room overlooking the garden courtyard, quite a pleasant spot really. After two hours he was getting restless, but did not expect much else really: life in the Seychelles involved a lot of waiting around, what ever you were doing. After three hours the doctor and another man, who turned out to be the surgeon, came out to have a word with Terry.

"All is well," he said. "We have removed the mole from your wife's toe; it took longer then we had hoped. The nurse is just completing the dressing and then you can take her home. We found it necessary to remove a large area above the toe, where it joins the foot, as a precaution. In some cases where a mole changes character, as this one appeared to be doing, it is sensible to remove a larger amount of tissue, just in case it should prove to be malignant. This is only a precaution."

"You mean cancerous do you Doctor?" Terry enquired.

"Yes exactly," he replied.

"Mr Reeves, I don't want to alarm you and I haven't said this to your wife, but the colour of the mole does tell us a lot. Mr Rao our surgeon here has a vast experience in the treatment of moles in India. His early thoughts are that it is likely that your wife's mole is the cancerous type. He has therefore removed the larger area to be sure that he has taken away any affected tissue. Even if it does prove to be cancerous, this action should have prevented it from spreading. He is hopeful that having done that all will be well. In order that we know what we are dealing with we are sending the mole off to the U.K. to check if it was malignant."

"How long will that take?" Terry asked anxiously.

"Normally about two weeks. We'll let you know as soon as we have the results. In the meantime, she must rest the leg, keep it up and keep it dry. We'll give her plenty of dressings and will need to see her and you again in ten days."

With that shocking revelation they shook Terry's hand and returned into the hospital, leaving Terry waiting for Ann. He fell back in his chair, stunned, trying to take it all in; he felt as if he had been kicked in the stomach.

The nurse wheeled Ann out to the car. "Think our date for Wednesday on the tennis court is off, don't you," she smiled.

"The length you will go to stop me from beating you, this really is the limit," Terry replied. Surprisingly, Ann was as bright as a button, probably the relief that it was all over.

With the help of Bertha she continued to care for Paul and Lynda, who accepted that their Mum had to have the mole removed from her foot. They themselves had a number of moles on their skin, so it was easy for them to understand what was going on. They had given Ann a walking stick for support and after resting the first day, she was up and walking about. The bandaging seemed huge, which they were told was to keep out the dirt and dust, but it must have been uncomfortable for her in the heat.

On the 14th August Ann was called to the hospital to have her foot redressed and to see the surgeon again. The foot seemed to be healing well so the dressing was very much reduced in size and therefore easier for Ann to move around. The surgeon explained to her that the result of the test showed the mole had been malignant, but as it had now been removed together with other tissues surrounding it, all should be well. They were pleased with the healing and they asked her to attend again in two to three weeks to be checked out. So although very shocked at the outcome of something so small, at least it was gone now and her foot less sore and healing well.

Life returned to something like normal and Ann went back to the hospital a couple of times over the next few weeks to allow them to check its progress. Healing was always slow in the humidity and heat of the Seychelles, even insect bites took ages to get over, some lasting for weeks, so there was no real concern that it had not completely healed. It would, given time.

They resumed playing tennis again, but perhaps not quite with the same vigour. The tennis was fun but they particularly enjoyed sitting outside the Reef Hotel looking out to sea after the game, and taking in the beauty that was the Seychelles.

On the 5th October they had their second visitors who were passing through the Seychelles and stopped there for a few days. Tony and Helen Andrews and their three children were missionaries in Tanzania and on their way to New Zealand for home leave. Terry and Ann had booked them into a local guesthouse. Chatting with them over those two days, rekindled Ann and Terry's interest in Tanzania, as they sat and chatted about old faces and places and remembered the days when they had worked in the country at Hombolo Leprosy Centre and how they had met there. It was hard to believe that was nine years ago, as it was all so real in their minds. It also brought back memories of the long separation they had endured, when Ann remained at Hombolo for six months after Terry had left, and the anguish of it all. Thank goodness, they thought, that is all behind us. It was fun renewing old acquaintances, and to wave them off at the airport, watching the enormous plane take off just meters away from where they stood. Planes always fascinated Paul, perhaps one day they might feature in his career they thought.

All this made them think of Africa, not that it was ever far from their minds. It also made them realise that their time in the Seychelles was fast coming to a close. They had decided to stay on for the full two years and had already been there for nearly twenty months. They would soon need to make plans for their future.

"Do you think we could get a job in Africa from here? Or would we have to return to UK to apply?" Ann enquired.

"I'm not sure; we would probably want to return to England to see everyone again and have a break, before we went off on another tour. It's time that we started to look around and see what's out there, don't you think?"

"Yes, we should," Ann replied. "I really would love to return to Tanzania if possible: the people are so lovely, it's a peaceful and beautiful place with so many wild animals; I'd love to see more of those. There are no wars like in the Congo or Mozambique; we certainly wouldn't want to take Paul and Lynda to anywhere like that."

"What about their future education in places like Tanzania?"

"There are International Schools which are excellent. Then when they go on to the next stage the fees are often paid for by the employer to go to private school." Ann said. "It would be very hard to see them go away like that, but we do see many children here doing it and they seem to love coming out to be with their parents for the holidays. Can you imagine at Holy Child School in Weymouth, at the holiday time, getting on a plane to Tanzania, that would have done wonders for your street cred!"

"Getting a ride in a car did that in my days," Terry laughed.

"I agree it would be great. Let's start making enquires and see what's on offer job wise. The UK government is pouring aid into Africa and continues to support people going out to work in the developing world, so I should be able to come up with something."

During October the humidity rose to eighty three percent and it became very sultry. The amount of rainfall increased as the season began to change towards the rains. The two million or so coconut trees that grew in the Seychelles would no doubt benefit from the rains, but for the humans it was uncomfortable at best. They longed for the evening breeze coming up off the sea to bring some relief. They had purchased an oscillating fan for Paul and Lynda's room and a small fan for themselves, which they mounted on the bedroom wall to provide some relief at night. The nights were the most difficult time and sleep did not come easily.

On 17th October Ann had her usual appointment with the doctor to check that the wound, still covered by a dressing, was progressing satisfactorily. Unfortunately the doctor was concerned about it and decided to check out some tissue around the wound that was not healing. He arranged for Ann to have a small operation the following Tuesday to remove some more tissue and send it to the UK for further analysis. Ann was pretty fed up having to go through that again, but did so bravely. It was then a case of waiting for the results to arrive, before the doctor decided the next course of action.

They busied themselves to try and take their minds off the problem, enjoying the beaches, the walks and an endless round of picnics which Paul and Lynda loved. The children (and Terry) enjoyed the warm sea, collecting shells and being buried by their Dad in the coral sand, although Lynda was never too sure about that process.

On Monday 3rd November there was a phone message left at the farm office telling Ann to attend the hospital immediately, as the results of her test were now back from England.

They both anxiously made their way to Victoria where they waited to see the doctor. The wait was short and they were quickly called to see him. Also there with him was his Staff Nurse, a religious sister who worked at the hospital, Sister Magdalen.

"Please sit down," the doctor invited.

"Mrs Reeves, I will come straight to the point, the results from the tissue recently sent to the UK have come back positive, I'm afraid. This means that there is still some cancer present in the toe. The result also showed that it is what's known as a 'malignant melanoma'."

They were both dumbfounded by this news and didn't fully understand it all.

"So what now? What can we do?" Terry enquired.

"It's my recommendation that you send your wife immediately to the U.K. for further treatment. In that way she will have the very best care. I'll provide you with a letter for her to give to the doctor and to the hospital. Where will you stay when you return to England?" the doctor asked Ann.

"Well my parents live near Bristol, so I would probably go there to start," Ann replied.

"That would be excellent as there is a very good unit at Frenchay Hospital. I'll make an appointment for you to see the specialist as soon as possible. Ring the hospital on your arrival in U.K. I'll give you the numbers and letters that you'll require. Come with me please, Mrs Reeves."

It was all happening so quickly, they had no time to think. As Ann went off to get the necessary letters from the doctor, Terry followed. As he did, the sister, Sister Magdalen, took his arm.

"Mr Reeves, I need to speak to you."

"Yes, sister, what is it?"

"You need to get your wife to England immediately. A malignant melanoma is the worst sort of cancer there is, I want you to know now that her chances of surviving long term are not good."

"But it was only a small mole sister, surely not," Terry replied.

She held his arm. "I wanted to prepare you. I'm sorry, but I felt you should know that this is about as serious as it gets."

He stared at her in astonishment, overcome, confused, tears in his eyes.

"No, surely not. How can it be?" he asked. "We have two lovely children. Surely there must be a mistake, Sister. It can't be that bad, can it?"

Sister Magdalen looked ashen, "Mr Reeves, I'm sorry. Please heed what I've told you and get her home as soon as you can; it's your best and only chance."

"But!" he stammered. "What about the children? How? What will I do? Oh God this is terrible. It has to be wrong."

She held his arm. "You have to be very brave, Mr Reeves," she said holding on to him. "Very, very brave. Can you do that?"

He just looked at her blankly.

"Go now and be with your wife. You know what you have to do."

"What was the Sister saying to you?" Ann enquired, as she rejoined him outside the doctor's office, clutching the letters.

"She was just saying that the earlier you get home to U.K. the better."

"Come on, let's go home," Ann said, tears in her eyes. "I'm so sorry, this is all my fault."

"Listen. Nothing is your fault, it just happens. It could so easily have been me, so don't ever think that. It's not your fault. I'll go and see Carly and Philip and explain the situation to them. If I forgo the gratuity due in February they will pay the fares and let me go early I'm sure. The first thing I have to do is get you booked on a flight."

They drove off in a cloud of dust, back to Sawa Sawa Farm. A silence descended on them both as they tried to take in the enormity of the situation. Surrounded by so much beauty it seemed so wrong, so impossible, tortuous, and unreal. Horror and beauty, what a poignant mix!

They couldn't speak: it hurt too much. Ann couldn't wait to get home and hug the children; she played with them on the veranda in a daze of disbelief.

"I'm going down to see the Brookes now and see what I can sort out. Try not to worry; I'll do everything I can." Terry set off down the hillside to inform Carly and Philip about the day's events. He was not looking forward to it at all.

The day was ending with strong windy gusts blowing in off the sea; the season was certainly changing. Ann had put Paul and Lynda to bed. She tried to explain that she would have to go and get further treatment for her foot and that Daddy was trying to arrange something. They seemed more interested in what story they would have that night, so she read their stories and kissed them goodnight. She felt hardly able to let them out of her arms; they were so precious to her, as indeed was Terry. She promised them that Daddy would go and say goodnight to them, like he always did, as soon as he arrived home.

Ann poured a large gin and tonic adding lots of ice and sat on the wall of the veranda, looking out to sea, trying to catch some of the passing breeze while she waited for Terry to return. What on earth was he doing? He had been gone ages and would be hungry, having eaten little since the call had come that morning for them to attend the hospital.

Light was fading before a tired, dispirited looking Terry staggered up over the horizon, having climbed up the side of the hill from Carly's house below. She rushed out, threw herself around his neck and cried bitterly.

"Come on now, there's no need for this," he said compassionately. I have managed to sort a few things out; we have a plan, let me explain.

Terry had never really seen Ann cry as she did, to be as deeply upset, as she was that night; she was inconsolable. He went to say goodnight to Paul and Lynda, but they were fast asleep. He kissed them and felt deep pain for them, as he gazed down on their peaceful faces, wondering what was before them.

They were going to need him so much. Would he be big enough for the task? He felt totally inadequate.
Ann had prepared a simple meal and placed it on a small table on the veranda; they sat looking out to sea with the new moon rising in the darkening skies.

"So go on tell me all," Ann said as she tried to recover and face the proposals.

"Well, Carly and Philip were of course sorry to hear our news and have been most helpful. They'll pay both our fares home and pay half the gratuity, as well as our holiday pay that's due, while allowing us to return to U.K. as soon as is practical, for me at least," Terry explained.

"What do you mean?" Ann asked.

"As you know, the doctor advised us that you should go home as soon as possible for treatment. Carly's daughter Valerie works for Caledonian Airways and she helped me book you on the next flight out. You leave the day after tomorrow, Wednesday 5th November departing at six in the evening. I'll follow with Paul and Lynda on Saturday 22nd November, giving me time to pack up here."
"Oh no, Terry, I can't go without you and the children."

"You can and you must. It will be far better for you to be free, to go and get done what has to be done, without having to worry about us. We'll manage."

"No, Terry, I can't leave you here, it's not fair on you all. You'll have far too much to do with the farm and everything, especially if you're to pack up all our belongings, arrange shipping and everything. No, I can't leave you with all that."

"Too late it's booked and you're going. Pat Cocks has said she will help and make some clothes for Paul and Lynda to travel back in, as well as to help all she can."

I've rung your Mum and Dad and told them. Your Dad is going to meet you at Bristol Station and you can stay there with them until I return and the hospital has seen you. I realise its all so quick, but it's best that way."

"You have been busy, haven't you? Poor Mum and Dad, I bet they were surprised. I don't want to stay there long term, you do know that, no matter what happens," Ann pleaded.

"Of course not. We'll find something as soon as I get home, in fact you can start to look as soon as you arrive back; it'll give you a project."

"Can't Paul and Lynda come back with me; surely it would be easier for you?" Ann suggested.

"No, you are the important one. This way you only have to think of one person and your own luggage while travelling. You can concentrate on yourself and getting to Pucklechurch to be with your Mum and Dad. I'm sure it's best. I can look after Paul and Lynda, with Bertha's help and Pat will help me too, I know she will, so don't worry."

"I don't like leaving you and with so much to do here, it's not fair. Terry we have had so much separation in the past, haven't we? I really don't want anymore. Please no more," Ann cried.

"I know, I don't want it either, but it's only a few weeks this time. I'll manage, really, I will manage."

"I think I want to go to bed now," Ann said tearfully.

"Yes it's been a long and difficult day. I'll follow you," he replied.

Terry poured another drink and sat in the chair looking out to sea; tears ran down his cheeks. He couldn't get Sister Magdalen's words out of his head.

A rat ran up the pole and along the electric wire that supplied the house, as they often did. Strangely it didn't seem to matter anymore. It stopped and looked down at him with a look of sympathy on its face, or was that just Terry's imagination.

He sat there as if he were in a vacuum turning over the day's events in his mind: it was a nightmare. Surely, Ann would recover from this? It was only a pea size mole; it could not possibly cause all this trouble, could it? How absolutely terrible Ann must feel, he thought, she does not deserve this.

He considered how on earth he was going to cope. I have to, he thought, for Ann's sake. I have to be strong enough, and then some more, to leave strength for Paul and Lynda. How was he going to explain it all to them? Then there was the packing, the organising, things to sell, bank to deal with, friends to see. Bertha, dear reliable Bertha, what about her? She had nothing and had become like a member of the family. Oh dear! What a mess. Then there was work and of course the big question of what on earth he was going to do once he arrived back in the U.K? He took a long deep breath, finished his drink, bade the rat goodnight and went to bed.

The next forty eight hours were a fever of activity as they prepared everything for Ann's departure. Terry had to get the necessary tax clearance with a certificate, in order that she could pass freely through immigration. Ann was busy packing and explaining patiently to Paul and Lynda what was going on. She went to see Pat and David to thank them for their help and to ask them to keep an eye on Terry and children. Pat being the great friend she was, happily agreed to do all that she could to help, and Ann took comfort knowing that she would.

Ann, being Ann, could not leave Bertha, their maid, without a future, for she had nobody and owned nothing. She went along to friends at "Seybake," the island's bakers to see if they knew anyone that might like an aging Bertha to help in the house. As luck would have it, they agreed to take her on themselves, to help out in their house, much to Ann's great relief. She had always thought about others in her life, before herself. Terry had always admired that quality in her, right back to their days at Hombolo.

The day of Ann's departure was a strange one. Everyone busy and trying not to believe it was happening. They had to check-in for her flight an hour before departure. Terry loaded up the cases and Paul and Lynda into the car for the short journey to the airport; they had expressed the wish to go and see their Mum off on the plane.

In the departure lounge were Pat and Dave with whom they had always had so much fun, and a few other friends that had been informed.

Dear old Bertha had somehow found her way to the airport and stood almost out of sight at the back of the departure section, with tears streaming down her cheeks. In her eyes was the timeless wisdom of a well-worn face, crazed with age, dark with sadness. Bertha gave Ann a gentle embrace: no words were necessary; the tears expressed all her feelings. Ann just gazed at her and quietly thanked her for caring.

It was time for the last farewells: Ann took Paul and Lynda in her arms, reassuring them that she would see them very soon and that they must take care of Daddy. They looked confused and bewildered as they kissed their mother goodbye. Looking weary, Terry embraced Ann and whispered, "It's not going to be like last time. This separation is only for a few days: we love each other, and nothing can break or destroy that, not ever."

Ann boarded the massive Caledonian VC 10; the droning noise of the jet engines took it quickly up into the evening sky until distance blurred it from their sight.

Things happen sometimes that you couldn't possible imagine, either when they are actually taking place, or indeed afterwards. As if you are not really part of them, you are conscious of what is happening, but feel outside of it. Terry felt like that on this occasion, and was numb as he drove back to Sawa Sawa Farm to put Paul and Lynda to bed and to read their usual bed time story, as if nothing was happening or had happened.

All this could not be, he thought, but it was, a sad day indeed for them all.

Next day, the morning air was crisp and clear at 4.30am when Terry arose. He could not sleep, although desperately tired; he decided to enjoy a cup of tea and sit with his thoughts, while watching the sun come up. The dull red ball arose from the sea as if floating on its surface; he wondered how Ann was and how the flight had been.

Somehow, for him, life had lost its shine, but he knew that from somewhere he had to find courage. It was so incredibly hard he had to dig deep. He had never had to face anything like this before. Could he do it, he questioned himself. Could he find the strength? He pondered these thoughts while watching the sunrise to its full glory, sending out shafts of light into the new day.

Then, delivered to his door like a parcel, his request was granted in full.

Paul, clutching his teddy, unable to sleep appeared on the veranda from his bedroom, half asleep, half awake, and he ran to his Dad who was sitting looking out to sea. Paul climbed onto his knee and together they sat looking out to the clear blue sea below. Yes, Terry thought, my new courage comes from these two, from Paul and from Lynda. His whole new purpose had been crystallised, his objective underlined. They needed him, they were as frightened and terrified as he was, and they were as upset as he was. They needed him more then ever and he was determined not to let them down.

He had just sixteen days to do everything that had to be done when packing up a house and a life; there was little time to lose. Over the course of that time he organised packing cases and shipping, taxation and banking, schooling and informing friends. There was the car and other items to sell, hospital fees to pay and flights to confirm, so much in such a short time. The packing cases were to be collected after they had left, to be sent by sea, so remained in the house.

On the last day, Saturday 22nd November 1975, he sat on the packing cases in the otherwise empty house, reading a letter that had just arrived from Ann, posted on Friday 14th November in Bristol. She was able to tell him that his Mum and Dad had rung her, showing their concern. Ann said she had tried to reassure them. He was pleased to hear that she'd been out to buy a new winter coat. She said that it was very expensive at £30, but the last one she'd had was ten years old.

Just at that moment he could forgive her anything to be back together. Like her, he had always hated being separated. They had hoped that it would be over once they were married, but somehow it seemed that they were destined to have these long periods apart.

Ann had been looking around for places for them to rent. She felt they would soon find something, but may have to pay £15 a week. She was looking at a winter let and sounded hopeful.

Regarding her treatment, she was waiting to hear from the hospital as to when she had to go in, but was expecting to be called any day, having already seen the doctors twice since she arrived.

As he was reading Ann's letter, sitting quietly on the packing cases, Pat and Dave arrived to take them all to the airport. Pat had made a lovely outfit for Lynda in which she looked a picture. They loaded up the remaining cases and said goodbye to the house, stopping off at Carly's house to say goodbye to the Brooks family and thank them for their help and understanding. Then set off to leave Sawa Sawa Farm behind them. They never were to meet any of the Brooks family again, but did correspond for a short time. A few years later Terry heard that the farm had been sold.

There is nowhere worse on earth then an airport at six o'clock on a dark November morning. That was where Terry found himself at Gatwick Airport after the long flight from the Seychelles, tired and exhausted with two equally tired children. In view of the long flight, Terry had arranged to spend the first night at his aunty's home in Horsham before going on to Pucklechurch.

A cousin who worked for the Datsun car company sorted out a car for him to buy which was a great help.

It was frustrating not to be able to go and see Ann immediately, but for the children's sake it seemed to be the best thing to do in the circumstances. They rang Ann on arrival and discovered that she was recovering from a second operation on her foot that had taken place a few days before. They had removed a larger area of tissue around where the mole had been, as the wound had not been healing well when she was in the Seychelles.

Next day Terry and the children set out from Aunty Eve's in Horsham to collect the car and settle up all the business attached to it, before driving over to Meadowland Cottage, Pucklechurch to meet Ann and her parents.

What a wonderful reunion they all enjoyed, even if the separation had only been for nineteen days on this occasion; it still seemed like a lifetime.

"I'm so glad to see you all again," Ann said happily, smiling as she took the children in her arms. "I've missed you so much." As she hugged Terry she said, "It doesn't get any easier, does it? Separation I mean."

"It certainly doesn't. But it sounds as if you haven't been idle. How's the foot? Was it very painful having to go through all that again?"

"I'll explain all that later. Let's go and see Mum and Dad. They're keeping out of the way so I can greet you first. Isn't that thoughtful of them?" Ann said.

She seemed to bounce along with joy, full of life, happy to have everyone reunited. Terry was shattered. But his share of the events had been nothing as traumatic as Ann's and if she could be so full of beans, then he should be too, for her sake, he thought.

They all enjoyed the next few days being together again and everyday Ann was walking more normally after the operation on her foot. The bandage was to come off the following week and then hopefully it would fully heal.

Certainly the heat had not helped the healing process in the Seychelles. Terry and the children were finding it so cold after the tropical climate, walking around in thick jumpers to try and keep warm; they realized just how much they had acclimatised to the heat and the humidity that they had endured.

On the Wednesday after Terry's arrival he and Ann went up the lane for a walk and then sat on the hill in the field outside

Meadowland Cottage that looked out over Bristol, far in the distance. They watched the colourful spectacle of hot air balloons rising from below where there was a club for enthusiasts. It was something of a favourite place for them, somewhere where they had made so many decisions in the past, including the one to get married.

Ann's mood had suddenly changed: she had lowered the mask worn for the sake of the children, and became very upset and tearful; her voice having a broken edge.

"It's all my fault this," she said, "dragging you half way around the world like I have, putting you through this hell, giving you all that extra work, upsetting all our plans. Don't think I haven't noticed how tired you look and I'm not surprised as I left you with everything to do, just everything."

"Stop there!" Terry interrupted her flow of self-attack. "It's not your fault as you put it, it's just the hand we've been dealt. You and I are one and together we'll fight this. I'm tired yes, I've had a long flight and, yes, lots to do; it takes a while to recover. You have to stop blaming yourself. We wanted to get out of the Seychelles; well we have, even if it wasn't quite in the way we'd have wished!"

"You were telling me last night that your doctor in Bristol wants you to attend Odstock Hospital, near Salisbury, a specialist unit for your after care. Well, I've had a thought," Terry said, "about our housing problems that is. It would work in well with moving to live in that area. I think it might be the answer, at least in the short term."

"Do you remember Major Rimmer, Lord Burnham's Land Agent? He has a house in Tisbury, not far from Salisbury that he'd done up for his retirement. I know he found it expensive to keep it going and may be happy for us to rent it from him for a while. What if I ask him if he would let it to us? At least he knows us well and it was fully furnished. It would certainly be a good area to live, as well as near to the hospital."

"What about your work?" Ann asked.

"Not sure. I'll continue to look around of course. I've one idea, but it's different. Lateral thinking has been applied, but I need to look into it in more detail."

"Sounds mysterious," Ann said with a smile.

"Not really. You know how I've often showed an interest in finance and the stock market, that sort of thing ever since we took out that savings plan with 'Save and Prosper' for our retirement when we were at Lillyfee Farm? Well, there is another large finance company that keeps advertising,

'Tambro Life,' it's part of Tambros the big merchant bankers. They are looking for sales people and the salaries look really attractive. I'm thinking of contacting them. They have an office both in Exeter and in Salisbury."

"But you're a farmer," Ann exclaimed. "Not a man in a suit. You don't know anything about finance and investment. What about our dream to dedicate ourselves to working in Africa? We have so much to offer that country. It was to be our future, our life."

"Well I know, but I guess there's training and if it means I get a job in the area, well it's all that matters at the moment, while you're getting fixed up. As for Africa, of course I want to return there to work, as much as you do. At the moment I feel I should try this. I might even like it, and lets face it I've not always found the best employers in agriculture, have I?"

"Well that's true, but it's your way of life. You love the countryside and living in the country, you always said you couldn't do anything else. This would be a complete change," Ann exclaimed.

She was very concerned that he would turn his back on his career, just so they could live near Salisbury, and she wasn't at all happy about that. She knew his roots were living and working in the countryside. He was never happier than when he was in the wilds of Africa; it was what he loved the most; it was what he was. If he finished up changing his life style for her, he may grow to hate it and her for forcing the change. No, she was not happy about this idea. She felt she knew him, better than he knew himself sometimes. He could never be happy working and perhaps living in a town. It was not for him that sort of living; it would be like taking a lion from the wild and putting it in a cage.

Terry was determined to give it a go. He realised that it would be a complete change of career, but wanted to give it a try, not just to be near to Salisbury, but also to prove to himself, that it was something he could do successfully. It gave him a chance of improving himself and his income if he was a success and, being between jobs, why not have a go, give it a try?

Chapter Fifteen

After spending Christmas with Ann's parents in Pucklechurch, on Tuesday 30th December 1975, Terry attended an interview at the office of Tambro Life Assurance in Salisbury. The Branch Manger, flamboyant Richard Carlyle-Clarke, interviewed him. He was a likeable charismatic character, full of life and enthusiasm. He gave Terry one of those American style tests to see the sort of person he was. This was supposed to show if Terry was suitable for such employment. When he had completed all the different sections by ticking boxes, Richard compared it with a chart, which was designed to show him if Terry was the right person to be a sales associate.

"According to this chart and the answers you have given, you are totally unsuitable for this type of career!" Richard told him with a smile.

Oh! Terry thought, so Ann was right after all.
"However," Richard said to him, "I like you and I like your attitude, so I'm going to stick my neck out and offer you a chance. The terms for an associate are not easy, but if you're successful then the sky's the limit and in a few years time you could be running your own branch, like this one here.

You will be given two weeks' training at Tambro Life House in Bristol at our Head Office, alongside other new sales associates. If you pass those exams you are given a licence enabling you to operate from this branch.

Financially, you are paid by commission only. The rates vary depending on the type of assurance or investment you have sold. To start with the company will credit your commission account with £600 until you have built up your own commissions, which will gradually pay off that amount.

He reported all this back to Ann and they finally agreed that he should go for it. At worst he could return to his roots and back into agriculture if he wanted to, once Ann had the all clear.

The other good news was that Major Rimmer was delighted for them to use his house in Tisbury, agreeing they could have it for about six months if they paid all the bills and the rates. That was indeed a fantastic result and they moved into Church Street, Tisbury, the first week in January 1976.

They also managed to get Paul and Lynda into Wardour Catholic School that was just outside Tisbury in a beautiful setting, a school with an excellent reputation. They both started there on 12th January.

The same week Ann had her first check at the hospital; the wound was healing well, only needing a small dressing, so far more comfortable for her. The doctors were delighted with her progress.

Terry went off happily to start his two-week course in Bristol, returning home at the weekends. It was hard work; he had not been used to studying. There was so much to learn about the different types of life assurance, the investment market, pension plans and capital transfer tax, together with a sound and useful grounding in income tax.

He thought his head would burst by the end of it, but he did manage to pass the examination and come away primed up to go out and make his first million! Or so he was led to believe.

In discussions with his manager Richard, they felt that he should concentrate on the farmers as he understood them and spoke their language, able to give advice on providing their pension requirements and protecting their farms from capital transfer tax, by means of life assurance.

For three long weeks Terry called at farms and businesses in Tisbury, Hindon, Warminster and Mere. He finally sold his first Life Assurance to a farmer in Warminster, which earned him the princely sum of £60 in commission. He was exhausted and somewhat dispirited; clearly it was never going to be easy. Every Friday all twenty-six associates at the Salisbury branch gathered for a weekly meeting. The manager used this occasion to lift the spirits and fire up the team for the following week. While there, Terry was able to meet the others and hear their stories. Some were highly successful; others were at the bottom and sinking fast.

At least Terry had made one sale; many of the others had made none and sat looking very fed up and forlorn at the meetings.

Ann continued to have fortnightly visits to the hospital in order for them to check her foot. The wound had now healed, but was very red and the skin very thin. On a visit to the hospital in April 1976 the doctor pointed out a number of small pinhead sized pimples that had appeared on Ann's legs. They were secondary growths: there were just a few and it was decided they would destroy them by freezing them. This apparently was a new technique and was done with a gun like device that froze the growth with a blast of liquid nitrogen. The dedicated doctor froze each one by holding the device over the spot for a few seconds, and giving it a shot of nitrogen to kill it. The spot would discolour when it froze but the skin tissues recovered after a few days. Alarmingly, within two weeks many more spots began to grow and so the process continued in an attempt to wipe them out.

In the first month after the initial outbreak the numbers became much reduced, but poor Ann was suffering from the constant treatment to her legs.

Terry continued on the path of being a sales associate, but increasingly felt Ann had been right, it was not for him. It was tough only earning from commission and it had none of the creativity connected to his previous employment. However, he could see Ann was fighting a battle with cancer and did not need any other upsets so he continued to try and make it work.

Early in May Terry had a breakthrough. He had visited a small farm run by two elderly ladies that bred horses. The two ladies enjoyed a chat with him, discussing matters agricultural. They invited him into their typical farmhouse kitchen for tea. During the conversation they explained they didn't require life insurance at their age or indeed a pension plan.

However, one of them said, "If you can stop all these share certificate documents coming in our mail then we'd be so happy. We don't understand them and we're far too busy with the horses to bother. Do you understand them all?" she asked. "I'm sure you do! I'll go and get all the share certificates for you."

She arrived back with heaps of certificates and notifications all in a muddle. Terry took a quick look at them and really didn't understand them at all, but did realise that they certainly owned a great number of shares, some of high value.

"I think I'll take all these back to our office for checking," he said. "I'll then let you know how best we can approach this for you."

They were delighted that he was to take them away and get them sorted as they worried so much about them.

He took them back to the office and put them on the desk of the manager Richard. "What do you think we could do with this lot?"

He was flabbergasted. "Where on earth did you get all those from?"

"I met two ladies near Gillingham and they want them moved into something less demanding. They don't have the time or the inclination to deal with them and are fed up with the level of tax attached. I wondered about doing a share exchange scheme as I remember something about them from the training course."

Richard was speechless. "Do you realise that there are thousands of pounds of shares here."

"I thought there must be."

Richard and his team checked through all the certificates and drew up a valuation for Terry to present to the ladies so that they would know the total value of their holdings. He also suggested how, by putting the money into bonds it would be much easier for them, with no tax worries and a five percent tax-free income.

They were delighted and said, "Well done Terry, where do we have to sign?"

Indeed, Terry went on to sign them both up and was able to earn himself a considerable commission, which improved his finances with Tambro, providing him with a guarantee of being able to draw down income each month for the next few months. Not only that, but the following month he went on to sign-up other financial schemes for one of the sisters, much to the delight of his manager, Richard.

At home, with the arrival of the month of June, they had been asked by Major Rimmer if they might find somewhere else to live and vacate Church Street: they had been there for nearly six months and he was in need of his house during the summer, due to various family commitments. Terry agreed to seek another place to rent as soon as possible, the Major having been so kind in letting them have the house rent free for six months. With the uncertain income from Tambros he knew that he wouldn't be able to take on a mortgage. They were desperate and Terry was getting more and more depressed by the situation. There seemed to be nowhere that they could rent and as they approached Whitsun weekend, they were both as low as they could ever remember being.

"How about we go to the vicar's farewell party in the church hall tonight? We've been invited to attend," Ann suggested, hoping it might cheer Terry up a bit.

Richard Hurford, the Australian vicar of Tisbury, had been Rector for seven years and good for the village. He was going to become the Precentor of Christ Church Cathedral, Grafton, New South Wales. Everyone was sorry that he was returning to Australia. But somehow Terry was just too low to feel like going out to be jolly and happy with him and everyone else in the village.

"Come on it will do you good," Ann persisted.

"No, I don't think I can do it."

"Well I'm going to go, you can stay here and feel sorry for yourself if you like."

"Oh, all right," Terry relented, "if you really want to I'll come with you."

They set off to the village hall in the evening sunshine of Whit Saturday and joined the crowds there. Terry did not feel like being happy and chatty; all he could think about was how on earth he could ever get out of the situation they were trapped in. He was desperate and very low in spirits.

He started to chat to a quiet weedy looking man who was also standing around looking somewhat lost.

"So what do you do?" Terry asked him.

Not the most original line to start up a conversation.

"I'm in chemicals," he replied.

How grim, Terry thought, imagining him standing in a tub of chemicals, thinking back to his own experience in the Seychelles, when he was standing in chemicals. Well, in the septic tank to be exact!

"What about you?" the weedy man asked.

"We've recently returned from two years working in the Seychelles. It's necessary for us to live in the area for a while as my wife Ann is having treatment at Odstock Hospital, so we're renting a house on Church Street. Well, we were, but we have to leave and find somewhere else as the owner, a friend of ours, needs to have it back. So to be honest we are a bit stuck."

Suddenly the weedy man looked alive. "Really," he perked up.

"Yes, really," Terry replied.

"My wife and I are about to go to Hong Kong for two years," the weedy man explained, "and we are desperate to find someone who we can trust to rent our house and look after it while we're away. I don't suppose you'd be interested, would you?"

Terry couldn't believe his ears. So there is a God he thought, Alleluia!

The weedy man's wife joined them and introduced themselves as Chris and Mary Henderson. They lived at Oddford Vale a house just around the corner from Church Street. Terry quickly caught Ann's eye and called her over to explain the situation and introduce her to Chris and Mary.

After chatting, they arranged to go to their house the following day to see if they would find it suitable. If it has a roof Terry thought, then it's going to be suitable!

The next day they found that Chris and Mary had a delightful three bed roomed bungalow at the end of the cul de sac with a beautiful garden looking out onto a field. It had a lawn at the front and a lawn and a vegetable area at the rear. It was just perfect and they agreed to meet their solicitor in Salisbury to sign a proper agreement. They moved in on 17th July with great relief.

Although the small pimple like growths on Ann's leg had reduced in numbers during May, suddenly in June they began to cover her legs like a rash. Every week the doctor patiently treated her legs with the search and freeze policy. The speed at which they appeared was terrifying, yet Ann continued to remain very calm about the whole thing. Her legs became increasingly affected by the severity of the treatment, becoming very sore and scarred.

By the third week of July they seemed to be fighting a losing battle, more and more pimple growths had to be frozen off her legs. The skin was not healing quickly enough before more little growths began to grow. Her legs started to get infected with the constant barrage of treatment.

The doctors were very concerned about her and she found it increasingly difficult to walk. Only her grit and determination kept her going.

At the beginning of August the doctor told Terry that there was a serious danger that gangrene would set in, with the resulting consequences as the infection began to take over.

He was absolutely horrified and began to fear for Ann's life. He hated to see the stress and horror she was being subjected to; it was so repugnant.

What had she ever done wrong to be given this hideous suffering?

Ann was not going to give in to the ghastly situation, her brave fight giving Terry the courage to watch with disbelief as she was consumed by the anguish and distress of her situation, but never for herself, always for Terry and the children. It was they that drove her on and gave her a fearless resolve in the face of such a scary and repulsive condition.

He listened for her to complain, but it never came, never once did she ask, "Why me?" Ann maintained the serenity that was always hers every day of her life, tranquil and calm, uncomplaining, and Terry wanting to scream!

Aunty Lesley arrived to stay a week on 11th August, something they could have done without at that time. But she turned out to be a great comfort to her niece, just when she needed it the most.

On the 14th August her condition was desperate; her legs were both so badly affected by the cancerous spots and the continuous treatment they had received that a severe infection set in. The doctors called Terry in to discuss the situation.

"Mr Reeves, your wife's condition has gone wildly out of control; it is now a case of trying to save her legs. Her condition is now critical. We would like to bring her in for three days and give her large doses of a drug to knock out the infection before it poisons her system. It's our last resort; at the moment it is the infection that worries us the most."

"I see," Terry responded glumly.

"If you like to go with the nurse to your wife's room, I'll come and explain the situation to her, but I wanted to let you know first," the doctor told him.

They listened with absolute numbness to what the doctor had to say, as he explained to Ann what they were suggesting.

Ann listened calmly, but her face dropped when she knew that she had to be admitted into hospital. The doctor left them to discuss it for a few minutes.

As always her concerns were not for herself, but for the children and for Terry. "How will you cope with the children on your own? Can you pick them up from school? What about your work?"

"Don't even think about all that, just let the doctors do what they have to do. We'll be fine." he lied.

"You know what this means?" she said with tears running down her face. "Again we have to be apart and you know how much I hate it. It seems to be our destiny, being separated like this. Why I wonder. Why?"

"Yes, it does sometimes seem that way, but what can we do? I'll come tomorrow once things are sorted at home and stay the night if they'll let me. It's handy that Aunty Lesley is staying with us. I'm sure she'll extend her stay to help out for a few days, if necessary. I hate the separations too, but you have to be in hospital for this treatment."

With the aid of Aunty Lesley, he was able to stay two nights at the hospital, going home in the day to check that all was well, to keep Paul and Lynda in the picture and to alleviate their fears. The three days became four as Terry sat and watched the drugs drip into Ann's arm. He prayed to the God that grants us all life that Ann might be spared, if not for his sake, then for the sake of the children. Sleep never seems to feature in hospital life and Terry felt that he had not slept for days, but how could he complain when Ann was bravely sitting on the edge of life.

On the fourth day he went home to collect fresh clothes for Ann and to get some rest. His nerves were on edge and he was desperate for sleep. He was told to return around 3pm.

Leaving dear Aunty to collect the children from the bus after school, he set off once more for the hospital. Heading off to where Ann was in a small side ward, a nurse stopped him and asked him to come to the doctor's consulting room. He sat waiting there, feeling cold and clammy. What now he thought, it's never good news to be asked to wait and see the doctor. He just wanted to go and see how Ann was.

"Mr Reeves. I've some news for you. As you know we have been fighting a severe infection in your wife's legs. I'm pleased to tell you that it appears we are winning and the infection is under control. But that's not all. We don't understand why, but the growths that were constantly appearing on her legs have now stopped completely. There is absolutely no recurrence of them, not a single one where as before they were growing like a rash. We are all baffled. We have never come across this before and can only assume that it's due to the infection in someway."

"That's all good news, isn't it?" Terry asked.

"Indeed it is. We will continue to monitor her condition and we'd like her to come in every three days for the next two weeks. Can you do that?"

"Yes, yes, of course I can."

"When the nurse is ready you can take her home, after all your children will want to see her."

"Many thanks, Doctor. I'll go and see her now and tell her we are going home. That will be the very best medicine yet for her."

Ann's health went from strength to strength over the next few months. Amazingly her legs healed showing little sign of all she had been through. She continued to have check-ups at the hospital, but all was well; they felt a great relief, allowing life to go on as normal. They enjoyed house sitting for Chris and Mary in Tisbury, always aware that they would, one day, over the next two years need to consider what they would do in the future.

A number of friends and family come to stay who all shared their relief that the cancer had been knocked out and they were able to have a normal life again. Terry took on an allotment at the rear of Church Street and Ann become involved with St John's Anglican Church taking the children for Sunday School and later in the year she was confirmed into the church. She had never previously been much of a churchgoer, despite the time she had spent in Africa, living with missionaries. Terry attended the Catholic Church in Tisbury, but would often join her at various services and events.

He was increasingly aware that the assurance business was not where his future lay. It had been interesting, but he was no salesman and was never going to be able to make the fortunes he had been led to believe were there for the taking. He hated not knowing each month whether he would have any commission or not to receive pay from; he could not live like that.

Apart from anything else he missed the contact with agriculture, the people and the countryside; he knew he had to start to look around for something else.

The large commissions he had received from sorting out the two sisters were fast running out as he withdrew £300 a month from his commission pot. It was just not working for him, he was not bringing in the business. By the end of November his commission was all used up, unless he brought in new business by the cut-off date for the December payments, then he would receive nothing. The family's Christmas was beginning to look as if it might be like Bob Cratchet's.

Terry increased his time out and about during November, trying to find business, revisiting all those that he'd spoken to in the past that had shown an interest in what he was proposing for them, but nothing. He looked every where he could, spoke to anyone likely to lead him to new contracts, still nothing. By Friday 26th November he arrived at the weekend exhausted. He had failed to sign up anyone all month, his commission bowl was empty and Christmas was looking bleak; he began to envy the turkeys.

He had only two days before the deadline for contracts to be in, to earn commission payable in December. On Monday he had an appointment with a farmer whom he had never met before, so not very hopeful there. On Tuesday he had another appointment with a farmer in East Stour, but he had rung to cancel the meeting. It was all looking rather hopeless. He dare not even think of how he would face Paul and Lynda at Christmas.

On the Monday he went along to meet a farmer from Charlton Horethorne, who had a 350-acre farm. He said how he was in a hurry so Terry quickly went through how he could protect his farm from the taxman in the event of his death. He explained that by taking out a Life Assurance in trust for his children the proceeds could be used to pay the inheritance tax, without having to sell off any of the land. He valued the farm, the stock and everything on it and worked out that the farmer would need to pay a premium of £350 a year to protect himself and the farm from the taxman.

"Ok," he said, "where do I sign? I've wanted to do something like this for a long time. You're the first person that has explained it in straightforward English. I have to go now, so let me sign the papers and you can fill me in on the details next Tuesday. Is that all right?"

Terry quickly produced the forms required, had him sign them and give him a cheque for the first premium. With that Mr Gooding left and asked Terry to close the door on his way out, once he had completed the forms!

Terry sat there in amazement; little did Mr Gooding know what he had done. Not only had he put his own business in a safe position for his family, he had also provided enough commission from the sale for Terry and his family to enjoy a good Christmas and right on the last possible day. Terry drove straight to the office on Milford Street with the papers to make sure they were processed that day in order for the commission to be credited to his account, ready for pay out in December. One thing for sure he never wanted to go through such an experience again. It was time to plan his route out and in the New Year he would be looking to see how he might move back into agricultural management again and perhaps if Ann were happy about it, to take up their dream to return to work in Africa, now that their troubles were behind them.

1977 started out all over the country with a sparkle: it was the year of the Queen's Silver Jubilee, when millions of people were to line the streets of London to watch the Queen and Duke on their way to St Paul's to start the celebrations. It gave a much needed lift to the people's sprits with the exception of the Manager of Manchester United, Tommy Docherty, who was sensationally sacked.

Terry started his year continuing to try and make a living from Tambro Life, while at the same time seeking a way out. He and Ann discussed their plight and agreed that they wanted to revert to their life's dream, to live and work in Africa. There were a few jobs around in East Africa but none really as suitable as the one advertised in the Farmers' Weekly of 8th April 1977.

A Farm Manager was required at the University of Malawi, Bunda College of Agriculture, Central Africa. There was one big problem, one that Terry had often found to be a stumbling block when applying for top jobs. They wanted someone with a degree!

"Just a minute, don't give in so easily," Ann said looking at the advert. "This is the perfect job for you and it's a wonderful agricultural country."

"I know," Terry said, "but I don't have a degree."

"If you read it carefully, it says should have a degree, not <u>must</u> have," Ann observed.

"You know you're right," Terry agreed. "It's worth having a go. It's a great post and in a very peaceful country and not too far for us to go and visit Tanzania sometime. You're a genius to notice that. Do you know that?"

"Should you ask your doctor about this first? See what they say. I know it's over six months now since all your health problems and the cancer, but we should get their view."

"Yes, ok I'll ask them next time I go," Ann agreed reluctantly.

Terry sent off three written applications to the University of Malawi, in Zomba, Malawi, together with his curriculum vitae and the names of three referees as requested. He was also asked to send a copy to the Inter-University Council on Tottenham Court Road, London that was fronting the appointment. He duly sent them off and waited. He hardly dare think that he might get an interview.

On 18th April he received a letter from the Inter-University Council in London, acknowledging his application and telling him that he would only hear further if the University had placed him on the short list of candidates for interview. On 22nd April he received another letter, this time from the Registrar at the University of Malawi telling him his application would be considered along with all the others and that he would hear from them again as soon as this process was complete, warning that it may take time. Then it was a waiting game.

On 9th June he received another letter from the Inter-University Council in London telling him he'd been short-listed and would be invited to an interview towards the end of the month. This duly followed when on 21st June he was invited to meet the Advisory Selection Committee on Thursday 14th July 1977 for an interview at 10.25am.

"I think this job has your name on it," Ann said, as she walked with Terry to the railway station at Tisbury where he was to catch the train to London. "I'm so excited."

"Me too," he replied, "a dream come true if we do pull it off."

Terry always found it particularly exciting to be interviewed for a job in London. There was something about being in the hub of things that really inspired and excited him. He arrived in London at 9.15am and made his way to Tottenham Court Road. There really was a special feel to being in the centre of London at the door of a new adventure into Africa. It awoke all his senses; he was determined not to let this one get away, whatever the opposition that lay before him at the interview.

As he was in plenty of time he walked up to the top of the road to view the Post Office Tower. He had heard much about it, but had never before seen it. He then walked back to number 90-91, the offices of the Inter-University Council on the first floor, introduced himself to reception and sat in the waiting area as instructed. He sat in the window looking down on the busy street below. He noticed a Rolls Royce flying a flag pull in outside the office. A large African man stepped out and walked across the pavement to the office. A few minutes later the door opened and he walked in to the large waiting area where Terry was sitting and then into another room. I wonder who that is Terry thought to himself.

After a few minutes Terry was called to his interview. He entered a long narrow room with a table down the middle. Nine people sat around the long table and at the head, opposite Terry, sat the African that he had seen arrive earlier.

They in turn fired questions at Terry about his past experiences and about his work in Tanzania and the Seychelles in particular. The African gent just sat there looking ahead at Terry, but never asked a single question.

"Mr. Reeves," said one of the board members, "I see you don't have a degree, only a Diploma in Agriculture."

"That's correct, but I'm a practical farmer. If it's someone to manage and run the farm profitably and in so doing teach the students, then I can do it. You'll see from my C.V. that I've managed other farms successfully; I don't consider a degree necessary to do that, as my history proves. I love Africa and its people and I'd like the opportunity to take on the University farm making it a leader in the country, and an example to others, putting Malawi University at the top in agricultural education."

They were all very quiet after that little speech from Terry; he hoped he had not overdone it. They asked him if there was anything else he wanted to know about the post or about Malawi. He asked a few questions about education for Paul and Lynda, numbers of students at the university, medical care and other general matters and left it at that. They thanked him for travelling up to London and told him that they would be writing in due course.

Terry left feeling that he'd given it his best shot, but he was a little unsure about the African Minister who had sat there the whole time motionless without saying a word!

He then took the underground train to Westminster that he liked to visit and where he always felt the wonderful sense of history about the place. He couldn't avoid popping into Westminster Abbey to sit alongside the tomb of his friend Dr Livingstone, while pondering the day's events. Somehow it seemed the only place to do it, like going to tell an old friend, especially one that had his roots in Africa. Then he set off to return to Tisbury and report the day's events to Ann who was waiting excitedly at home.

Terry's sales at Hambros did not progress much, but he kept his head above water. In fact, for most of July and part of August Terry was the branch leader in commission earned. Much of that was due to the reinvestments from the ladies at Gillingham.

As the days past since his interview in London, Terry felt the chances of his being appointed as Farm Manager for the University of Malawi were slipping away. His heart sank with every postman that passed the door.

Their friends Pat and Dave came to stay for a week on 15th August so that gave them a much needed lift. They knew what it was to work overseas and the frustrations of waiting for things to happen. Perhaps it was appropriate that on 17th August, a telegram arrived from the Registrar of the University of Malawi offering Terry the job.

"Offer you Bunda Farm Manager K3627 p.a. plus BESS supplementation of £3754 p.a. if eligible. Plus gratuity. Cable reaction – letter follows." Registrar University Office Zomba Malawi

They were all sitting around the kitchen table enjoying morning coffee as Terry opened the telegram, knowing what it was, but not knowing what it said. Ann, Pat and Dave held their breath as they watched his expression.

"That's it then," he said with a beaming smile. "We are off to Malawi!"

Silence fell as everyone stared at each other! Not a cry of excitement as one might have expected, just a stunned silence. Pat broke the stillness. "Well, that is good news."

"Yes, congratulations," Dave said, "we'll be all right now for our holidays!"

Ann looked across at Terry with a half smile on her face, which said," Yes, you did it."

Terry, too, was so delighted and relieved; he saw Malawi with its agriculture, as his country, made for him. He was so pleased to have this wonderful opportunity, even more so to have got out of the financial world, back into the career that suited him best.

Then, as anyone that has ever gone to work overseas will know, the fun started: the endless chores until the day you leave, medical examinations, vaccinations and malaria precautions to organise, a new contract to negotiate and agree, and the old contract with Tambro's to break, employment permits to arrange and immigration clearances to obtain, shipping and shopping and banking, and a thousand other such tasks. All that, and the emotion of leaving and saying goodbye to everyone had to be coped with, as well as their own personal fear. Yes, fear! But it was very exciting.

Chapter Sixteen

The reverse of joy is sadness: in many ways the greater the joy, the deeper the sadness. November brought with it one of the saddest events in anybody's life, the day when their mother dies. It is true what they say, that when anyone dies, a part of you always seems to die with them, especially when they have been close to you, but when you lose your mother that is really something.

Terry's mother, Daisy, had been unwell for only a few months as far as he knew. He had been to visit her a number of times to take her out on trips to Portland, which she loved to visit, and to the sea front at Weymouth, to sit in the car and have a change of scene. He was not aware of anything seriously wrong with her. Early in November while at home she took a turn for the worse and was taken into the Weymouth hospital.

On Friday 4th November Terry went along to the Weymouth and District Hospital at 6.00pm to see her. She was either in a deep sleep or under the effect of drugs, but Terry could feel that she was not long for this world. He sat with her for a while holding her hand, trying to reassure her that all would be well, that God needed her and was calling her home. Her breathing was rapid and he feared the worse, but there was no conversation between them. At 7.30 he left the hospital to return to Tisbury, where Aunty Evie, Daisy's sister-in-law from Horsham, was due to arrive and stay for a few days in order to visit her.

On his drive home, overwhelmed with grief, Terry realised his mother was dying, and he cried and prayed for her all the way home to Tisbury, that dark wet evening. At 9.30pm a phone call from the hospital confirmed that she had in fact just died.

She had been very upset that her end was near at such a comparatively young age of sixty-five. She felt very let down by God. She loved her grandchildren, Anna-Marie fourteen years and Craig eleven, Paul seven and Lynda five. They were just at an age when they were giving her so much pleasure. She was disappointed and upset at not being able to go on being with them, to watch them grow into adults. She wanted that so much, but was to be deprived of it, making her feel understandably bitter.

Terry grieved for the loss of his Mum, sad that she had been snatched away from them at such an early age. Her life had never been easy. All she ever had and loved most were her own children and grandchildren. It was not at all surprising that she hurt so much when the time came for her to say goodbye.

Daisy's mother, an illiterate under-house parlour maid from a family of fourteen, had been forced to give up her and her twin brother to a children's home at birth, where they remained until classified as adults. Daisy didn't even know that she had a twin brother, Arthur, until she was eighteen. They had both lived in separate children's homes, as was the way in those times. It was always assumed they had been the result of an upstairs downstairs relationship. Someone had financed their years in the children's home, someone of considerable means.

Later in her young adult years a Mrs Stone from Easton, Portland, adopted Daisy. She wanted someone to do the work in her bed and breakfast business and to adopt a child was a useful source of free labour about the house. Daisy's life did not go on to be much easier, she craved the love of family life but was not to find it with her newly adopted mother. Her life was never easy with Mr and Mrs Stone, but that is another rich and sad story.

A lot of goodbyes had to be said before Terry and Ann could leave for Malawi. Their parents yes, but the one Terry dreaded the most was having to say goodbye to a very special lady, whom he had always known as Aunty Potton. She was now eighty-one years old. She had befriended his mum during the war years, having looked after Esmee, his sister, for the first five years of her life and followed them both in all they did in a special mother-like way. In turn they loved her, having been very close to her every day of their lives. It was hard to say farewell and when he kissed her goodbye, he gave her such a hug on parting, both instinctively knowing in their hearts that they were unlikely ever to see each other again.

She died less than nine months later, on 7th October 1978, two days after her eighty-second birthday, while Terry was in Africa.

Her death opened a secret that rocked the family to its core. It also created a date in Terry's life that for reasons yet unknown to him would become very significant.

Terry found it especially hard having to leave his father, so soon after his Mother's death. Frank continued to live at the family home at 1 Tennyson Road, Weymouth, enjoying pretty good health. At least he had his daughter Esmee who lived nearby and cared for him and his needs and he enjoyed going out and about, not being one to sit at home alone. Terry felt that his being in Africa would give his Dad a new interest in following his life and experiences.

At that time there was another sadness for the world, when it had to say farewell to Charlie Chaplin, the comic genius of silent films, aged eighty-eight years, the passing of a long celebrated and funny man.

Perhaps 1978, which came in with less sparkle than 1977, would prove to be a happier year for everyone.

As the year came towards its close everything was set for Terry and Ann's new life and adventure in Malawi.

On 24th January 1978, Terry, Ann, Paul and Lynda set off on the Super VC10, Flight BA 141 at 5pm from London Heathrow, to embark on their new life, to follow their 'calling' to live and work in Africa. Their long-standing dream and desire had at last come to fruition. There had been so many difficult hurdles and serious obstacles to overcome to get to that point, but there they were, at last, and so happy to reach out into the future and their new life in Africa.

They flew over the south coast of England at dusk, with lovely views of the Isle of Wight, over Paris and Italy, then Cairo, to land at Khartoum at 1am local time. It was seventy-seven degrees, a bleak little airport in the middle of the desert, not awfully desirable, but they were impressed with the strict security.

They flew mile upon mile across open bush country, all seemingly uninhabited. The Sahara desert laid out before them; the full moon illuminating the barren land with the Nile snaking its way eerily through the landscape.

They had decided that as they were passing near to Tanzania on the way to Malawi, they would take the opportunity to make a return visit to the Hombolo Leprosy Centre, another long-held dream. They arranged to stop in Dar es Salaam for two nights and then take the Air Tanzania plane inland to Dodoma. It was an exciting prospect returning to the very place where they had met and fallen in love, back in 1966 and they looked forward to it with delight.

Ann had, with her Sunday school group, raised some £43 to take out to Hombolo to give to the mission for their use, a gift from the children of Tisbury.

They arrived in Dar es Salaam ('Haven of Peace') at 6.45am, a little late, on the morning of 25th January 1978. The flight had been somewhat bumpy over Africa, but nobody had been sick. It was only half full so they had plenty of room to spread themselves out and to get some sleep. The airline staff were very helpful with the children and gave them their meals first. They also provided colouring books and crayons, which made all the difference. Paul and Lynda loved it and were so excited by the whole experience.

A very tedious customs and immigration department slowed their progress through the airport at Dar, causing queues. There was no sense of hurry or urgency. The customs officer asked Terry if he had any coloured televisions in his luggage!

They made their way to the Motel Agip in the city centre. It was wonderful to feel the breath of Africa on them again, the warmth and humidity of Dar es Salaam, always intense at that time of the year. Their room was not yet ready so they ordered some refreshments. They waited over an hour for a glass of rather weak lemon juice and a cup of tea so strong the spoon could stand up in it!

After they all had a nap in their air-conditioned room they explored the city, as far as they could with two young children and looked at places they had both known from their last stay in Dar in the mid sixties, playing the, "Do you remember?" .... game.

Dar depressed them with its scruffiness; things had really deteriorated in the years since they were last there. Nothing was available in the shops even the bookshops were empty. They couldn't get an airmail letter and stamps had only just come in after a long break. Everything was a luxury, a dreadful state of affairs. Whisky was twenty pounds a bottle, not that they were looking to buy it! They were so pleased they were only passing through and that they had not saved for years to go to Dar es Salaam for an exotic holiday!

It was really hard to believe it was all happening: the changeover from Tisbury to this tropical city had happened so quickly once they accepted the job. On the following Friday, the 27th January they arranged for a taxi to collect them from the hotel to take them to the airport. There they would catch the Air Tanzania plane to Dodoma where George Hart was to meet them and take them out to Hombolo.

A rather beaten up old taxi arrived at the Motel Agip to collect them early that morning. The happy Tanzanian driver greeted them with a "Jambo Bwana" and loaded their cases in the car.

"Habari Bwana?" (How are you). "Where am you a going to please?" he enquired.

"To the airport, asante." (thank-you) We are going to Dodoma," Terry replied.

"So you know Tanzania?"

"Yes a little, we used to work here at a Leprosy Centre north of Dodoma in the sixties."

"It is good you come again to be with us. Welcome!"

The driver drove off through the streets of Dar up Nkrumah Street to the airport. As they approached the airport, three armed soldiers stepped out in front of the taxi, pointing their guns at them.

"Stop! Stop!" they screamed at the driver.

He skidded to a halt and leapt from the car.

"It's OK. It's Ok," he shouted at the soldiers. "You can have anything you like from me."

He looked terrified and Terry and family were none too happy either as they watched the event unfold.

The soldiers pointed their guns at Terry and screamed, "Get out of the car."

He, Ann and the children quickly obeyed their demands. Paul and Lynda stood there at the side of the road, clutching their teddies in fear.

They were all rooted to the spot as the soldiers searched the car. The driver was dancing around excitedly, saying something in Swahili to the soldiers and waving his arms around.

One of the soldiers came over to Terry and with his gun indicating that he wanted him to go to the back of the car where the second soldier was standing. Terry was reluctant to be separated from Ann and the children, but at the same time wanted to do as they asked so as not to upset them unduly.

They asked Terry to take out the cases and open them, this he did, feeling very uncomfortable at having to do it at gunpoint. They poked around in the contents, showing little interest. They ordered Terry to put them back in the boot again. Meanwhile their taxi driver was still dancing around screaming and shouting at the soldiers.

Terry, without invitation, then went back to put his arms around Ann and the children, while awaiting the soldiers' next move. The three armed soldiers approached them, went up to Lynda taking her teddy from her and examined it closely then did the same to Paul and gave them back after having carried out an intense examination of the bears.

With that, they waved them into the car, the driver too. He roared off to the airport buildings a few meters away and stopped outside the departure area.

"What was all that about?" Terry asked the taxi driver.

"Bwana, you have to understand, this is Africa! I go now. I go now. You no pay, no pay, too much trouble. I go."

But Terry gave the driver a handful of notes, "You must have this and thank you."

"Thank you English. I sorry, I sorry," he said, leapt in his car and took off at high speed towards Dar es Salaam. (Haven of Peace?)

They never knew what it was all about, but were only pleased to have got out of the situation and glad to be inside the safety of the airport buildings to check in for their flight to Dodoma.

They sat in the departure lounge having been through all the checks. There were no other passengers to be seen. 10.30am, the time for departure came and went. At 11am Terry went to ask why there was a delay and at what time their flight would leave for Dodoma.

"The plane it is broke," the lady replied.

"I see, so when will the flight now take place?"

"It should be ready for you in three days," she replied casually!

"So what do we do now?" Terry asked the lady.

She just shook her shoulders and walked away.

Terry took this information to Ann, still recovering from being held at gunpoint.

"Whatever are we going to do now?" she asked.

"Perhaps we should return to our hotel and seek other flights." Terry suggested. "We may even have to cancel our visit to Hombolo and go on to Malawi next week as planned. That would be so disappointing, but it's no good staying here. Come on, let's get a taxi back to the Motel Agip."

They staggered into the Hotel again in the heat of the day and enquired if they could have their room back as their flight had been cancelled.

"No sir, I'm sorry the hotel is fully booked for the next few days. You'll have to try somewhere else."

"Guess what?" Terry reported to Ann. "The place is booked. I'll have to go and find somewhere else. You stay here with the children and I'll go and see what I can find. First, lets have some food and some cold drinks; it's so hot and sticky here."

After they'd taken a snack at the Motel Agip, Terry set off to look around the city in search of a room for them all, rather then try and use the telephone system. He felt it better to do that before sorting out flights to Dodoma, it was hot and everyone was feeling a bit on edge, and it was unlikely they would get another flight that day.

He went from one hotel to another; everywhere was booked. There was apparently a political gathering in the city so all the rooms were taken, or held in case a politician wanted to have one. Exhausted in the humid conditions, Terry returned to Motel Agip to check how Ann and the children were coping.

"It's no good, every where's fully booked, what on earth are we going to do?" he exclaimed.

They had another cup of thick brown tea, and fanta for the children, and asked reception for the local phone book. As they were skimming through the accommodation lists they noticed the Salvation Army listed.

"I never knew they worked overseas," Terry said. "Let's give them a ring."

He spoke to a lady who told him they had plenty of rooms and to go along immediately. She told him they had a restaurant too. It sounded perfect. As they were about to gather up their cases to go and get a taxi, a member of the hotel staff approached them.

"Are you Mr and Mrs Reeves?" the man asked,

"Yes we are."

"There is a message for you at reception."

Whoever can that be, they wondered, as nobody even knew they were there. On picking up the message they found it was from George Hart in Dodoma. He had of course been to meet the plane, only to find that it had been cancelled. He therefore arranged for the Mission Aviation Fellowship (MAF) who had a small plane flying up from Dar to Dodoma the next day to pick them up. MAF would fly them direct into Hombolo Leprosy Centre. He instructed Terry and family to catch the plane at 10.30 the following morning at Dar es Salaam airport.

Since the 60's George had built a dirt airstrip for the MAF plane to drop in with supplies and take out any really sick people for treatment elsewhere. This was fantastic news. How amazing to be flown into the Leprosy Centre. What excitement.

They took a taxi to the Salvation Army centre where they were given a small but clean room in a purpose built area. It had wooden shutters on the small windows and was very hot inside, but they made the best of it. At least they had somewhere to spend the night. It was a lifesaver. The food was excellent, well prepared and served in a large clean hall. They were always grateful to the Salvation Army for taking them in that night and from that day on were great supporters of them, a wonderful Christian body, who really do care about people and try to do something to help.

The following morning they made their way to the airport to pick up their MAF flight. They were greeted there by the Australian piliot and put on board a small six-seater Cessna aircraft. Terry sat next to the pilot, with Ann and the children behind and the cases behind that. It was tiny inside; they had never before been in such a small aircraft. For Terry sitting next to the pilot with earphones on, it was a new and terrifying experience. The plane taxied out on to the runway, looking like a fly amongst the large jet planes that surrounded them.

It was 11am as the plane 5H-MPX lifted up into the blue sky leaving Dar es Salaam with all its problems behind. It was a bumpy noisy ride as the little plane rode the hot air currents, rising up from the green plains below. Ann became very sick and Terry tried not to look at her too much for fear of her starting him off. It was exciting to fly over the African bush, recalling its long history but little progress. As the plane approached Hombolo they tried to spot something familiar. The first thing they saw was the lake next to the Leprosy Centre: it had been formed in 1957 by placing a dam at one end. This allowed them to collect water for irrigation and drinking, to breed fish and provide a source of protein. The plane circled around until the clearing at the north of the centre could be seen. They gently dropped from 6,000 ft and touched down onto the dirt runway at 2pm. As the plane rattled along and finally drew to a halt, the pilot turned off the engines. Terry opened his door, aware of the green all around and the absolute silence. They had come home.

They almost fell out of the plane, as a land rover approached. George and Joan were there to welcome them back to Hombolo after twelve years away. It was an emotional moment for them all with much hand shaking and hugging going on. George was keen to show them around and to explain all the changes since they were last there. Terry had difficulty orientating himself, not unexpected after such a long time away. However, he soon recognised a few things and gradually put it all together in his mind.

That evening, George and Terry sat enjoying the sunset together on an old tree trunk by the rain gauge outside George and Joan's house, like two old friends who had never been apart.

"Well, mate, how's the old place feel to you? Is it good to be back home?" George enquired having ushered Terry all around the farm, proudly showing him all the improvements that had taken place.

"Is it good being back in Africa? Are you going to make this your life?" George asked in his usual quizzical manner.

"Is this God's plan for you do you think?"

"You know George, you are the first person to ask me that and I guess the only person who really knows me well enough to ask such a question."

"So what's the answer then, mate? Don't forget I saw you grow up here, grow up and mature. You were the son that I never had. You'll never know how I wanted you to stay and work here alongside me. We were such a good team, you and I. In our short time together we grew close and not many people can I say that about?

Do you remember what you wrote in our visitors' book when you left in November 1966 after your year as a VSO?

'From Boyhood to Manhood.' Never truer words, mate."

"Oh yes, I had forgotten that," Terry replied, smiling at the thought of what he had written all those years ago.

"We've always been honest with each other George, sharing our deepest thoughts. I'm happy that you enjoyed our time together, short as it was. I certainly did. The year I spent here was the most profound of my life and shaped it for all time. I grew in respect for the work and sacrifices you had to make, battling against the odds and all in the name of Christ. It was an inspiration."

"You asked if we're going to make this our life here in Africa. Well, Ann and I have given it much thought over the years; our hearts are definitely in Africa. We've felt that we were being pushed along that path and despite all the obstacles that we've had to overcome, particularly Ann with the cancer she had to fight, we still want to work here. So yes, I do feel it's God's hand on our life. It's what he wants us to do, and we both feel that, our destiny you may say."

"Following the way of Christ is never easy, mate, but if we can help these people in this country and show them the face of Christ, then we'll have done the right thing, even if, after we have all gone home it falls apart. We are sowing seeds here, mate, in more ways then one."

"Come on its getting dark and we still have some nasty beasts here that would love to eat you, fresh meat from the old country. Not to mention the snakes, hope you haven't forgotten them."

"Do you remember that time when ....?"

They walked back slowly to the house, in the fast fading light of the day, deep in conversation. Terry in his white trousers and hat and George in his usual khaki shorts and slouch hat, with long brown leather boots laced up to his knees: unlikely friends from opposite ends of the world, sharing a very special moment of friendship, deep in the African bush, two people that had influenced each other's lives so much in the past and would go on to do so again. But that event was as unimaginable to George, as it was to Terry and was hidden in the future.

Terry and Ann enjoyed walking around Hombolo and remembering the early days when they were both young and single. They visited their old houses, pausing in thought at the spot where they had both sat having afternoon tea, the day he told Ann how he felt about her. They went into Ann's Occupational Therapy building, built during her time at Hombolo, amazed at the trees that had since grown around it. They looked around the hospital chatting to some of the leprosy patients, also around the farm looking at this and that and remembering.

Unfortunately they had just missed Dawn and Guy who had left the year before, after fourteen years of service at Hombolo, having originally agreed to come for two years! They had now retired to the Blue Mountains of eastern Australia, as indeed had Win Preston, the nurse.

The two clear days at Hombolo were a wonderful experience, but it was time for Ann, Terry and family to leave, returning to Dar es Salaam to embark on the next part of their journey and to their new life in Malawi.

George and Joan took them in the Land Rover from Hombolo along the muddy, rutted and bumpy roads to Dodoma. There they waited at the Dodoma Hotel sipping cool drinks on the veranda, before going to the airport for the Air Tanzania flight back to Dar, due to depart at 6pm.

It was sad to leave George and Joan when the time came to say goodbye, but it had been wonderful to spend time with them again, to reminisce and to see Hombolo Leprosy Centre once more.

Two more days were spent with ex Seychelles' friends Lyn and Ross in Dar es Salaam, before flying out to Blantyre, Malawi, on Friday 3rd February 1978.

They arrived at midday. The country was very green and well cultivated, as they looked down from the plane. All international flights to Malawi flew into Blantyre in those days; from there they took the Air Malawi plane up country to Lilongwe, about an hour's journey. As the plane dropped down into Lilongwe Airport at 18.00 hours the light was fading. They were met by the Executive Officer of the University who was holding a card with their names on it.

"Mr Reeves, I'm your executive officer, Mr Jumea. I've come to take you to Bunda College. Follow me please to the Land Rover."

Mr Jumea quickly loaded the cases into the back and they set off the fourteen miles to Bunda College University Farm and Campus. The first three miles took them along tarmac roads around the edge of the city. It looked very modern and a great deal of money had clearly been invested in new buildings and landscaping, making it like any European city. They travelled on through to the old town of Lilongwe, which was more typically African, with its dukas (shops) and Indian shops lining the streets. The road took them south onto the Blantyre road out of Lilongwe. After a few miles they turned off the main road to bump along a dirt road, full of holes and corrugations. There was well-cultivated land on each side of the road with small mud houses scattered amongst the crops of maize and tobacco. Darkness was falling and the African night taking over.

Terry and Ann said nothing, sitting in the dark as they bumped along the road, both were wondering just what sort of accommodation they would find at Bunda, following their terrible experience in the Seychelles. It could only be better they felt! By this time everyone was feeling tired. Paul and Lynda had done so well and enjoyed the experience of the past few weeks, but were ready to settle and have their own rooms in the new house.

The journey to Bunda College took nearly an hour. They finally drove into the campus which was, surprisingly, lit by mains electricity; apart from the college buildings it was an area of houses and roads lined with hedges, the main college buildings on one-side, houses on the other. As they drove along they noticed numbers on a post outside the drive of every house. Their house was number 16, where they turned off the road down a driveway some twenty metres long to the bungalow that was to be their home. There was a small house on the left of the drive that was the houseboy's dwelling, surrounded by a green hedge. The Land Rover pulled up in front of the brick-built bungalow, set in a beautiful large garden.

"This is your house," Mr Jumea announced. "It's very nice. Yes?"

"Thank you," both Terry and Ann replied with some relief, "it's very nice. Yes."

At the door of the bungalow was a short and smart looking Malawian man wearing a white apron, looking out at them through the darkness.

"Greetings, I'm John. I'm your cook-houseboy. I cook and I clean the house for you, very much clean. I have cooked for you this evening rice and roasted chicken. I bring your cases, thank you. How is England?"

"Hello, John, we're pleased to meet you." Terry replied. "England is very cold; we're enjoying the sunshine of Malawi." They both replied shaking his hand. "Thanks for preparing such a lovely meal. We've had a long day and we're ready to eat."

"But first we would like to look around the house. These are our children, Paul and Lynda. They are so excited and ready to explore the place."

"It is how you wish Bwana? I am ready to serve you please in ten minutes."

"That's perfect," Ann replied, "and thank you so much." Paul and Lynda rushed into the house running from room to room; they were so full of energy and delighted to see their bedroom was large, light and airy. They could not wait to see the garden, but it was too dark to see far. There was a large long kitchen with plenty of workspace. It had a door into the dining area and there was also a useful serving hatch.

The living and dining area were all one, but very spacious indeed and all the floors were of polished smooth concrete. The rooms all contained the usual hard furnishings, right down to a writing desk in the corner of the sitting area. There was a floor to ceiling window looking onto the garden and a large brick fireplace. Apparently in August you needed to have a log fire when the evening temperatures fell for about six weeks. Another door took them out onto the veranda that looked down the long wide garden, currently in darkness.

There were three large bedrooms each with a mosquito net draped over a large metal frame, looking rather like a four-poster bed. The main bedroom had two single beds butted together under one large net. Off the corridor to the bedrooms there was a huge bathroom with rows of cupboards. Throughout the house the windows were covered with weld-mesh in order to deter burglars: this allowed you to have the windows open by night reasonably safely. Pole burglars were a problem, like everywhere in Africa. They would put a long pole with a hook on the end through the bars of the weld-mesh, to pick up anything like trousers and handbags and with their other hand remove items of value, replacing the hooked item where they had found it so you would never realise.

"Come on, let's eat. I'm starving," Ann suggested. "This is all absolutely amazing, isn't it, and dinner prepared too? I think I could get used to this way of life quite quickly."

"Yes! Me too as there is no washing-up. Good for John." Terry laughed.

They enjoyed the wonderful roast chicken meal that John had prepared for them and were overjoyed with the first impressions of their new home.

"This is how it should be, not like we found it in the Seychelles," Terry commented. "I think we're going to enjoy it here. I can't wait to see the garden. It looks vast. Paul and Lynda will love that."

"It'll all look much better once our boxes and trunks arrive from the U.K. with our belongings and we've put a few rugs down on this concrete floor. In the meantime," Ann said, "I'll make new curtains throughout the whole house. These look very tired, don't they? I'm sure someone will let me use their sewing machine until mine arrives. It's so good to have a houseboy-cook already employed here for us. It'll take some getting used to, having someone around again, but so necessary in the heat and of course it provides employment. John seems very pleasant, doesn't he?"

The University had provided bedding, until their own arrived, so they quickly made up all the beds, then it was time for Paul and Lynda to try out the new bath and snuggle up for the night in their new beds. They seemed very content and chatted away until sleep overcame them.

"What an exciting few weeks it's been," Ann said, as she and Terry sat on the veranda wall outside with a well earned gin and tonic in their hands, listening to the crickets. "All a bit of a dream really, leaving Tisbury, going to Dar es Salaam, returning to Hombolo, flying in a small plane across Africa and then arriving here. My head is spinning. But you know, it has certainly been the right thing for us to do, don't you agree?"

"Without a doubt, no question; it's what we always wanted and dreamed of doing. A bit daunting taking on the new job, but in a way that's going to be the easy bit," Terry replied.

"Tomorrow if you like, I'll get a lift to Lilongwe with Choen Sichinga who has been acting as Farm Manager. Apparently he's coming to see me here in the morning to fill me in and help in any way. Felix Pereira, the last manager, left a few months ago, I understand, so there's been a bit of a 'holding job' going on until they found a new Manager. I'll get some supplies to keep us going, open a bank account and research the purchase of a car for us. Apparently good second-hand cars are difficult to find, a bit like it was in the Seychelles. It's a case of if you see one, buy it, as it might be a long time before you see another!"

"Good idea," Ann said. "I'll go and meet some of the neighbours around, find out about schools, and sort out things here a bit."

They enjoyed sitting in the darkness under the stars. There was no light pollution, giving them the full benefit of the African sky lit by a million, million stars that went on forever. It was awe inspiring and reminded them just why they loved Africa so much and why they'd returned to make it their life. The last quarter of the moon was showing on its back in the clear night sky, the Southern Cross visible to the south, something never seen in the northern hemisphere. The drums rang out giving their urgent message for those that understood their beat. They were totally immersed in their surroundings, hypnotised by the mysterious voices of the African night, intoxicated by its evocative smells that stimulated all the senses. They were both without doubt still very much in love with Africa.

Surprisingly they all slept well in their new beds. Sleeping inside a mosquito net always felt a bit like being in a tent, but you did feel very secure knowing that no insects could get at you.

John had prepared breakfast: it was wonderful to find it all set up and ready on the table, a real treat. They were amazed at the size of the garden, which was laid mainly to lawn and flowerbeds. Outside the window of the sitting area were two twelve-foot high Poinsettia trees and a lovely guava tree. The view from the garden looked out over grassland where there were a few cattle in the distance, probably some of those for which Terry would be responsible.

Choen Sichinga arrived to meet Terry as planned. He was a tall Malawian, who was qualified as an engineer. He explained that he had been out to the States to obtain his B.Sc. Terry was not quite sure why he had been chosen to stand in as Farm Manager, but that is what he had been doing for the past few months. He soon found that Choen was the sort of person who made the simplest things sound complicated, never giving a direct answer. He was a bit of a wheeler-dealer and used the farm Toyota pick-up to transport a lot of his own produce to sell in Lilongwe, as well as the College's.

Choen drove Terry to Lilongwe and pointed out all the places that he might need, both for his personal needs and for the farm. First Terry went to the National Bank of Malawi to open an account and pay in some traveler's cheques. The exchange rate was 1.65 Kwacha to the pound. Choen explained that the best exchange rate was always acquired from an Indian shop in Lilongwe Old Town. He took him along and introduced him to Mr Musa, the owner of the hardware shop, as well as many other similar establishments in the town.

They had a sort of "four candles/fork handles" type of conversation, but Mr Musa was going to be a useful contact, explaining that anything they needed, he was able to obtain. At a price no doubt!

They then went along to Stansfield Motors to see if they had any second-hand cars available, but there were none. It was suggested that they buy a copy of the Daily Times as there were often cars advertised when other expatriates were leaving and needed to sell.

Choen pointed out the Capital Hotel on the edge of the new town of Lilongwe. Apparently the farm supplied them with chickens and vegetables, when available. He also showed him David Whitehead's shop, where you could buy excellent material for furnishings. That would be useful to show Ann, Terry thought. He then took Terry to "Farming and Engineering Services" who supplied spares for machinery and all sorts of equipment for the farm. Then on to Mandala Motors to see if they had any cars, but no luck there either.

They drove past the Drive-in Cinema, which was useful to know about, it was currently showing "That Man in Istanbul," starring Horst Bucholz and "The Hell Fighters" starring John Wayne and Katherine Ross. Clearly spoilt for choice!

From there they went on to the all-important supermarket 'PTC', where everyone seemed to go to buy their groceries. The local market in the old town was a wonderful source of every type of tropical fruit and vegetable, so they went there too. Terry bought a few pawpaws that he loved from his days in Tanzania, as well as strawberries which he was surprised to find, huge melons and beautiful mangoes, lemons and limes. The whole market thronged with people on bikes and on foot, carrying everything on their heads from a single tomato to a load of firewood so big that it would take two men to lift it. There were clay pots and galvanised watering cans, which had been made locally; piles of old clothes, some laid out flat, others in heaps; small stacks of dried insects and round black cakes made of flour and flying ants, all piled high in individual lots; fish, from Tilapia to Catfish, every shape and size from Lake Malawi, brought in from Salima fresh each morning. English and sweet potatoes, cassava, cabbage and maize all added to the colourful display.

The local witch doctor was dispensing his medicine to those in need and there were beggars on every corner hoping for a coin from the passers-by. Added to this mix was the continual buzz of flies hoping for their share of anything that was on offer.

After a refreshing drink and a sandwich at one of the small hotels, Terry found an advert in the Daily Times offering a car for sale. He spoke to a Mrs Cornwell who told him they were returning to the UK the next weekend and needed to keep the car until then. It was a white Ford Zephyr and they wanted K1,600 for it. Choen drove Terry to the Cornwell's house on the edge of Lilongwe and he gave her a post dated English cheque to secure the purchase which he would collect the following Saturday. She had no idea what the mileage was, and told Terry that it must have been around the clock at least once, but it was a good steady plodder.

Choen agreed with Terry that the next day they would go around the farm to introduce him to the staff. In the meantime the Toyota pick-up was Terry's as part of the job.

At 7.30 the following morning they set off on a tour of the farm. Bunda College of Agriculture was designed to provide agricultural training to Diploma level. The Government of Malawi had constructed the campus in 1966/67. The total area of the farm under production was four hundred hectares, but there was in total one thousand three hundred available. A new combined curriculum was devised for a three-year diploma and a five-year degree programme.

The college buildings consisted of one large auditorium and five classrooms and other rooms for chemistry, plant biology, home economics, laboratories and an engineering workshop. It had a modern library with over eighteen thousand books with a seating capacity for a hundred people. Two hundred and fifty male and female students had enrolled for the 77/78 academic years.

The mixed farm was used for teaching the students, also for research with a commercial aspect. Nobody admitted to that, until the end of the financial year when they wanted to see that it had made a profit! The day-to-day co-ordination of the farm activities was the responsibility of the Farm Manager. There was, however, a Farm Committee under the Chairmanship of the Principal, which discussed and advised on general policy. They met each month.

The farm was giving over more and more land to the growing of tobacco, which was said to be primarily for teaching purposes. However, it was widely thought that due to the high profitability of the crop it was as much for its commercial value and promoting the Principal's status. The fourteen tobacco barns were in the process of being increased by the addition of eighteen new barns and a new grading shed, all at considerable cost. Four hundred and fifty hectares of Virginia tobacco and seventy of Burley tobacco were to be grown on the farm.

In addition to the tobacco, the farm had a fifty cow dairy herd of Ayrshire cows, with three hundred beef cows and their calves. There were twenty crossbred sows with their progeny reared for pork. Two thousand laying hens supplied the egg needs of the campus, allowing some to be sold. Fifteen thousand broilers a year were reared from imported day old chicks to produce birds of up to five pounds in weight, for sale to the college and outlets in Lilongwe.

The farm supported one hundred and fifty ewes, fifty goats and fifty rabbits that were sold mainly for meat and to show how protein can be produced in small village environments. The fisheries were expanding and producing profitable supplies of fish from five man-made ponds.

There was also a slaughterhouse, butchery, farm shop and large market garden with a full drip irrigation system, and a large workshop for the maintenance and repair of all the college vehicles and farm equipment. The Farm office was fully staffed with clerk, typist, messenger and storekeeper. No doubt Terry would inevitably spend much of his time attending to the administration there. A team of night watchmen were employed to guard the stock and livestock, but one wondered how much they slept at night and how much guarding took place!

That all seemed to add up to a very busy life in the days ahead. Choen explained all the day-to-day happenings, introducing him to everyone as they toured around. The main everyday work was in the efficient hands of Mr Munthali, the foreman, a fatherly figure who controlled the considerable work force under Terry's guidance. He employed the field labourers as necessary depending on the workload; they were paid thirty tambala a day (one hundred tambala = one Kwatcha – K1.65 = £1).

The tobacco section employed large numbers of people; at peak times over four hundred were taken on. This was in the very capable hands of Jack Banda, a sincere and hard working man who, Terry discovered, was quite a remarkable character.

Each section had a head of department, which made Terry's day-to-day duties easier, as he had only to deal with each department head. The trick was to circulate around each enterprise and then speak to its head regarding anything that was not being carried out as it should be. Terry made twice daily visits to the tobacco section where Jack Banda, the head of the tobacco section, always treated him with great courtesy.

On their first meeting Terry walked around the curing barns with Jack, to see the progress of the Virginia tobacco.

"This is leapings one" Jack explained in his very measured English.

They inspected the contents of the barn together; the large leaves had been tied on long strings and were stretched across the barn, rising some twenty five tiers high. Around the bottom of the barn was a large metal pipe that carried hot air from a wood fire at one end. The heat rose up through the tiers of tobacco and in so doing dried the leaves.

They moved on to the next barn.

"This is leapings two!" Jack explained. They inspected the contents of that barn and then moved on to the next.

"This is leapings three!" Jack again explained, and they inspected that.

This continued to "Leapings seven," as they went to each barn in turn.

By this time Terry was somewhat confused, wondering what a 'leapings' was, but not wishing to show his ignorance.
"Jack, can I ask you something?" Terry finally asked.
"Sure, sure," Jack replied.
"What is a leapings?"
Jack looked puzzled by the question.
"It is the first cut of the crop," he explained.
It suddenly dawned on Terry that what he had meant was "Reapings" not "Leapings!" Everything suddenly became clear!

When the tobacco was dry it was moved to a large grading shed. To be able to do this, the dry crisp leaves hanging in the barns had to have a blast of steam, in order to make them pliable enough to move. Otherwise they would just shatter into pieces.

A hose from a steam boiler was placed in the barn just long enough to condition the tobacco for moving to the grading shed. There it was graded into different sized leaves and tied into 'hands,' small bundles of tobacco. It was then placed in a large baling machine that made it into a hay-like bale and wrapped it in hessian. It was labelled and ready to go to the auction floor when the sales commenced.

"So when does your day start?" Terry asked Jack.

"I start work at 6am when I have to be here to check in all the workers. At the moment there are about two hundred. It varies from day to day. They carry out the grading, and attend to the barns and the firewood. Others are working in the field, leaping the tobacco leaves and transporting them here to be cured. It is a very big job," Jack explained.

"What time do you finish at night?"

"It is usually around 7pm as it is getting dark, but I look out again in the evening to make sure the night watchmen are not sleeping."

"Then," Jack told him, "I do my studies."

"Studies? What are you studying for?"

"I've just finished doing seven "O" levels and now I'm doing "A" levels in Maths, English, Biology and Religion."

Terry was astonished. It was surely enough, the hard physical work that he did each day, but to think he was studying, too, was truly amazing. Even more amazing was that Jack lived in a small brick built house with five children. It had no electricity and no water on tap. He studied by oil lamplight surrounded by all his children after a full day's work, from late evening until midnight in such poor conditions. He really was a remarkable man the like of which Terry had never met before. He was totally honest, reliable and very skilled at his job, turning out some of the best tobacco in the country.

Ann had met up with so many of the other expatriates on the campus, and from many other countries too: America, India, Pakistan, Wales, Canada, U.K. Columbia, Nigeria to name just a few. Many had children, so there was a college bus that took them into Lilongwe each day to the school, returning in the early afternoon. Paul and Lynda were enrolled at Bishop Mackenzie, International School and they were able to start there straight away.

She had made friends with Mary Reynolds who lived at Bunda with her husband Len and two children, Paul and Sue, who were the same ages. They were also newly from England. Len ran a goat project at the college.

"One evening we should invite them here and a few others to have a small dinner party with us," Ann suggested. "I wonder if John is up to it?"

"Everyday we get people coming to the door asking if we need a houseboy or gardener, but I have to turn them away. We must have had eight this week alone," Ann explained. "Do they think we can employ the whole of Malawi here? I guess they are so desperate for work. One came this morning with a glowing reference from a past employer, there was nothing he couldn't do, but it had been typed in red ink! Mary told me that if it's in red, it's a signal from the past employer not to employ that man, irrespective of what the words on the reference say! John tells me he has a friend, Mandraz, who can do garden work, so I think we should employ him. We need someone and you are never going to have time with all you have before you."

"Yes, that's fine, you employ whoever you need, anything to make life that bit easier for you. I'm going to be kept pretty busy I can see that and it's always better to have someone recommended," Terry suggested.

"Are you sure that you can manage your new job?" Ann asked, rather concerned, "as you never seem to have a minute since you arrived here. The job sounds huge, not to mention all the meetings you're expected to attend, being part of the administration of the university, and some held in Zomba too. You've certainly taken on a big responsibility and it sounds quite political."

"Yes, it is. I think one of the worst things about the job, surprisingly, is the wretched farm shop. At present everyone fills in a form to order his or her needs from the shop once a week. This has to be received by the farm office each Thursday. The orders are made up and taken to the college on Friday lunchtime, when the houseboys collect it from the hatch of a small storeroom. As you can imagine it's chaos of the worst sort, a scrum, with everyone milling around asking for their order of chicken, beef, pork vegetables, eggs etc. It's a wonder they ever get to the right person. Then on Saturday mornings my phone never stops with people ringing me to say, 'I ordered pork and yet received beef,' or

'I ordered cabbage but didn't receive it,' 'my eggs were cracked,' and so on.

It's driving me mad. The answer is so simple too; all they need is to have a couple of deep freeze units and a few shelves in a small room, which could be topped up from the farm, like a shop. Then the staff can go there to buy what they want and when they want it. For some reason the Principal Nick Lungu will not hear of it and so the chaos continues.

It's become so bad of late that I now make sure I'm out of the office on a Saturday morning when the complaint calls come in!"

Chapter Seventeen

Dinner parties were one of the main forms of social life on the campus. Terry and Ann decided it was time they invited a few friends around to get to know others on the campus and exchange views and concerns about life at Bunda. Terry arranged to have a large rib of beef from the farm and as vegetables were nearly always in abundance it was easy to prepare quite a feast. That, plus one of Ann's specialities, lemon merangue pie, would go down a treat.

Ann found John the houseboy/cook very good at basic things, but needed advice and help with many other things, including how to set and prepare the table. He was fine with one knife and fork, but beyond that had little experience. She explained to John all the little things, like where to place the glasses, which glasses to use, the size of the plates to be used and their position on the table.

On the evening of the dinner party Ann and John prepared the table together. He watched carefully as she explained what she would like him to do and how to present the food on the various plates and serve them. She provided him with a nice fresh white apron and told him he should put the food on the serving plates and keep them warm until she asked him to serve.

Then, instead of bringing the food to the table as he normally did, she suggested he should serve the food through the hatch. John looked a little confused and concerned, but agreed to do as asked and would await the sign for him to commence serving.

Later after the guests had finished their starters, Ann rang the small table bell for John to commence serving. There was a certain amount of clattering in the kitchen, and then John opened the hatch from the kitchen to the dining room. Everyone was astonished to see John trying to climb through the hatch with a plate of food in his hand.

"What on earth are you doing?" Ann demanded.

"You asked me, madam, to serve the meal through the hatch. It is what I am doing. It is what you asked me to do, but it is much difficult."

"No! No! John you just pass the food through the hatch and place it on the table on this side, where I will serve the guests. You do not have to climb through!"

There were often such misunderstandings when dealing with the work force. Most were not too serious and considering the cultural differences, it was never really a serious problem.

On one occasion there had been a minor problem with the health of some of the sows at the piggery on the farm and Terry thought it wise not to allow students and staff to go near the pigs for a few weeks. He sent a memo to the College to be placed on their notice board stating that the Pigs were 'Out of Bounds' for the next two weeks. At the end of this period he received the following hand written note from Doctor Makhembera the Vice Principal of the college:-

"I would like to know if the Pigs are still out of lbs (pounds). Thanks. Dr. Makhembera.

Such were the misunderstandings that often took place between the cultures.

In order to upgrade the pigs and to bring in new blood lines, Terry ordered two young boar pigs to be flown in from South Africa. After a few weeks he received the following telegram from the telecommunications department in Lilongwe:-

'Pegs arriving Chileka airport flight SA184
Friday March 2nd 9am
Please acknowledge this advice.'
Barnes

An American family at Bunda asked Terry if he could provide a suckling pig for them to roast for a dinner party, as was their tradition. They roast the suckling pig whole and serve it on a roasting dish at the table, as a centrepiece. Terry agreed to have the suckling pig delivered to the Americans' house, where they prepared it for the meal, together with the help of their cook. It was explained to the cook how to roast and baste it and how to present it on the large dish with the vegetables all around. The cook was told, just before you carry the dish into the dining room, put a large apple in the mouth and place the dish in the centre of the table.

The guests were all sitting around the table, waiting in great anticipation for the arrival of the roast suckling pig. The cook walked in with the steaming dish, beautifully laid out as had been explained, but with the apple in his own mouth!

So many of these events took place and will be remembered and spoken of for years to come.

The Ford Zephyr car proved to be a great success and was indeed a steady plodder. It had little acceleration, doing naught to sixty miles per hour in about ten minutes! But it was extremely comfortable and excellent for going to watch films at the drive-in cinema, as they often did in Lilongwe. From time to time bits fell off and either Terry or the farm mechanic would bodge a repair to carry it on for a few more miles. On the bumpy roads the accelerator linkage under the bonnet would sometimes come apart, but it was a simple matter to stop the car, lift the bonnet and put one of the linkage arms back into position.

Ann often went to the local village of Mutundu to the colourful market, where you saw every form of life. It was a busy and lively place. There was a large choice of vegetables, some not available at Bunda Farm. The journey was about four miles, but unfortunately on one occasion half way along the bumpy road to Muntundu the accelerator linkage fell apart and the car came to a halt.

Ann had no idea of the cause and did not know the trick with the accelerator linkage. She sat for ages hoping to see a friendly face on the way to market, but none came. On her feet she only had flip-flop sandals. She found them most comfortable, following the operations she'd had on her foot, which was always somewhat tender. In the end she decided to lock the car and proceeded to walk back the two miles or so to Bunda to find Terry who was in the farm office. She finally staggered into his office in quite a state.

"What on earth have you been doing?" Terry enquired.

"That bloody car broke down and left me on the road and nobody was around so I had to walk here," she replied exhaustedly.

"Oh no! I bet it's that damn linkage again. It's easy to put it back in position. Didn't I show you?" Terry enquired. "Oops! No, clearly I didn't."

Terry's clerk, seeing Ann's distress brought her a cold drink to help her recover from her ordeal. They then drove in Terry's farm pick-up to recover the car. In seconds Terry had opened the bonnet and fixed the problem, being careful to show Ann what to do, should it ever happen again.

As they were getting back into the car a white pick-up pulled in behind them. They couldn't believe what they saw: in the back was a large live turkey jumping up and down, and sitting in the passenger seat was a huge fat pig, not what you expect to see on a dusty rough road in the centre of Africa. A tall thin dark haired, slightly wild looking young European man stepped out.

"Can I help you? Have you broken down?" he asked.

Ann and Terry could hardly believe what they were seeing. Why would anyone drive around with a pig in the passenger seat?

"No, it's fine now thanks. It's fixed."

"My name's Luigi Borgnis. I'm Italian. I run a tobacco farm not far from here at Zanzi Estate."

"Hello, Luigi, nice to meet you. I'm Terry this is my wife, Ann, from England. We recently moved to Bunda College where I'm the Farm Manager."

"You must come and see my farm sometime," Luigi suggested. "I have few visitors, being deep in the bush, so would be very pleased to see you. Would you like to come tomorrow and stay for dinner? Say around 5pm then I can show you my farm."

"Sure we would love to and thanks for inviting us. We have two children. Can we bring them, too?

"Yes, please do. They are welcome."

"So what's with the pig?" Terry asked curiously. "It's not very often you see a pig in the cab of a van."

"That's Julio. He's a pet. I had him when he was just a baby, but he's grown so fast. He eats all that I don't eat, clears up all the old bread and everything and just grew and grew. I really don't know what to do with him."

"And the turkey in the back?" Terry hardly dared to ask.

"Ah that's Philip; he is a pet too. He is a bit stupid looking I know, but he just likes to ride in the back of the van and he sleeps there too.

I guess you think I am totally mad."

"No, no," Terry quickly responded. "Eccentric, but not mad!"

Luigi quickly wrote down some instruction on how to find his house and sped off along the dirt road, with Philip jumping up and down in the back, as they disappeared in a cloud of dust. There began another life long friendship, as so often happens in these far away places.

The following day Terry and family set off to visit Luigi's farm, looking forward to seeing their new friend's farm. Eccentric as he was, he seemed a very likeable and kindly character. They turned off the Mutundu road as per their instructions and down a long sandy track with deep ruts.

After about a mile they came to a barrier across the road. Ann got out and lifted the barrier, allowing them to continue on their way. They drove on up the sandy track, with its splendid tall blue-gum trees with their grey peeling bark, on either side. The track continued through open land planted to maize with red termite mounds rising fifteen feet into the air along side the track. At a junction in the road they saw a large plough disc mounted on a pole by the side of the road. It read, "Manager's House." They turned right by the sign along a pathway that took them to a magnificent colonial style bungalow, with wide veranda and orange tiled roof. In front of the house the garden had been laid out almost in an Italian style, with a roundabout made from a low hedge and covered in colourful shrubs. In the middle was a tall white pole with the Italian flag flying from it! Terry drove around the roundabout and pulled in at the side of the house.

They all jumped out of the car and looked with wonder at their surroundings: it was a truly beautiful setting, rich in colour, growth and fragrance from the roses, frangipani, and bougainvillea, a delight to the eye. They stood there admiring the lushness of the garden, undoubtedly helped by the oscillating sprinkler distributing life-giving water to the plants. They stood taking in the wonder and surprise of the environment, created with such care deep in the bush.

There was no sign of Luigi, so they called out, "Hello. Anybody home!"

There was no reply at first, then, they heard a voice, but could not see anyone around. They walked around the garden through a group of blue-gum trees reaching high into the sky and around to the side of the house, past a BBQ, table and chairs. As they sat in the chairs they heard a rustling high in the trees above.

"Hello. Welcome to Zanzi Estate," a voice called out from the branches of the tree. They then caught sight of Luigi, high up in the tree and making his way down.

"I thought I'd look out to see if you were coming. I often climb the trees," he explained.

He quickly slid down to greet them in the normal manner as if it was not unusual to be found half way up a tree! Luigi spoke very good English, if sometimes a little broken. They introduced him to Paul and Lynda, who gazed at him as if he were a monkey from the wild!

"Thomas! Thomas!" Luigi shouted, "Where are you? We have visitors."

But no Thomas came.

"Thomas," he shouted again. "It's no good, I'll have to go and find him.

That man, he is old and he is deaf, but I employ him. He came to me as a houseboy and cook, but he can do neither of those things. Why do I continue to employ him? Everyday I tell him: "Soon you must return to your village." What use are you to me? You are too old to learn and to work. But everyday he tells me that he has nowhere to go, so what can I do?

When I ask him to go to the garden to bring me some tomato for a meal, he brings me green tomatoes. Why do you bring me green tomatoes to eat? I ask him. Then I realise that he is colour blind as well. What can I do with him?"

Then a short bent over man shuffled out onto the veranda. He was dressed in very old, torn, and dirty trousers, a bright coloured shirt with the buttons done up unevenly and wearing the white gloves of a butler from Victorian days.

"Yes, Master," he said to Luigi.

"Thomas why don't you come when I call you? You know this evening we have visitors from Bunda College."

"Yes, Master. Shall I make scones?"

"No Thomas, do not make scones. You know I spent the whole afternoon doing your job for you and cooking a chicken for our guests."

"Yes, Master." Thomas replied.

"No scones, Thomas. No scones please! He thinks that because you are English then you eat only scones. It is crazy employing such a man. His last employer must have explained that English people like scones. So every time he sees an English person come to the house he makes scones! Not just a few, but hundreds of them. He would give you scones for breakfast, lunch and dinner. I tell him, Thomas, please, no more scones. But still he makes scones. He is a very old man and I can't cast him out, so what can I do?"

Luigi took them around his farm, which was mainly a tobacco-growing farm with vast brick tobacco barns and mountains of wood for curing the tobacco. He showed them the bales of tobacco in the grading shed, ready to go to the auction floors. It had been a very good year and as he grew two hundred acres there were a lot of bales, graded and ready to be sold.

They returned to the house and sat on the veranda where Luigi served them cool drinks, while preparing the meal, popping along to chat when he could. They learnt that Luigi was not in fact a farmer, but a teacher. His great, great, great, great, great, grandfather was Giuseppe Mattia Borgnis, a famous painter from the 1750's who lived in northern Italy.

Luigi had been teaching in Milan when he met the father of one of his pupils. He asked Luigi if he would be interested in going to manage the farm he owned in Malawi. Even though he had no experience of agriculture, he accepted the offer and here he was some two years later, and enjoying it. Luigi was certainly an eccentric, but a kindly man who loved Malawi and its people, and was loving the adventure too.

Thomas served them a lovely chicken meal in the large open kitchen. The room was vast with high ceilings, plain walls and minimal furniture, but homely. They sat and chatted and got to know each other a little more. Paul and Lynda had gone off with Thomas who was showing them a pet guinea pig that lived in Luigi's scullery and to show them Julio the pig and Philip the turkey that lived in the yard at the back of the house.

"So where is your Boss now? Does he come here very often?" Terry asked Luigi. "Is he still in Italy?"

"No," said Luigi, "he is behind you."

"Behind me? How do you mean?"

"He is in the cupboard!"

"In the cupboard?" Terry exclaimed, sounding like a parrot repeating everything Luigi said.

"Yes, he died a month ago and his ashes are there in an urn waiting for his son to come and scatter them as per his wishes."

Terry and Ann were speechless as they listened to the story of Luigi's boss; this really was a most unusual set-up here at Zanzi Estate.

Ann was very busy home making in the first few months, creating new curtains throughout the house, buying things like rugs, bedding and items of furniture needed for the new home, dress making for herself and for Lynda and taking care of the children who had settled well into the new way of life making many new school friends, both local and from overseas.

It was also a time of making new friends themselves and getting into university life on the campus. There was always some function to attend in Terry's position as Farm Manager, social evenings, when they would be invited to attend a dinner or BBQ at the Principal's residence. Invitations would flood in. Terry felt it was never appropriate to turn down these invitations, for he was expected to be there.

The Principal and Mrs B.F. Lungu
request the pleasure of the company of
Mr and Mrs T.F. Reeves
at a drinks/dinner party in honour of new and returning members of staff at their residence at 7.00 pm on Friday 12th May 1978

RSVP
(Regrets only to Principal's Secretary)

or

Please come to meet the Senators
The Principal and Mrs B. F. Lungu
Invite all Senators to a LUNCHEON on the
Occasion of the meeting of the UNIVERSITY SENATE
At BUNDA COLLEGE
On 16th June 1978
RSVP (Regrets only to Principal's Secretary)

N.B. Those interested in purchasing beef, pork, chicken, eggs, fish, mutton, goat meat, vegetables, caterpillars, ants, and other produce from the College Farm should please contact the Farm Manager in advance.

or

The University of Malawi
Invites

Mr and Mrs T.F. Reeves
To witness the presentation of academic awards by
The Vice Chancellor
Dr. David Kimble, O.B.E., B.A., Ph.D.
In
Congregation
At Chancellor College, Zomba, on Saturday, 29th July 1978

N.B. You are cordially invited to a reception in the empty cafeteria, Chancellor College, immediately after the Congregation and thereafter to a buffet luncheon at Kuchawe Inn at 1.30p.m.

These were fairly typical of some of the events that took place during the year.

Ann continued to enjoy her new life at Bunda, getting the house set up, meeting new people and making new friends. Terry had purchased new bikes for everyone and Ann often went out with friends into the wooded areas to follow her life long interest in bird spotting. Using her bicycle was excellent for this, as it caused the minimum of disturbance to the birds. Malawi had a rich and diverse bird life, from the simple Cattle Egret, Grey Heron and Pied Crow to the Hammerkop, Weaver and Red-billed Wood Hoopoe. By habit she took to going for rides in the bush with a notebook and pencil to record the birds that she had seen, later marking them in her book on East African birds. She would often find a spot to sit, and stare up through the canopy of branches to the blue African sky, waiting for a passing bird to reveal itself, thus giving her the simplest of pleasures and joy.

Walking and riding her bike in the bush gave Ann a great feeling of peace, of being in touch with a greater being. It focused her mind and provided some of the happiest days of her life. She seemed to have an awareness given to her by the years of illness and sorrow that she had endured. Her fight with cancer and her wish to create a better world, for her children and for those less fortunate than herself, all served to deepen her love affair with Africa.

Terry was slowly getting to grips with the farm and making his mark, but it was never easy. He enjoyed the job even if he did wish it were less bureaucratic. However, that was the nature of a University with all its different department heads and committees to satisfy, while still keeping it a commercial enterprise.

There were many battles with the administrative staff, one to one, and in administrative meetings, but on the whole he kept good relations with Principal, staff and students, despite all. The farm staff under his firm but fair control looked to him to represent them and fight their corner when dealing with the Principal, Registrar and Bursar. In turn Terry tried to involve his own heads of department and keep them informed and feel that they were not individuals but working as one body for the good of the University as a whole. The sheer number of staff was quite overwhelming at times, many were part time and for a seasonal task like harvesting the tobacco, but over four hundred on the payroll was quite an administrative task however you looked at it, as well as the day to day problems that arose from such numbers.

Ann herself had quite an administrative task with all the household affairs. John was very good and reliable and the garden boy Mandraz kept the garden in order, but needed constant direction and advice. Paul and Lynda went off to school on the college bus each day, but you could never be sure at what hour they would return. The Principal's daughter used the bus but had a habit of going off with a friend after school without telling anyone, leaving the bus driver with a mini bus full of children, but one missing. He realised that if he returned to Bunda without the Principal's daughter he would certainly lose his job. So when this happened the children on the bus had to sit and wait, often in the hot sun, until the Principal's daughter decided to turn up. This resulted in all the Mums waiting at Bunda for their children, not knowing what was happening. Ann often found herself in this position and continually had to monitor the children's comings and goings!

Never-the-less Ann thought she would enjoy doing something to bring her more in touch with the local people, a job of some sort, now that the house was complete.

"What do you think?" she asked Terry, "I would really like to use my skills with the people. There must be plenty of need?"

"I can see you might like to do something more fulfilling, but not sure what's available. I've heard there's a Catholic Mission Hospital not far from here, over near Luigi's place. Could be worth a visit."

"I'll go over there tomorrow and see what goes on; if there is anything I could help with, even on a voluntary basis, that would be fine," Ann said.

The next day she drove the four miles to Mlale Hospital, a general hospital run by the White Sisters (Missionary Sisters of our Lady of Africa). White Fathers also shared the mission, looking after the pastoral needs of the people and running a large church, but they lived independently of the sisters.

There were four Missionary Sisters running the hospital, from four different countries, Spain, Holland, USA and Canada. They all stopped their work to welcome Ann and sat chatting for a while enjoying a coffee with her. Sister Laura from Spain explained that she held a sewing class at the mission once a week where she taught local women to sew and make clothes and would be delighted to have Ann come along and help. Laura was full of life and worked hard for the people as well as looking after the house and preparing all the meals for the other sisters.

Ann agreed to go to Mlale each week to help Laura and there again started another lifelong friendship and association with all the sisters.

Ann enjoyed so much the contact with the indigenous people of Malawi and to be able to help them with their needs. She also found great joy being with the sisters who radiated love and were always so happy and inspirational, a true example to all. They worked hard running the hospital and training the staff. Patients came from far and wide for help and treatment and to have their babies.

The sisters were keen to hear of Terry's work and enquired about the family, wanting to know all about them and why they had come to Africa. Ann promised that one day she would bring Terry and the children to meet them and also invite them all to Bunda College.

Ann was delighted with her day; she had found an outlet for her energies, a new challenge and use for her talents, giving her renewed purpose and a chance to serve the people who needed so much help. It was also good to get away from Bunda once a week and find such wonderful new warm friends at the mission. She couldn't wait to get home to tell Terry all about it.

On driving home through the woodland close to Bunda she saw one of the farm tractors smashed up and half way up a tree. One of the wheels was missing and it looked a rather mangled mess. No one was around and it looked as if the John Dere farm tractor had crashed. Poor Terry she thought, he will be pretty fed up to have one of his tractors out of action.

Shortly after her arrival home, Terry returned for lunch.

"I saw the tractor just now," she said. "What happened?"

"I've no idea, these drivers would smash up anything. They drive too fast and think they are in a racing car. It'll take ages to get the parts and to repair it, to say nothing of the expense. Meantime I'm expected to continue to run the business with one tractor less at this busy time. What a country this is," he said gloomily.

"Come and have your lunch. I want to tell you all about my visit to the sisters at Mlale Mission, they were so welcoming and such wonderful people. It's been agreed that I'll go along and help out there at the mission once a week."

Ann rang the bell in order that John would know they were ready to eat. He had prepared a salad and brought it to the table.

"Bwana, I sorry to see the broken tractor when I going to the farm shop. It looks very sick, sorry for that."

"Thanks John, it's a big problem for me," Terry replied. "Except it's not near the farm, but in the woods."

John looked puzzled.

"Bwana I sorry, but it was on my way to the farm shop."

"John it couldn't be," Ann joined in. "The tractor is up in the woods on the road to the campus. It's the green John Dere, and I saw it myself just a few minutes ago."

"No madam, I sorry, but it is red and it is laying in the field near the tobacco barn. It's quite dead."

"But that's in the opposite direction. Are you sure?" she replied.

"Oh yes, I sure," he replied. "Maybe there is two tractors sick!"

Terry looked at Ann in disbelief. "Surely not? Oh no, it can't be, not two in a day. Sorry, going to have to go!"

Terry shot off to check John's statement and sure enough out in the field near the farm was the red Massey Ferguson lying on its side with a trailer attached to it. On further investigation he found that one of the drivers had overloaded the trailer, the wheel went in a hole and the whole lot turned over. So now of the four tractors on the farm, two were out of action!

That evening, as Ann and Terry sat on the veranda with their gin and tonic, as they liked to do, enjoying the African night, she told him all about her day and how she had agreed to go and help Sister Laura.

"I'm pleased for you; it will be good to meet others, outside of the campus. I know we have Luigi, but this is different."

"The sisters are keen to meet you and the children. One day we must go over. You would really like them, they are so warm and lovely." Ann explained. "In a strange way I felt they need our friendship as much as we need theirs; they are so isolated."

"Yeh, that would be nice. When things get a bit quieter I'll take time and go to see them with you. Strangely enough my Dad has a lot of sister friends from the Sisters of Mercy. He is often at their place on Wyke Road having a meal or for Mass. They are so good to him. He always speaks highly of them." Terry commented. "I guess my view of sisters comes from my contact with them during school years; I've never really known them personally on a one to one basis."

"I have some other news for you," Ann hesitantly said, as they looked down the moonlit garden, enjoying the peace of the evening.

"Not sure you are going to like it. I wish I didn't have to tell you, after all you've had to put up with today, with the tractors and everything."

There was an immediate look of fear in Terry's eyes.

"Is it the old trouble," he asked, "is it back again? I know you said the foot was a bit sore around the scar."

"No, no, it's not the 'old trouble' as you put it, well not in that way. My foot is often sore, but no it's not that, thankfully."

"You're not pregnant, are you?" he asked rather alarmed.

"No I'm not, anyway would that be so terrible?" she said smiling at him.

"But you said the old trouble, so I thought that's what you meant."

"I picked up the post today at the college," Ann explained. "We had letters from England, well just the one to be exact. What were the three things you always said followed us around, wherever we went? Blocked drains, smoking chimneys and .... ?"

Terry thought for a moment, and then the penny dropped.

"Oh no, it can't be can it, not already?" he exclaimed.

"Yes that's right, Aunt Lesley wrote to say that she is arriving on Friday 4th August at 17.30 in Lilongwe and will stay for eight weeks!"

"Eight weeks!" Terry again exclaimed. "You receive a lesser sentence for murder!"

"Will it be so terrible? You know how she loves to be in Africa," Ann pleaded.

"No, of course not," Terry laughed, "You know I love her really and she was such a fantastic help to us when you were ill, allowing me to visit you in hospital at our time of great need. We can take her to a game park for a few days, perhaps up to Kasungu Reserve and feed her to the lions," he joked.

"That sounds like a good idea, except there are no lions at Kasungu Park. The kids will be on holiday so we could go as a family: its time we got out and about to see a bit more of the country. I'll look into it and see if I can book it for us. I understand the accommodation there is at Lifupa Lodge, just outside of Kasungu village, it has a number of rondavels that you stay in and a central restaurant where you take all your meals. Aunty Lesley would love that."

Luigi, was becoming a good friend and seemed to breeze in and out of their house at will as he passed to go to the farm shop for produce or to visit other friends he had made at Bunda College. He was not a very relaxed person: he smoked too much, drank too much red wine and was always on the move as if he could not settle in one place for long. At times he seemed lonely and loved to drop in for a chat, but he was always busy carrying a big responsibility at the farm, which he took seriously. He knew the Sisters at Mlale and was a close friend of the Spanish sister, Laura, who Ann helped. The Spanish and the Italian mentality were very similar and drew them close. He was very generous to the sisters and often entertained them at his place, took them to town and brought things for them. Life was like that in the bush, everyone helping to support each other.

Luigi, on hearing that Terry and Ann were to celebrate their tenth wedding anniversary asked if he could give a party for them at his place; he loved to entertain and did it well. So on Thursday 8th June he worked hard, with the doubtful help of Thomas to prepare a feast to which he had invited the sisters from Malale Mission, as well as a number of people from Bunda College. He enjoyed entertaining, preparing the food and wines, writing out the invitations and being the Master of Ceremonies. He assured them in his little complimentary speech before the feast began that there were no scones! About twenty people gathered on the veranda of Luigi's house that evening enjoying the buffet feast that he had prepared. It was warm, but not hot at that time of the year, with just a hint of a breeze. The veranda was covered with greenery and flowers and lit by candles. Luigi must have spent hours decorating it and making it look nice, but that was his way.

The electric light provided by the generator was erratic at best and the only source of power at Zanzi Estate, miles from an electricity supply. It seemed to be a little irregular in its output: sometimes the lights were so bright that you needed sunglasses, and then so dull you could hardly see. It was a magical evening full of fun, memories, music and friendship that continued into the small hours at this magnificent colonial house, with its beautiful garden in the middle of the emptiness of the bush and a star-studded night deep in Africa's warm heart.

The school year moved quickly to a close in order that those going abroad for the summer holidays could do so easily. Paul was doing very well and enjoying the day-to-day school life. Lynda, too, was enjoying the junior section in her way, always pleased to return home to her pet guinea pig, Olga. They loved to play with the children of their Malawian neighbour, the college registrar, Bill Mvalo, riding their bikes around the campus and all jumping into the back of Terry's pick-up to go to the farm to see the livestock whenever they could. The free lifestyle seemed to suit them well. Terry and Ann were delighted to see them settled at last and gaining in the knowledge and love of their idyllic surroundings. Would they ever really come to understand how very different their childhood had been compared to that of their contemporaries at home? It had to have an effect on them, the wilderness life, the scenery, the contrast of peoples, places and cultures, the understanding that the world was indeed a large, varied and exciting place. It would be interesting to see the effects on their lives.

July and August were months when the temperatures dropped, being much lower by day and cold by night. Jumpers and coats were worn which seemed strange in Africa and not what you expect. The fire was lit early of an evening; it was a joy to sit by and to smell the wood burning just as if they were back in the U.K. The tobacco season was over so there was less pressure at work and fewer numbers of workers around to care for and to create problems. All of the tobacco had now gone to be sold at the tobacco auction in Limbe in the south of the country and soon they would be able to assess the success of the year's crop. The university was always buzzing with people coming and going with their various activities. Exterior examiners arrived and left, Government Ministers had to be dealt with and there were endless meetings with staff and students, but also some enjoyable evening parties both at the college and with the many staff.

Ann and Terry prepared Auntie Lesley's room for her visit that was soon upon them and began to plan trips out for her and for themselves during the school holidays. Ann enjoyed her visits to Mlale mission, helping the people make clothes for themselves and some to sell to raise money for their families. She became very fond of the sisters and they of her. Terry had been busy so had not yet gone over to visit them, but was happy to see that Ann had found an outlet for her talents that she enjoyed.

Just before 6pm on Friday 4th August, Auntie Lesley dropped out of the sky at Lilongwe Airport on a still, cool evening. She was delighted to be in Malawi and to be with them all again. She was amazing for her age and would celebrate her 70th birthday while staying with them, and was always game to travel the world when an opportunity arose. She was never one to give up easily; having worked nearly thirty years in Africa, she was full of determination and courage. Terry and Ann admired her and all that she had done with her life, and welcomed her to their home. She soon settled into her surroundings and got on very well with John the cook/houseboy. John was not sure what to call Lesley: his name for Ann was 'Madame' so he couldn't call Lesley by the same name, and so he called her 'Big Madame.' This, of course, was nothing to do with her considerable size, but with her age. Big in years! It did make them all laugh and the name stuck with her for the rest of her days!

Ann went to see the doctor at the Kamuzu Hospital for her three-monthly check-up; her foot was still sore in the area of the skin graft so she asked him to check it to see if anything could be done. Lesley went with her, and then they planned to do some shopping and show Lesley around Lilongwe.

Terry had managed to get the parts for one of the tractors. He was happy to see them arrive and to get the mechanic to fix at least one of the tractors ready for ploughing and to help with the sowing of the tobacco nursery for the new season. He spent most of the day with Jack Banda setting out the seeding of the nursery, which seemed vast due to the extra tobacco acreage they had to provide for in the coming year as the farm expanded. After the long day with Jack, he was pleased to get home early, keen to hear how the day had gone and if Lesley had enjoyed her visit to Lilongwe.

Ann and Lesley were in the sitting room with a tray of tea.
"So, girls, how was the trip?" he asked.

As soon as he had uttered those words he saw Ann's face, frozen and distraught, eyes red with tears.

"Whatever has happened? What's going on? Terry asked.

Lesley sat looking at the floor, glum, shaken and traumatised, most unlike her.

"They want to operate again on my foot, the cancer is back," Ann replied. "The doctor said the skin around the graft has cancer cells developing and I need to have another operation to remove them; he has also said that one or two toes should be removed."

"Oh my God!" Terry exclaimed, and rushed over to put his arm around her.

There was a sudden coldness in the air as they held on to each other sitting in complete silence, fearing to let go.

Lesley excused herself, saying she was going to her room to pray.

Terry and Ann sat there holding hands, staring at each other in disbelief.

"What's happening to us?" Ann asked. "What is happening?"

"Where are the kids?" Terry asked.

"They are still at Mary and Len's playing with their children. I've not seen them yet," she replied.

"The doctor, he is certain of his diagnosis, is he?" Terry asked.

"Yes, he said he was, there was no question of doing tests. He said they could do the operation at Kamuzu Hospital if we wanted, but they don't have the after care, so suggests I return to the UK."

"I see," Terry replied gloomily. "I see."

Neither of them knew what to do or say next, they both just sat staring into space, holding on to each other.

"Mummy, Mummy, look what I've got," came an excited voice as Paul and Lynda rushed in followed by Mary. They were both holding new comics they'd been given by Mary and Len.

Ann immediately switched into their world, greeted them and admired the comics.

"I hope you both thanked Mary for those. They are very rare here in Malawi. Once you have read them be sure to pass them on to one of your friends."

Terry could see Mary was aware that she had just walked in on something and said, "Are you all right you two, you look a bit shattered? Did your aunty have a good day?"

Ann took the children off to their rooms to get them ready for their baths; they shouted, "Thank you," to Mary and off they skipped.

Mary was no fool; she could feel something was not right.

"Mary, thank you for meeting Paul and Lynda from school and giving them tea. It was very kind of you," Terry said. "I'm afraid we've had some shocking news. Ann has, I know, told you about her past health problems. Today she went for her regular check up and they found the cancer is still there and affecting her toes. It's not good I'm afraid; they need to operate and suggest she returns home for that."

"Oh Terry, that's terrible news, just when I was getting to know her too. What will you do?"

"I've no idea yet. We've only just had chance to discuss it as Ann and Auntie only arrived back from Lilongwe an hour ago."

"Oh right, well I'll leave you to it, Terry," Mary said in a fluster. "Let me know the minute you decide what to do and anything, just anything I can do, tell me and I'll do it. I will call in again tomorrow to see Ann. Oh that is terrible." Mary rushed out sobbing as she went off back across the campus to her house.

Terry could hear Paul and Lynda enjoying their bath and went to join them. First of all he knocked on Auntie's door to check that she was all right. She was sitting there, her face as white as a sheet, looking out the window across the brown savannah grasslands, tears rolling down her cheeks in the fading light of the day. "My dear Terry," she said, "My dear Ann, you two don't deserve this, you and your lovely family. People so often say to me, 'Lesley, how good to have a strong faith like you do as a missionary, I wish I could be like you.' Today my faith is tested to the utmost and I ask God. Why? Why? Why?"

John had lit the fire which brought cheer into the house, the African rug stretched out in welcome, inviting everyone to come and sit by its flames now licking around the logs burning fiercely in the grate. Wisps of smoke were curling around the edge of the fireplace and into the room, filling it with that special smell of a wood fire. It was just like any other evening in August, except this was unbelievably and horrifyingly different.

They all sat in silence over their meal, picking at it leaving John to wonder if he had done something wrong.

"Madame is there something wrong with my cookings? The cabbage was not so good from the farm today. Please may you consider that?" John said earnestly.

"It is not your meal John. That was first class, as always; we are very happy with that. Today we have had some very bad news and we are all feeling very sad, but it's not your fault," Terry explained.

"I'm sorry for that, Master, if the news it is not good," John replied with concern.

"Thank you. We'll explain to you tomorrow. If you like you can go home now. We have kept you very late, and we'll clear up later."

"OK Master, I am gone now to my house. I will be back in the morning. Until then its goodbye."

The three of them sat there looking into the fire.

"What happens next?" Terry enquired. "Where do we go from here?"

There was no reply, just a stunned silence.

Ann looked at Terry, Terry looked at Ann and Lesley looked at them both.

"Shall I go home? Would that help?" Lesley suggested.

"Lesley, our home is your home, you know that. You should stay here with us, if you are happy to," Ann responded.

"Of course I am, but I don't want to be in the way," Lesley replied.

"If you don't mind I will go to my room and leave you to discuss your plans."

She set off in a quiet thoughtful manner, the like of which Terry had never seen in her before. Usually she was so full of life and good humour, if sometimes very full on and demanding. This evening she was walking around like a scolded child as she went off to her bedroom with a heavy heart.

"I can't believe this is happening," Ann said. "I really did think this was all behind us. The doctor said he really would prefer me to go home for the operation and although ever fibre in my body wants to be here, I feel he's right; I have no option. I have to go home. So once again it looks as if we are going to be separated. Why does it always come back to this? The thing I hate the most keeps presenting itself. Every time I say I can't ever do it again and then I have to. It makes no sense. It's not fair. It's really getting me down, the operations I can take, but our separation from each other is just awful. I can't explain why it is; I guess it's simply how I am. We didn't marry to spend our lives apart, then why does it keep coming back to that? "

"I wish I had an answer to that, I really do," replied Terry.
Ann rushed off in a flood of tears to the bedroom.

Terry was left staring into the fire where he sat until the small hours. He paced the room, sat in this chair and that chair, made cups of tea and coffee, drank several glasses of gin and tonic went out on the veranda and sat there listening to the African night, the cicadas and the distant cry of hyenas. Where ever he went he could not find the answer or the solution.

The next thing he remembered was Ann standing at his side calling him to wake up; he had a sharp pain in his back from lying so long in the chair.
"What are you doing out here?" she asked. "I woke up and the bed was empty. Do you know what time it is?"
"I've no idea. Why am I out here on the veranda?"
"It's what I'd like to know," she replied. "It's 3.30am. Come to bed."
"I can't move. I'm frozen in this chair," Terry said as he slowly gathered himself together.
"Come on inside. I'll make us a cup of tea," Ann said giving Terry a smile.
"And will that make all things right?"
He struggled to his feet and returned to the fireside where there were just grey cold ashes. He felt terrible.
"What are we going to do?" Ann asked as she brought him a mug of tea. "We have to start things moving in the morning."

"It is morning." Terry replied sarcastically.

"Yes, and you've not been to bed. You're not going to be much help to me like this. It's no good you falling apart; I need you! So pull yourself together. I realise it's been a terrible shock, it has been for me too don't forget."

"I'm sorry," said Terry, "it's just knocked the stuffing out of me. Like you I am tired of pulling myself up to find again the strength to fight back, getting to the point where we feel we have overcome the problem and won the battle, only to find we haven't, that it's sneaked in the back door and we have to do it all yet again. I'm so sick and tired of it, as I'm sure you are."

"Where is your faith then?" she replied. "You're the one that is the Catholic, has all the answers. Where are they now?"

"Don't you think I've been thinking the same thing, looking for the answers? I didn't sit out here all night for the good of my health you know. I've been searching too."

Ann kissed him and sat on his knee while they wrestled with their torment, lost in their personal grief seeking an answer, looking for a way out.

"There is no question you have to return home for the operation. There you will receive the best possible care. I don't see you getting that here." Terry relented. "The doctors might allow you to return here again after, but probably not for a couple of years."

Ann looked mournful, "So can we all return? We've only been here six months. What does it mean in terms of your contract?"

"We would have to repay all the University costs, our fares out, baggage allowance etc, as well as our fares back to U.K. That's a lot to ask." Terry explained.

"The alternative is that you return, perhaps with the children, and I stay here for another year. That way all our fares will be paid and the only financial loss is the gratuity we were due at the end of the contract. That's as I see it, but I will need to check the situation with the Registrar in Zomba."

"Do you know what you're saying?" Ann asked. "A whole year? Are you mad?"

"I know, not sure how I'd cope without you and the children here. I'd miss you all so much. It would be desperate," he explained passionately."

"You don't know how you'd cope? What about me?" she screamed."

"Terry, no I can't do it, I can't and I won't let you do it either. Don't forget there is Paul and Lynda to think about. We have to consider them in all this."

"Don't you think I do? Paul and Lynda will always be our top priority; they always have been and always will be. But what life will it be for them, returning home with no income, in debt up to our necks with the University, and with nowhere to live?" Terry pleaded. "A whole year without you and them will tear me apart too, but I don't want you stressed, worrying about all our financial problems when you have such a big operation before you."

"I don't really see that we have very much option. You could, I'm sure go to stay with my father in Weymouth. Paul and Lynda would be able to get in to St Augustine's School if we have a word with the sisters. I could return there in August next year when I'd served the necessary eighteen months of my contract."

"No! No! There has to be another way, there has to be," Ann said with renewed determination in her voice.

"I don't see it. I really don't. We are bound by the contract." Terry pointed out. "After all you've made a wonderful home here and I have John to look after me to keep things going. Time will pass and as long as you are all O.K. and you recover well, what else matters? My Dad will, I'm sure, be glad of the company if you were to stay with him, and my sister Esmee is not far away."

"No! I can't and won't do it; I can't even think of that idea, it's totally out of the question. I'm sorry Terry I just can't and I won't let you." Ann said.

"Let's get some sleep, its very nearly time to get up; I can't think anymore, I'm exhausted."

As they went to their bedroom they noticed Auntie's light shining under her door; she too was having a bad night.

Chapter Eighteen

When in the midst of a catastrophe like this you realize there is one bonus. When you are at the bottom there is no further to go, you have no choice but to fight your way out. You have to face the problem head on. It requires persistence and action, and a plan to take you out of it. This so often requires a change of attitude and some lateral thinking; Terry awoke with the urge to do just that. He went down to the farm office and rang the registrar in Zomba who was responsible for contracts of employment. He verified the situation was as they had thought it to be. He asked the registrar to confirm this in writing and send it to him at Bunda as soon as possible.

Terry had another thought during the night that would help them somewhat over the problem of their long proposed separation and he put this to Ann.
"How about if you and the kids go home now, as soon as we can get a flight and then in the middle of March, next year, come out for a month for Easter which is mid April. That would break it up and it wouldn't seem quite so long."
"I don't know. I can't and don't want to imagine it," Ann said thoughtfully.
"I hate the whole idea, I really do. Is there no other way?"
"Except for us to return owing thousands to the University and all the complications of that," Terry explained.
"Then it seems I have to I suppose. What choice do I have? I'll have to go along with it. It would be easier than a full year apart and could work if there is no other way," said Ann with a slight misgiving in her voice.
"It would give you time to get over the operation and it has to be better than us all going back and having to pay off such a huge debt before we can get back on our feet. If the doctors advise against returning to Africa as they might well do in the short term, then I will return in August next year when it'll all be over and everything paid off. What do you think?"

"How about you in all this?" Ann asked.

"Look if you and the children are all right, then I'll manage. I'll miss you all like you could never imagine, but I'll do it for their sake and for yours. Together we can do it, but it's never going to be easy. We all have to make a sacrifice in order to get out of this mess and this seems a good compromise."

"Yes, it does seem the best way, but it does blow our dream out of the water," said Ann reluctantly.

"Forget dreams for now," Terry said, "this is reality, hard tough realism. Dreams can follow."

Over lunch the decision was explained to Lesley: she could see that this was probably the best answer. She offered anything she had to help them, which was much appreciated.

"If you can just help us with the children while we get all this organised then that is the biggest help you can give at the moment." Ann said, thanking her for the offer. "I'm afraid it's not going to turn out to be the sort of holiday we had planned for you Auntie, but that's life!"

When Paul and Lynda returned from school, Terry and Ann explained that their Mum had been to see the doctor who said it was vital that she had further treatment to her foot as soon as possible. Therefore it was necessary for them to return home with her and for Daddy to stay to keep his promise to the university to go on working until August the following year. They both looked sad and upset and wondered about their guinea pig, Olga. What would happen to him? It was suggested that as he was not able to come on the plane with them, their friends Sue and Paul Reynolds might look after him for them. They agreed reluctantly to this arrangement, saying they really would prefer to stay at Bunda. It was explained how they would be able to return to visit Olga at Easter, which did seem to soften the blow.

Terry's feet never touched the ground, once the decision had been made for Ann and the children to return home to England. There was so much to do and no University support for such an event. The first thing was to get flights booked and after hours spent in Lilongwe at the travel office Terry was finally able to get them all on a flight, from Blantyre to London on Thursday 24th August. It meant that he would have to drive them the 140 miles to Blantyre as there was no connecting local flight, but that was the earliest available and it gave them six days to prepare. He had to write formally to the University and to the Principal of Bunda College to inform them what was going on, to reassure them that he would be remaining as Farm Manager. As to the future, Terry felt he should keep the door open until Ann's operation was over and the doctors had given their thoughts and advice.

Terry's sister, Esmee, was a tremendous help in agreeing to have the children stay with her when Ann was hospitalised and helping with getting the children into the local Catholic school. Terry's father agreed that they could stay with him until Terry returned to England, which was a tremendous help. He was very concerned for them all and wanting to assist in whatever way he could. Ann was glad to know Paul and Lynda had a school to go to that was near-by and so close to their Grandad's house.

The days flew by, Ann found she couldn't go to say goodbye to the sisters at Mlale, time ran out and she wouldn't have found it easy after all their kindness. Terry promised to go over and tell the sisters as soon as he got back from Blantyre. It was very hard for her saying goodbye to their lovely house at Bunda after having worked so hard to turn it into the home they had planned to stay in for many years. Ann realised how hard it was going to be for Terry to have Lesley staying for another five weeks. She was never the easiest person to live with!

Terry kept busy and as long as that was the case all was well. He couldn't stop to think about the direction in which he was going, or the emptiness he would undoubtedly feel once they had left. When he did think about it, he felt a colossal pressure numbing his senses: the beauty and gracefulness that was Ann, slowly being dragged away from him, day by wretched day, was a living nightmare.

On the day of departure the 24th August 1978 they decided to leave early. Nobody had been told when they were to leave. Ann could not face the goodbyes that would have arisen. Lesley was to stay at Bunda in the care of John, and only those two knew the day of Ann's departure. Terry loaded up the car at 7.30 that cold misty morning. John had prepared food for the journey to Blantyre and Terry had booked a hotel room to go and stay after he had seen the plane off at 5pm.

Ann said a tearful goodbye to Lesley and made her promise to keep an eye on Terry. John and his wife and their four children all stood in a line by the door as Ann made her way to the car, the little children all dressed in their Sunday best. Each one squeezed her hand shyly and smiled in that special way that only African children can. They shook Paul and Lynda's hands and said goodbye to them in Chichewa.

"I shall take care of Big Madame and the Bwana and give them the good cookings that you have showed me to do. We wish you a good trip and you arrive in the good condition, as we are when you leave us. Please greet the doctors in the United Kingdom and tell them to mend your foot quickly that you may return to show me more cookings. You have been very kind to Margaret my wife and my children for which we say a big thank you."

Ann took one last look at the house; a tear rolled down her cheek as she looked down the garden, took a deep breath and stepped into the car with the children.

Slowly the Zephyr gathered speed, past the college buildings and out onto the dirt road that took them the twelve miles onto the tarmacked M1 to Blantyre. The car bounced along leaving a dust cloud behind that seemed to carry all of Ann's dreams silently with it, as she surrendered to the events of the day, leaving the people, the landscape, and the birds that she loved, having studied their habits and their ways, all now lost to her.

They travelled mile after endless mile along the broken and uneven surface of the M1 towards Blantyre, as fast as they were able through Nathenje, and on to the high plateau of Dedza, with its own brand of early morning freshness. Then on along the border of Mozambique, with its refugee villages extending the length of the road as far as the eye could see, the smells of decay and wood smoke drifting into the air. They took it all in as they passed over bridges and dry riverbeds with thin weak looking cattle seeking to graze amongst the dry bush grasses. They travelled along in silence, each with their own thoughts, and each with their own sadness.

Eventually they pulled in for a break at the side of the road near Ntcheu. At a high point in the landscape overlooking Mozambique, far in the distance they could see women working in the fields preparing for the new season. They enjoyed the sandwiches that John had prepared for them and it was a chance to stretch their legs and for the children to run around after the long journey.

Terry was amazed that Ann never once complained about her lot. She could easily have been forgiven for being totally consumed with all that lay before her; nobody would have denied her that. But no, as always, her thoughts were with others, confirmed to Terry by a gesture that seemed to summarise everything that was Ann and what he loved about her.

Two young boys were about fifty metres from where they were eating, peering out over the rocks in their direction. Ann picked out two oranges and a packet of biscuits from the basket of food that John had prepared for their journey. She held them up and walked towards the two young boys offering the items to them. The boys, half afraid, and like wild animals that receive food from a human hand, slowly edged forward towards her. Terry watched in admiration for what she was doing; he had not even noticed the boys, being totally taken over by the day's events, absorbed in his own distress. But Ann, carrying her own personal sorrow, still managed to see these two boys and to recognise their needs, giving them great joy and pleasure, clearly visible as they devoured the food with speed and thankfulness and smiled, waved and continued on their own journey by foot into the bush.

Ann, Terry and family continued on with their journey, through Liwonde, over the Kamuzu Barrage into Zomba with the splendid Zomba Plateau rising 7,000 ft above the town. They stopped there to refuel and to rest before going on to Chileka Airport, just outside of Blantyre. The flight was, thankfully, leaving on time at 5pm; to drag out the departure would have served only to make things worse, the whole situation already feeling very unreal.

There was much hugging, kissing, tears and goodbyes as they went through into the departure area. The airport at Chileka was such that you could see the passengers walking out onto the plane and watch it take off, not the impersonal event that it is in today's modern airports. Terry stood looking out from the raised observation bay as Ann and the children made their way to the British Airways flight BA 58 to London Heathrow. He watched them slowly walk away from him, across the tarmac, up the steps, and at the top turn and wave before disappearing inside. He watched the plane take off burying itself in the evening sky, leaving him feeling broken, desperate and alone. He remained there staring up into the sky as if they would suddenly reappear. Not knowing what to do next, his world had just been shattered and he was devastated.

He finally took himself off to the city and the Ryall's Hotel in Blantyre where he spent the night. Those distressing events left a mark on him that would last forever. The next morning he rose early, making his way back to Bunda College to be reunited with Lesley. She was pleased to see him safely home.

When Terry had finished work the following day he went to the Mlale Mission to see the sisters to tell them about Ann's departure to England. He drove down the long dusty single-track road to their mission station and knocked on the door that he assumed was their living quarters. He introduced himself to Sister Laura who answered the door and immediately invited him in for a cup of tea and to meet the other sisters. One by one they came to the kitchen for their tea, all greeting him and making him feel so welcome. He explained to them about Ann and all that had happened; they were shocked and dismayed. They insisted that he come for a meal with them the following evening and to bring along Aunty as well. That day started another life long friendship with them all, despite the fact that many of the sisters retired and moved to other parts of the world over the years.

Five days after Ann's arrival back in the U.K. she was taken into hospital at Odstock, near Salisbury, where she had four toes removed all of which were affected by the cancer. Terry's sister took care of the children, and organised their schooling at St Augustine's School on Hardy's Avenue in Weymouth, just a short distance from their Grandad's home. Terry was in touch by telephone, and desperately wanting to be with them all at this incredibly difficult time.

Ann, as ever, was unbelievably brave and was soon looking forward to coming out of hospital to be with the children at 1 Tennyson Road, where they would spend the next year. Within weeks she was beginning to think about and plan for the trip out to Malawi the following March, such was her bravery. She made a remarkably good recovery from such a big operation and soon managed to walk again, taking over the care of Paul and Lynda from Esmee and her husband Roger who had stepped in at such a difficult time.

Ann learnt to live with Grandad and together they managed very well. It must have been difficult for him too, an intrusion into his daily life at seventy years of age. However, he loved his grandchildren and was very happy to go along to Hardy's Avenue to meet the children from school in an afternoon, always stopping to buy them some sweets as he waited on the corner at Hatton's shop. He was so generous to them all.

Everyone on the campus at Bunda was very kind and helpful to Terry, inviting him to their homes and generally keeping an eye on him. The days with Aunty were not easy, as his heart and mind were elsewhere; they both felt the emptiness of the house without the family. An American couple, Ed and Mary Lawson, invited Terry and Auntie to join them on a trip to Lafupa Lodge, at the Kasungu Game Park north of Lilongwe, where Terry and Ann had hoped to take her. It was just a three-day trip, so they decided to take up the offer. It was a wonderful expedition and a lovely change after the horrors of the past few weeks; they saw many different birds like the Pied Kingfisher, Saddle Bill Stock, the African Fish Eagle and the Woolly Necked Stork. There were many animals there too, the fierce Cape Buffalo being the most menacing of them: they had a habit of blocking off your road and then surrounding you, not an easy situation to get out of with their fierce looking horns and powerful necks. Lafupa Lodge was made up of thatched rondavels for sleeping and a central thatched building for the restaurant that in the circumstance served excellent food. The three days' break gave them a real lift and they felt more able to face all that was ahead.

Terry's birthday was on 15th September so the sisters asked him if he and Lesley would like to go with them for the weekend to another mission station at Mua over by Lake Malawi, where they were going for a few days. Mua was in its early days a leprosy centre, now it was a mission run by White Fathers and White Sisters with a large hospital and a school. It was at the bottom of a steep escarpment below the mountains of Dedza and alongside the lake, Africa's third largest, three hundred and fifty miles long and fifty miles at its widest point.

The lake was of course a great source of fish for everyone, and had fine sandy beaches with every sort of recreation. It was good to witness how another mission station was run, to see the dedication and hard work of those that managed and developed it, whose task it was to eventually hand over to the local people. The Sisters of Mua, like sisters all over the world were so welcoming and full of a reflected love and peace, making them feel very 'at home'.

The rooms at the mission were simple but clean and the food always excellent, despite restricted budgets and the availability of supplies. On the evening of Saturday 16th September, there was a spectacular event, not only a full moon but also a total eclipse of the moon for over an hour. They all sat on the steps of the mission at 7pm to watch this quite unusual happening, a moment that they would always remember, both for the eclipse and the togetherness they had shared in the midst of Malawi's isolation.

Aunt Lesley enjoyed meeting the sisters of the Mlale mission who often invited her to stay with them for the day: they enjoyed her company, also they realised how difficult it must be for Terry, who had a very demanding job at Bunda. Furthermore he had to deal with the difficult situation of Ann and the children being miles from him. So they were a tremendous support during Lesley's visit, helping him to survive. Although her holiday had not worked out quite as planned or as she could have imagined, she enjoyed her stay and the experience of being back in Africa, a place in which she had spent so much of her life serving the people for more than thirty years. In the last year at her mission station at Mkalinzi, a few miles north of Kigoma in western Tanzania, she, working alone attended to 468 in-patients and 26,684 out patients, vaccinating over 7,000 people for smallpox. It was no surprise that her people referred to her as "The Warrior."

It was with some relief that Terry put Lesley on the Air Malawi plane at Lilongwe Airport at 2.30 on Friday 29th September 1978, at the end of her visit. It turned out to be the last time Lesley would ever see Africa, which had been her second home for so much of her life.

Terry drove back to Bunda after seeing her off, suddenly feeling very alone as he sat drinking tea on his veranda at house number 16, Bunda College, while thinking over the events of the last few weeks. He missed Ann, Paul and Lynda so much it hurt; it broke his heart being separated from them, so much so that he wondered now the wisdom of that decision. He cursed the cancer that had smashed their lives and destroyed their dreams.

He found it impossible to go into Paul and Lynda's bedroom; he had not been able to since they left, it would have been too upsetting. He had locked the door and wondered now if he could ever go back in there while they were away; it would distress him too much. He sat feeling quite miserable, thinking of his predicament. What now he wondered for him, for Ann and for the children?

Work forced Terry on with the dry planting of the new tobacco crop due to start at anytime, resulting in an increase in the labour force with all its problems. There seemed to be a run of staff with wives having their babies. The head herdsmen had knocked on Terry's window in the middle of the night, declaring, "My wife is sick. Can you take her to the hospital?"

So at 3am Terry arose, picked up the man and his wife from their house and took them to the maternity unit at the Mission

Hospital four miles away. On arrival Terry helped her out of the pick-up, and her husband took her into the hospital while Terry turned the car around. Within minutes he returned and Terry asked, "Has she settled in all right?"

"Oh yes," he replied. "It was a boy!" Their seventh child!

That was about as close as Terry wanted to be to having someone give birth in his car or alongside the road!

Ann was continuing with her remarkable and brave recovery and settling down as well as possible, given the circumstances. She had found a second hand car, which would give them all new freedom and allow them to get around more. She started a pottery class, took Paul and Lynda swimming and it enabled them to be able to go out and about, and away for weekends to see Margaret and Philip in Devon or home to visit her parents at Pucklechurch, near Bristol.

The protest against fuel taxation was gaining strength causing shortages everywhere. The Prime Minister James Callaghan had even considered calling a 'state of emergency' as the protests developed around the country in what became the "Winter of Discontent." Ann often had problems finding a garage with petrol, but going out of town, she was able to find fuel more readily available, but of course risky in case there was none and the petrol ran out. Shades of Africa!

She spent so much of her time writing letters to Terry, every two or three days one was posted off to Malawi, with pictures and a few words from the children. She knew and understood the value of letters and she herself lived for the next one from Terry. She often thought how much of their lives had been spent communicating with each other in this way, far too much; in fact it had to stop.

Terry only had access to the telephone through the farm office at work; it was very expensive to call England at £10 for six minutes. However, they tried to have a chat once a month and it was on such an occasion that Ann had to convey the sad news that his Aunty Potton had been taken into hospital at Dorchester and died on Saturday 7th October 1978. Terry was devastated; she had been like a mother to him, always there in times of need or for advice. She had at all times been kind and loving, never demanding and so grateful for any help he gave her in the way of shopping, repairing things around the house, cutting firewood or delivering the washing that she took in to make ends meet.

She was of the old school, knowing absolute contentment, never craving for anything and quietly accepting what life bestowed on her. In thankfulness she knelt by her bed every night to say her prayers to a Father she totally trusted in with absolute faith. Her greatest joy was to have half a pig's head for her Sunday roast, washed down with a 'Green Top' (a light ale). Most evenings she would walk the mile to the Railway Arch public house, on Chickerell Road. There she would stand at the same place every night in the corner of the bar and enjoy her 'Green Top' and a chat with anyone. It did not matter how many drinks she had during the evening, she would always walk home clutching two full bottles, one of which she drank sitting at her table before going to bed, come what may!

Every morning you could time your watch by her: at ten minutes to eight you would see her walking down Bradford Road on her way to do the cleaning at the Railway Arch public house, never late by a minute. She cleaned house for a doctor and his wife once a week on Wyke Road and afterwards, on her way home, she would cut through the convent grounds where Terry attended his senior school. His bicycle was always parked on the driveway: she would stop at his bike and place a chocolate bar in his saddlebag, such was her love.

The first rain of the year at Bunda started at 6pm on Friday 20th October, and welcome it was too. Dry planting of tobacco had started early in October as it usually did, so, unless it was to be replanted, rain was essential. It was a very special time, to smell the rain on the dry African soil, an aroma that stays with you always.

Christmas 1978 was of course the hardest time for them all. Ann and the children spent it with Grandad at Tennyson Road and then went down to Devon to stay a few days with Margaret and Philip. For Ann it was the peak of the hill, once past that, March and the month's holiday in Malawi was not far away, when at last she could be reunited with Terry. She was so glad they had made that plan; it did make it feel like a much shorter separation.

For Terry Christmas was a unique celebration. He attended midnight Mass with the sisters at Mlale Mission and Luigi was there too. Christmas dinner was had all together at the Mission with the White Fathers; there were twelve different nationalities around the table for lunch. Terry brought along a large pork joint and a rib of beef and every vegetable you could think of from the college farm. Luigi brought a turkey (No, not Philip!) goat and many bottles of wine, some from Italy! Sister Laura, Anny and Genevive all joined in to help and although Terry missed his family desperately, he did enjoy the unusualness of the day with them.

1979 made a welcome entry. Ann was battling with snow and shortage of fuels everywhere as she went to Devon to visit friends Margaret and Philip. Terry on the other hand was battling with heat, the tobacco and maize crops of Malawi. On New Year's Day he enjoyed the day with the sisters. He and Anny, the Dutch sister who was a midwife at the hospital, went for a walk in the bush. They got on so well together. She always had words of comfort and wisdom for him. They grew very close during that time; she was a marvellous support while he was in Malawi and during the years that followed, until she was "lost" to Alzheimer's Disease in later years while retired in Holland where she is today.

The New Year brought news that a Sister Claire was coming to stay at Mlale mission. She had been taken ill at one of the missions and was forced to return to her home in Canada. Claire, now well into her 70's, had been the Provincial for the whole of East Africa, and well respected for her many years of service. She was very weak and needed to rest and gain in strength before making the journey to Canada with her friend, Sister Marcelle, who would look after her.

Terry grew to know and admire Claire, finding her a brave, fearsome lady, with a strong faith and a wonderful sense of humour.

He enjoyed sitting chatting with her when she was feeling strong enough, listening to her numerous and fascinating stories relating to her years in East and Central Africa. Sadly her health was failing and it was not expected she would live for very long, but they hoped long enough to return to her beloved home in Quebec.

Terry often dropped in to have afternoon tea with the sisters, for a bit of light relief from his work. He would drive the few miles from Bunda, often with piles of tomatoes, cabbage or whatever the farm had in abundance, to give to the sisters, and the patients of the hospital. Laura who ran the kitchen and organised all the cooking was of course delighted to receive these gifts. He would often sit and enjoy a conversation with Claire, if she was up to it.

"Well, Claire, how are you today?" he would ask her as she sat quietly taking in her surroundings.

"I'm being well looked after for which I thank God," she'd reply. "The trouble is I have no appetite, the only thing I fancy to eat is fish, which we don't have. We're too far from the lake or the sea so I have to manage!"

"I've plenty of fish at Bunda Farm. We have ponds and a large lake where we breed them and sometimes sell them in the shop," Terry explained to her, "If you like I could bring you some."

"Would you really? That would be wonderful. You are kind."

The next day Terry brought her some fish and every few days after, whenever they were available from the farm. She did enjoy them and slowly with the love and support of her fellow sisters grew in health and strength, so much so that the doctor told her she was strong enough to make the journey to Canada.

The day she left Mlale with her friend and carer, sister Marcelle, to fly to Canada, Terry went to say goodbye, knowing that he would probably never see her again and to thank her for her friendship and the happy times they had shared.

"Your fish has saved my life!" she said, as he gave her a big hug. Climbing into the car that was to take her to the airport, she said, "I'll write to you from Canada." He waved her goodbye and could never have imagined the wisdom and support he would receive from her in the years ahead or the circumstances of their next meeting.

Ann's foot healed well and she managed with the disability of losing four small toes. Never complaining, she attended the doctors regularly to make sure all was well. There seemed to be no further problem with the foot and everyone was happy that the cancer had now all been removed.

All thoughts were now set on Ann and the children going to Malawi for Easter: the date was set and the flights booked for Thursday 22nd March 1979, six days before Lynda's seventh birthday.

Terry happily drove to Blantyre to meet them on a glorious sunny day, showing Malawi off at its best. He had booked a family room at the Ryalls hotel in Blantyre in order that they could have a night's rest before setting out on the long journey to Bunda College. Terry arrived a full hour before the plane was due in; he scoured the sky for the first sight of it. He had his cine camera ready to record the event and their arrival; he felt sure that Paul would enjoy seeing himself fly in, as he was still very keen on aircraft and flying. Right on time the Super VC10 touched down and slowly pulled in to the buildings in front of where Terry was standing. He trained his camera on the door of the aircraft as it opened; excitement was high, making it difficult to hold the camera still.

One by one the passengers came down the gangway, but no Ann, Paul or Lynda appeared. The numbers slowed and then stopped, everyone was off the plane. Terry's heart sank. What on earth had happened he wondered? Then suddenly there they were, slowly making their way down the stairs to the tarmac, the last ones off the plane. What a relief!

"Don't ever do that to me again," he said when they came into the arrivals' area and he held them all in his arms.

"I hope we'll never have to," Ann replied. "Sorry but we were gathering everything together and I wanted to make sure nobody stood on my foot!"

"It doesn't matter, nothing matters now. We are together again," Terry said with glee.

They drove off to the hotel and while Ann and Terry had tea, Paul and Lynda were quickly into the swimming pool, keen to show their Dad how well they could swim, with armbands of course!

"How are you really?" Terry asked Ann, as they sat by the pool enjoying a cup of Malawi tea. "You certainly look well."

"I feel well and the doctors all seem happy with me, so yes I guess I must be fine. The foot is healed and I manage well, better then I thought I would. At least I have my big toe, which, they say, is half of the foot." She smiled bravely.

"It has all been such a terrible ordeal, and I don't mean the operation, I mean our separation. Your Dad has been lovely and so generous in everyway, so sweet. He gave me £10 when I left to spend on the children while we are away and is always buying them bags of sweets or giving them pocket money. Your sister too has been marvellous. I don't know how I'd have managed without her and Roger, but I've found it so very hard, being without you and alone."

"Sorry to blurt all this out to you now, so early, but I have to tell you."

"No please do. Paul and Lynda are fine there in the pool for a while, happy to be free and work off some of their energy after your long flight."

Ann looked intensely at Terry with some anguish and sadness.
"I've had to make a decision I'm afraid. I hope you won't be too hurt and upset by it."

Terry listened to her intently, wondering what to expect.

"You know how we've always said we wanted to work in Africa and to make it our life's work. We always said that, right back when we first met at Hombolo Leprosy Centre. Well, Terry, I'm sorry, but I can never, ever, go through these separations again, never. Do you understand? I just can't do it."

"If I was to return here to live and we carried on as before and then something like I've just been through happens again, well

I couldn't go through with yet another separation, not again, not ever. Sorry I just couldn't. Can you understand? Can you forgive me?"

Terry gazed at her in silence, trying to take it all in, the full implications of it. Clearly she was deeply troubled by the separation they had just been forced to endure. It had hit her hard, as it had Terry, but she had made a decision, and there was no going back.

"You realise what this means, don't you?" Ann said. "Our African life, our work, our dream is over, forever. We can never again consider working in our beloved Africa. Terry, I'm emotionally drained. I married you because I loved you and wanted us to be together, that's to live together, not on opposite sides of the world like we've had to do. I'm not prepared, or able to put us in the position of having ever to do that all over again. When you come home in August after all this is over, that's in five months time, it has to be forever."

"Of course I do understand," Terry replied. "This has been the longest and most difficult of all the times that we've been apart. I feel as you do, I can't do it again. It broke my heart to see you, Paul and Lynda leave as you did. It tore me apart; we have to give up the madness that is Africa. I know we do."

"We just have to live through the next five months, then given time I'm sure we'll settle into something else and will find other ways to love and serve Africa and its people. We can't go on fighting against the odds as we've done. Enough is enough!"

"I'm so glad to hear you say that," Ann said. "I sensed from your letters that you would. You sounded so low at times; I wanted to jump on the next plane to be with you."

They both felt in sombre mood the next day as they made their way to Lilongwe and to Bunda College. "I feel as if I have never been away. It's strange, but it's so nice to be back. I'm glad we decided to do this," Ann said happily.

The following evening Terry had organised a dinner party at their house. All the Sisters, Luigi and some of the Bunda friends came along. He had acquired the largest rib of beef possible from the farm for the celebration and John, their cook, pulled out all the stops for the occasion.

"Bwana," he enquired, "this time I serve through the hatch again? But I 'm not climbing through, you see I learn!"

"You do well, John, you learn very quickly," Terry replied.

Luigi arrived with what at first looked like a large bouquet of flowers; on closer examination you could see that it was huge tobacco leaves and their flower heads, all wrapped in a large clear oven bag. It looked just like something from a flower shop. That was typical of his kindness and creativity. He presented these to Ann to welcome her back home as he put it.

Ann enjoyed her return to Bunda. There was no doubt that it had been absolutely the right thing for them to do. She took her bicycle out into the bush to view the wonderful bird life as she had so often done before; the beauty of them overwhelmed her as they silently glided around in the depth of the forested areas. She loved the trees too and had her favourites; she would sit for ages with her back to a tree as if to draw strength from it, sketching a picture and becoming absorbed in her surroundings and in her own solitary thoughts, trying to make sense of all that had taken place in their lives. Did she ever find the answers? Her reflective and placid personality would indicate that perhaps she had.

As Terry and Ann had been forced to give up their life in Africa, deciding he would return home in August for good, it was necessary to write to the University Registrar in Zomba and to the Principal of Bunda College to tender his resignation. It was a tough thing to do, especially after all the heartache of trying to find the job in the first place. He'd grown to love the country and had enjoyed the work; he was getting to know the people and to see the development of the farm as it grew in size and productivity. Of course his resignation also marked the end of his working life in Africa, which saddened him.

Like a favourite box of chocolates that you never want to end, the holiday drew to a close, the dream to an end. The day before

Ann and the children left Bunda, the Sisters of Mlale mission invited them all over for supper. Terry took along some films that he had borrowed from the British Council, and showed them on the old college Bell and Howard 16mm projector. They all sat in the long kitchen as he projected them on to the white wall that acted as a screen. They enjoyed the evening but it was more than tinged with sadness. Terry began to wonder if the strain of it all was getting to him, he was not feeling himself at all, but weak, tired and exhausted. He did not say anything to Ann, but he felt really ill, hot and cold, weak and shivery. He confided in Sister Anny. She said that he could be getting flu or even malaria: his head throbbed and at times he did not know which way to turn. Ann did ask him if he was sickening for something, as he looked pale; he told her it was just a cold, but he couldn't wait to get back to bed.

On Friday 20th April 1979 Ann and the children left Bunda for the last time. Terry once again drove them to Blantyre to catch their BA flight to London. He was feeling really flu-like, his head and his heart heavy that day as he put them through the airport formalities and they checked in for the flight. He stood watching them in the scalding heat, as once again distance was to separate them. They walked away up the steps of the plane and disappeared inside. It took off shortly and in minutes they were no more than a dot in the sky, as the jet took them from him and on their long return journey to England.

Terry, with head throbbing, managed to drive back to Bunda and immediately took to his bed. By the middle of the night he realised that he must have malaria, one minute he was hot the next cold, shivering and sweating in turn. He had violent nightmares and a head that felt as if there were a thousand hammers banging away inside. Fortunately Sister Anny had given him some tablets in case it was malaria, which he decided to take. He had no memory of when or how many he had taken; all he could recall was that he was either hot or cold, shivering with hot water bottles around him one minute and then so hot he felt he was cooking from within. He was afraid to sleep because of the nightmares, but sleep he did, almost without knowing, until he awoke, either freezing or sweating profusely.

John, the houseboy, was very alarmed and sent to the college for the medical nurse. Her reputation was that she would prescribe either a plaster or an aspirin, neither of which were currently in stock, but she confirmed that he did indeed have malaria and he should stay in bed. The way Terry was feeling he wondered if he would ever have any other choice. After four days of this he began to feel slightly better and was able to stand the sight of food, but not to eat it. He drank as much fluid as he could. This he knew was important. On the sixth day he felt able to eat and slowly over the course of the next week dragged himself back to something like normal. He felt weak but returned to work after ten days, wondering how on earth he had picked up the malaria because he had been taking all the necessary protection.

Ann and Terry soon had to return to their old way of life, taking some comfort from knowing the end was in sight. Terry worked away at Bunda with long hours and the many frustrations, enjoying the company and support of people like Luigi and the sisters. Ann and the children were back with Terry's father at Tennyson Road, Weymouth, supported by visits to see Esmee and Roger and to her parents at Pucklechurch and friends in Devon. Letters were always a great help even if they did take a week to ten days to arrive and with all the strikes it was often much longer. An air letter (a bluey) was priced at ten and a half pence with a full letter by air around eleven to twelve pence so it was quite a part of their budget. Ann was starting to prepare for Terry's return by taking his suit to the cleaners ready for his interviews. She thought that the charge of £1.50 to have it cleaned was a bit steep, but it had to be done. While out shopping, she decided to buy a new king size quilt for their bed at Tennyson Road as VAT was shortly to rise to 15%.

Lynda had started dancing classes, which she enjoyed and was already working towards an exam in July; she did seem to have a certain 'feel' for it. They continued to attend swimming lessons at the pool in Weymouth and Lynda and Paul were both improving. Grandad, always so generous, liked to pay for them to go swimming. Petrol shortages continued: it now cost £1.20 a gallon, if it could be found. Ann had managed mostly to get her tank filled up and acquired a 'Regular Customer' card from the local garage. She had mentioned to a few people how she enjoyed sewing and had been asked to shorten eight railwaymen's trousers, not her favourite job, but she was paid fifty pence a pair. Esmee often visited Ann and had asked her if she would answer some questions for one of her research questionnaires that she often carried out in a part time job. Roger had made Ann a flower press, which would help her in her hobby of pressed flower card making.

"Tomorrow is our Wedding Anniversary," Ann wrote in her letter to Terry of Thursday 7th June. "Happy Anniversary. I feel very sad here on my own as I contemplate our wedding day eleven years ago. You should be here but you're not! Roll on eight weeks time."

"What a wonderful surprise it was when Esmee walked in about 10.30am with the most beautiful bouquet of flowers from you! Russet coloured chrysanthemums, red carnations, some white stocks and freesias and some maidenhair fern with a big red ribbon around them. Thank you very, very much. They are super, also the lovely card you had written. I can't stop looking at them. Esmee suggested that I put the flowers in a bottle of lemonade; she said her pub landlady always puts her flowers in it; something to do with the bubbles keeping them fresh! Your Dad went out this morning to get a card for us. It's a lovely one, but he handed it to me in its cellophane wrapping; he hadn't written in it. He is a case, isn't he?"

"By the way I went to Poole Pottery Shop where you can buy very good seconds. It's full of lovely things and with the VAT about to go up and knowing our need to replace items that we've sold, I went ahead and purchased some thirty-five pieces, jug, teapot, tea plates, cereal bowls, dinner plates and oval plates, tea cups and saucers. They are greyish/white with slightly fluted edges all for £38.62. I'm thrilled with it all and can't wait to use it in our new home, where ever that'll be!"

On 3rd June, Whit Sunday, Terry, Luigi and the sisters from Mlale took a picnic to the top of Bunda Mountain behind the college. It was quite a steep climb over the rock face to the top: the views from there were magnificent as they all sat enjoying the view and rest while eating their picnic. They wrote a card from the summit to post to Ann, so she would know they had all been thinking of her. Then all signed it and took a few pictures and cine film to record the event. Occasions like this were a godsend for Terry as he ticked off the days and his return to the family. Their separation was made worse due to a postal strike in the U.K. that was holding up all letters; he had not heard from them for over three weeks and even worse they were not getting his letters either. Strangely a cassette tape he had made with the sisters had got through and the one Ann had made in reply arrived in eight days. They were, on both sides of the divide, counting the days and planning for the reunion. Ann was taking the Farmers' Weekly to see if there were suitable job vacancies and forwarding them on to Terry in the hope that he may be able to find something to apply for.

Terry began to put up for sale items that he would not be taking home. The main one was the Ford Zephyr car. It had been a faithful friend and on the whole reliable, so he was sorry to see it go. He placed an advert at the golf club and at the butchery in Lilongwe, as was traditional when expatriates left the country. He had the use of the college pick-up for his everyday needs so could manage without it. It was only a few days later that a newly arrived couple to Malawi bought the car for the same price he had paid for it, fifteen months before, so he was happy to dispose of it satisfactorily.

Excitement was all around in Malawi as the Queen, the Duke of Edinburgh and Prince Andrew were to make a short visit on Monday 23rd July to the new capital of Lilongwe that was moving from the old colonial headquarters in Zomba. They would be welcomed by His Excellency the Life President, Ngwazi Dr. H. Kamuzu Banda and his ministers at a reception at the palace, before leaving for a visit to Botswana on their four nation African tour.

No doubt Ann would be watching closely at home to see if she could recognise anyone or the places shown on the news clips.

Terry received a letter from his father, full of excitement about the fact that his nephew Laurie had been in touch, and with his father George was coming to see him at Tennyson Road. They had never been in touch for years for some reason, but had now suddenly decided to make contact. Terry's dad was delighted. He also said how much Paul had been helping him in the garden and enjoyed it, cutting the grass, watering and planting for his grandad.

Terry's last week in Malawi was full of emotion. Most of his things were either packed up ready to be shipped back to U.K. sold, or in the case ready to leave. The Farm office was busy with farm reports and letters to complete, as he handed over the farm to Choen Sichinga who would be the acting Farm Manager until the new appointment had been completed. There were so many farm staff to say farewell to and he was touched by their kind words.

The week before he left, Terry took his cook/houseboy John to Salima, on the banks of Lake Malawi, to the village where he had his home. Terry drove John, his wife and children with their few possessions in his pick-up truck to the lakeside village. It was sad to say goodbye for John had been a faithful and honest man in all his dealings with them. He and his family all shook hands and waved as Terry left them at seven in the morning standing in the dust on the lakeshore as he made the return journey to Bunda.

Every day there was either a farewell dinner or a lunch with someone, such as Janet a volunteer working at the college, Len and Mary Reynolds lecturer and friends from Bunda, Wanda an American teacher, Ed and Mary Lawson also from the states, Luigi, of course, and last of all the Sisters of Mlale. They invited a Dutch White Father, Fr Cola to say a Mass, after which they provided a lovely supper, when they all sang "Till We Meet Again" by Jim Reeves; there wasn't a dry eye in the house.

Terry was due to fly out on 3rd August. Ed and Mary Lawson offered to take him to Lilongwe Airport, where he would get the local flight to Blantyre. There he would pick up the BA flight to London. In the morning he had been asked to go down to the farm to bid farewell to the men and leave the pick-up outside the farm office. Terry suspected nothing and drove to the farm. As he approached he could see a large body of people milling around and wondered what was going on. Oh no, not trouble he thought, not on my last day!

He pulled up outside the farm office as he had done so many times before.

Mr Munthali the farm foreman greeted him as he stepped out of the pick-up.

"Bwana, we are all here today to say goodbye to you, all the men that work here and some that you employed in the tobacco fields last season. Many have come miles to greet you."

Terry was amazed, the colour drained from his face in surprise as the crowd gathered around him. Someone had put a long trailer by the office so that some of the men could stand on it to see him.

"There are over three hundred men here from the farm and around one hundred and fifty workers from the tobacco section," Mr Munthali informed him.

"Mr Segula your office clerk would now like to say a few words."

He stood on a box outside the office so he could be seen, a short grey haired sincere man, who had worked closely with Terry. All the staff gathered around. There was absolute silence as he read the letter that he had prepared and was to give Terry after the ceremony.

ON YOUR DEPARTURE

"It is a matter of a few hours before you leave us for the United Kingdom. It is regrettable that you will do so alone, without your beloved wife and children who are currently at home on doctor's advice.

We do not have much to say at this moment except mentioning that we had in you a Farm Manager who was always kind and understanding. And as a token of our appreciation for this, we have unanimously decided to present this small gift to you. We hope you will accept it.

When you are in the United Kingdom or elsewhere, do please remember us always.

We wish you good luck, ZIKOMO. (thank you)"

Sincerely yours,
BUNDA COLLEGE FARM STAFF - LILONGWE, MALAWI

With that he was presented with a number of ebony woodcarvings of African people. After which it was his turn to stand on the box and say a few words, which he asked Mr Segula to translate for him, as most did not understand English only Chichewa, the local language.

Terry was deeply touched by the presence of so many people that had gathered there to say goodbye; it crossed all language barriers and would stay with him always.

A few pictures of them all were then taken, gathered around the trailer; they divided up into different groups for other pictures before saying the final sad farewell.

Terry left Lilongwe Airport at 14.30 to fly Air Malawi to Blantyre, from where all the international flights operated.

At 17.30 on Friday 3rd August 1979, he sat looking out of the plane window, while they awaited clearance for take off. The sun was dropping to the horizon, an enormous orange ball set in a deep red sky the like of which he had never seen before. It seemed to symbolise the end of Terry's short career in Africa as he gazed out across the landscape with a lump in his throat watching the sun and his life in Africa sink out of sight.

Chapter Nineteen

Arriving 6.30am at Heathrow Airport in August is only slightly better than at the same time on a wet and windy day in November. But for Terry just to catch sight of Ann, Paul and Lynda waiting to greet him made it all worthwhile.

He caught his breath as he saw her beaming with joy and happiness in a blue-striped dress that set off her fair hair, standing between the two children, his long suffering children, and they so young, so fragile, so trusting in the decisions that had been made to bring them to that day.

There was a frenzy of hugging, kissing, tears and excitement as he scooped them all up, sitting Paul and Lynda on the luggage trolley, then pushing them along through the corridors to the car park, laughing and joking as they went.

Ann had booked a caravan just outside Stonehenge near the village of Newton Tone. She had already spent a couple of days there with the children to prepare things before his arrival and had driven to the airport from the caravan that morning. It was quite an isolated spot on a farm, but she felt, very suitable for them to spend a few days together, before plunging Terry into the challenges of life back in England.

They loaded up his cases into Ann's Morris 1300 and she drove them confidently around the fast moving roads of London and on to the caravan parked on the edge of a quiet field, just outside the village. It had two bedrooms and was very well equipped with a near full size kitchen, rather like a small cottage. Terry was in a daze; everything seemed to be moving so fast, the cars, the people, everything, with everybody in such a rush, a very different pace to that of Malawi that he'd just left.

"Why is everyone in such a hurry?" he asked Ann.

"Yes I know, it seems like that when you first arrive back, hard to believe, but soon you will pick up the same pace, it's life here in England I'm afraid!"

Terry was so glad to be able to stop and rest and take it all in. There was so much for him to absorb, with his mind still back in Malawi and the sorrows and joys of the past few weeks.

He had brought gifts for them all from Malawi, a hand made wire car for Paul made by a young Malawian boy out of galvanised wire, wooden dolls dressed in traditional Malawian costume for Lynda, perfume for Ann from the plane as well as Malawi Gin and Malawi tea, which he distributed while Ann made some coffee. Paul and Lynda were keen to show their Dad around their room in the caravan, as well as all their toys and books. They did not want to leave his side for a minute following him everywhere he went.

"So now it is my turn to ask you," Ann said, "how are you? How did it all go? How do you feel now you're back in England?"

"First and foremost I'm happy to be back and with you all: it blocks out everything else and makes you realise what the important things are in life. Everything I want is here; let's leave it like that for now. I'm relieved that it's over now and all behind us and we are back together, as it should be. I'm very tired and need to rest and come to terms with everything and then I'll be all right."

The caravan was a wonderful environment for them to spend the next few days, a place to step off the world. It had been very perceptive of Ann to choose such a spot, Terry thought. The children enjoyed the wide open spaces, playing football, riding the farm ponies and being with their Dad as they got to know each other again. Paul in particular had missed his Dad and so enjoyed having someone to kick a football with and to enjoy some male company. Terry had missed them both so much; he was totally overwhelmed having them back again. Ann watched him reading to them with tears of joy running down his cheeks. He could not bear to let them go and in the end they both fell asleep in his arms. Ann watched with pleasure before prizing them apart and into their beds.

In the evenings Ann and Terry at last had time to themselves, their wounds were deep, and they needed that healing time together. They had to get to know each other again, to try and feel and to understand what they had both been through in their totally different circumstances, separated by horror and providence. To listen to each other, to have the opportunity to talk over the events that had taken place, in both their lives over the past few months, while at the same time getting stuck into the Malawi gin! Terry had been a stranger to sleep for the past month, living on nervous energy, so was able to catch up, to the extent that Ann wondered if he was suffering from some tropical disease again, he slept so much. She remembered he had twice suffered from malaria during his time in Malawi. He was quite drawn and gaunt, and so she let him sleep when he needed to. He did seem to spend quite a lot of his time sitting outside gazing towards the hills, as if in a trance. It was a total change for him, the climate, the surroundings, the routine and the sudden lack of responsibility that had been his with all the people and the politics that surrounded his job at Bunda. He had put on a very brave face, but Ann's illness and being separated from Paul and Lynda sat heavily on his shoulders. As he often said to her, he felt he really was not equipped to carry such a burden. It seemed only now that he had the time to absorb all that had taken place; it was as if he was trying to understand and come to terms with it all, as he sat staring blankly ahead. He was certainly in a state of shock.

The time and effort that had gone into finding the right job in the right place, being appointed as Farm Manager at the University of Malawi against all odds, only to have it snatched away made no sense to him. Somehow he had to put all that behind him, pick himself up and get out there and find another job, difficult when he felt he had had his ultimate job but was forced to give it up.

After the treasured days and nights together, resting, pondering their joys and sorrows, the time came for them to return to everyday life. The challenges ahead were enormous; they were to be their most difficult yet. Sometimes we wish we could see into the future but our creator was entirely right in not permitting us that faculty.

Terry was delighted to see his father again; he was older but retained his youthful face, never really looking his now seventy one years. They chatted about Malawi, but Frank had never travelled out of the U.K. so had little understanding of having to live and work in a foreign country and all that goes with it. None the less he was delighted to see his son safely home again with his family. The next few days were a whirl of visiting friends and family around the place and of course seeing Ann's parents in Pucklechurch. He was able to thank Esmee and Roger for coming to his aid in taking care of the children when Ann first had to return home, something he would always be grateful to them for doing.

The most important task now was for Terry to start looking for new employment. He felt instinctively that this was not going to be an easy undertaking, partly because his last position had been a totally satisfactory one for him. For once it had not been his choice to leave it. He could not continue to dwell on the past and had to go forward. After all, the last time he only had to write off for a few jobs and then managed to have one offered to him. He poured over the Farmers' Weekly, his only real source of advertised appointments, selecting a few that might be of interest and wrote off with his C.V. and detailed letter explaining his current position. He had already written off ten applications from adverts Ann had sent to him when he was in Malawi, most of those were not prepared to consider him as he was too far away at that time, or else they told him they would, 'hold his name on file'.

He only applied for jobs south of a line from Bristol to Buckinghamshire, as they did not really want to live in the north. He applied for farm managers' jobs in Swindon, Hampshire, Henley on Thames, Burford, and Buckinghamshire. Then lifting the line he went on to apply for posts in Oxford, Gloucestershire, an Aylesbury Mushroom farm, as well as Melton Mowbray, Berwickshire, Yorkshire and with Lord Forbes in Aberdeen to name but a few. These often resulted in no reply, or a 'thank you, but no thank you,' type of letter. Panic and depression set in as he began to realise that it was not as easy to find a job in 1979 as it had previously been.

He bought a small table at the local furniture store to use as a desk in their bedroom at his father's house on Tennyson Road, so he could work without disturbance. Many an hour was spent writing letters and filling forms and by this time he was prepared to move anywhere a suitable job could be found.

By the end of September he was beginning to wonder if he would ever find a job or indeed be invited to an interview. He decided to go and sign on at the Employment Exchange to register as unemployed, something he had never had to do before; it meant that he would receive £30 a week in unemployment benefit payments while he was seeking work, so he felt it to be worthwhile. To go through the process was quite an experience, being passed from one desk to another, filling forms, answering questions. There did not really seem to be a category that he fitted into, so they were not quite sure what to do with him. They didn't have that many farm managers just returned from Africa on their books! Every two weeks he had to go and join the queue at the offices on Westham Road in Weymouth to sign a form to say that he was still unemployed; if he failed to do that he would not receive his payment. He hated that.

His spirits were low. When not writing letters of application he took himself off on a walk along the old railway track to Sandsfoot Castle. There he went down onto the small beach below to gather winkles as he had done as a child, fruits of the sea that he loved! It gave him something useful to do and he enjoyed the walk and the sea air to blow away the cobwebs.

On the 2nd October he saw a very small advert the size of a postage stamp in the Farmers' Weekly, asking for an Estate Manager, near Harrogate, in North Yorkshire. Terry decided to apply, not holding out much hope for the job, with the advert being so small and having little or no impact. He had applied for so many he thought, why not have a go. There was nothing to lose.

On the 24th October he received a phone call asking him to attend an interview at the offices of the Bowman Estate, North Park Road in the centre of Harrogate. So on Tuesday 6th November he took the 6.15am train from Weymouth to Leeds and Harrogate in time to arrive for his 3pm interview with Peter Quigley the group manager. It was a strange interview, as Mr Quigley seemed to know very little about the job, what the acreage was or how many farms they had on the estate!

It seemed to Terry as if they owned many farms in different parts of Yorkshire, centred on the area around York, all let to tenant farmers. The post was really more of a land agent, or as the Scottish would say a 'Factor'. Quigley was very vague about the whole thing, even when Terry asked him about the salary that was being offered.

"What salary were you thinking of Mr Reeves?" Quigley asked him.

"I was thinking about £7,000 per annum, plus a house and car," Terry replied, tongue in cheek.

"That's just what we were thinking to offer," Mr Quigley replied.

Terry had the feeling that not only did Mr Quigley have no idea, he had not even given it any thought! "I assume that there is also a pension scheme within the company too?" Terry enquired.

"Yes," a nervous reply came, "we are about to look into setting up a new scheme for all the staff."

Again Terry felt that Quigley had no idea what a pension scheme was, that it was all very new to him. He did seem incredibly naive.

With that the office door opened and in walked a smart, suave looking man in a grey suit. Terry was introduced to him.

"This is Andrew Bowman who owns the estate," Quigley rattled off.

Terry shook his hand. He had a very slivery handshake and his eyes were all over the place in a nervous sort of way.

"Very pleased to meet you. I trust Mr Quigley has told you all about us. I gather you have just returned from Africa; that will have been interesting. Well I'll leave you to it, hope to see you again!"

That was it. He was out of the door as fast as he had come in.

Terry tried to extract more information about the job from Quigley, but little was forthcoming. All he could gather was that the tenanted farms were being managed by a local estate agent and auctioneer. Andrew Bowman was not happy with the service they had provided, so decided to manage it in-house and therefore needed someone with agricultural knowledge to take over the job.

There were, apparently, a number of houses available for the successful applicant and Terry would be free to choose one of five if appointed.

Quigley was then very keen to see that Terry had his return train fare of £39.60 repaid to him, together with a generous payment for his meals while travelling to and from the interview. They shook hands and Quigley said he would be in touch by the end of November. Terry then took the 17.10 train from Harrogate and arrived back in Weymouth at 23.35, somewhat exhausted after the long and rather confusing day.

"How did it go? What's the job like?" Ann asked Terry when she met him at the station in Weymouth.

"Well strangely, I'm not actually sure. It really was the most bizarre interview I've ever had. I'm sure if I'd told them the moon was made of green cheese they would have believed me!"

Terry related the day's events to Ann, and they both came to the conclusion that it was an odd set up, but could be interesting and worth going for should it be offered.

"It'll mean moving all the way to Yorkshire and 'up north'," Terry laughed. "I've heard it's all cloth caps and ferrets, but yes let's give it a go if we get the chance. It's a long way from all the family, which is a shame, but we have to go where the work is if we want to make something of our lives and for the children's sake too. It's supposed to be a very beautiful county, somewhere that neither of us knows and as far as I could see there are no lions or hyenas to worry about this time!"

The salary was way above what Terry would have asked, but Ann's father, when discussing the job with him when they were last in Pucklechurch, suggested he asked for £7,000 per annum, if he had the chance, so Terry was eternally grateful for that advice.

Ann had other news for Terry: she had been to see the doctor in Salisbury for her usual check up. He had carried out an x-ray and scan on her stomach as she had been feeling some discomfort in that area for a few weeks. He wanted her to have an operation at Weymouth and District Hospital on Tuesday 20th November to investigate the situation. Terry's heart sank to a new low. Oh dear, here we go again he thought.

Ann was almost pleased to have the investigation, given all the discomfort she had endured over the past few weeks. The worry of something else breaking out was never far from the surface, yet always bravely carried. She wanted it done, when hopefully it would put a stop to her problem once and for all and take away the distress. Terry had been worried and could see that she was often in pain, which grieved him. It was only after they had asked for a second opinion that the doctor decided to take this option.

Terry took the news hard this time. He hated to see Ann suffer; it felt as if God was taking advantage of her bravery and demanding more each time. Every time it was harder for him, dragging him ever lower, even if he did not always show it. He became deeply depressed about the whole thing. Nothing seemed able to shake him out of it: the lack of a job, money worries, Ann's health, the children and coming to terms with the considerable change in their lives, after the excitement of their time spent in Africa that they had loved so much and hated to leave. He was finding it all a bit too much. His heart ached for Ann, for he knew the tremendous burden she was carrying. He hated to see her suffer as she had. He felt as if they were sitting on a time bomb.

All the time he would recall the words of the sister in the Seychelles: they rang loudly through his head. He felt so maudlin, trying to lean on his faith, trying to be strong for Ann and the children, but it was not working, he was sinking fast, uncontrollably. He would stand in the church as he attended Mass on a Sunday, unable to pray, unable to find the words or the thoughts, feeling totally devastated and rejected by the God of love. Darkness enveloped him: it was for him a living nightmare that became darker and more unreal by the day.

On Saturday 3rd November they received the sad news that Terry's Auntie Hartie from Horsham in Sussex had died in hospital at Guildford, which all added to the gloom. Terry felt that she had always understood him as a child, more than many, when he went through some complex stages in his early life. Although he never saw her that much, he always felt close to her; she was so understanding and caring, having herself known a lot of sadness in life.

Ann's braveness in those dark days inspired Terry: her courage was extraordinary. She told him she loved him and the children so much that she was determined to fight and to overcome her illness, if only for them.

It was, he thought, he that should be lifting and supporting her. Instead, he found it was her bravery in dealing with her suffering that gave him new energy and courage to pull himself up, out of his depressed and selfish state, to carry on and assist her in the fight, however dark the hour.

Ann suffered a great deal of discomfort at this time; in many ways it was the worst time for her physically and emotionally. It was a very welcome boost to her spirits that the day before going into hospital for the operation, Terry received a letter offering him the job in Harrogate, starting on Monday 7th January 1980. They were both delighted with the news. At last something good was happening in their lives, news that carried Ann through the three hour operation the following day. The surgeon found another growth that had been causing a blockage in her intestine; they removed it and took a long time checking out the whole area to make sure there were no other growths lurking around.

Terry visited her twice a day and always came away with renewed courage from her attitude. Grandad Reeves collected Paul and Lynda from St Augustine's School each afternoon, which allowed Terry to go and spend as much time as possible with her. Ten days later she was allowed home much to everyone's delight and together they started making plans to move to Harrogate for Terry to take up his new job as Estate Manager for J. J. Bowman Properties.

He felt able to splash out and purchased a three year old Austin Princess Car for £1,845; it provided more space and comfort for Ann and would be good for the long journey north. It would be far easier for Ann to ride in and drive as she recovered from her operation.

Lynda had a party to celebrate her success at ballet; she had been attending lessons at the Pavilion in Weymouth and collected her certificates with a merit award at a presentation on Friday 7th December. She was thrilled. The following week Terry drove up to Harrogate to look at the houses that were on offer with his new job.

Andrew Bowman met him and showed him around the properties. In the end Terry choose 'Riverside House' in the small town of Boroughbridge. The house was alongside both the River Ure and the main stone bridge over it. There was no garden, only a yard with two large old garages and an old factory building next to it. It was a three bedroomed house with plenty of space and a large open lounge that he liked. Alongside the house was the entrance to a lovely walk along the river to Milby Lock, where the canal met the river. So, on that side it was in a lovely setting, with good walks, while still in walking distance of the small town for the local shops. Terry was able to drive back to Weymouth and tell Ann all about their new home. It gave her the tonic she needed and she couldn't wait to go up to Yorkshire to make a real home for them all.

Christmas 1979 was spent at Pucklechurch with Ann's parents; they had a week there and enjoyed it very much as always. Meadowland Cottage was such a lovely open and light modern house, set in such a beautifully landscaped garden, with its shrubs, hedges and vegetable garden. Terry always felt totally at home there. It took a lot of Cecil's time looking after it, most of their school summer holidays were given over to caring for it. But it gave them much pleasure too and would always be a very special place for Terry and Ann. They returned to Weymouth for the 30th December as Paul and Lynda were to receive their first Holy Communion at the 9am Mass at the Convent chapel on Wyke Road, a lovely service with all the family.

On Monday 7th January 1980 they arrived at their new home in Boroughbridge with great joy and excitement after the long drive from the south.

"It's really lovely," Ann said when she saw it, having had a good look around the house and surrounding area.

"This will be so good for us all. We're very near to the town and all the services we're likely to need, but still with a feeling of being in the countryside. The river makes a delightful setting with the footpath and it's a beautiful walk up to the lock. I love it."

The next day their furniture arrived from storage and the packing cases from Malawi arrived too. There was paper and packing everywhere and more excitement as forgotten items came out; it was like Christmas all over again. Ann was busy making lists, things to make and things to buy in the January sales. They made an appointment with the local Catholic School in Knaresborough and were able to fix a day to meet the headmaster Mr John Pay.

There was a school bus that would collect Paul and Lynda from Boroughbridge and return them to the town centre later in the day, so all very convenient.

On Wednesday January 9th Terry went to his office in Harrogate to meet again Mr Quigley to get his instructions and be introduced to his new job. It all sounded very casual. He was asked to arrive around midday, when Terry had expected to be there for 9am! He duly arrived at the given time and he and Peter Quigley had a general chat.

"I expect you'll want to get on with your unpacking," Quigley said, "So see you again next Monday then I'll take you to your office in the village of Arkendale, where you will share the Old Reading Room with Jeremy Ashworth our Forester!

What a luxury Terry thought to be given all this time to settle in while still being paid. He had never experienced that before.

When the unpacking was complete, they enjoyed exploring Boroughbridge a small town, centred on the square, which had a good feel to it. There was no supermarket apart from the small Co-operative Wholesale Society, but there was a baker, a chemist, a good fish and chip shop and a post office!

Terry went into the post office where the postmaster was at the counter.

"Where tha from lad?" he asked.

"Pardon?" Terry replied, not understanding what he was saying.

"Where tha from lad?" he repeated.

"We've come from Weymouth, in Dorset," Terry replied, hoping that he had understood the second time.

"Oo arr. That's down south int it?"

"Yes it's on the south coast," Terry explained.

"Aah! It might be a long time before we accept you up ere lad," the postmaster said in a loud gruff voice.

"Really," Terry replied, "It might be a long time before I accept you too!"

After that brief and amusing exchange they were always the best of friends!

Back at Riverside House things were already taking shape. Paul chose the room at the front of the house and Lynda liked the look of the one over looking the yard and the apple tree at the back. They quickly arranged their books and toys and Terry agreed to get a desk for Paul's room and a dressing table for Lynda's. It was also agreed that they would have their rooms redecorated, once they were settled in. Terry wanted to form a vegetable garden and was planning to ask if one of the long garages could be removed and the area turned over to a vegetable growing area. The other old garage would be fine for their car, bikes and storage.

The next day a car was delivered to the house: it was the company car to be used by Terry in his work as well as for his own personal use. It was a bright red Alpha Sud, made by Alfa Romeo, a neat car that would suit the purpose well.

They used it to go to Knaresborough about seven miles away, to meet the headmaster Mr John Pay at St Mary's School. The school at the end of a cul-de-sac had a very homely feel to it. The Head was very friendly and helpful, explaining that they would both be in the class of Miss Veal to start with and then see how it worked out.

Lynda and Paul seemed happy with their new school and it was agreed that after the first week they would catch the school bus from Boroughbridge, which would return them there each afternoon around 4pm where Ann would meet them.

Ann found a Brownie Pack in Boroughbridge and went along to enrol Lynda, as she wanted to join a pack, if there was one around. Paul decided that he would like to join the table tennis and Judo club and so Terry took him along to sign on with Mr Faulkner who ran the clubs in Boroughbridge.

Ann was stronger by the day and had recovered well from the operation she'd had in Weymouth. They both went to meet her new consultant Professor Jocylyn, at Cookridge Hospital on the edge of

Leeds and dates were fixed for her to be monitored, which was reassuring for them both. It was quite a long drive but it was considered to be the centre for the treatment of cancer in the north, so they were fortunate.

Terry liked the look and feel of the Ripon Catholic Church and decided he would attend weekly Mass there. Ann had heard that the Anglican Church in the village of Kirby Hill was very active and took herself along each Sunday, while Terry, Paul and Lynda went to Ripon. They both became involved in their respective churches and would sometimes attend each other's, which worked well.

On his first real day at work Terry was taken by Peter Quigley to meet Jeremy Ashworth the Forester for the Bowman Estates and to show him his office. Jeremy was a tall, dark haired, quiet and deep thinking man, slightly younger than Terry. Their office was 'The Old Reading Room' in the village of Arkendale, just south of Boroughbridge. A tiny building divided into two small offices, with a sink in one and a toilet in the entrance hall. Jeremy greeted Terry with a certain amount of suspicion and amusement as Peter introduced them to each other. A list of the properties owned by the company had been given to Jeremy who had been charged with showing Terry around them all, being the only person who seemed to know where they were situated. Together they pondered the list dividing them into areas and made a plan to visit a different area each day until they had completed the task. Jeremy did not know most of the farms or where in fact they were, but did seem to know the general areas and so the two of them set off each day to see what they could discover!

"Have you any idea of the number or acreage of farms owned by the company?" Terry asked Jeremy.

"No, I've no idea. I don't know many, but I can point them out to you as we drive around and mark them on a map for you to revisit later," he replied.

"There are so many different properties in the company, farms and woodland yes, but also houses, garages, large country houses, an old Victorian mansion, opencast coal mines and a hotel or two I believe. I hope you are free for the next thirty years!" Jeremy laughed, with his large brown eyes that twinkled as he smiled in a knowing way.

"Are there no records then?" Terry queried. "Somebody must know what the company owns surely?"

"You would think so, but there don't appear to be any records. They have all been managed by different estate agents and purchased at different times by different solicitors, so it's all a bit of a muddle as you will find!" Jeremy explained.

"You see, Andrew Bowman is the eldest of six children, three boys and three girls. Their father died recently and left the estate in trust. Andrew was made Chairman, so he has to come to terms with it all. The father was, I'm told, a bit of a rough diamond and made his money through a building company in York just after the war. At that time they didn't ask for estimates, just for the job to be done. They built houses, schools and public buildings including a large public swimming pool for the council and in so doing made a lot of money. As the money piled up he began to wonder what he should do with it and was advised to buy land. So he took the advice and bought land wherever it came up for sale and then more land, farms and woodland, anywhere and everywhere, wherever it became available. He then purchased some houses, not just one house at a time, but rows of houses in and around Leeds, not far from where the building company was based. He purchased rough grazing land near to Leeds only to find that underneath was coal, which was then mined by open cast methods and of course created more money. So he then bought more land and farms and so it went on. Talk about the Midas touch. He certainly had it."

"Apparently, J.J. Bowman, Andrew's father was a rough looking character and dressed like a tramp. At one auction when he was bidding for a farm over at East Heslerton near Scarborough, the auctioneer thought he was a tramp. When the farm was knocked down to him, the auctioneer went off to check with the bank that JJ was who he claimed to be and good for the money!" Jeremy explained.

"He really was very eccentric indeed; he lived in a small village over near Ilkley and drove each day to the building company's offices in his Rolls Royce. He struck up a friendship with Wilfred Langford a local auctioneer and estate agent in Otley. Langford purchased a lot of the properties on his behalf and went on to manage them for J.J." Jeremy explained in his enigmatic and dry manner.

"Wilfred Langford didn't do very much management and was more of a rent collector, doing nothing for the farms or the farmers, so a lot of the tenanted farms have fallen into disrepair, so you'll have plenty to get your teeth into," Jeremy smiled.

"Well thanks Jeremy for giving me the background. It's a great help. How long have you been here?"

"Nearly two years now. Like you, the woodland I care for is scattered around the farms and estates. There is much to do as you might imagine. It's an interesting job and I enjoy it. I'm fairly free to organise my own day which is always good, especially now that we have our young baby Marianne."

Terry felt Jeremy was going to become a good friend, one he could confide and trust in. They got on well during the tours around the farms, having pub lunches and picnics in some fairly remote places, and peering over hedges at farms that were on his list. Both of them were amazed at the goings on in the company. Jeremy was a naturally reserved sort of chap and did not trust others easily, perhaps a bit shy too. But Terry got the impression that he would be a good and trusted friend, which he certainly became, far beyond the call of friendship, as the next nine years would go on to prove.

After touring around all the areas with Jeremy, Terry tried to gather together plans and documents of the properties, as well as the rent roll from the estate agents that were supposed to be managing the farms. Only then would he be able to make sense of it all. They were all very reluctant to hand over much detail and were rather upset at having to lose the commissions they received from collecting the farm rents, so were less than co-operative. Terry then had to resort to the solicitors for plans and tenancy agreements, but that was not easy either, as so many had been involved over the years. However, from all sources he slowly began to gather some details of the properties. Clearly Andrew Bowman had no knowledge of them, but he had notified all the estate agents of Terry's appointment, instructing them to pass him all their files.

Once he had gathered something of a base to work from, he decided to tour slowly around some of the farms, meet the farmers and see what was what. This was no easy task as he did not even know the geography of the area, so had to find the towns and villages first and then the farms. Many were in obscure places, on the moors around Leeds, Ilkley and Harrogate. Others were as far apart as Scarborough on the east coast to Horton in Ribblesdale in the west.

There were three major estates of land with a variety of tenancies: one estate, north of York with six different tenants; another near the Yorkshire Moors at Kilburn surrounding the White Horse of Kilburn, home of the famous 'Mouseman' wood carver, which had ten different tenants; then there was a large estate around Arkendale and Boroughbridge of some fifteen tenancies on some of the better producing arable land. So there was plenty to discover, some wonderful characters to meet and obstacles to overcome.

The estate agents were all losing considerable income from the loss of the rent collections on behalf of Bowman's so would do all that they could to trip Terry up and to make it difficult for him. As far as they were concerned he was bad news: they had had it too easy for too long, receiving a high income for little or no work when up from the south, of all places, comes this chap to stand in their way and cut off their income. They were not happy! The tenants themselves had had a tough time, having experienced rising rents and no landlord input, either in the way of repairs or development. Terry could already see that an active landlord could achieve a great deal in so many ways, like merging land holdings, freeing development land, selling off some holdings and reinvesting. Then there were agricultural grants on offer, which could be taken and used to improve the farms to the advantage of both the landlord and the tenants. The opportunities were endless and Terry began to feel the job ahead had the excitement he needed to replace the loss and the challenge of Africa.

There was a large estate north of York at Kexby of some 1500 acres split into six different farms. Terry thought he would start by going there to look around and meet the farmers. He had no idea where York was in relation to Boroughbridge, so before setting out he had to consult the local map and plan his route. Once there he had a very rough plan of the area that Jeremy had helped him to plot the farms onto, with the names of the tenant farmers. Having found his way to Kexby after driving through the centre of York he decided to visit Kexby Old Hall Farm. He drove down a rough unmade farm road just outside of Elvington village, to a group of very old farm buildings with an ancient red brick farmhouse. As he approached the house he saw a man standing in the adjoining field, so stopped by the side of the track to see if he was the farmer.

"Good morning," Terry called to him, as he stepped out of his shiny new car onto the edge of a very muddy field.

The roughly dressed character slowly approached Terry with a glint and half smile on his face.

"Ow–do," he said.

"I'm looking for Mr Beevers," Terry said.

"Oh aye!"

"Can you tell me where I might find him?"

"Aaah well," he replied as he eyed Terry with suspicion. "Aaah, I could."

"Well?" Terry replied after a lull.

"So where tha from?" he asked.

"I'm Terry Reeves the new land agent for J.J. Bowman Properties, the landlord."

"Oh aye lad."

"I need to speak to Mr Beevers please if he is around."

"Oh aye!"

"Thought Langford was Land Agent for Bowman's?"

"Well he was, but not anymore, I am."

"Oh aye!"

"So can you tell me where I might find him?"

"Aye I could!" he said as he looked at Terry with one eye squinting at him as if trying to sum him up.

"You're speaking to him. I'm Harry Beevers."

"Oh pleased to meet you," Terry said, smiling at this wonderfully eccentric character from another age.

"Oh aye," he replied, "Oh aye."

"So what tha done to me friend Langford then?" he asked Terry. " 'As someone finally shot the old bugger?"

Terry laughed and was already beginning to warm to Harry Beevers. At first he had wondered if he was drunk, with his strange manner and ways. He was difficult to understand too with his very local dialect.

"Did you see much of Mr Langford?" Terry asked.

"Oh aye, saw him once every three years when it were time for rent review."

"Is that all?" Terry exclaimed rather surprised.

"Oh aye," he replied.

"He'd drive into yard 'ere and blow his horn until I or Babs came out of t'house. He'd then shout out of car window, "Hey! Rent's going up. You have three options. Sign here. Get out! Or go t'arbitration? Come on, hurry up wot you going to do? I have to get back t'market."

"That would be last time I'd see him 'til next review."

"That's amazing," Terry said. "Did he not do anything else for you on the farm? Repairs and things like that?"

"Nowt!" Harry replied, "Never in over fifteen years."

"But you're paying £30 an acre."

"Oh aye lad, I knows that!"

"So what's the land like here?" Terry asked as he stepped out into the field and stood talking to him. "Is it very heavy land?"

"Oh aye!" he replied, "You could say that, specially down t'Ings land next to river."

"So what crops do you grow here?"

"Tatties, wheat, barley, we've a lot of sheep, pigs and some beef cows as well as turkeys, geese and poultry for Christmas market. We're a real mixed farm. It's only way, then they all help each other depending on the market."

As they were standing talking, Terry was suddenly aware that he and Harry were slowly sinking into the ground.

"What goes on here then, we seem to be sinking?"

"Oh aye, t'whole farm is like this. Some places worse than t'others."

"But you can't farm land like this. Don't you know there are EEC grants to drain farmland. You can get 60% of the cost back."

"Oh aye, is that so?"

"Look Mr Beevers?"

"Nay lad, Harry is me name, YOU, don't call me Mr Beevers, landlord an all! Harry, lad, is me name. It's Harry!"

"O.K. Harry. If I investigate having the drainage done and do the paper work for the grants from the EEC, would you be O.K. with that?"

"But tha'll want more rent?"

"Probably, but not that much more, as you're already paying a good rent for very poor wet land. I'll give you some figures and then you'll know the new rent after the drainage, and after the grant. At least you will then have land that you can farm and make more profit per acre that will more than cover the extra rent. You have over 400 acres here I understand, including the Ings land."

"Aye Lad, near enough."

"Leave it with me Harry and I'll come up with a proposal for you with some costings."

"Aye, I expect you will," he said with a smile.

Terry then walked around the farm with Harry, to get a feel of the land and establish where the boundaries were so that he could then draw up a plan of the farm.

Chapter Twenty

Ann was a little nervous, as it was time for her to go to Cookridge Hospital, near Leeds, for a check up again. This time they wanted to do an x-ray and liver scan to make sure all was well and settled down after the operation she had in Weymouth. Terry drove her there, to be of what little support he could at these difficult times. She protested and wanted to go on her own so as not to take him away from his work.

"The next time I want to drive myself," Ann said as they hurtled down the A1 to Leeds. "There's no need for you to give up your work to escort me. I'm a big girl now," she laughed.

"I've never really thought of you as being that big," he laughed.

So on Thursday 7th February, she drove herself to the hospital for the results and floated home having been given the "all clear." They were both delighted and went out to celebrate that night.

Things were looking up. Paul and Lynda's new school of St Mary's in Knaresborough was proving to be a great success: they were both very happy and making good progress, while at the same time making good friends, both at school and around Boroughbridge. Terry too was beginning to enjoy his new job; his friendship with his colleague Jeremy grew and he was more and more fascinated with the Yorkshire farmers that he was meeting and the exchanges that took place between them, as unbelievable as many of them were!

"You know," he said to Ann. "I really didn't think I would ever settle back here in the U.K. again after all the excitement of Africa, but I think I will. Yorkshire and its people are wonderful: a spade is a spade here and that suits me; it's my sort of language. I'm really beginning to feel at home and settled."

"Me too, I wondered if we ever would? I can never forget the beauty and people of Africa. It haunts me, but this is the right place for us to be now, I'm sure of that," Ann said. "Maybe in time we can go back for a holiday that would be fun and do all the things the tourists do, that we never had the time for before."

Letters were starting to arrive from their old friends in Malawi and from the Sisters at Mlale. It was always a joy to hear from them and to catch up on life there. They had also received a letter from an ex colleague, now in the States to tell them that Professor Don Mac Lusky, who had been the head of the Livestock Department at Bunda College when they were there, was now living in Knaresborough, near to Harrogate. They were delighted as they had got to know Don quite well when they were all at Bunda College and never imagined they would see him again back in England. They decided to surprise him and one afternoon went to his house and knocked on the door. His face was a picture; he was very surprised, but delighted to renew their acquaintance again after so long. Over thirty years later the rich friendship continues and grows.

Terry continued to search out the farms and land owned by Bowman's, an interesting if sometimes frustrating task. The Yorkshire farmers, Terry was learning, were a tough and canny breed, often with a dry sense of humour that was sometimes difficult to separate from the truth.

It was not perhaps the best time, Ash Wednesday 20th February, to go off onto the moors around Beamsley, nestled between the A59 to Skipton and Ilkley, but Terry decided to go and meet the farmers over that way to see something of the farms. Two of the tenant farmers that were within a mile of each other, on the moor, had the same surname; one was Gerald and the other Harold. He drove along the twisting single track road from Ilkley to Harold Grange's farm.

"Good morning, I'm the new agent from Bowman's," he said to a short, sharp featured man in the cow yard. "Are you Mr Grange?"

"Aye tha got that reet. T'aint time for t'rent to go up is it?" he enquired.

"No not as far as I know, just wanted to come and meet you and see the farm."

"Tis a cold wet farm and we can 'ardly make a living it's s'poor. I tell that Langford, but ee don't listen and just puts rent even higher. Guess tha'll be doing same lad?"

"The reason I'm here is to get to know the farm and the farmers. Maybe I can help you, we shall see."

"Tha gonna come and milk cows then? I could do with some 'elp."

"Don't think that I couldn't," Terry replied. "I used to relief milk for four dairies when I worked in Dorset."

"Oh aye, thas a farmer then?"

"Well I know my way around a cow, shall we say, having milked hundreds and made the milk into cheese and butter."

Harold showed Terry around a very clean and tidy old-style milking shed. The milking machines were all laid out spotless and shining clean. The milk was piped into a mobile milk tank that each day he towed out to the side of the main road, for the dairy's tanker to suck out the contents.

"So Harold, are you and Gerald Grange brothers? I see he lives just over the hill from you at Beamsley?"

"Aye lad, dats reet."

"I suppose you both work together and share machinery do you?" Terry asked.

"Naa, 'aven't seen him for nearly twenty five years now!"

"Twenty five years! why's that?"

"We fell out. We don't get on! He is an awkward old bugger is Gerald."

Later that day Terry was to find out just how awkward Gerald could be.

The visit to Gerald was going to be different as his rent was due to be reviewed, so Terry thought he would kill two birds with one stone, see the farm and at the same time review the rent. Unlike his visit to Harold, he had rung Gerald first and explained what he intended to do, and that he would arrive at midday.

The single road down towards Beamsley twisted this way and that; Terry spotted the farm sign on the right side of the road. 'Ling Chapel Farm.' That's a strange name he thought, sounds Chinese! He drove down the rough unmade road to the stone built farmhouse and buildings. Out of the house came a short man wearing a ripped jacket with the inside spilling out. He smiled as he greeted Terry.

"What's he done with Langford then? 'Tis over three years since he was here. I see him at market some weeks, but he never speaks to me."

"You'll have to put up with me now. Langford is no longer looking after the farms for the Bowman's" Terry explained.

"Ah tha better come in then, and tha'd be wanting a cup of tea eh?"

"That would be nice, thank you. It's just coming on to rain too."

Terry went into the house that was well cared for and met Gerald's wife, a kindly, busy lady who soon produced a cup of tea and put it on the table in front of them.

Terry took out the papers from his brief case and started to fill in the legal form of notice for the rent increase. It was necessary to record the new rent on a form, which both parties had to sign, that is, once it had been agreed with Gerald Grange. That was always the tricky bit!

From the information Terry had managed to acquire from the solicitor about the tenancy, he found that the legally required notice that should always be issued six months prior to a rent review, had not on this occasion been served, an omission by the previous estate agent. But the rent review was well overdue and Gerald Grange realised that, so Terry was sure it wouldn't be a problem.

They sat at the table looking at a plan of the farm and discussing what the new rent would be. Terry put forward his proposal and Gerald would give reasons why he thought it should be lower and so the negotiation continued for over an hour. They finally seemed to get to a figure that both could agree.

"Now then, before I sign anything I wanna show you state of t'landlords boundary wall which you must agree to repair. Come with me I'll show you," Gerald demanded.

They went outside, where it was now pouring with rain. Terry took his jacket from the car and followed Gerald. They walked behind the house, up a steep incline and across two fields. They were wet, muddy and covered in cow manure that had recently been spread across the field, then on through a small wood and over a steep-sided ditch. Terry was getting soaked as the rain poured down relentlessly, his feet caked in mud, and one of his boots was leaking. He had meant to get some new ones, but somehow had never got around to it. Gerald climbed over the stonewall, up another steep hill, across a stream and up to the highest point of the farm. Terry was struggling to follow him and felt Gerald was doing this on purpose, just to make a point! There he showed him the wall that formed the boundary, a small portion of which had collapsed; it looked as if it had been that way for many years!

"That's it, "Gerald explained." That's the wall you have to repair. It's your obligation under my tenancy agreement. Are you gona do it lad?"

Terry stood there, now soaked to the skin in the pouring rain, one boot half full of water. "If it's our responsibility then I'll see it is done," Terry replied, "but only when you have signed the new rental agreement."

They turned back to make their way to the farmhouse again, the rain was coming at them sideways. Terry could feel the water inside his jacket and his suit underneath it was soaked. They staggered into the farmhouse. Terry was wet to the skin, and was feeling very cross with Gerald, realising now that he had dragged him up there on purpose.

"Right Gerald, we've settled the rent, and I've seen your wall and agreed to repair it," Terry said sharply, as he sat in a puddle of water dripping all over the floor.

"Aye lad, we've done that!"

Terry filled in the details on the form, trying not to get it wet from the water now running off him.

"It just remains for you to sign the form now please, Gerald," Terry said with authority, passing him a pen.

Gerald slowly put on his glasses, read the form even more closely, took the pen in his hand and was just about to sign it when he looked up at Terry with a quizzical expression on his face.

"You know, I don't think tha ever served that legal notice thing to tell me tha was going to review rent, did ee?" Gerald asked with a gleam in his eye." So I can't be signing this, wouldn't be right."

Terry was furious; this old rogue knew all along that the notice had not been served and that legally it had to be. He never had any intention of signing a new rent agreement. He was just playing with Terry, with him being the new boy, and trying to make a point. Terry realised that Gerald was, legally speaking correct, and there was nothing he could do but return to his office and send out a notice giving Gerald the six months' notice that he was legally entitled to.

Gerald sat there with a broad smile on his face as Terry squelched his way out of the house. He turned to Gerald and said, "I'll be back. I'll be back."

It was certainly a lesson for Terry; farmers may not always look so bright or seem to know what they are doing, but don't underestimate them ever. You do so at your peril; they are no one's fool!

It was turning out to be a fascinating job with plenty of challenges. The Reading Room office in Arkendale was a comfortable but sparse place to work, where Terry and Jeremy spent hours discussing all the unbelievable goings-on within the company. Occasionally Andrew Bowman would attend an informal meeting with them both; otherwise they depended on seeing him at his office on North Park Road, Harrogate. Relationships with him were good, but there was always a strange faraway air about the man. He spent a lot of his time at the building company they owned in York that was run by his brother David; it seemed to give him a lot of heartache for some reason.

Gradually, Terry found all the farms in the company's ownership and gathered together files on each of the properties, prepared all the rent invoices and collected the rents. Improvements were made; land drained; rents reviewed and farms merged into one where appropriate. This resulted in the freeing up of development opportunities for the company, which was rewarding for Terry to have achieved and for the Bowman family financially.

On a visit to the farms on the Kilburn Estate, Terry called on one of the farmers to discuss the building of a new barn under an

EEC grant scheme. The farmer was busy dealing with his vet, so Terry watched.

"Tha knows who this is lad?" he asked.

"Your vet from Thirsk, isn't it?"

"Aye, that's Mr Herriot, you know, he that writes all those books and is on T.V. Well that's not his real name, his real name is Alf and a damn good vet he is too!"

It was the only time that Terry ever met him, a kindly man whose reputation went before him. They had a good chat about the state of farming and the economy before they both continued on their way.

Life outside of work was good too, as they all slowly settled into life in Yorkshire. Ann was enjoying making the house into a home and made new friends locally. She attended the Anglican Church at Kirby Hill, near Boroughbridge and was involved with the children's group. She still enjoyed making greetings cards and the church was delighted to sell them to raise funds. She made many new friends from this connection.

Terry found the Catholic Church at Ripon suited his needs, the priest preached well, leaving Terry with a good message each week. Paul and Lynda seemed to enjoy the singing too, although a bit young to take too much meaning from it all. Nevertheless, he hoped, that one day their faith would grow, for what else was there in the end?

Terry's life was his work, Ann and the children. They drove out to explore the moors and got to know some of the beautiful little villages around Wensleydale and Swaledale. He loved to take them out on bikes too. Often on a Sunday afternoon they would cycle up through Milby to Dishforth where there was an airstrip, always a favourite for Paul, at other times south through Boroughbridge to the small village of Minskip or around Aldborough. Walks along the river bank to Milby Lock were a favourite and always entertaining. If they were lucky they would see the startling blue kingfisher speed past, or be there when the boats passed through the lock gates. Some weekends when Weymouth FC, from the 'Conference League,' were playing a team not too far away, like Boston or

Altringham, Terry and Paul would go off to watch the game, reminding them of the times when living in Weymouth with Grandad. Lynda was enjoying Brownies and was starting to attend a dance class in Knaresborough every Friday following her success at the Weymouth class. They had both made lots of friends from school including Emma and Oliver who also lived in Boroughbridge and were originally from Southport.

Africa, never far from either of them, was kept fresh in their minds with correspondence and news from friends. Janet Halley a friend from Bunda had met Trevor Croft while she worked in Malawi and they wrote to tell them that they were getting married on Saturday 1st March at her home in Devon, but later that week would drop in on their way through Yorkshire. Another friendship made in Africa!

Sister Claire for whom Terry had provided fish when she was ill at Mlale Mission, kept up a stream of correspondence every few weeks. She had grown back to good health and was living at Sillery in Quebec, and happy there after her long life and service in East Africa. She always accredited her good health to the fish that Terry provided and they often laughed about those days.

On the 12th April they all went to Aylesford in Kent for a week to see Ann's Auntie Smith. She lived in Rose Cottage, right next to the old bridge in the picturesque village and was the retired headmistress of the junior school. They loved to stay there and to take a walk up to the Aylesford Priory, home of the Carmelites, and a short distance up the road where they enjoyed the grounds, the pottery and all the delightful chapels. They attended Mass there on a Sunday and often enjoyed having a chat with the friendly monks that lived there. It was such a peaceful, prayerful place and remained a favourite retreat place for Terry to visit in the years ahead.

As they were in Kent they went to pick up Auntie Lesley from her flat at Major Clarke House in Cranbrook and took her with them to stay in Boroughbridge for a couple of weeks. She was so pleased to see them all so happy and well and to see their new home.

Over Whitsun time they went to see the family in Weymouth and then on to Pucklechurch; it was always a joy to return there, one of Terry's favourite places nestling in the countryside not far from the wonderful city of Bath.

Ann had another check up at the hospital in Cookridge, near Leeds, and to everyone's great relief was again given the all clear.

They had received other news from Tanzania. George, Joan and their daughter Anne, now twenty two years old and studying to be a nurse at St Bartholomew's hospital in London, were coming for a four night stay with them on 14th June. George and Joan were on leave from C.M.S. in Tanzania, where they were still working, now at the blind school at Buigiri, just south east of Hombolo. It was wonderful for Terry and Ann to see them again, to catch up on their life and to have news of Hombolo, a place that would always be very special for them, following their meeting and experiences while working there in the 60's.

They could not believe how grown up Anne was, for she had only been a child when they were at Hombolo together, but that was of course in 1966. Now she was busy carving out a career for herself and it was interesting to chat with her to see how her early life at Hombolo had affected her and her sister Margaret. She had grown into a beautiful young lady with her father's piercing sapphire blue eyes. George now sixty years old, looked older, as they all did of course, but still with the enthusiasm he always had to serve the people of Africa.

"So how's it going mate?" was George's opening question, as always in his true New Zealand manner.

"You going to be able to settle here then?"

"That's a very good question George. Ask me again in a few years."

"Well you ain't lost your humour mate, I'm pleased to see that!"

"You've been through some mighty tough times the two of you and we just had to see how you was doing while we were here on leave and staying with Joan's sister Meg in Lapworth. You two had set your cap at Africa and were going to make it your life, but He (God) had other plans for you mate! That's rough. Our hearts went out to you."

"Will you be able to show me around some of your farms while I'm here mate, I'd love to see what you are doing?"

"Yes, of course I will George," Terry replied. "We can go over to Kilburn tomorrow and then around some of the farms near York, both very different but interesting for you. We can leave the girls to go shopping in York. They'll enjoy that."

The next day Ann drove Joan and her daughter Anne off in the car for a day out in York, while George and Terry spent a wonderful day together reminiscing, and exploring the Yorkshire countryside. George loved to see the farms and being introduced to the local farmers. You could see him examining everything he saw and filing away the detail in his mind for later use in Africa. That was his way. Seeing things through George's eyes was like seeing them for the first time: he would study the smallest points, being amazed by the detail and the way it had been constructed, when most would just rush by.

They had taken a picnic lunch and so they sat by the River Derwent under a tree at Kexby, north of York to enjoy it in the warmth of the June sun.

"We could almost be back in Tanzania," George said, as he leaned back against an old oak tree of some two hundred and fifty years.

"Yes we could be, perhaps a bit cooler here with fewer flies!" said Terry laughing.

They say that you can tell the nature of a tree by its texture and its fruits. Seeing George lean back against that old oak, his arm resting on the tree, with his craggy sun-burnt skin, almost the same texture as the tree, spoke to Terry, then again later when he saw the fruits of George in his daughter Anne.

"You know mate we were so sorry about Ann's health problem and all you have both been through, you both had your hearts in Africa and you seemed to have found such a wonderful job in Malawi. You'll have been very disappointed that it had to come to an end. It's hard to understand the will of God sometimes; our hearts went out to you at that phase in your life."

"Thanks George. It was a terrible ordeal."

"Those idyllic days we had spent at Hombolo led us to believe that it was the sort of life that we wanted and were destined for; it fed our great love for the country and its people. However, for us, it was not to be but why, we shall never know."

"God's will mate, God's will!"

Looking around the farms of Yorkshire, George yearned for the same type of soil at his farm in Tanzania. "We can only dream of such fertility," he said. The mix of soil in that part of Yorkshire was unusual: the clay was solid and yet there were seams of sand within it. This caused so many problems when draining the land. George was able to see how the rolls of plastic drainage pipe that were being placed in the soil to carry away the water, were also wrapped in hessian to prevent the sand entering them, an unusual mix.

George, Joan and Anne enjoyed their reunion over those four days, coming together from different parts of the world, renewing their friendships and their memories, their various encounters touching their hearts, feeling privileged to be together again, always looking forward to the next opportunity, which sadly was never to be.

Soon after George left, Terry's father came up for a week's holiday with them. He so enjoyed seeing it all and had never been to Yorkshire before. Terry took him around the farms and to see the Dales and the Yorkshire Moors where he was able to ride on the steam train at Pickering and journey across the moors thus taking him back to the days of steam that he knew and had worked with in his first job at Portland Railway Station in Dorset. He loved the Train Museum at York and went back there three times over the next few years. It was of course every railway man's dream to see all the wonderfully restored engines in the centre of York.

The summer of 1980 saw the arrival of a new member of family. In August, Duke, a handsome fourteen month old long-nose collie from the R.S.P.C.A. who was in need of some love and care, soon became a firm favourite with them all.

Many of the family and friends came to see how the nomads had settled down after their trips across the world, following their love of Africa. It was a busy summer for them all, Terry in his work and Ann entertaining everyone. She was alive with health and so glad to be free of the cancer that had caused them to move around the world and had instigated so much heartache and stress.

Ann was so full of life, she decided to approach Terry with an idea.

"What would you think about me getting a job, back in Occupational Therapy? I would really like to put something back and to be doing something useful again. The house is now well set up and I feel I need to be doing something. I've enjoyed coming around with you sometimes and seeing the countryside and the farms, but I would like to be earning again and the money would be useful too, not that we are short these days."

"Have you a job in mind?" Terry asked.

"No it's just an idea. I've another health check and scan in November and thought after that I'd like see what is out there. Maybe on a part time basis, if that's available? I've kept up my registration so I can return to work as a therapist if I wish."

"Part time would be better, as I don't want you to get stressed or under any strain. I can see how you would want to do something; after all you're not used to being a kept woman," he laughed!

"I'll start looking around and see what's out there; it would be exciting to get back to work again."

Andrew Bowman had agreed to sell one of the farms that he owned out at Ilkley: it rather stood alone and for some reason best known to him, he had asked Langford's to market it. Terry was asked to attend the auction of the farm on Andrew's behalf. The auction was to take place at Craiglands Hotel in Ilkley at 3pm. Terry made his way there an hour before the auction was due to start. The agents Langford and Son had produced and distributed the details and taken all the enquiries. The 120 acres with farm house and buildings were in good demand, even if some of the land was very wet and in need of drainage.

The main room at the hotel was used for the gathering farmers to assemble. Chairs were all laid out like a theatre with a head table where the auctioneer and his team would sit, alongside the solicitor acting for the vendor and of course Terry who was to represent the owner. There must have been over one hundred people in the room as the excitement grew. Many were just there to see what it fetched and for a bit of a day out. There were of course many, too, who were there to bid in the hope of getting a good deal in buying the farm or to add it to their adjoining land.

Terry had never been so closely involved with the sale of a farm before, so it was all new and exciting to him. He really did not have a part to play just to be there to represent the company. It had also been put upon him at a very late stage. Andrew had never told him of his intentions and Terry never really knew the farm. It had all been set up without his knowledge; he was very much the new boy and feeling his way.

At 2.30pm the main team started to gather at the head table, the excitement started to flow through the room, everyone looking at everyone else to try and spot who might be making the bids and were interested in the farm.

Terry sat next to Mr Langford with the solicitor on his other side. It felt like a jury, Terry thought.

"So what's the reserve to be?" Mr Langford asked Terry.

"Reserve? I've no idea," Terry replied rather surprised to be asked.

"Mr Andrew said he would not tell me on the phone but I was to ask you," Mr Langford responded.

"Well he never said anything to me. I've no idea what figure he has in mind."

"You'd better telephone him to find out straight away, as I'll have to start the auction in fifteen minutes, but can't sell it if I don't have a reserve price!"

Terry rushed off to find a phone. He rang Andrew's office, but he was not there. He rang his home but his housekeeper said he was not there. Panic set in. What were they to do?

Terry returned to the auction room to find Langford was already on his feet going over the details of the sale and the auction to the excited room of potential buyers.

"Well what did he say? What's the figure?" Langford asked impatiently.

"I can't find him, I've tried everywhere." This is crazy Terry thought.

"Well you have to keep trying to find him," Langford whispered to Terry. "I'll continue as slowly as I can, but you have to find him and bloody quick."

Terry rushed out of the room with the solicitor following him.

"I can't find Andrew and we don't have a reserve," Terry explained to the solicitor, Kenneth.

They both took a phone in different rooms to see if they could find him. Terry rang Andrew's two sisters, no joy there. He rang the hotel that the company owned in Boroughbridge, but he was not there. He rang the company garage, not there either. They rang the building company in York, spoke to his brother the M.D.; he had no idea where he was. They rang again to his office and left messages everywhere, but nobody could find him.

Terry rushed back to the auction room to tell Langford he was not having any luck. Langford was at the stage where he was starting to take bids. He was going at a very slow pace, slowly extracting bids and kept going over the qualities of the farm to slow the process down. He was already taking bids of £150,000 and therefore into serious money, but still had no reserve or sign of Andrew to provide the figure. Langford drew the bids on and on and they were now over £200,000. Langford was looking pale, Terry was feeling sick, the bidders unaware were getting excited and were smelling victory, the end was in sight for the buyers. Just as the last bid of the day was made and Langford was again telling everyone what a wonderful farm it was in order to slow the progress, the solicitor had made contact with Andrew and thrust a reserve price under the nose of Langford on a scrap of paper and the hammer fell at £210,000, £30,000 over Andrew's reserve!

Chapter twenty-One

With her usual determination and spirit, Ann applied for the post of part-time Occupational Therapist at the Ripon and District Hospital that she had seen advertised in the Ripon Gazette and she was offered the post. She was delighted for so many reasons and looked forward to starting work on Monday 5th January 1981. Ann's latest health check in Leeds had given her the all clear, so she was on top of the world. The year for both of them and the children was ending on a much happier and more contented note and with the first snow fall of the year at the end of November, they were beginning to look forward to a Christmas the like of which they had not enjoyed for so many years, together and in their own home. Paul and Lynda had settled well into their school and enjoyed many activities in and around Boroughbridge where they had made new friends. In many ways Africa and their old life seemed far in the distant past but always in their hearts.

Terry discovered an uncanny and strange coincidence surrounding their move to live in Boroughbridge. The old coaching house hotel in the centre of the town, the "Crown Hotel" had, during the Second World War, been a base for troops. They had taken over the rear of the hotel, now the car park, and used the outbuildings to house the Army.

Terry found a number of letters amongst his mother's belongings after her death. One of the letters was from her brother-in-law, Terry's uncle, Jonathan Robert Reeves of the 1st Battalion Dorset Regiment, who had been stationed in Boroughbridge in 1941. One of the reasons was to guard the bridge that crossed the river Ure. It formed the A1 link road from the south to the north of England and into Scotland.

'Riverside House' that Terry, Ann, Paul and Lynda had moved into, was just a few yards from the Crown Hotel and had itself, at that time, been a pub. So, maybe, Jonathan had been to their house to have a drink, never, of course, knowing that it would one day be home to his, as yet unborn, nephew.

As it happened, in 1945 the bridge did collapse, under the weight of a heavy transporter that was carrying an eighty ton steel mill on its way to Falkirk from Sheffield. The Army had to build a replacement Bailey bridge whilst the old bridge was being repaired. Sir Donald Bailey, an obscure civil servant in the British War Office, had for just this purpose invented the Bailey bridge in 1939. Over two thousand were in use by 1947.

Christmas 1980 was on a Thursday, which seemed to make the holiday period very long. Terry had not been used to having such long breaks, as in the past there had always been livestock to attend to. It was wonderful to finish work on 19th December and not have to return to work until 5th January. The excitement grew for them and for Paul and Lynda as they all looked forward to sharing the days ahead as a family, remembering the past occasions when they had been separated and, indeed, even in different countries. Paul and Lynda both had new watches for Christmas and so many presents and gifts from family and friends. Everyone seemed to have remembered them in a special way and it was good to have time to play with them and enjoy the days of fun and relaxation together.

"It's so good to see Paul and Lynda happy, isn't it? They have been through so much with changes of country, home and school and who knows what they understand, and fear, regarding my fight with cancer." Ann expressed her concern.

"Yes, it certainly has been a traumatic time for us all, but now we can look forward, you to your new job and me settling into this most unlikely position as Land Agent. We seem to have come out of it all pretty well; I feel we'll be happy living here on the River Ure, even if there are no hippos!" Terry said laughing.

On New Year's Day the sun shone to start the year. In the afternoon they decided to go out for some fresh air and a walk. They drove about ten miles north to the village of Kilburn in North Yorkshire. Terry had seen the White Horse that was carved on the hillside when viewing some of the farms; it looked similar to the one carved on the Dorset hillside at Osmington near Weymouth. They drove up the steep embankment to moorland above the horse, parked the car and walked along the top of Sutton Bank. The footpath took them above the horse on one side with a gliding club on the other. Paul enjoyed seeing the gliders and asked if one day he might learn to fly from there! There was a glorious panoramic view of what seemed to be the whole of Yorkshire twinkling in the sunlight below them and into the distance.

For the first time they realised what a vast and beautiful county Yorkshire was, truly as was said, 'God's own country'. It seemed to have everything: the beautiful beaches of Scarborough, Filey, Whitby, Staithes and Robin Hood's Bay, with charming and delightful villages throughout, retaining much of their old character and history. Then there was the dramatic austerity and isolation of the North York Moors, now declared a National Park, which ran from the Hambleton Hills to the rugged cliffs of the coast. These were totally different from the magic of Wensleydale, Swaledale and the exceptional Coverdale, home of a thirteenth-century Catholic Premonstratensian Monastery. Add to this heady mix all the market towns like Ripon, Northallerton and Skipton plus the mighty city of York and you begin to realise something of the flavour of Yorkshire.

Terry returned to work refreshed on 5th January 1981 and ready to face the New Year. Ann started her new job at Ripon Hospital and was soon out visiting her patients in their homes helping them with their needs. It was not long before she settled in to become a vital member of the staff bringing a wide experience to the job.

Terry continued to be fascinated by the many eccentric Yorkshire characters that he met within his work. They had a certain charm, wisdom acquired over the generations and handed down, all with a twinkle in their eyes. Some were out and out villains to be wary of, but mostly they were a warm and gritty type, probably best embodied in the world famous mariner and navigator Captain James Cook.

One such character he met in the village of Kilburn, under the shadow of the White Horse of Kilburn. The village found fame through Robert Thompson, the world famous wood carver who was born there and started out in life as a wheelwright. Opposite where he was born lived Annie Cornforth.

As she told Terry, "I was born here, christened here, confirmed here, married here and I expect to be buried here."

He first met Annie on a visit to her house. It was part of Kilburn Hall, the farmhouse that was in the centre of the village and owned by Bowman's. Annie was then a widow but had lived there all her life and was then in her mid 80's, wiry fit and caring for herself. Terry called at her house one rainy day to see the property for the first time. He knocked on the rear door. When slowly it opened Annie stood looking at him with a puzzled expression.

"Good Morning Mrs Cornforth. I'm Terry Reeves the new Agent for Bowman's. I've come to meet you and would like to look around if it's convenient?"

"Aah, you'd best come in," she said.

As he went in he noticed a large, wide oak staircase and on each step of the stairs was a bucket or a can, placed there to catch the drops of water that were falling from the ceiling.

"What's going on here?" Terry asked.

"Tha might well ask," she replied, "it's been like that for years."

"Have you never reported it to Mr Langford the previous agent?" Terry asked.

"Course I have, for over six years. I'm fed up with reporting it, he never does anything. It's like an orchestra here when it rains 'ard as water drops down and I 'ave to keep emptying buckets. You see I'm not as young as I was and can't do it like I used to do."

"This is terrible. I'll get a builder out to fix the roof for you as soon as possible. This is nonsense and has to stop," Terry told Mrs Cornforth.

"That'd be a great relief. It's not nice having water come in your house, is it?"

Terry had a good look around the very old farmhouse. It had been divided into two, many years before. There was little in the way of any comforts throughout, the oak floor boards had only the odd rug to cover the floor. Most of the walls were covered in wood panelling and looked centuries old. There was no heating except a large old black range in the living room where Mrs Cornforth had her chair by the side of the fire. The kitchen consisted of a large brownish flat sink with a brass cold tap and wooden draining board. There was no hot water system. The only toilet was outside across the cobbled yard next to the coal shed in a lean-to building with leaking roof!

After his tour around, they sat either side of the fire, which was burning away brightly in the black range as the water from the rain plopped into the cans and buckets on the adjoining open stairway a few feet from them.

"Would you like a glass of sherry?" Mrs Cornforth asked with a twinkle in her eye.

"That would be very kind, thank you."

She carefully measured out two glasses of Bristol Cream Sherry as if it was a vital medicine and handed a glass to Terry.

"So how many years have you lived here?" Terry asked.

"I was born 'ere and I've lived 'ere ever since."

"Do you have any family?"

"Yes, I 'ave a son but he and his wife live in America so I don't see them very often. He tries to come over every year to see me."

"I see, that must be very hard for you, Mrs Cornforth."

"Aye, I'd like to see him more, but that's his life. I've lots of friends in the village that come to see me. Vicar is good too and often comes to see me to make sure I'm right tha knows."

"Don't suppose you get out very much these days?" Terry asked her.

"No, not so much. I 'ave a friend Mrs Barker up t'hill. I go up there for tea when I can and often at Christmas. But sometimes she's bad so I can't go."

"Me son's very good when he comes; he makes sure I 'ave all I need, but I don't need so much these days, well you don't when you're old, do you? He loves to visit London when he's here and goes on train from York. It's nice for him."

"Have you ever been to London, Mrs Cornforth?"

She thought long and hard.

"I once went to York, but that was about twenty years ago now. I went on bus that used to come through village, but we don't 'ave one now!"

"You see, we were always used to working all day and growing a lot of our own food. We kept a pig or two and some hens, had a house cow and made our own bread. Old Kirk (the tenant farmer and her employer) always made sure we had food and he did always give us Sunday afternoons off work. He was always very good about that was old Kirk. He told me that whatever 'appened I would never 'ave to leave 'ere, there'd always be a place for me to live. Well then he retired and went and died so I wondered what was going to 'appen to me? His daughter told me t'speak to agent, but I never saw him until now, when you came today. You see I worry about it, there is nothing worse than worry. It makes ya bad! But Sheila, his daughter, told me to speak t'agent and find out, but I worry in case tha threw me out."

"Well, don't you worry, we'll not be throwing you out, and you can stay here as long as you want to."

"Aah! well tha says that, but what about Mr Bowman, what if he wants me out, that's what matters?"

"I can tell you, Mrs Cornforth, Mr Bowman will not throw you out. You have my word for that and one day I'll bring him to meet you and he can tell you himself."

"Well, young man you've made me feel a lot better, right worried I was. I've lived 'ere all me life ya see, and I'm not wanting to move now. They asked me if I wanted one of them there new bungalow things in village. Well what would I want with one of them, daaaaaa? There's nowt as bad as worry is there? I was right troubled I can tell you."

"Will you come and see me again?"

"Oh, yes, I will, of course I will. I'll be here so often your neighbours 'll think we're having an affair!" Terry said with a smile.

She liked that and laughed out loud.

"I'm going to fix up with a builder to come and repair your roof as soon as possible. Then we can take away all those buckets and cans from your stairs."

"I see you have no hot water in the kitchen. How do you manage?"

"Well I carry it up from range of course."

"I see. That's not very good is it? I'm going to arrange with the builder to fix an electric heater that will provide hot water over your sink."

"Naa, what you want to spend tha money doing that for? I'll never use it, the old range does me fine," she replied.

"It will make it much easier for you. I see you do your washing in the sink there too, so you must need a lot of hot water."

"It's no good I won't use it, be a waste of money!" she said with fierce resistance.

Terry could not believe her reluctance but was equally determined.

"Look, Mrs Cornforth, I'm going to put a water heater in whether you like it or not."

"Daaaaaaa waste of money," she replied shaking her head.

"I tell you what," he said. "I'll have it put in and if next month when I come again, you still don't like it or use it, then I'll have it taken away."

"Are you going to have some more sherry?" she asked, changing the subject.

Two months later when he suggested removing it, Annie would have none of it.

Ann's job was going so well that they increased her hours; she enjoyed every minute with such vitality, endearing herself to both staff and patients. She was so busy that they gave her the use of a car to avoid having to charge mileage in her own.

She continued to have regular check-ups at Cookridge Hospital near Leeds, always driving herself to the appointments, insisting Terry get on with his job. At her check on 24th March they asked her to return on 27th for a scan. Terry was a bit unnerved by this, but felt it was just a precaution. Just the same he decided to be around when she returned home and worked away in the garage doing some repairs to a chair, while awaiting her return.

She arrived back around two that afternoon, and when she stepped out of the car the look on her face spoke a thousand words. As he looked out of the garage window he could see her devastated face; instantly he knew. His blood ran cold. He ran across the yard to greet her. He could see she had been crying by her tear-stained face. She said just two words. "It's back."

Duke, the dog rushed up to her wagging his tail in greeting. Ann patted him with trembling hands. She was broken and shattered. Terry noticed as she stood there with her back to the river bank, the fresh new leaves of the weeping willow hanging over the fence, framing her at that heart-rending moment that he would remember forever.

"I have to attend the hospital on 31st March to see Professor Joslin who will tell us the next step. Sorry Terry, but it's not good. I fear we may have lost the fight; we have to face it. What are we going to do? Paul and Lynda too?"

Terry went along with her to the hospital; they were told that arrangements had been made for Ann to go into St James's Hospital in Leeds on 5th April for an operation on her stomach, as there was a new growth that had to be removed.

All this had to be relayed to the children and to the rest of the family and on 5th April Terry took her to St James's where she remained until recovered and strong enough to return home on 18th.

On 23rd April they had an appointment again with her surgeon Professor Joslin to let them know his findings and what he would then be able to do. He explained that the growth in her stomach was too large for it to be removed; they would begin drug treatment immediately to try and shrink it.

While Ann was seeing the nurse, filling in the inevitable forms, the Professor told Terry to prepare himself: time was short; he was really sorry but there was nothing else he could do, only to make sure her end was as painless as possible, and he would contact her doctor to inform him.

Terry told the Professor that Ann would want to remain at home, that he wanted to do all he could for her, that somehow he would care for her himself, with their doctor's help and advice.

About this time Terry spoke to his Parish Priest to tell him about the terminal nature of Ann's illness. He asked him if he would kindly go to see her as he felt she would gain great benefit from such a visit. He agreed to pay her a call. Terry also informed the church Ann had attended at Kirby Hill of her condition and asked if the vicar would call to see her.

Terry was shocked and amazed that neither of the church ministers responded to his request. He was absolutely dumbfounded that those who he had always thought would be there in an hour of need should treat them so heartlessly. It left him outraged, reeling, angry and feeling alone, but determined to carry on; if that was the way it had to be then he would fight on unaided.

He began to wonder if he had failed to underline the urgency of his request so, unbelieving of their failure to visit, he again repeated his request, pleading for them to go and see Ann before it was too late. They both failed to accept the challenge and for no apparent reason.

Ann was not beaten yet. She was determined to carry on with life and with her work and they continued to have friends and family stay, while they all prayed for a miracle to happen. The radium treatment was severe at best and each time knocked her back for a couple of days.

Terry's father from Weymouth came to stay for a week in July, about the same time that Ann gave her notice to her employers at Ripon Hospital that she could no longer continue with her work. They kindly told her that the job was hers anytime she felt able to return, which softened the blow considerably and gave her hope.

In August their dear friends Margaret and Philip came for an overnight stay to see Ann. They all enjoyed a walk along the river path that sunny afternoon, watching the boats pass through the gates at Milby Lock as if they had not a care in the world.

Early in September, Joan Hart, on a short visit to England from Tanzania to see her sister, also made an overnight visit, which they enjoyed.

Friends from Paul and Lynda's school and their mums had been so kind in coming to help in a much needed and practical way, once they heard about Ann's problem. They helped Terry with the day-to-day things to keep them all going and to be there for Paul and Lynda whose lives were continuing amongst all this as normally as they could. Terry tried to keep them informed of their mother's condition; they were, no doubt, having to cope with their own emotions, sadness and fears, which they did bravely. Terry worried so much about them and the long-term effects all this was having on them and their lives.

Then one evening in mid September, around 6pm an extraordinary thing happened. The phone rang just as Terry and the children had finished their meal.

"Can I speak to Terry Reeves?" the gruff voice asked.

"Yes, I'm speaking."

"This is Father Jerome from St Mary's Catholic Church in Knaresborough. Your children go to our school and I understand from the school that your wife is very ill."

"That is correct Father, but I don't go to your church, I go to Ripon."

"That doesn't matter to me. Could I come along to see her?"

"Yes of course, I'd be delighted," Terry replied.

"I'll come tomorrow evening at 5pm. Is that convenient?"

"Thank you so much. We will be delighted to see you."

The following day Fr. Jerome, who was a Benedictine priest, came to the house and sat and chatted to them both.

To Ann he said, "Would you like to receive communion? I can bring it to you every day if you would like that."

"I'm afraid I'm not a Catholic," she replied.

"Well we can soon change that, if you would like?"

After a short chat with her it was agreed that the following week on Tuesday 29th September, Fr. Jerome would hold a short service in their sitting room with a few of Ann's friends, when she would be welcomed into the Catholic Church. Until then he came the ten miles to visit her faithfully each day.

Ann's mother and father then came to stay for five days on 22nd September and Terry met them off the train in York. They wanted to see her and to be with her for her forty first birthday on 27th September.

On the 29th September, as agreed, Wendy, Pat and Clare, fairly new friends from Knaresborough, gathered in the sitting room at Riverside House with Father Jerome for the service that was to welcome Ann into the Catholic Church. Terry had been talking to Ann during the day about the step that she was about to take into the church. She was happy and determined to embark on this new venture, seeming very pleased to have been able to come to this decision after so many years of no real commitment.

She was feeling very weak and they had to spend a long time getting her dressed and down from the bedroom, but she heroically did it to be with her friends on this special occasion. It was a very spiritual and simple service, followed by a Mass. They were all very moved by it and delighted to have shared that moment with her. After, they then all enjoyed a light supper and thanked Fr. Jerome for his kindness and resolve in making it all happen. He continued to bring Ann communion every single day thereafter giving her much comfort and strength.

The following day Ann was bright but tired. The doctor had made his daily, sometimes twice-daily visit and the children had gone off to school. Terry lay on the bed by Ann's side as he often did, holding her hand. She seemed to want to chat to him and so they did for over an hour, a very special intimate time of sharing.

"I know that I'm going to die soon," Ann said, quite bluntly to Terry.

"I want to talk to you while I still can and I want you to write these things down, so that you'll never forget. Will you do that?"

"Of course I will, if it's what you want," Terry replied, rather surprised.

Even now she was still thinking of others. What an amazing person she was, always others before herself!

"I'd write it, but I can't focus to write well. It would take me too long and my hand is shaky, so I want you to do it. I've written diaries a great deal, as you know over the years; it's something I've always had the urge to do."

Terry went off to find a sheet of paper as she insisted he wrote it as she spoke.

"You see I've had a great deal of time to think in the last few weeks. I feel somehow, that I want you to record, for me, my thoughts at this time, for the children mainly; they are my life, my all. I want them to know how much I love them, or perhaps I should say how much we both love them. They can't be here now, being so young, so I can't tell them. You know the love I have for you and I can tell you that, but for them, how else will they know? I want them to hear it from me, not second hand from you. Does that make any sense?"

"Yes it does, perfect sense. I'll do anything you ask, as you know I will."

"Firstly, please, don't force Paul and Lynda to come into the bedroom to see me if they prefer not to. I'll quite understand. I can see they are shocked at how I look, having become so thin. I'm pretty horrified myself," Ann said with a tired half smile."

"Of course I'd never force them to do that. I always ask them if they want to come and see you, then I leave it to them," Terry replied.

"How will they take it when I go I wonder? What will you do?" Ann asked with brave concern.

"I really have no idea. It's something that I can't even think about," Terry replied gloomily, taken aback by her questions.

"But you must think of these things, you have to. You will keep them at home with you won't you, after I've gone?"

"Of course I will, they are part of you, and you are part of them. They will always remind me of you and in that way you will be with me forever."

"They're fortunate to have you for their father. I want them to know that, so write it down, tell them I know the depth of you and the love you have for me, Paul and Lynda. I know how you love them and will guide them in their lives the very best you can. I'm sorry this must be difficult for you to have to write this, but you must and one day I want you to give it to them. You'll know the right time, or else leave it for them to read."

"They must know these things from me their mother. They will always love you, when they are old enough to understand and imagine the situation you are now in, and for all that you have done for them. I'm sure of that, but they will never really know all that we have had to do and sacrifice. Perhaps it's how it should be, what all parents have to do?"

"Will you, one day, when they are older, tell them about this. Tell them I loved them so much and wanted to stay; they are so dear to me. I live for them and for you. I would have done anything for this not to happen. I did fight, tell them, but now I'm so weak, so very weak. Tell them I tried, tell them I love them and always will. I want them and you to know how much I loved you all and will go on caring for you all in my new life." Ann gazed at Terry longingly.

"I will take care of you all from above. I wish I understood why this has had to happen; we had only planned to do good things in our lives. There are so many unanswered questions."

"Why has God always wanted to separate us? All our married life we have had to fight to be together. I've lost count of the weeks, months and years that we've had to be apart. You know how much I've always hated it, as you have. Now we have again to separate, the greatest separation that anyone can endure and the thing I hate most."

Ann stared looking into the flowers that were all around her in the room. Tears rolled uncontrollably down her cheeks, and his; her hands trembled as she hung on to Terry, watching carefully as he wrote her words down.

"What will you do? Will you marry again?"

"Oh Ann, don't speak like this. How can I even think like that?" Terry replied.

"Well, I want you to think about it. I don't want you to be on your own; you're not good on your own."

She gripped his hand as if in pain and then laid back on the pillow to rest, breathing deeply.

"Will you promise me something else?" she asked.

"Of course, anything."

"Will you always look after my Mum and Dad, go and see them and take Paul and Lynda to see them, keep an eye on them in general. Will you do that for as long as they live, just for me?"

"Yes, of course I will, I promise. Now, please, can we stop all this?"

"No, I have to say these things. I have to. If not now, when? Please let me. I know it hurts, but I worry for you all."

Terry took both her hands and tried to reassure her as he lay at her side. "I'll do all that you have asked me to do, of course I will and I'll do everything in my power to care for Paul and for Lynda, you know that, as I will for your Mum and Dad too, so don't worry and concern yourself anymore."

"Thank you. You are so good. I feel at ease now. I lay here thinking of all these things. The days are long and I think too much sometimes! I'm very fortunate. Thank you so much for looking after me here at home. You have had to do things that I know you find hard and no man should have to do."

"Promise me one last thing. You will keep me at home, won't you? I don't want to go anywhere else, only to stay here with you in our home. Promise me that."

"You don't have to ask," Terry replied. "Of course I'll keep you here. I'll never leave you, you can be certain of that."

"I've just had to say these things: everything plays on my mind laying here like this."

"Pat Cocks is coming for a few days to see you and to help me, so that will be nice, and you know how well you two get on, so you don't want to be too tired. Perhaps you should rest now." Terry explained. "I'm going to pick her up in York at 2pm off the train. Claire's daughter, Susan from Knaresborough, is going to be here while I go to York. She is a lovely girl and wanted to help us."

"I'm blessed to have so many lovely people around me," Ann said as she drifted into a deep sleep.

Pat spent three days with Ann. They chatted when they could and Pat would just lay on the bed with her while Ann drifted in and out of sleep. They were good friends and Ann enjoyed Pat's warmth and companionship as much as she could and the comfort of knowing she was there. It also enabled Terry to do all the things that were crying out for his attention and to try and create some sort of normality for the children. He tried to explain to them how ill their mother was and tried to take in, himself, the magnitude of what was going on around him.

Pat's three days with them were tough for her. Terry had got used to all that was going on, but for Pat it was something of a shock as well as having to cope with her own grief. She was a marvel and gave them all courage. They were so grateful to her and David for giving up her time to be with Ann at that most difficult of times.

On Sunday 4th October Terry was able to spend the whole day with Ann and with the children who on the whole busied themselves playing with friends or in their bedrooms, where he was sure they tried not to think about all that was going on around them.

'The Flame Trees of Thika' was showing on television and normally Terry and Ann would have enjoyed watching the series. They had seen the early episodes together, the story having been all about life in Kenya, so right up their street. But by this time Ann was not able to get out of bed and spent the day drifting in and out of sleep. Terry sat with her most of the day, hardly able to keep awake. He could not remember the last time that he had a full night's sleep and seemed to just exist, snatching an hour here and there for the past few weeks, forcing himself on, while at the same time trying to cope with his heartbreak and grief.

Paul and Lynda looked like two frightened rabbits caught in the headlights, never knowing what was going to happen next. It concerned them so much to have their mother ill and to see their father walking around exhausted. Everyday they saw yet another person come to the house to help: there was a trail of doctors and nurses calling at all hours, phones ringing and callers at the door. Their whole life was turned upside down; they had no idea what to expect next. Quite rightly, they buried themselves in their own needs.

On Monday, Claire Taylor a friend from Knaresborough came to spend the day with Ann. By this time Ann was asleep most of the time but would have felt the comfort of having a kind friend at her side.

The following day Tuesday 6th October Terry, now off work, spent the day with Ann. By this time she was moving into a coma and not able to converse. He sat with her from dawn through the day until evening, just answering the phone and the door as callers came along.

In the afternoon, Jean, a lady that worked in Terry's office, came to be with him to allow him to spend some time with the children, wash and eat. Seeing him so distressed and at the end of his tether she decided to stay the whole night in the house. Terry looked so desperate with no family living in the area and she did not want him to be alone when it looked as if the end was near.

Terry would not leave Ann's side for a minute, knowing just how much she hated them to be separated. This at least was one occasion when he did have some control over it. He sat holding her hand. She knew that she was dying, but had not been afraid. She drifted into a coma, her breathing shallow, but sometimes rapid. A tearful Jean came along at times to heroically sit with them and to bring tea or coffee to Terry, the anguish and distress lining his face as he sat there hour after torturous hour. By midnight, Ann's breathing was very shallow and became irregular until at 0.39am on Wednesday 7th October 1981 Ann took her last shallow breath with Terry holding her hand as her spirit left her and the mystery of death confronted them both.

He sat the whole night in a confusion of emotion and contradictory feelings, wondering at the justification for such a waste of a good and beautiful life, lost at such a young age, forty one years and ten days.

He had to brace himself to face the children in the morning and endeavour to explain to them the night's events. With their being so young at nine and eleven years, to lose their mother and face such tragedy, how could he ask them to face such desolation?

At 7am he heard voices, so he went into their room. They looked at him his eyes swollen and puffy with tears; he had no need to say a thing. He spoke gently and quietly, confirming that in the night their mother had died, that she was no longer with them. They were white with shock, their broken hearts merged in agony as he hugged them in silence. If only he had been as brave as they were he thought as he left them in their room to digest the news.

Ann's parents needed then to be told, so he picked up the phone to tell them. The familiar voice of her mother answered. For a few seconds he lost the power of speech.

"I think I know what you have to tell me," she said.

"Yes I'm afraid so, at 12.40 last night. We were together and Jean was in the house with me."

"Paul and Lynda, are they going to cope?" she asked.

"How will any of us? We are all very traumatised. Sorry but I have to go. I'll ring again later."

Terry then rang his family, followed by Doctor Green who had cared for and supported Ann all the time that she was at home. Even on occasions when Terry had to call him to come out in the middle of the night, he was always uncomplaining and on this last occasion came immediately.

Terry was devastated, broken, but strangely routine took him over. With their dog Duke, he set off for his usual walk along the river path by Riverside House, desperate to feel a freshness on his face. He had not been outside for days and had not really taken any notice of the weather, having no idea what the conditions were. The brisk morning air hit him, leaves were flying around and dark black clouds hovered menacingly low overhead.

As he started out alone with Duke, along the riverside he felt the wind so strong in his back that it was almost possible to lean back and allow it to support him totally; he was amazed by its strength. There was a wildness and violence about the force of the wind, an almost spiritual ferocity about it, as if outside of the house, as well as inside, there had been a tremendous fight against evil.

As he continued to walk along the path towards Milby Lock with these thoughts in his mind, he noticed that every tree along the riverside, and there were many, some in excess of twenty five feet high, had their tops ripped off and broken. The tops of some hung down still partly connected to the tree, others had been aggressively smashed on to the ground below with fierceness and power. To this day the signs and the damage to those trees can still be perceived. Terry had never before seen, or was to see again in his twenty-four years living in Yorkshire, such devastation.

There was no doubt that on the night of Ann's death a dramatic spiritual fight took place with far-reaching consequences for the family, symbolized by the vast destruction of the trees. It changed everything but the trees continued to survive, albeit in a transformed way, as indeed did Ann, now passed and gone ahead to a new freedom, their final separation.

Lightning Source UK Ltd.
Milton Keynes UK
178444UK00001B/7/P